DEFENDERS OF THE FAITH

JEAN PLAIDY

ISIS
LARGE PRINT
Oxford

Copyright © Jean Plaidy, 1956 and 1971

First published in Great Britain 1956
by
Hodder & Stoughton Ltd.
under the pseudonym of Ellalice Tate

Published in Large Print 2012 by ISIS Publishing Ltd.,
7 Centremead, Osney Mead, Oxford OX2 0ES
by arrangement with
The Random House Group Limited

British Library Cataloguing in Publication Data
Plaidy, Jean, 1906–1993.
  Defenders of the faith.
  1. Great Britain - - History - - Tudors,
  1485–1603 - - Fiction.
  2. Great Britain - - Church history - - 16th century
  - - Fiction.
  3. Inquisition - - Spain - - Fiction.
  4. Historical fiction.
  5. Large type books.
  I. Title II. Tate, Ellalice, 1906–1993.
  823.9'12–dc23

ISBN 978-0-7531-8844-6 (hb)
ISBN 978-0-7531-8845-3 (pb)

Printed and bound in Great Britain by
T. J. International Ltd., Padstow, Cornwall

CHAPTER
ONE

It was a summer's day and there was perfect peace in the Chelsea garden. The Thames, flowing quietly by the steep bank now decorated with purple loosestrife and scorpion grass, washed the privy steps with a gentle rhythmic murmur, and a cuckoo stammered out a few notes from a bush in the nuttery. One of the kitchen-maids came out into the garden to feed a peacock which had perched on the low stone wall, impatiently waiting for his dinner. She stood, her hand outstretched, that he might peck at the pulse she held in her palm, and putting her head on one side, muttered to the gorgeous creature: "You greedy thing! You vain old greedy thing!" Her lips were full and soft, her eyes gentle, and her body heavy beneath her worsted gown. She was clearly destined for almost immediate motherhood.

"Get along with you, then," she said. "Can't you wait for your dinner?"

She shaded her eyes and looked across the hundred yards or so of garden to the river. The serenity of maternity became her.

"Nan! Nan! Where are you?" called a voice from within.

Nan went slowly through the porch, pausing to give a quick glance at the big bay windows and the large casements as she did so. The latticed window on the second floor opened from Master Charles' chamber; and every time she passed into the house she glanced at it.

The sun burned down on the walls, which were covered with golden moss and stone crop; it brought out the smell of newly cut hay in the home field and mingled it with the perfume from the walled rose-gardens. The heat shimmered on the gables; a dog barked suddenly; and a maid put her head out of an upper window to shake a duster.

In his favourite wicker seat, Sir Ralph Grendell, the master of the house, sat back, letting the sun warm him while he listened with deep contentment to the sounds of the afternoon. He was forty-two, inclined to be plump, and his expression was one of tolerance and lazy enjoyment.

From where he sat, by looking along the river he had a clear view of the City of London. He could see the noble houses with their gardens, running, like his own, down to the river's edge; the meadows and the wooded hills were delightful; he could see fruit-laden trees in orchards, and flowers both wild and cultivated; and in the distance were the Bridge and the grey bastions of London's mighty fortress.

Although he had not turned his head, he had been aware of the girl who came out to feed the peacock. Nan. The kitchen wench. He smiled tolerantly. She was but fifteen and young to have fallen, but it was certain to happen early to Nan, for, poor, sweet, silly creature, she would be unable to prevent its happening. She was meant for motherhood.

She would not say who was the father of her child, but both he and his wife Jane could guess; and, for that reason alone, they would have said that Nan should have her child in their house: and they had promised that it should be well cared for.

At his feet, in a basket, lay his grandson Roger — a strong and beautiful boy, whose solemn blue eyes now studied Sir Ralph as though he read his thoughts. The baby began to kick furiously. He had been lively from his birth — the sort of baby to delight everyone who saw him. There was not a woman in the household who did not worship him; and young Roger seemed, in his nine months of existence, to have realised this. He was imperious, at times querulous; and it was as though he knew already that one day he would be Sir Roger Grendell, heir to the Grendell estates and fortune.

And how like Roger would Nan's child be? Well, it was lucky for her that the father of her child was Charles Grendell instead of some wandering pedlar who would have plucked her as he might a ripe plum or peach and then passed on.

He smiled, seeing himself as Jane saw him. She had said that his kindly tolerance would have made a saint of him if it had not grown out of sheer laziness. Contentment was necessary to him; and if he was to enjoy it, those about him must be contented too, for he was a man who could not be happy unless he shared that which brought him pleasure.

He heard the sound of footsteps on the flagged path and looking up saw Dolores, his Spanish daughter-in-law — the one he loved best — coming towards him. She carried a basket and was on her way from the rose-gardens. Watching her approach, he marvelled, as he had when he had first set eyes on her, at her strange, exotic beauty. Her body was heavy now, for she, like Nan, was to bear his grandchild.

She knelt down to look into the solemn eyes of the baby, who stopped kicking to look at her.

"But," she said, "he is so beautiful."

Ralph made room for her on the wicker seat. "You should not exert yourself," he said. "It is too hot this afternoon."

She shook her head. She was, he thought, almost more beautiful than she had been when he had first seen her. The bulkiness of her body made her thin, olive-skinned face, with its high cheek-bones and those lustrous dark eyes, seem more ethereal than before; the black hair seemed too heavy for her small head.

He was glad that his son Richard was not the one to betray his wife with little Nan.

"I do not feel the heat," she said in her quaint foreign accent. "I like it."

"It is more like your own country, eh?"

"A little like it, dear father."

"Those roses are beautiful."

She held out the basket with one of her pretty gestures.

"Dolores," he said, "will you ever feel that England is your home?"

"Home," she answered, "is where my husband is . . . and where my child will be."

"It makes me happy to think that in a little while I shall have my second grandchild."

"The child will be half Spanish. You will not like?"

"I shall like it. The child, remember, will also be half English."

"There will be two grandchildrens, yes!" she said, smiling down at Roger. "That little one and mine."

Nay, he thought, there will be three. Yours, Roger, and Nan's little bastard. A servant in his own house! He should be angry with his eldest son. It was regrettable. Were there not girls enough outside? Yet how could he blame the boy! He was young and lusty, not studious, sensitive, as his younger brother Richard was. Why, thought Ralph, my two sons are so different in character that if I were not pleased with one I must be with the other.

Dolores said: "I wonder which you will love best. The little boy there . . . or mine? Which, I wonder."

"I shall love them equally," he said, but he did not believe it. One did not love two people equally. That was clearly a grandfather's duty, but when could the giving of affection be brought down to a mere duty?

She smiled at him. Although she could not always understand the English idiom, she understood him well.

"You must take great care, Dolores. I would not have you tire yourself. Remember, you are not as hardy as our Cecily."

"You think of Richard's birth, yes?"

She was right. Twenty-one years ago it had been, on a summer's day like this. He had sat in this garden with Jane beside him; they had talked of the child who had become Richard; and little Charles, not then two, but already showing signs of the lusty, self-willed person he would become, had played on the grass, defying their instructions to keep away from the river bank, urgently wanting to pick water plantains and cream-and-codlins simply because they grew close to that part of the bank which was forbidden territory; just as now, a man, he could not leave simple Nan alone when he was married to his pretty, buxom Cecily.

Jane had all but died at Richard's birth, and he had known that there would be no more children.

"It makes you sad," said Dolores. "I should not have called it to your mind."

"Nay," he answered. "I am not sad. I have had a very happy life."

"You look at life, and you make it good by looking."

"That's a pretty thought, my dear. But it has been a good life; and I look forward now to the days when my house will be filled with my grandchildren."

"But you were not pleased that your son should marry a Spanish woman, dear father."

No, he had not been pleased. She had visited England with her father, who came to the Court on an embassy from Spain. That was how Richard had met her.

"I have become pleased," he answered. "If I can go on as I am now, I ask nothing more of life." He found it easy to talk to her, and he went on: "Oh, once I had my dreams. I thought to go to Court. I planned to enter the service of the great Cardinal . . . or to go on a mission to some foreign country. A place was found for me at Court, but nothing came of it. I had not the special charm which would attract the King. I had not the ability. For a while I was bitter, but soon I learned contentment. I knew that it was better to lie in the friendly shade than in the hot blaze of dangerous noon. I had a friend once, Dolores. He lived nearby. Look! You can see his house from here."

She followed his gaze and saw the house that stood back from the river; it was very like the one in which they lived.

"Once there was not a happier man in England. There was not a happier household than that one. But he was a brilliant man, so brilliant that, though he did not seek greatness, it came to him. His name was More . . . Thomas More. He asked for domestic peace, and instead he was given a King's favour; and that, my dear, is a fickle thing. He was England's greatest statesman . . . for a time. He held that position which I had dreamed of holding. He was famous and many sought his favours. He was a great man, a good man. And a year ago, when I sat in my garden, I saw him set out in his barge. I saw him go past my garden; and he called to me as he went. I was sitting here with Jane beside me. I knew that he envied me my peace, my happiness, my contentment. 'Ah, friend Grendell,' he called to me, 'you do well there, sitting in the shade.' I have never forgotten those words. And later I saw him go down the river from Westminster to the Tower. He went in by the

Traitors' Gate; and he came out only to walk to Tower Hill that he might lay his head on the block."

He turned his head away that she might not see the tears in his eyes.

"So now," he continued after a pause, "I ask for peace, to live my life with my family about me; for that is the good life, that is the life for me."

"You are a good man, Father. Like your neighbour who died, you are a good man."

"He was a saint," he murmured.

"And you," she told him, lifting his hand to her lips, "are just . . . a good man."

Cecily had come upon them. She saw the Spanish woman kissing her father-in-law's hand. Cecily pursed her lips. What nonsense! thought Cecily. Many things were nonsense to Cecily.

She swooped on the child and picked him up. "You should not have let him lie in the sun. His little head is quite hot." Her prim face under the rather severe headdress softened for the baby. Beyond everything she loved her son; more than her dignity and her position in this house she loved the baby. Her pride in him was greater than her pride in her domestic skill, and that was great.

Cecily was fair-skinned and flaxen-haired; and her very efficiency called attention to the inadequacy of others. There was no need, thought Ralph, a little impatiently, for her to look so complacent. They were all aware of the excellent qualities of Cecily.

"Did you not hear the supper bell?" she demanded.

Her face was flushed; she had been watching the maids in the kitchen. Jane said that life had never been so easy before Cecily had joined the family. She knew just how peacocks should be served, how to make lapwing into a rare delicacy. She had more than one pair of eyes, the kitchen girls said; and if they so much as took theirs off the roasting beef they would feel Mistress Cecily's hand about their ears; the hand was hard and did not match her soft Devonshire accent. She was the daughter of a country knight and had brought Charles a substantial dowry. She was healthy, very interested in food, so devoted to cleanliness that she insisted on changing the rushes once a week. A burnt piecrust could move her more deeply than the infidelity of her husband. The child alone could soften her; and Ralph wondered whether her pride in him was similar to that which she had in her cooking. She said: "This is *my* child; therefore he must be perfect!" as she said: "This is my bread. I made it. Therefore it must be the best bread."

It was wrong to feel critical. She was a good girl; and he was lucky in his daughters.

"A nice state of affairs," she grumbled indulgently as she took Roger and sat down on the seat to adjust his garments. "A nice state of affairs, Master Roger." She kissed him. "It is because he feels his strength that he kicks so. He kicked everything off when he was little . . . all his swaddling clothes. It was impossible to keep this one covered."

Her sharp blue eyes were studying her sister-in-law a little maliciously. Poor thing! she was thinking. She'll not find it easy when her time comes. The daughter of a Spanish nobleman! She fancied herself too noble to interest herself in kitchen matters. It would be far better for her if she were a bit more active. A woman was a fool to lie about too much when she was expecting her first child.

"The day Roger was born, I was out in the orchards, helping with the apple harvest," she said, in that tone of pride and reproach which made her father-in-law smile.

"Ah," said Dolores, "you are very strong and very brave."

Dear Cecily! thought Ralph. It was wrong to feel this faint dislike because she was possessed of many virtues and aware of them. She would have been a fool had she not been so aware. Why should it be necessary for the good to be ignorant of their goodness in order to be loved, when ignorance in other matters was so tiresome?

"The beef will be spoiled," said Cecily, and her mouth watered at the thought of the beef.

"Dolores was tired," Ralph explained. "We talked and so . . . did not hear the bell."

"If Dolores would exercise herself more, the gathering of a few flowers would not tire her."

"Listen!" said Ralph. "Who is that?"

Dolores stood up. "A boat has stopped at the stairs," she said.

Ralph stood up beside her and, shading his eyes, saw a man getting out of the boat; he was tall and lean; his beard was grey and flowing; his strange garments proclaimed that he was a foreigner.

10

Cecily's expression was one of exasperation. Another of her father-in-law's queer friends! He had so many and they invariably called at meal-times, being sure of a place at his table. There would be endless talk about matters which Cecily considered of no importance.

Ralph went forward to greet his visitor. He had met him a week or so before at the house of a friend and being interested in his views had invited him to call when he could spare the time.

Ralph held out his hands and bade Emil Pretzel welcome to his house.

In the great hall, which was the centre of the house, the family sat at table. Sunlight shone through the great bow windows so that the silver dishes gleamed. About the hall was the gallery, the walls of which were hung with paintings and tapestry. Beyond the raised dais on which the table was set, there were doors leading to other rooms; and at the far end of the hall were more doors leading to the kitchens and the servants' quarters.

The guest sat at Ralph's right hand; Jane Grendell was on his left. The maids and serving-men hurried back and forth. Cecily's eyes were on them, and each was aware of Cecily.

The beef was roasted to a turn; so was the lamb and the capon. Cecily's eyes glistened as she looked at the pigeon pie, specially flavoured with pork, onions and herbs; it was made as she had learned to make it in her mother's Devonshire kitchen. She hoped the visitor would remark on the lightness of her pastry, although he did not appear to be a man who would appreciate good food.

Lady Grendell was delighted with the company of the guest because Ralph was obviously pleased to have him at their table. After the meal, she expected, they would wander in the gardens, down to the river, where they would sit and talk. And later, when darkness fell, and she and Ralph lay in their big bed together with the curtains drawn to shut them in, they would talk of the visitor, exchange opinions, share private jokes.

But Jane Grendell was less pleased with the visitor as he grew more talkative, for she recognised the fanatic in the burning fervour of his eyes; and she wanted no fanatics to ruffle the serenity of their lives. Fanatics were disturbing people. Sir Thomas More had been a fanatic in his way, and she had been angry with him. Why, she had demanded of Ralph, could he not take the Oath of Supremacy? Surely it would have been so easy to mumble a few words and restore happiness to his family. Yet he would not do it, and so he had died and his family had suffered great anguish. Ralph and Jane, his neighbours who had loved him, had found their pleasant lives disturbed and uneasy. No, Jane wanted no fanatics, no martyrs bringing their uncomfortable ways into her home.

Emil Pretzel was telling them about Germany, and how he had come to England some months ago. There was a similarity between the two countries, he said, which could not but delight him.

"A similarity in the character of our peoples," he explained in his low, guttural voice. "We are simple

12

disciplined people. We are a people attracted by clear thinking, by a religion which is not clogged by the trappings of that ceremony which makes an appeal to minds given over to emotion rather than to logical good sense."

Ralph was smiling at Jane. Here was one of those Reformers. Their conversation was always interesting.

"Is it possible," the visitor was going on, "that by consecrating bread it can really be turned into the body of Christ?"

"That is what we have been taught in the gospels," said Jane quickly. Her eyes were on the servants. This was dangerous talk. Fanatics . . . martyrs . . . suffered death because of disputes over pieces of bread. It should not happen in this house! thought Jane fiercely.

Ralph was smiling lazily at his guest. Ralph was a little careless. He liked to make people talk; he liked to put forth challenging opinions. Often he would take an opposite view merely to force a discussion. Jane's eyes appealed to him not to do so now . . . not before the servants.

Charles momentarily saved the conversation from being dangerous. He did it quite unconsciously. That was Charles' charm; he did most things without deliberation.

"This cob loaf is good, sir," he said. "I'll warrant you'll find no better than this made in our house . . . no matter where you look for it . . . be it consecrated or not."

His father laughed. Charles always amused him. Jane laughed with relief; and Cecily with pleasure. Cecily it was who had shown them how to make cob bread the Devon way.

"And how long do you propose staying in this country, Herr Pretzel?" asked Jane.

"For some months, Lady Grendell. That is, if there is still a welcome for me."

"You must rest awhile with us," said Ralph. "Cecily, my dear, you can have them prepare a bed for our guest, can you not?"

"Indeed yes," answered Cecily. "I set the maids to work before we sat down to eat, for I guessed you would not allow Herr Pretzel to leave us without sleeping under our roof."

"You see," said Ralph, "how well we are looked after. We are singularly blessed in our daughters . . . both of them."

Dolores bowed her head in acknowledgment of the compliment.

"Dolores," went on Ralph, "the wife of my younger son, comes from Spain."

"A sad and tortured land," said Pretzel.

"How so?" asked Richard.

"You say 'how so'?" The fanatical eyes blazed suddenly. "I refer, my dear sir, to the terrible Inquisition."

"The Inquisition?" said Dolores. "It concerns itself only with those who are heretics."

"Heretics!" cried Pretzel. "What are these heretics? Those men . . . those women who love . . . who love *die Wahrheit*! These men and women . . . are they not those who have seen . . . the Light?"

14

Jane sighed. Thus must it always be with fanatics; they must court danger; they could not bear to see the flames subdued; they must blow them to greater ferocity; it was almost as though they *hoped* to burn themselves in the process. Did the man not realise that to talk thus of his doctrines could prove disastrous, not only to him but his friends?

"There will always be disagreement between men on these matters of religion," said Ralph soothingly.

The German placed his hands on the table and said as though addressing a meeting: "This Inquisition is a monster. My felicitations to the lady. She has escaped from that barbarous land. She has become *die tochter* in this house. That is a happy thing, for soon in this land we shall see the Catholic doctrines . . . gone . . . and in their place the truth of Martin Luther will flourish."

Jane said with a smile: "Herr Pretzel, you are a stranger in our land. Therefore you may not know that we accept the religion of which our King is the head. We do not discuss these matters."

"My dear!" Ralph admonished.

Richard said in his thoughtful way: "But my dear sir, the Inquisition was originally set up in your country. Most European states have been under its sway at some time. There was a time when both France and Germany submitted to its jurisdiction."

"Ah! We did not have it long!" cried the German.

"And in this country," went on Richard, "we had it not at all. Nor shall we . . . good Catholics though we may be."

"It is only in the barbarous land of Spain that it has become a monster," went on Pretzel. "Ferdinand and Isabella, with Torquemada, fed it . . . enriched it . . . enlarged it . . . and now . . ." He spread his hands eloquently. "It *is* Spain."

Richard was angered on behalf of his wife. She seemed so gentle, but she was filled with Spanish pride. The German, when he insulted her country, was insulting her. Richard realised that the man did not understand this. How could he, he asked himself, with his crude German manners, understand the dignity of a Spaniard?

Richard pressed Dolores' hand — he loved her devotedly — while, looking sternly at Pretzel, he said: "All that is done, is done in the name of God. And I know of no better reason."

"Well," said Charles, "who are we to talk of the iniquities of the Inquisition?" He smiled at his sister-in-law. He was ready to defend her because she was a beautiful woman; and he liked all beautiful women, while he distrusted all foreigners if they were masculine. "I remember what happened to the monks of the Charterhouse. I saw them die. I'll swear their deaths were as cruel as those meted out by the Inquisition. I remember . . . why, it must be five years ago, when I was a young lad . . . I saw the death of Richard Roose. Dost remember him, Father?"

"No," said Ralph, "that I do not."

"He was a cook in the kitchens of my lord Bishop of Rochester. He had poisoned someone by putting a brew in the soup. It was in Smithfield that I saw him

16

die the poisoners' death as decreed by the law. They put him in a cauldron of water which they brought slowly to the boil. His screams were terrible."

Jane said quickly: "Let us talk of more pleasant things, I beg of you. I am going to take Herr Pretzel into the garden as soon as the meal is over. I want to show him my herbs and explain their uses to him. Do you try this pickle, Herr Pretzel. It contains the glasswort, which grows in our fields."

Ralph smiled at her indulgently; he was amused by her fears. But she would not allow herself to be laughed out of her caution. Fanatics alarmed her.

She kept control of the conversation and would allow no sitting over the meal.

"Come, Herr Pretzel," she cried, as soon as they had finished eating. "The sun still shines, and although it is a good thing to sit over dinner, it should not be done over supper, so they tell us. Come into the garden, and my husband and I will show you our estate."

And as they walked among the flowers and trees Jane was relieved. Out in the open, they could talk to their hearts' content.

Dolores lay on her bed and Richard sat beside her, holding her hand.

"How do you feel, my love?"

"Only tired."

"Did that man upset you?"

"Oh . . . no. He is a German, and it is thus that Germans conduct themselves."

"I thought his words concerning your country hurt you a little, my darling."

"Hurt? No . . . no. By a German? By a . . . heretic?"

He laughed and laid his head on the pillow beside hers.

"I could almost wish that there was not to be this child," he said.

"But you must not," she answered.

"I love you so much. I do not want children. Why should I? Are we two not enough for each other?"

"You are afraid," she said. "You must not be. I will be well. I will be as the good Cecily."

"Poor Cecily!" He laughed. "Why is it that that girl, possessing all the virtues, makes us want to slap her?"

"Is it because she, who is so right, must make us feel so wrong?"

"Why should we feel wrong?"

"I, because I am not strong . . . and brave and clever as she is. When you feel ill, it is she who makes a posset for you. She looks to the comfort of all."

"Poor Cecily! And . . . dearest Dolores!"

"You say my name as you did on that first day."

"The day I first saw you. I shall never forget it."

"I was weeping."

"And your tears made me long to see you happy."

"Richard . . . *amigo* . . . how I love you! See, there are tears now. This time for happiness. So perhaps you like them better than the tears of sadness? Now I weep because you are here with me and I am in this happy home . . . because although my home is far away, I have another here with your father and mother, who have become as my own. The day we first met I wept for the Queen. She had just died, you remember . . . so sadly in the castle of Kimbolton, not allowed to have the comforts her friends could bring her. And afterwards, when we loved and were married, I was frightened because I could not forget the Spanish Queen who had married an English King. Is it that a Spanish woman cannot live in happiness with an English husband, I wondered."

"You have proved that to be not so."

"Perhaps *she* thought she had proved it . . . when she had been married but a year. It was not until she was growing old that he found he no longer wished her for his wife."

"That had nothing to do with her being a Spaniard, you foolish one. He had since seen Mistress Anne Boleyn and become enamoured of her. My dearest, the executioner's sword has now taken Anne's head from her body; and that because he saw Jane Seymour."

She put her fingers on his mouth. "I am afraid," she said.

"What have I done?"

"I am filled with dread. It is that man. He frightens me."

"Poor Pretzel! Why, he is just a simple uncouth Lutheran."

"I wish he had not come."

"In a few days he will be gone, and it will be as though he never was here."

"Will it? I wonder . . . will it?"

He lifted her heavy black hair from her face and kissed her. When he spoke again it was in Spanish — which she was teaching him. His accent never failed to make her smile, and he wished her to smile now.

"You could never be a Spaniard," she said.

"But I improve, do I not?"

"Ah yes, my love, you improve."

"When we are old and grey, I shall speak your tongue as well as those who were born in your sunny land."

"When we are old and grey! I like the sound of that. I could wish we were old and grey at this moment . . . and our lives behind us."

"You would wish our lives away!"

She said: "I am full of wishes today. It is because that man is here. I wish he had not come today."

"You have allowed him to upset you with his crude German talk . . . with his Lutheran manners."

"Perhaps it is so. Yet there is a feeling within me . . . I wish he had not come today."

Then, to draw her thoughts from the stranger, he began to talk of the child soon to be born; and they lay watching the deepening of the twilight.

Cecily was in the kitchen, superintending the maids as they cleared away the dishes. Her bright blue eyes missed nothing; they sparkled below her prim headdress. She patted her lovely golden hair, which was taken off her face and held in a golden net at the nape of her neck.

"Come, Betsy, put the beef away. But first let me see what is left. I shall turn that into a good pie. Did you hang the pheasants? That is well. Now, Gillian, to the well for water. Nan, go with Gillian and take another pail."

Cecily watched the girl's awkward gait. Her time must be near. Cecily hoped the girl's bastard would not be embarrassingly like Roger. She would never forgive Charles because the girl he had chosen to seduce was one of the maids in the house. Cecily's position in this house, her dignity, the respect accorded to her, were of the utmost importance; she could not forgive anyone who impaired them. Looking at the girl now, she hated, not the poor silly creature, but Charles. They should have forced her to marry one of the men on the estate, but neither Sir Ralph nor Lady Grendell would force Nan into marriage. Affairs in this house when not conducted by Cecily were, in Cecily's opinion, very badly managed.

When the two girls were at the well, Gillian looked slyly at Nan.

"Mistress Cecily all but killed you with her looks," said Gillian.

"Why so?" said Nan. Her voice was soft; it suited her gentle dove's eyes and sensuous mouth.

Gillian dug her elbow in Nan's side. "And don't you know?"

Nan looked placidly down the well. She would die rather than speak of Master Charles.

"You're a dark horse, Nan. But not so dark as you think."

"I'm not a horse," said Nan.

"You're big enough for one!" Gillian rolled about in glee. She liked a joke, and, if that joke happened to be of her own making, the more she liked it.

"Hey!" called Betsy from the kitchen window. "What are you two about? Does it take you all day to fetch a pail of water?"

When they returned to the kitchen, Betsy cuffed them both — Gillian lightly and Nan severely. There were times when the sight of Nan was more than she could bear. Nan knew it, but she bore no grudge. She knew that Betsy longed for Master Charles, and she believed he had once had a fondness for her. Nan had seen him touch her thigh as he passed. Nan knew the gesture well. Did she not know all his gestures? He had a way of touching a woman as he had of touching a horse; and he touched a horse in a different way after he had ridden her.

Therefore Nan accepted the cuff.

I feel sinful this day, she thought. The strange gentleman looked so solemn and good. He made me feel how bad I must be.

And she, like Dolores, could not help wishing that he had not come.

Jane was saying: "Here is the burdock. It improves many a dish. Have you ever tried its flavour? This purple orchis and old man's pepper will add much to a mess of pottage. Look! Do you know this herb-twopence? It will cure many things. And if ever you have a toothache, Herr Pretzel, you should try a little camomile. Is it not wonderful to think that God gives us these things . . . growing wild about us? It is only for us to learn their uses."

"So it is with the faith, my dear lady. The truth is all about us . . . and we have but to see it . . . and gather it."

Ralph said with a smile: "Dearest Jane, it is of the herbs of truth our guest would talk."

"But," said Jane, "it is wiser to talk of these earthly herbs."

"And Herr Pretzel is our guest, Jane. Let him choose his herbs."

So they talked of the new faith, the new learning; and how could they remain untouched by the fire of this man?

They sat in the gardens until the twilight came and the glow-worms appeared beneath the bushes.

"Thus," said the visitor, "the lights are springing up all over Europe . . . a little one here . . . another there . . . so small that they are not always seen . . . but soon, my friends, those lights will be multiplied, and so will illumine the whole world."

Nan could not sleep that night. She lay on her pallet in the room she shared with the other women and watched the leafy branches of a tree sway gently in the moonlight.

On such a night as this, she thought, Gillian took me to the wood.

She had forgotten her visit to the wood for many months, but the presence of the stranger had reminded her tonight.

It was difficult to lie comfortably; there were pins and needles in her side and her coarse brown hair seemed unbearably hot. She could see Jennet on her pallet, sleeping peacefully. Jennet had come safely through her trouble. It was nearly eight years ago when Jennet must have felt as Nan did now, for the boy sleeping by the door was past seven. Jennet's mouth was slightly open and she snored faintly; she was at peace. But then perhaps Jennet had never been persuaded to pay a visit to the wood.

An owl hooted suddenly. It was the big grey one who had his home in the barn. Meg Pornack, the midwife, said that evil spirits entered the bodies of birds and animals; and Meg Pornack knew of such things.

What's come over me? asked Nan of herself. It's that German gentleman. He's so good; it makes badness seem more bad today than it was yesterday.

She wished she could sleep as the others did, but although her body ached with the exhaustion produced by the day's work, sleep would not come. In the morning she would be drowsy and Betsy would give her a cuff — two cuffs — one for sleeping late and the other because of the child she was to have.

She began to think of it all from the very beginning, when he had seen her at the washtub with her sleeves rolled above her elbows, and her hair tumbling over her face. He seemed to notice her for the first time, for it was four years before that when her mother had sent her from an overcrowded cottage to work at the big house.

"Hello," he had said. He was beautiful and his eyes crinkled up with laughter.

She had curtsied, lifting her arms out of the tub. "Good morrow to you, sir."

"Who are you?" he had asked.

"I'm Nan, sir."

That had happened more than a year ago when there had been a Queen Anne on the throne. He had said: "You have a queenly name. Nan the Queen and Nan the maid. I'll swear Nan the Queen is no prettier than Nan the maid!"

She had curtsied again, not knowing what to do, blushing under his scrutiny; for there had been that in his looks to make a maiden blush.

Then he had kissed her on the mouth. "I like you, Nan," he had said; and he had gone off singing:

"The hunt is up, the hunt is up,
And it is well nigh day.
And Harry our King has gone hunting
To bring the deer to bay . . ."

He had turned to look at her and had repeated:

"To bring the deer to bay,
To bring the deer to bay."

Then he had laughed and thrown her a kiss; and she had thought: Surely there never was such a kind and beautiful master.

But Betsy came out and boxed her ears for wasting time.

It had happened the next day, in the copse beyond the hay field.

"Sweet Nan," he had said, "I'll swear there was never another like you."

She remembered those words every time she was hurt and frightened.

It seemed very soon that she discovered she was going to have a child; she had trembled with fear when she had told him about it; but there was nothing unkind about Master Charles. First he had looked blank, then he had laughed; for what looked like plain wickedness to her was comic to him. He had told her not to fret and he had kissed her bare breasts which were changing already to betray her secret.

"Never you fret, Nan," he told her. "Our little one will have brothers and sisters . . . many of them . . . so he'll not be lonely. I'll see you're cared for. There's naught to fear. This is happening at every hour . . . in every part of the world. Think of that, Nan. But Mistress Cecily . . . she'll not be pleased."

Nan had trembled at the thought of Mistress Cecily.

"Be still, little one. 'Tis a matter easily settled. It shall be credited to one of the men, but you'll not say who. Marry! I'm not ashamed of getting a fine girl like you with child. Nor should you be to bear it. Yet . . . for the sake of the peace of us all, Nan, we'll keep our secret."

"Yes, master."

"So . . . all will be well, Nan, and you must not fret."

When she was with him, she felt that to be so; but alas, she could not always be with him. Betsy's eyes had followed her, sly and scrutinising. "Marry," she cried, "you're fattening." Betsy had hitched up Nan's skirts and pretended to look beneath them. "Have you been staying out in the copse too long?" All the girls tittered then, as they did when Betsy made a joke; and Nan had become frightened, for Mistress Cecily was watching her too.

Gillian had been her friend; when they had cleared out the rushes together, Gillian had said: "I know what you've been at. Betsy's right. You've been staying too long in the copse."

"You lie!"

Gillian poked Nan. "That don't lie. You're thickening, girl. Come a few weeks and you'll not be able to hide it."

Nan said nothing; her fear was great then.

Later Gillian said: "I'll take you to see Mother Roach, the old witch in the woods."

"What will she do for me?"

"She'll make you a maid again . . . or as near as makes no difference."

"How will she do that?"

"By giving you a potion."

"She'd want my soul in exchange."

"Nay! Bread and meat would suffice!"

"And where'd I get bread and meat?"

"From the pantry. Where else?"

"'Tis not mine to take."

"There's some would say it belongs to him as had played his part in this."

So Gillian had taken Nan to Mother Roach's hut, and there the old woman made Nan sit on a pile of logs. Bones lay on the floor; herbs were drying on strings attached to the walls; and the fire sent out black smoke from under an evil-smelling cauldron.

"What's your wish, girl?" Mother Roach asked.

Nan was too frightened to speak, so Gillian spoke for her.

"She wishes to be a virtuous maid again."

"Then we must take away that which makes her not so," said Mother Roach.

She hobbled about the hut mixing a brew in a cup; then she looked at the food which the girls had brought with them, and as it was to her satisfaction, she handed the cup to Nan. The taste of the liquid made Nan retch, but she drank it all.

When they left the old woman's hut, Gillian said: "You'll feel ill in the morning." Then it was that Nan first noticed the owl, and there seemed to be the laughter of demons in his screech, so that she began to believe that she had sold her soul to the devil. The pains came next morning but they were not enough to make her keep to her pallet. She went about her work feeling sick and ill; the sickness persisted for a week, but the child still grew within her.

"I don't understand," said Gillian. "'Tas never been known to fail before."

Nan was glad then, glad it had failed; for after her visit to Mother Roach she had been filled with a terrible depression which never in the whole of her life had she experienced before. It was as though the old owl screeched "Murderess!" to her; it was as though he told her that when her child ceased to live he would have her soul for ever.

The child had become real. It was not merely a symbol of shame, but her own little baby. She loved little babies. More than anything in the world — except Master Charles — did she love little babies. She could not forget that she had tried to kill her own baby.

But as the weeks passed and she no longer felt the effects of Mother Roach's potion, she grew placid; and she cared for nothing but that the child lived and that she was not a murderess.

The mistress, Lady Grendell, sent for Nan one day.

"Nan," said her ladyship, "you are going to have a child. Who is responsible for this?"

And, simple girl that she was, Nan saw that in her ladyship's face which implored Nan not to tell.

"So," went on Lady Grendell quickly, "you refuse to tell me? Nan, although I should not say this, it does you credit. This man has betrayed you and you wish to protect him. That is so, is it not?"

"Yes, my lady."

"Well, Nan, you have behaved shamefully, but you are only a child. How old are you, Nan?"

"I shall be sixteen in two months from today, my lady."

"Well, you shall stay here and have the child, and I doubt not that when it is born we will find a place for it as we did for Jennet's boy."

"Yes, my lady. Thank you, my lady."

She had curtsied and gone; and that night she had cried with happiness because not only did she serve a kind, good mistress and master, not only had she been loved by Master Charles, but, in addition to this good fortune, Mother Roach's potion had failed.

It was only because the very pious Herr Pretzel was in the house that she must be reminded that her happiness had its roots in wickedness.

In the bedroom over the porch, Jane said: "I have never before been so moved by such talk."

"Nor I," said Ralph.

"There is a beauty in all that simplicity. I am glad he is staying a little while. I look forward to his conversation."

"We shall have plenty of that, never fear."

"But in the garden, Ralph. Let it be in the garden. We should not speak rashly before the servants."

"We are lucky in our servants, Jane. They would be loyal."

"In many ways, yes. But when there is religious conflict, many will put their faith before loyalty to a master. The servants love you — as well they should — and I would trust them in most things. But in religious matters I would not be sure."

He kissed her gently. "You alarm yourself too easily, Jane."

"We have been happy. That is why I fear change."

"Have no fear. We are of no importance. We live in our backwater and watch the world go by."

She clung to him saying: "I pray that you will never be called to high office."

"Our neighbour haunts you still."

"Yes, he haunts me. I think of him often. I think of him, sitting in his gardens, reading aloud from a book printed by Wynkyn de Worde as he loved to do. I think of him sailing up the river on his barge . . ."

"Don't, Jane. Don't. He walked in the rays of the sun. I am in the shade. Rejoice that you have married the laziest man in England."

"I shall rejoice," she answered, "if you will but stay as you are."

They laughed, and outside the grey owl hooted, but it did not disturb them as it had disturbed Nan. To them it was one of the peaceful sounds of the night.

It was a week later when Dolores' pains started.

Gillian was sent running to the village for Meg Pornack, the midwife. Meg came, wheezing along the lanes; she was looking forward to a pleasant stay in the big house.

A midwife's life was a good one, as Meg saw it. "Look," she would say, "you eat like the quality; you stay in their houses; you have the ladies at your mercy, for their lives and those of their children depend on you."

She liked to have the ladies at her mercy. It was a comforting thought that the beggar girl and the Queen were much alike when it came to bearing children.

Meg liked to pose as a wise woman, but she was too clever to be thought a witch. She was not going to run the risk of the ducking stool and worse. She was going to get all the fun she could out of life; let others bear the pain. Her profession had made her bold; and although she would drop as low a curtsy as any to the gentry, there would be a knowing glint in her eyes when she did so, as she thought: Ah, my fine lady, you did not cut such a grand figure in child-bed, did you? There wasn't much difference 'twixt you and the watercress-gatherer, there wasn't!

She went to the bedchamber and saw Mistress Dolores. Her practised eye told her that there would be some hours to wait yet.

"Just you lie down, my lady, and you just wait," she told her. "Soon you'll have a lovely young son, I shouldn't wonder, for look! you're big in the front, and that's the sure sign of a boy, so I've always found."

Master Richard waylaid her as she came down to the kitchen to get herself a bite to eat. He was one of the worrying men, and those she did not admire. Men, as a whole, she respected. They took the fun and dodged the pain. That was what she herself had done, and she must admire any who were like Meg Pornack. She liked to think of herself as wily and to hint at the gay adventures she had enjoyed in her youth. Fun, she implied, she had had in plenty; and there had been no paying the piper for Meggie Pornack. So she had a fellow-feeling with the men, but not with Master Richard's kind, because he was going to suffer in his own way as much as Madam Dolores; and a man who did that was a fool, for whereas Madam Dolores' sufferings were imposed by a law of Nature, Master Richard's were brought on by himself.

"Meg," he said, "she will be all right? There's nothing *wrong* . . . is there? I mean . . . everything is . . . as it should be?"

"Bless your kind heart, sir, there's nothing wrong at all." She smiled at him. "Don't you fret. You'll be laughing in a little while from now, that you will . . . wondering what all the fuss was about. I must get myself something to eat, then I'll be back, sir. I've got my work to do and I'll need my strength to do it."

"Yes, yes," he said.

He went back to his wife, and Meg met Charles on the lower landing.

She dropped him a curtsy. There was a man, if ever there was one.

"So *you* are here, Meg?" he said.

"Thank you, yes, sir."

"What a life yours is! Are you flourishing, Meg? Are you bringing many babies into the world?"

"Aye, sir. And I feel I shouldn't let the opportunity go by without thanking you, sir."

She was insolent, but it was diplomatic insolence. It was the sort he liked; it made him laugh, and he liked anyone who made him laugh.

"You are not thanking me for this one, Meg?"

"No, no, sir. But it's gentlemen like you that puts business in the way of a poor woman like myself."

"You're a saucy old woman, Meg."

"Why so, sir? For saying a thank-you to a kind gentleman?"

She had her head on one side; if she had been even slightly handsome he would have kissed her.

"Get on your way," he said with a laugh. "You wicked old woman!"

She grinned and curtsied before she passed on to the kitchen.

There she was treated with respect. A piece of beef and a chete loaf were set on the table before her while Betsy sent Nan to the buttery for a gallon of ale.

She smacked her lips with relish while the girls waited for her to speak. It was homage such as this that she loved.

"'Twill be the first foreigner I've ever helped," she said.

"Will it now?" said Betsy.

"Foreigners!" She rolled her eyes and smacked her lips. "I don't like it much. Foreigners are queer. They say some of them have tails."

The girls were awestruck, picturing a queer animal running about the house playing with Master Roger.

"One thing you can be sure of," said Gillian, "this child will be no Master Roger."

Meg had spied Nan. "Here," she said. "You, girl."

Nan came forward timidly.

"Your time's not far off."

"No, Mistress Pornack."

"You girls!" Meg snickered. "You don't know how to live. What do you want to get into trouble for? Feeling all right?"

"Yes, Mistress Pornack."

34

Betsy caught Nan's shoulder. "It seems to me she ought to have had her baby by now."

"I'll take a look at her," said Meg. "It would be a bit comic if I was to deliver the two at the same time. You go to your bedroom, Nan, and I'll be along to see you."

Nan went out obediently; and when Meg had finished her meal, she said: "I'll go and look at her before I go to Mistress Dolores. I don't quite like the looks of little Nan."

In the room which she shared with the other girls, Nan looked in alarm at Meg Pornack.

"Lie down, girl," said Meg. "When did it happen, eh? You mustn't mind my question. These things have to be known."

"I can't say when."

"You ought to have more sense . . . but as I always say, it's the people without sense who make work for Meggie Pornack." She leered at Nan. "He's a bonny man, and it's hard for the likes of you to say him nay, eh?"

Nan was silent. Sensing a certain fear in her eyes, Meg became alert.

"You haven't been *up* to anything . . . since it happened, have you?"

Nan's eyes filled with sudden tears. "Oh, Mistress Pornack, was it very bad . . . what I did? I wished I hadn't. But it seemed all right . . . afterwards. My baby will be all right, won't it?"

"What did you do?"

"I went to Mother Roach . . . and she gave me something to drink."

Meg took Nan by the shoulders and shook her.

"You little fool!" she cried. "So that's it. Why . . . you might have done murder . . . That's what you might have done."

"Murder . . ." Nan felt the return of all the horror she had known. She lay staring at Meg Pornack.

Nan went about her work with tears in her eyes. To her the world was a dark place. She would follow Master Roger with her brooding eyes, but Tansy, his nurse, would not let her touch him. Tansy guarded the boy; he was hers.

Nan dreamed of little babies, her little baby among them. When she awoke, she thought she must have dreamed of Heaven, for that was where her little baby was now. It had been a little girl, and an hour after her birth she had died. "That," Meg Pornack had said, "is all along of visiting wicked witches in the wood."

There was another baby in the house; he had been born only a few hours after Nan's baby.

How should Nan have known there was so much misery in the world?

She met Master Charles on a turn of the staircase, and he took her face in his hands and kissed her. "Well, Nan?"

But she had no smile for him, her eagerness was gone.

"What ails you, little Nan?" he asked.

"I killed my baby. I murdered my own little baby."

"Nay! 'Tis not so. The child died as many children die. Smile, Nan. You'll have more, never fear."

And his hands on her body were a suggestion and an invitation, but she shook her head and the tears streamed down her cheeks as she ran away to hide herself.

She would lean out of a window to shake her duster, and see the good man walking in the gardens talking earnestly to Sir Ralph and Lady Grendell; that only made her feel the more wicked.

Richard touched her arm one day when she was carrying dishes to the kitchen.

"You have not seen my son, Nan," he said. "Would you like to?"

She looked into his face and saw a sadness and a fear there which equalled her own, and she began to cry again.

"Come, Nan," he said, "come and see my son."

Mistress Dolores, looking pale and ill, was lying in the big bed.

She said: "Ah, Nan, I heard of your trouble." She took Nan's hand. "You must try not to grieve so, Nan."

Nan knelt by the bed and wept afresh.

Dolores sent her to look at the baby, who was lying in a cradle decorated with blue ribbons. Nan had never seen such a wan little baby. He looked like a tired old man. "He is going to die . . . as my baby died," she murmured to herself. "But he will not be murdered."

As she turned away from the cradle, Dolores said to her: "You like my baby, Nan?"

"I . . . I don't want to see any more little babies. I don't . . ."

She stopped, astonished at her temerity; but Richard laid his hand on her shoulder and gently pushed her out of the room.

A month after that day when Ralph, Dolores and Cecily had seen his arrival, Emil Pretzel went down to the barge which was moored at the privy stairs.

As the boat slipped away, all those who had gone to say farewell waved to him. Each knew that his visit had wrought a change; he had sown those seeds he had come to sow: some had fallen on stony ground, but others were stirring in fertile soil.

On the wicker seat sat Nan; her face was placid, and there was a deep contentment in her smile as she looked at the baby at her breast.

Miracles could happen. Nan had come out of an ugly experience and was happy again. She had a baby, and the boy in her arms seemed more like her own than the girl-child who had lived but an hour.

"Little Felipe," she murmured. "Nan's baby — that's who you are, little Felipe."

It was the prettiest name in the world, though it was so foreign, and Betsy and Meg Pornack had said he should have been Ralph or Charles or Richard.

He was hers. She fed him with her milk that had been meant for another. But what did that matter? The memory of the other was fading, for the miracle had happened.

"Nan," Sir Ralph had said to her, "you have saved that boy's life."

Sir Ralph was not only kind but clever; he knew of the terrible haunting fear that had been hers; he knew of her guilt, though he had never spoken of it. And when he said: "You have saved the boy's life!" she felt he meant that Felipe was her child in place of the one she had lost. She was his nurse; his care was her concern and she no longer worked in the kitchens. She was nothing but Felipe's nurse. She hardly ever thought of Master Charles; and she never gave a thought to Mother Roach.

Felipe grew stronger every day. He was going to live, and she had saved him. From her body, which she had hated during those days of agony, had come the nourishment which had saved Felipe's life; and in Nan's mind were vague and shadowy thoughts. But for her sin and her shame, she told herself, this baby would have died; she was convinced now that only she could have nourished his little body. He was her joy, her life and the means of her redemption.

She looked for a brief second from his little face to the barge which was slipping away from the privy stairs.

Much had happened since the stranger had come among them.

CHAPTER
TWO

In the summer of his ninth year Felipe first became aware of change. Before that he had accepted everything which life had given him, without thought that others might not enjoy his good fortune; he had taken for granted that life would go on as it had during his nine peaceful years.

He lived in a beautiful house in which there were many to love him. Life was made up of lessons and play; there was skating in winter, hay-making in summer; riding, swimming, tennis and kayles. At these he did not excel as did his cousin Roger; but he could better Roger at their lessons. There was no rivalry between the cousins. It was understood between them that Roger should allow Felipe to write his Latin essays in such a fair imitation of Roger's bold hand that Mr Heath, their tutor, thought Roger had written them; Roger naturally took the lead in sports.

On that May day when Felipe first became aware of change, the two boys were together in the schoolroom.

"Roger," said Felipe suddenly, "what is happening in this house?"

Roger wrinkled his sunburned brow, as he did when he was trying to concentrate. His blue eyes sparkled. "There's roast pheasant for dinner," he said.

Felipe smiled at his cousin. He was almost a year younger than Roger, but with his solemn, olive-skinned face and his dark eyes he seemed, at times, older. It was only when they stood up and Roger towered above his cousin that Roger showed he was the elder.

"Nay," said Felipe, smiling, "I meant not what was cooking in the kitchen."

He continued to smile because he knew that what was happening in the kitchen was of the utmost importance to Roger, who, with the largest appetite in the household, was always hungry. Roger hung about the kitchen and helped himself to pies and cakes, and the women in the kitchen encouraged him to do this. They adored him. Of all the children, he was the favourite. They said he was wicked, but they loved his wickedness. They would click their tongues and laugh when they talked of it. "The young rogue, what has he been up to now?" How often were those words used about Roger? His grandfather and his grandmother used them. So did his father and mother, as well as the servants; but they all used them indulgently, as though — which indeed was the case — they loved him more for his sins than they could for any virtues.

"What then?" asked Roger.

"Have you not noticed? They are quieter. They whisper. Something is afoot, depend upon it."

"You imagine too much," said Roger.

"Do I? That is what they all say."

"You dream. Sometimes, cousin, I think you should have been a girl."

"But your sisters do not dream as you say I do."

"Nay. But to dream is for girls, not for men." Roger studied his cousin critically. "I know what you will be when you grow up. You will be a scholar." There was great scorn in Roger's voice.

"And you?" said Felipe, for he loved his cousin, and he knew that there was nothing that pleased Roger more than to discuss his own future.

"I shall go to sea," he said. "I shall sail the Spanish Main. I shall go to Peru and Mexico." He looked out of the window at the river flowing past the garden. "I would that river were the sea. I would I could sail where none has been before . . . right out past Westminster and Gravesend. I would I were captain of a ship that I might sail right over the edge of the world."

"And what would you do when you had sailed over the edge of the world?"

"Find new lands. Men to be my slaves . . . lions, tigers which I would tame to obey me." His blue eyes blazed. Who was the one who was dreaming now? Felipe wondered. Roger would say: But these are not *dreams*: they are *plans*.

Felipe let him go on talking, while he wondered why there was a strangeness in this house. It was something to do with the visitors who came at night; it had something to do with a book he had seen in his grandparents' bedroom.

Once he had taken a message to his grandmother from his grandfather, and when he entered the room, she was not there; but he had seen the book lying on a table, and because he loved books, he had looked at it. A second later his grandmother had come into the room.

"Felipe, what have you there?" she had said.

"It is a Bible, is it not?" he had answered.

It might have been when she had taken it from him that he had first become aware of the strangeness, for she had looked very anxious. Hastily she had put the book into a drawer.

"It is nothing . . . nothing," she had said, with a sharpness that was not natural to her; it was as though she was angry with him for his inquisitiveness. When he had given her the message, he had felt that she scarcely listened to him.

"Felipe," Roger was saying, "you shall come with me. You shall be my second in command. Then if we meet a Spanish ship and take her captive, you can talk to the prisoners."

"Thank you," said Felipe.

Roger studied his cousin with seriousness. "I often think it is strange that you should be my cousin and yet almost a Spaniard. Your name is Grendell, but you are not really English. Felipe . . . and Grendell. Half Spanish, half English."

There were times when Felipe wished his cousin to know that if he were not as tall as he was, if he were not completely English, there were many things he could do a good deal better than Roger. He turned to his books. "Have you done your translation?" he asked.

"I have not. Nor can I make sense of the thing."

"Give it to me. It is easy."

He began to write Roger's translation, and Roger was momentarily subdued. "Sometimes," he said, "you shall take command of the ship."

"Thank you, cousin. That is good of you."

It was very comforting to be able to feel superior to Roger at times; and whilst Roger swatted flies, Felipe thought of all the reasons why it was better to be Felipe than to be Roger.

For instance, how frustrating it must be to see a page of Latin and not be able to construe it! How humiliating to be told by Mr Heath: "You are lazy and inattentive." Yet Roger felt no humiliation. He *was* lazy and inattentive; his brain would not absorb Latin, French or Spanish. Yet what did they say? "The rogue . . . what has he been up to now?"

And when his sins were so great that he must be whipped, the whole household seemed plunged in mourning. Grandfather and Grandmother went into the garden so that they should not hear Roger's yells: Roger's father would grumble: "Boys must be boys." Even his mother would say: "Now, Mr Heath, remember he is but a boy." His youngest sister, Kate, would cry in sympathy. And Tansy, who had been his nurse, said that she would like to lay the stick about Mr Heath, for what was more natural than that boys should get up to tricks?

The one least concerned would be Roger himself; and though he would yell lustily while the punishment went on, he would quickly recover and greatly enjoy the condolence of the household.

Felipe was hardly ever whipped at all. He knew that some thought that was unnatural for a boy; and they did not like it. Aunt Cecily, Roger's mother, said there was something sly about a boy who was never caught. She did not believe that a boy could keep out of mischief as successfully as Felipe did.

Aunt Cecily disturbed Felipe because she showed such dislike for him. When he had been a very small boy she had more than once locked him in a dark cupboard and pretended it was an accident. He remembered standing in the dark, with the sweat of fear on him. Naña (as he called Nan) had rescued him. In those days Naña had told him she was one of his mothers. He had found great comfort in laying his head on her big bosom; when he had been frightened in the night he would go to her, and she would take him under her blankets and hold him close to her.

Aunt Cecily had seemed to him more unlike Naña than anyone else could possibly be. He often felt that the more she loved Roger, the more she hated *him*; and that the two emotions grew side by side.

None of the children hated him; Roger and his three sisters were all Felipe's friends. This applied particularly to young Kate; yet when Aunt Cecily saw them together she would call Kate away.

When Felipe had been very young Aunt Cecily had made faces at him if she found him in a dark corridor alone. That was before he could speak very well; sometimes he had gone screaming to Naña. Then Aunt Cecily had said: "That child's not right in the head. He's nervous. He's not a bit like Roger." He had never said anything about the faces, even to Naña. He was a secretive boy. Roger never kept anything back. No wonder they all loved Roger; he was so natural, so easy to understand.

It might have been thought that one so endowed with natural gifts, which commanded so much love from those about him, would have been spoilt. Not so Roger. He was selfish perhaps, inasmuch as he saw himself the centre of the world, as the hero of all adventures, but he had inherited his grandfather's natural kindliness, so that although others might seem pigmies to him, he could not be indifferent to their sufferings. He wanted to enjoy life, and enjoyment — as with his grandfather — to be thoroughly relished, must be shared.

It was small wonder, Felipe often thought, that everyone loved Roger. But there were three people in the household who loved Felipe best.

First there was his father, and Felipe dearly loved his father. It seemed to him that in the grave man there was infinite wisdom. His father was a deity to him — omniscient, omnipotent, all-loving. That was how God was, Felipe believed, only his father was much kinder than he could believe God was; he would never have asked Isaac to sacrifice his son; he would not have slain or punished anyone. Felipe faced the alarming fact that he loved his father better than God.

Then there was his mother; and if his father represented Goodness, she was Beauty. She spoke in soft, sweet tones; she would lie on her couch, for she was not strong, and that caused his father much anxiety; she would tell him about her beloved *España*.

She would call him *niño*, her little *rey*, her *hijo*. And all these names were love-names when she said them.

Neither his father nor his mother seemed to him quite human; they were perfect, and human beings were not perfect. The best of them were like Roger, attractive, but far from perfect; and Felipe suspected — for he was a little boy who liked to use his reasoning powers to solve all his problems — that Roger was so greatly loved because he was more human than anybody.

Then there was Naña, who loved him completely. *He* had first called her Naña. Her real name was Nan. Everybody in the house called her Naña in imitation of his Naña. She would refer to herself as Naña. "You should have come to Naña. Didn't you know Naña was waiting?" "Naña's boy," she called him.

He did not run to her as much as he used to. One must grow up. But he never forgot the comfort of her big, warm body. "Naña . . . Naña . . . I'm frightened. There are lions in the room. There are fog-dogs coming for me." "Shush," she would say to the shadows. "Shush away. You shan't come after Naña's boy."

"Naña," he asked her once, "whose boy am I — yours or my mother's?"

"You're mine," she said fiercely. "Mine first . . . hers second."

The logical Felipe could not be satisfied with that. "Then why is Roger my cousin?"

Then she told him the story of how he all but died because his mother could not feed him, and how the saints had come to her in a dream and told her that although she believed her own baby had died, the soul of that baby had gone into the body of the baby that would drink her milk. "You were that baby, Felipe. That's why you are Naña's."

He had been contented with that explanation. It was pleasant to have two mothers. "The earthly and the heavenly mother," he had said. For if there could be an earthly and a heavenly father, why should there not be two such mothers?

Mr Heath expressed himself satisfied with Roger's translation, and the two boys left the schoolroom and went into the gardens.

That was the beginning, thought Felipe afterwards. Until then it was just any day.

"Shall we ride?" asked Felipe.

"No." Roger's dreams were still with him. "Let's go to the river. Let's go to the barge."

"We are not allowed to."

Roger looked scornful. "Are you a coward, Sir Felipe?"

"I am not, Sir Roger."

"Then come to the barge, and do not act as though you were."

"The rope is not safe. Grandfather said so. He said we are not to play in the barge until a new one has been fixed."

"Do you think I could not manage the barge if she broke away?"

"That I cannot say. But Grandfather said we were not to."

But Roger wished to play in the barge. The fact that it was forbidden made it the more desirable.

"Grandfather thinks we are children."

"So we are."

"You may be, Felipe, but you forget that I am much older than you. Come. I will be the captain, and you shall be my second. We are going to sail down the river . . . out to sea. We shall Capture a Spaniard laden with treasure . . . and we'll hang her crew. Ahoy there! Ahoy!"

Roger was already running down to the river bank, and Felipe followed.

The bushes grew thick about the privy steps and the willows drooped into the water at that spot; and as Felipe came panting after Roger — for Roger ran faster and had soon outstripped him — he was aware that he had stopped and was signalling to him not to speak.

When he reached Roger, his cousin seized him and forced him down into the bushes, putting a finger to his lips.

Felipe thought this was some new game, but when he heard the sound of a boat's scraping against the stairs, followed by that of men's voices, he realised why Roger had forced him to hide.

Three men were getting out of a barge. They were in official uniform.

One man said: "This is the house of Sir Ralph Grendell."

"Well," said another, "what of it? We have orders to search the place. Don't forget — if we find what we seek, we are to arrest Sir Ralph first."

"I don't like it," said one of the men. "He was good to me when my wife was sick."

"Fool!" came the retort. "These are the King's orders."

The men walked up the steps and started to cross the lawns. Roger was about to leap to his feet, to run after them, to demand what they meant to do; but with a sudden intuition that this was even more dangerous than Roger could understand, Felipe held him back.

"Hush!" said Felipe.

"Did you not hear?" whispered Roger. "Did you not hear the insolence of those rogues? They would search our house. They would arrest our grandfather."

"On the King's orders!" said Felipe.

He remembered suddenly the book he had seen in his grandmother's room; he remembered her strangeness because he had found it. He believed this visit had something to do with that book, and that if those men found it they would take it . . . and his grandfather with it. Why should a book be a bad thing? He did not know. But he did know that books were important. You read them and grew wise.

His face was pale, yet his black eyes burned.

He said: "Roger, I know . . . I think I know!"

"What do you know?"

"It is about a book. They will search and find it. They must not find it. We must take it and hide it. I believe it is in a drawer in Grandfather's and Grandmother's bedroom."

Here was adventure such as Roger loved, even though he might not fully understand what it was about. Impetuously he prepared to run after the men.

"Not that way!" cried Felipe. "To the back. We must use the back staircase. We must get to the room before they do."

They sped across the grass. Felipe was running as fast as Roger now. Fear was with him — fear such as Roger would never understand.

He knew that he was right. Evil was in their house, threatening their contentment. Unless he was very quick and clever, they would take his grandfather away, and there would never again be happiness in this beloved home.

They ran to the back of the house and through the kitchen quarters. They could hear the strange rumble of voices in the hall.

"Quick!" whispered Felipe and they ran up the stairs.

In the drawer they found the book; there were other books there with it.

"Take them all," urged Felipe on sudden impulse. "We must hide them all."

Roger was ready to obey, for Felipe was in command of operations. They took the books and ran out of the house by way of the back staircase.

"We must hide them," panted Felipe. "We must hide them where none can find them."

"Like treasure," said Roger. "I have it. In the orchard where the new trees have been planted."

"Yes. It should be easy. Keep the books hidden, Roger. If we are caught, Roger . . . if we are caught we will say the books are ours."

"Let us say that we sailed down the river to the sea and that we captured a Spanish galleon and . . ."

"Nay, nay. We must say we bought them from an old pedlar and that we have not yet looked at them."

In the orchard they worked feverishly until they had buried the books. They trampled down the earth and stood back to admire their work.

"And now?" said Roger.

"Let us to the house, to see what is happening."

Dolores was lying on her couch. Richard sat beside her holding her hand. They watched the men turning out the drawers.

"You'll forgive us, my lady," said one of the men. "These are the King's orders."

"What do you hope to find?" asked Richard.

"We hope *not* to find what we are looking for, sir," was the answer.

Richard could feel his wife's trembling. She believed that, although they might find nothing in this room, they would do so in another. She could not bear to think of what would happen then. She knew that there were books in this house which were forbidden books — forbidden by the law of the land. Before the coming of the German Pretzel, her father-in-law had been a good Catholic. But neither Catholics nor Protestants were safe now. Those Catholics who believed the Pope was head of the Church were called traitors; those who turned to the new learning, the teachings of Martin Luther, were called rebels.

Her father-in-law was a rebel; yet he was not fervent in his new belief. He was interested, that was all; he liked the new ideas. He wished to discuss them, so he entertained men and women at his house who had similar interests; and because it was forbidden to gather together and talk of such things, these people came in secret after dark.

Richard attended those gatherings; he, too, read those forbidden books. Oh, why need they meddle?

"It is not that I believe in the new faith," Richard had said. "Indeed I know not what I do believe. But not to read what is written by scholars — that seems to me to be shutting one's eyes when it may be that the truth is waiting to be seen."

And now, because one day a man named Pretzel had called upon them, fear stalked the house.

She knew why these men had come at this time, because she and Richard had often talked of these things. Anne Askew, the friend of the Queen who made no secret of the fact that she was a Reformer, had been arrested; it was said that they were trying to make her talk in the Tower so as to implicate others, and that Thomas Gardiner, the Bishop of Winchester, and Sir Thomas Wriothesley, the Lord Chancellor, really aimed to implicate the Queen because the King was tired of her and wished to replace her by another wife. All knew that if the Queen were arrested and died the heretics' death, the King and his ministers would need others to die with her.

So Dolores thought of the father-in-law, who had become dear to her, that good, kind man who had once asked nothing but to live peacefully with his family; and she trembled that he might at any moment be taken to the Tower to join Anne Askew.

The heat in the room seemed stifling. Her heart was beating in the uneasy way it did at times of stress and excitement. She wished that she did not so often feel ill. Poor Richard! She was afraid she was being a disappointment to him. She was sick and fragile, having miscarriages instead of children, unable to be the wife to him that Cecily was to Charles. Yet how much happier they had been than Charles and Cecily. But would any of them be happy after today?

The men had gone, and she could hear them in the room of her parents-in-law.

"Richard," she said, "they cannot fail . . ."

"Hush, my darling; who knows?"

"But we know. Do you hope for a miracle?"

They waited.

Now, thought Dolores. Now . . . at any moment.

The house was quiet. The men had gone. The miracle had happened.

Jane looked at her grandsons. Two little boys . . . and because of them this was not the house of mourning it might have been.

Roger was excited. It was a great adventure. Already he thought of the books as buried treasure; he was born to be an adventurer. Felipe's eyes were melancholy. He was the one who had saved them, and Roger had been but his henchman in this; to Felipe was the glory, but he was too thoughtful to see it as such. Fear had been implanted in Felipe.

"Shall we go out now and dig up the books?" asked Roger.

"Nay," said his grandfather. "Leave them hidden. Who knows when they may return?"

"Grandfather, what books were they?"

Ralph hesitated, but Charles said: "They must know, Father." He looked with pride at his son. "They are old enough to understand, and do not forget what we owe them."

"My boys," said Ralph, "those books were written by clever men who do not think on certain religious topics as do our masters. Therefore the people of this land are forbidden to read those books."

"But for your action," said Charles, "your grandfather and possibly others in this house would be the King's prisoners."

"We should have rescued you all," cried Roger; his expression was almost regretful. If they had taken his grandfather he would have had an opportunity of storming the Tower.

"I doubt not that you would, my son," said Charles. "But it is better that the books should not be found; and for that we have to thank you and your cousin. Now you are no longer boys. You are men, Not a word of this to any. Do you swear?"

"I swear!" cried Roger; and Felipe echoed him.

Dr Cresset, the physician, who had always been a friend of the family, arrived at that moment. He was rather breathless. Word had come to him that the Grendells' house was being searched.

Felipe knew that Dr Cresset was one of those who called at the house after dark to read and talk.

"I heard the news," said the doctor. "What happened?"

Charles said: "The sun shines brightly. You boys should be out in the fresh air."

They went, but reluctantly, and when they had gone Dr Cresset was taken into the small winter parlour, where they talked in low tones. It was alarming to think that they were known as Reformers. The doctor was amazed by their miraculous escape.

"It was as though Providence was guarding us," he declared. "How could Felipe have known the importance of that book?"

"He is a strange boy," said Jane. "Not bold and dashing as his cousin, but thoughtful, grave and deeply affectionate. I think we must have betrayed the importance of the book in some way. It is to Felipe that we owe our safety at this moment."

Richard joined them. He looked relieved to see Dr Cresset.

"I heard news of what had happened, and I came to see for myself," said the doctor.

"A miraculous escape."

"And it is to your young son that we must be grateful."

Richard smiled. "Felipe sees more than we realise, I think."

"God bless him," said Jane.

The doctor turned to Richard. "You look shaken still," he said.

"It is . . . Dolores."

"This is upsetting for her."

"This, yes . . . but she does not grow stronger. We thought that after she had lost her child she would recover. But no. It seems that she is weaker than ever. She coughs too much. I am wondering whether she will ever be well while she has to face our damp, cold air. I wonder, would she recover her strength if she went back to her native country? What do you think?"

"There is a possibility that she might."

"I would do anything . . . anything to make her well again."

Ralph turned to his son. "Richard, it might be well for you and Dolores to take a trip to Spain. There is peace just now, and there are her estates which need attention. Moreover, who knows what the next move will be? We know that we are watched. We know that we are suspected. It might be wise for you to go away for a while."

"Dolores loves this place. And . . . what of the boy?"

"She must want to see her home. As for Felipe, he will be happy where you two are. Besides, there is her health to think of first."

"I will speak of it to her."

Jane looked at her son with troubled eyes. She hated the thought of parting with any member of her family. She was fond of Dolores, but how she wished Richard had not made a Spanish marriage! How she wished that Emil Pretzel had never come to this house! It was he who had brought trouble into their lives. It was always thus with fanatics.

Night fell uneasily over the house.

In their rooms the servants, lying on their pallets, whispered together. What was the meaning of the search? Who were the men who had come? For what had they been looking? When the houses of the quality were searched, when the quality was suspected, it sometimes happened that their servants were taken and tortured, that they might give information against those they served.

Cecily sat up in bed waiting for Charles to join her and douse the candle. Her hair, in two golden ropes, lay over her shoulders; she looked as prim without her headdress as with it.

Cecily was shaken. She had always known that things over which she had no control in this house were badly managed.

"Life has never been the same since that man Pretzel came," she grumbled. "I remember the day well. It was just before Felipe was born. He put ideas into your father's head. I do not know why he must meddle in such matters."

Charles shrugged his shoulders; for once he was almost in agreement with his wife.

"What if they had taken him?" demanded Cecily. "They might have taken you too. And you know well what happens to heretics. They take all their lands and goods if they are proved guilty."

"I see," said Charles, "that the loss of my estate would mean far more to you than would the loss of my person."

"There are the children to be thought of."

He was silent. There had been too much bickering. In the first years of marriage he had thought: This is a good enough union. She is fair; she is healthy; and she is what is called a good wife. Cecily had thought: He has fortune and standing; he can give me children. Both had thought they could compromise, but with the passing of the years the little irritations, piled one upon another, made a great barrier between them. She loathed his infidelities; he loathed her carping small-mindedness. Theirs was not a happy marriage.

There was one thing they had in common: their overwhelming affection for their firstborn. Again and again Roger had been the means of averting the quarrel, as he was now.

"To think," said Cecily, "that but for our boy's having the courage and the presence of mind to bury those books, your father would be the King's prisoner now."

Cecily had forgotten Felipe's part in the adventure; she had not for a moment believed that his could be the major share.

"What a boy he is!" said Charles. "What a man he will be!"

They looked at each other and, their irritation temporarily forgotten, they smiled.

He snuffed out the candle and got into bed.

It would be a good thing if they could have another son like Roger.

There was moonlight in the room. Jane had not drawn the curtains of the bed. She lay still, waiting. Her heart was beating wildly. Ralph was aware of it; he reached for her hand and held it firmly.

"Why are you not asleep?" asked Jane.

"Do you expect me to fall lightly to sleep after the events of the day?"

"I have been lying here, waiting for you to sleep."

"Why is that?"

"Because there is something I must do. It is two of the clock. I heard the clock strike. Why do you lie awake like this?"

"For the same reason that you do."

They were silent for a while, then Jane said: "There is something I wish to do this night. I cannot live through another day with it undone. What if those men came back and searched the orchard?"

"They could not dig up all our land, looking for the books."

"They would see where the earth had been disturbed." She sat up. "I can wait no longer. I hoped to do this while you slept."

She rose and lighted a candle. He thought that in her long bedgown, with her hair streaming about her shoulders, she looked like an apparition. He also rose and put on a few garments.

"We must be quiet, Jane," he said. "We do not wish the servants to hear us."

Silently they crept down the stairs. In the porch they took a lanthorn which they lighted from the candle; then they made their way across the damp grass to the orchard.

Every now and then Jane looked over her shoulder as though she feared they were being watched. She noticed that Ralph did the same.

Felipe also could not sleep that night. He heard the creaking of the stairs and, when his grandparents crept out of the house, he was at his window watching their cautious progress through the gardens to the orchard.

He knew they were going to the spot where the books were buried. He believed that they were going to retrieve them and bring them back to the house.

He thought: If the men come back I must be ready to bury them again.

He was poignantly aware of their fear.

Change was everywhere. This time last night he had been an ignorant boy; he had believed that grown-up people were afraid of nothing; he had thought that his grandfather was the most important man in the world. Now he understood that grown-up people could know such fear as he had known in the darkness of the cupboard in which his Aunt Cecily had locked him. Growing up did not, then, release one from fear. Rather did it bring worse fear.

He pressed his cold hands against the window-panes and waited there until he saw a thin column of smoke rising among the orchard trees.

He understood; they were burning the books.

He went back to bed and lay there, shivering, for a long time.

Dolores sent for Nana. Nana went to her apprehensively; visits to Dolores usually meant that there would be a discussion concerning Felipe. Nana was always afraid that they would take him from her.

Nana thought that Dolores looked very ill. She seemed as though she were wasting away. Looking at the blue veins on the white hands, Nana was conscious of her own short, thick fingers, so sturdy and useful. She was for ever comparing herself with Dolores, and it seemed to Nana that there had never been two women more unlike.

"Naña," said Dolores; and she said the name in the soft foreign way as none other but Felipe said it. "I have something to say to you, Naña. Will you sit, please?"

Nana came forward. She was twenty-four, but she did not look as old as that, though bearing a child had made a woman of her. Her breasts were as big as her hips, but her waist was trim. Her face had lost none of its softness, and her eyes were still gentle; her warm mouth proclaimed her sensuality, but it was now touched with motherliness; everything about her suggested the mother.

She brought a stool and sat awkwardly by the couch.

"I have some news, Naña."

"Yes, my lady."

"We are going away, my husband and I. We are going to my country."

Nana felt that her heart was going to leap into her mouth. Her eyes were momentarily wild, like those of an animal who suspects an attack on her young.

"Yes," went on Dolores, "our son will come with us; but Naña, let me say this quickly ... we should not wish to take him from you. And how he loves you! Naña ... if we should go to Spain and you wished to come with us ... we should take you. We should not separate you from Felipe."

Nana sat very still. It was too much to expect her to understand. She ... to go away ... She ... who rarely went into the nearby city, to go to a strange land!

"Naña, you must not be distressed. There is time for you to decide what you wish to do. Naña ... you must think of this. I tell you now because I would not wish you to hear of it from others ... and to think that we wished to take Felipe from you."

Nana said: "To leave this house ... To go to Spain ..."

"Do not be frightened. My country is a beautiful place."

"Do you go ... for ever?" asked Nana harshly.

"No. We shall return. It is my father's house and his lands ... which are now mine. We have matters to attend to. And it is thought it will do good to my health."

"He is happy here," said Nana. "He is happy learning and playing with his cousin."

"He would not be happy if we went without him."

Nana said slyly: "He would forget soon after the parting. He would look forward to the day when you would come back."

"We could not go away and leave him, Naña. He is our son. I wish him to see his grandfather's country."

Nana, whose emotions were primitive, began to cry suddenly, covering her face with her hands.

"Oh, Naña . . . Naña," said Dolores, "you must not. It is not to hurt you that we would wish . . . You shall not lose him. Do not I, his mother, know how you feel?"

"He is *my* boy," said Nana. "Ever since he was so small and so ill . . . he is my boy."

"Naña, I would not separate you. Go away now. Think of what I have said. There is no need for you to say at once that you will come. I tell you now, that you may not hear it through others . . . and fear that we should take our son away."

Nana got up slowly. Her face was already patchy with her tears.

She folded her hands across her breasts as though she held a baby there.

She went out murmuring: "But he is mine. None could take him from me. He is mine . . ."

Nana lay sleepless on her pallet which was in the little anteroom adjoining Felipe's; she had slept there since he was a little boy.

She would never forget the exquisite joy of those nights when she awakened to see a small figure standing beside her pallet, and heard a voice say: "Naña

64

. . . Naña . . . I cannot sleep tonight." Then she would take him in beside her and hold him in her arms; she would call him her baby, Nana's boy.

She had been happy. Her life was bounded by love; there could be nothing of any importance in her life but love. She gave out love — intense love — and never measured what came to her in return. While she could love she was happy.

But this great love was divided between two people; for her, the rest of the household, the rest of the world, scarcely existed. She was primitive in her emotions; she would have died for the two she loved; but she was not asked to die. A more painful decision was put before her. Not since those days when she had paid a visit to Mother Roach had she had such a problem to face. It was her nature to act on impulse; so now, given a choice of action, she was bewildered. There would have been no problem if her love had not been divided and the trip to Spain did not mean that those two whom she loved would be in different countries and far apart.

"You must choose, Nana," she kept telling herself.

How could she live without Charles? That would mean never to enjoy those moments which somehow, even after nine years, seemed always to bring surprise. To hear his laughter, to accept his embraces and to hear him say: "There is none like you, Nana!" meant as much to her as the love of Felipe . . . almost as much perhaps . . . or more? She could not be sure. Charles had playfully called her Nana when Felipe had renamed her, and he had continued to do so. She *was* Nana now; Felipe had made her that; and she seemed to have had no life which had not contained Charles and Felipe. To her they were husband and child. They satisfied her completely.

Now she was being asked to decide whether she would give up Charles or Felipe. It was a choice which could bring only misery, and her poor brain was incapable of making it. She could not picture a life without Charles; she could not picture a life without Felipe. So she wept and prayed; but neither her tears nor her prayers could help her.

This afternoon when she had been spreading, on the bushes in the shrubbery, the sheets which she had just washed, Charles had ridden into the stable yard, and he must come past the shrubbery on his way from the stables to the house. He came up from behind, caught her and kissed her neck. She had laughed in confusion, afraid that they would be seen; there was always the utmost joy in the terror he inspired.

"Nana . . . you tremble like an aspen. Why do you tremble, Nana?"

"You should not . . . you should not . . ."

Then he ran his hands over her in the way he liked to, and which she liked so much that her body tingled with pleasure.

"Nana," he said, "this is as good as the first time. Do you remember?"

What great joy had been hers, with the clothes flapping about them, for he had not given her time to put them down, and the sheet she had been setting across the laurel bush was trailing in the dust.

But he saw the shadow in her face. "What ails you, Nana?" he asked.

"It is the boy," she said. "They will take him to Spain."

"Yes," he said. "Yes." He was quicker than she was, and she did not have to say everything that was in her mind to make him understand. "And, Nana," he went on, "they want you to go with them."

She nodded, and he looked at her in dismay.

"I must talk to you," he said. "We cannot talk here. Nana . . . in the copse. Yes, I must talk to you. I'll go there and wait. Be quick."

She nodded. She was always obedient in love.

She trembled as she hung the clothes, and then, not stopping for anything but to take the basket back to the bolting house, she ran as fast as she could to the copse. He was lying on the grass, and he held out his arms to her.

"Nana, you would never leave me!"

"But the boy," she said.

"Children!" he cried indignantly. "What are children? They love you while they need you, then they forget. And he is not even yours."

It was the first time she had ever contradicted him. "He is mine," she said. "He *is* mine."

"Nana, you would not leave *me*, would you?"

Her silence alarmed him, and suddenly he understood all that she meant to him. Before that moment she had been Nana, the serving girl, always ready to come when called, delightful, more satisfying than any he had known; and he had believed this was chiefly because she was so different from Cecily. Nana was warm; Cecily cold. Cecily was arrogant; Nana was meek. Cecily was coldly critical; Nana was warmly appreciative.

He realised with astonishment that he had ceased to think very much about any women other than Cecily and Nana. To keep the peace with Cecily, to enjoy peace with Nana — that was how he was spending his time. She was more important to him than he had realised, this plump girl with her heavy brown hair, her large brown eyes whose expression was always soft or loving, her full soft lips that could never say No to her lover.

"Nana," he said in panic, "you could not leave *me*!"

And still she did not answer.

He looked at her as he had never looked at her before, and he knew then that there were two sides to her character; previously he had been concerned only with one side. There was the mistress — the perfect mistress, he now realised — who had lured him without words, without demands, from all others. But there was also the mother, and her he had completely overlooked. He had a rival; a small, pale-faced boy.

He gave her a gentle shake. All desire for love-making had left him. This was incredible. He was here alone with Nana; always before he had known how to make good use of such moments, laughing lightly, caressing lightly, loving lightly.

"Nana, look at me." Then he remembered that he was calling her by that ridiculous name — the name the boy had given her.

"Nan!" he said. "Nan!"

But she did not seem to hear. Her large eyes were sad and bewildered; she was trying to picture her life as it would be when she had no Felipe; as later, when she stood by Felipe's bed and tucked him in, she would try to imagine a life without Charles.

He was in great danger of losing her, and he knew it.

He pulled her down, lavishing kisses and caresses upon her until she could not but respond. It was so easy to arouse her desire. But desire was fleeting; and such satisfaction was not what he wanted now.

"Nan," he said, "put your arms about me, Nan."

But she said: "I must go."

He would not release her.

"You must stop this folly," he said. "What would you do in Spain?"

She shook her head. Her eyes were full of tears, and she looked distressed.

He knew that she was undecided between her affection for him and that which she bore to Felipe.

"You have no idea what it would be like," he went on. "You would hate it. Do you know, Nan, that you would be among people who are quite different from yourself? You could not understand their language."

Still she said nothing.

She was a stupid woman, he told himself. He could not reason with her.

He was angry because he had failed to make her accept the fact that he was more important to her than Felipe could possibly be.

"I shall not let you go," he said.

Again he pulled her down and held her fast; and she lay quietly in his arms. But when she left the wood her problem had not grown less; and all that night and all the next day she went on asking herself: "How can I leave the master? How can I leave the boy?"

The mistress implored the mother; but the mother was firm. Nan and Nana fought together.

The boys rode out from the stables. Roger, full of a secret enjoyment, led the way.

"You must ask no questions," he said. "Just follow me." Three weeks had passed since Felipe had stood at his window and watched the smoke rising from the orchard trees in early morning. Three weeks seemed an age; he could almost believe that life was as it had been before the day of The Search.

He had waited during the days that followed, apprehensive, not caring to stray far from the gardens, for fear something should happen while he was gone. But the days passed and security seemed to have returned.

Roger was chattering as they rode along by the river. He was now regarding his cousin with something like awe. He was envious of Felipe.

"To think that you should be the one to go to Spain! I wish I could go to Spain. You will sail on the sea. Just think! There may be a shipwreck. You may be taken by pirates . . . Spanish pirates. But they would not harm you, for you could pretend to be a Spaniard, and none would know that you were not entirely so. I asked my father if I could go to Spain. He was angry. He said,

'Do not talk to me of going to Spain!' I do not think he wants you to go to Spain, Felipe. I wonder why."

"We shall come back," said Felipe. "We shall not be away for long."

"How I long to go with you! Why could I not come? Felipe, I shall run away. I shall hide on the ship on which you sail. When you are a day out I shall make my presence known . . . and your father will have to take me with you."

Felipe listened respectfully while Roger went on to tell of the adventures he would have.

"Whither are you taking me?" he asked.

"Be patient. You will see."

They rode through Westminster to the village of Charing. The City lay glittering before them. Felipe looked at the great Tower which dominated all other buildings; he could not help thinking of the prisoners within those walls.

Now they saw people coming into the City — some on foot, some on horseback. There was a festive air about the crowd.

"It is some holiday," said Felipe. "What is it? I cannot remember. It looks like May Day."

"May Day in July?" laughed Roger.

Felipe watched the beggars and pedlars mingling with the respectable merchants and their apprentices. They were all bent on pleasure, all going the same way.

"Why, this is Smithfield Fair," said Felipe. "My father brought me here last year when he bought a horse."

"They are not selling horses in Smithfield Square today, cousin."

"What then?"

"Patience . . . and you will see."

Now they were actually in the square, and about them were the swelling crowds. People stood in groups, chattering, looking about them eagerly. By the church of St Bartholomew sat several men; their clothes proclaimed their standing and importance.

"You may well gape, cousin," said Roger. "There is my Lord of Norfolk, and with him the Lord Mayor of London and the Lord Chancellor himself."

"What do they here?"

"You are impatient."

Then Felipe heard words spoken by someone in the crowd which made him tremble with fear as he sat there on his horse. "To the stake!" were those words. "Death to the heretics!"

The heretics! They would have called his grandparents that if the books had been found.

Suddenly the day was too warm. The air was full of smells — hot meat and spiced food, which the pedlars were selling to the crowd; sweating people; the odour of horses which always hung about the square.

Roger was looking about him with excitement. Felipe, longing to leave this place, thought it must be comforting to be like Roger, for when something happened that was dangerous, he enjoyed it, providing the danger excited him.

"Why have they put a fence round the centre of the square?" asked Felipe.

"To prevent the crowd getting there."

"But why?"

"You will see."

"What are those poles with the chains attached to them?"

"You will see soon enough. Look! They are bringing them."

A shout had gone up, and the air was filled with the cries of the people.

"God bless you! God bless you!" cried one, quietly, very quietly.

"Death to the heretics!" cried many others loudly.

"To the stake!"

"These are heretics!"

"These are martyrs," muttered a few.

Felipe felt that the blue sky was pressing down upon him; he felt that if it came nearer he would faint.

Then he saw the woman they carried. She sat on a chair, and he realised why, for her legs were wrapped about with bloodstained bandages. Her eyes burned brightly in her pale face. Three others were brought with her — three men who marched between halberdiers.

The sight of those four people filled Felipe with anguish that turned to horror, with pity that merged into anger.

"Do you know who she is?" Roger was asking. "She is Anne Askew. She is the heretic friend of the Queen. She has been racked nigh to death, they say."

"Be silent," said Felipe. "Be silent."

Roger looked at him in astonishment, but he had turned his head away. His eyes felt hot, his throat dry.

"She is condemned to be burned at the stake," said Roger, who could not be silent on an occasion such as this. "Now you know why all the people are here and why I brought you."

"I . . . I shall go back," said Felipe.

"What! It has not started yet. You could not go before it started."

"I do not wish to stay here."

"Why not?" Roger's eyes were incredulous.

"I . . . I do not care to see it."

Felipe looked at his cousin and saw that the burning of a heretic meant no more to him than the killing of a rat. It was cruel; it was horrible. Yet he, Felipe, was the strange one. Most of these people felt as Roger felt. They had come to see the show as he had. Perhaps some of them had brought their friends to make a holiday of it.

"I . . . I do not care to see it," he repeated.

"Do not go," said Roger. "Who knows? There may be a pardon. There often is. They will say 'Recant and save yourselves.' There is time for that yet."

Felipe found that there was such a press of people that he could not turn his horse. His eyes were drawn to the woman in the chair; now she stood on the other side of the fence; and those who carried her led the procession to the stakes.

They set her on her chair by the first of the stakes and began to put the chain about her waist. In her hands she was holding a cross.

74

And Felipe felt that it was about his waist that they were setting the chain, that it was his nerveless fingers which held the cross; he felt that he had suffered on the rack as the woman had suffered.

A priest stood up and began to preach; he begged the woman and the three men to recant and live to worship God in the true religion. Proudly they refused.

Felipe could not see their faces clearly now, but every line of their bodies proclaimed their determination to die bravely. They fascinated him; a moment ago he had wanted to turn away, to put as great a distance as possible between himself and this foul place. Yet now he felt compelled to stay.

The day of The Search was vivid in his memory. This seemed like a sequel to it. He wondered whether, but for his action in hiding the books, his grandfather would have been one of the men standing there chained to the stake. Even more horrible — might not his grandmother have been like the woman in the chair!

Roger said: "Look! Now they are showing them the King's pardon. It will be theirs if they but recant. Look! look!"

Felipe closed his eyes and prayed for the three men and the woman in the chair. "Let them recant, God. Let them recant. You will not mind whether they are Catholics or heretics. But do not let the fires be lighted at their feet because . . . I cannot bear it."

He kept his eyes shut; he could not look. For ever he would remember the blue sky, the warm sunshine, the smell of horses and people . . . the shouts, the threats and the blessings.

"She would never recant. She is a martyr."

Those words spoken by a man who stood nearby made Felipe open his eyes. Now he saw that faggots were being laid at the foot of the stakes.

A loud voice called: "Let justice be done!"

Then, to Felipe's horror, the flames were applied to the wood and the smoke began to rise.

He could bear no more. He forced his horse through the crowd. Curses followed him. Then . . . suddenly he heard the never-to-be-forgotten shrieks of agony.

He left the crowd, and he could not forbear to look back. Through his tears he saw the smoke from the fires of Smithfield.

He rode on, not caring where he went; and the tears were falling slowly down his cheeks.

CHAPTER
THREE

It seemed to Felipe that he had been a long time in Spain, and that the voyage across the sea, which had been so full of alarms that he had more than once believed he would never survive it, had surely taken place when he was a very little boy. Yet it was only six months ago when he had first set foot in the land of his maternal ancestors.

He would never forget his first glimpse of Spain — the tall mountains, the strand of gold with the sea caressing it, the town of Santander rising from a rugged arm that jutted into the ocean. He believed he would always remember riding on his mule over the mountain passes, and the fear which had ridden with them that their presence would be detected by outlaws and they themselves robbed and murdered. He remembered the changing landscape — the grey, uncultivated soil and the vineyards; the rugged mountains and the plateau; the towns built of stone which had turned golden with age; the heat of the days and the sudden cold of the nights. The people he had seen on the journey had interested him; although his mother was Spanish she was not like them. Their moods changed quickly; he had seen laughter and love change to vituperative anger and hatred in a roadside quarrel. He wished to remember everything he saw so that he could tell Roger of it when he returned to England; he wanted to make Roger see the strange landscape, the women with the flowers tucked in their hair, the men with their knives stuck in their *fajas* — knives that were sharp and ready.

The vast estates which his mother had inherited were some few miles outside the town of Valladolid — between that town and Zamora.

They had come through Zamora on their way to the mansion which had been their home during the last months. To Felipe, as he had paused on the banks of the Douro to look up at the town, it had seemed like a mirage in the air, with its golden-hued buildings which looked as though they were suspended on the edge of the cliffs.

But they had rested there for only a short time before taking the road to Valladolid, and they had reached the great house just before sunset, weary after the journey under the hot sun of the late afternoon — for they could not travel in the heat of noon — grimy and weary.

Felipe had ridden, during the journey, between his father and mother; but Nana had ridden just behind. He was in a strange land, but he had his three loved ones with him and, greatly as he missed his cousin Roger, he was happy.

At the house, which was of the familiar golden hue, there were many servants to greet them. They were dressed in black and they smelt of onions as, so it seemed to Felipe, did most of the people in this country.

They bowed ceremoniously; they kissed not only the hands of his father and mother, but his also; and they addressed him as Don Felipe.

He had been so tired that he had almost fallen asleep on his mule, and one of the men came forward to lift him down; but Nana was beside him, fiercely possessive, as she had been when they had ridden across those frightening mountains. Dear Naña! Felipe loved her deeply, for he knew that she had undertaken this journey for him.

It was fitting, on his first night in his new home, that Naña, his old nurse, should help him to bed.

The house had seemed strange at first, but now he had grown accustomed to it. It was vast; its staircases were wide, with oddly carved banisters; its rooms were lofty and dark because the sunblinds were invariably drawn. The columns of marble, which were a feature both inside and out, were beautifully wrought, and some were inscribed with words which Felipe could not understand until his father translated them for him and told him that the house had been built for a Caliph many years ago when the Moors ruled Spain, and that the inscription was taken from the Koran. "Only God is the Conqueror," his father read out. The floor of the great hall was made of multicoloured tiles laid in varying patterns; the roof was supported by graceful marble columns, a representation, said his father, of Arab tent-poles.

Everything about the house was of great interest to Felipe; he felt when entering it that he had stepped into another world, a world of strange men, the Moors who had conquered and in their turn been conquered. "Only God is the Conqueror." The men who had inscribed those words were Moslems; they too had a God, and what they said of Him in the inscription, told Felipe that he could not be very different from the God he had been taught to worship.

This strange house was built round a *patio* — a beautiful tiled enclosure in which a fountain played and flowers bloomed. Felipe was happy lying in the *patio* looking up at the sky, feeling secure and sheltered with the house on every side.

He had many friends now. The servants vied with each other in their efforts to please the little Don. When he rode out from the house and grounds, on his father's instructions he was always accompanied by Pablo. Pablo was a solemn young man; and the knife he wore in his *faja* was long and curved. He was in love with Marina, the cook's daughter, who could not decide between Pablo and Tomás, who was a servant in the house. Pablo told his troubles to Felipe, and through him Felipe learned much of life; and as life to Pablo meant love and death, Felipe began to attach great importance to these. "One day," Pablo would say, his eyes flashing, his teeth gleaming, "I will kill Marina. Or I will kill Tomás. Perhaps I will kill them both." Then Felipe would beg him to do no such thing. "What good would it do you if Marina was dead?" he would ask in his logical way. "You would be no happier than you are now. And if you killed Tomás you would be killed for killing him." It delighted Pablo to be entreated not to kill, by the little Don; eventually he would allow himself to be persuaded to put back his knife.

There came a day of *fiesta* when the girls wore flowers in their hair and danced the *jota*. Felipe enjoyed that; and gradually he began to learn a little about this strange country to which he felt part of him belonged. Pablo was beside him on the day of *fiesta*, snapping his fingers, spitting with contempt. It was an Andalusian habit to wear flowers in the hair, he said. The Andalusians were the vainest women in the world; and they wore flowers in their hair to call attention to themselves. Marina was an Andalusian. "I would kill them all!" said Pablo.

And it was Pablo who taught Felipe more of the strangeness of life than did his learned tutor, Don Manuel Garcia.

The beggars called out to Richard and Dolores as they rode into Valladolid. They flocked about the pair, exposing their hideous sores and deformities.

"For the love of the saints, Señor. Spare a *peseta*, Señora, for the love of the Virgin."

Richard threw a handful of coins to the ground; and while the beggars scrambled he and Dolores rode on.

They rode into the Plaza Mayor; at the windows of the houses plump ladies sat fanning themselves to keep off the flies. The air was filled with the smell of *olla podrida*, the mutton stew strongly seasoned with onions, which seemed to be brewing in every house in every town in Spain. Townsfolk were squatting on the cobbles talking about the last bull-fight which had been held in the Plaza and of the next *fiesta*, the crowning event of which would be an even better fight than the last. Two children were listening entranced to the conversation of the men, and every now and then one of them would leap up and play the matador, dancing daintily on his toes, while he waved a red kerchief to tease an imaginary bull. On a balcony sat a woman plucking the feathers from a live fowl and letting them float down on to the cobbles; starving dogs prowled about looking for food, snapping at the myriads of flies grown drowsy in the hot air.

"Let us go quickly to the church," said Dolores. "Then . . . we can go home."

Richard led the way to the stables, and there called for a groom to take their horses and look after them until they should return.

It was a short distance to the church, through narrow streets in which many of the shops displayed the goldsmith's sign, for this was Valladolid, the town of the goldsmiths.

They paused for a moment to look up at the magnificent façade of that church which had been built by the fanatical zealot of the Inquisition, Torquemada; and standing there, Richard was reminded of a long-ago day at Chelsea when a stranger had sat at his father's table and talked of the Inquisition. He had said that Torquemada was one of those who had enriched and enlarged the Inquisition until it *was* Spain. Was that true? Richard wondered. The people in the streets —

those women at the balconies, those men talking of the latest bullfight — were they, at every moment, conscious of that great monster which, according to Pretzel, was Spain?

What right, Richard asked himself, had he to enter their church? They might call him Infidel, for if they knew his mind they would consider him as much an infidel as the Jews and Moors whom they had tortured. He did not know whether he entirely believed in the teachings of Martin Luther, but he leaned towards them. He would not tell Dolores of this tendency, because, as a good Catholic, she would be disturbed. He watched her make the sign of the cross; he followed her actions and sank on his knees beside her.

He would offer thanks to God, who, he felt sure, would not mind whether a man was a Catholic or a Lutheran, a Jew or a Moor, for he was full of grateful feelings on this day. Dolores' health had improved since she had set foot in her native land. She had seemed to bloom again, and for that he was deeply thankful. He himself was homesick for green fields, for his father's house; he could never feel at home in this land of alternate lushness and barrenness, with its great mountains, its arid plains, its hot sun, its cold winds, its passionate people who could be more gay and yet more solemn than any.

He longed for a glimpse of the quiet river and the primroses on its banks, the wild violets in the copse and the daffodils growing under the trees, the sun that did not scorch, the winds that were not so bleak; he thought with regret of the people of his own race, who

83

lacked the mercurial temperament of these Spaniards and did not fly into sudden rages which demanded death as the payment for an insult.

Yet, here in her native land, Dolores had regained her health, and she wished to come to the church of San Pablo, which she had attended many times in her childhood. This time she wished to pray that her hope of a child might be fulfilled.

Rarely had he seen her look so well as she did now. He must remember that the great house, almost fantastic in its oriental splendour, which was built round the *patio,* was the home in which she had been brought up, the only child of indulgent parents. Her father must have loved her dearly, he realised now, to have raised no objection to a marriage which, while it brought her happiness, made of him a lonely man.

Dolores had finished her prayer and she rose.

"I know," she said, "that this time my child will live."

As they came out into the sunshine, he said: "Shall he be born in England?"

"That is what you wish, is it not?"

"I wish what is best for you. If we are going back, we should go back soon, before you find the journey too irksome."

"I could put my cousin from Toledo in charge of the estate," she said. "And later, perhaps Felipe will wish to come back and claim it. If you want to go back to England . . . soon, then that is what I wish."

"But you have been so well here. I am afraid that you will not be . . . if we go back."

"I was born here, Richard. Perhaps our bodies demand their native air. For me . . . I could always be happy where you and Felipe are."

"It will be seven months before the child is born. Dolores, I think we should be unwise to go back before that. I think the child should be born here. When our baby is a few months old, then we can return. That will give us time to put our affairs in order."

She was well content.

They paused, on their way back to the stables, before one of the many goldsmiths' shops.

"Let us go in," said Richard. "I wish to make a purchase."

The goldsmith came forward to meet them, bowing ceremoniously. He knew Dolores, for more than once in the past her father had brought her into this shop. She was a lady of great nobility; he was not sure that she was not distantly related to the Emperor himself, or was it the Archbishop of Toledo?

It was a great honour, he said, to see the noble gentleman and his lady in his shop; he was at their service; he asked nothing but to be able to obey their slightest command.

Dolores chose a ring for Richard and he chose one for her. They slipped them on each other's fingers; hers held a ruby, his a diamond.

"And," said Richard, "there is something else. I wish to see a cross . . . a small one set with precious stones. I want it for a child."

Dolores said in English: "You wish it for our child?"

He nodded, and Dolores talked to the goldsmith of the cross, for he found Richard's accent somewhat difficult to follow.

"A delicate cross," she said. "Filigree work perhaps, set with sapphires and diamonds . . . rubies or perhaps emeralds. And there should be a slender gold chain . . . that it may be worn by a child."

They chose a dainty cross of gold set with sapphires and diamonds; and a fine gold chain was selected on which the cross would hang.

When they left the shop, Richard said: "The cross and chain shall be placed about the child's neck; whenever we see it we shall remember this day."

"I am afraid suddenly," she said. "I am afraid you tempt the Fates."

"No," he answered, "I am showing my faith. This time God will grant us a child."

He took her hand and kissed the ring which a short while ago he had put there.

And as they went back to the stables and mounted their horses, he was dreaming of this time next year, when they should be at home in Chelsea; he pictured Dolores sitting on the wicker seat which overlooked the river; and the child was in her arms.

It was difficult to sleep during the hot nights, and Nana was filled with longing for home. Constantly she thought of Master Charles, and her body yearned for him. Yet she had chosen as she must choose. She had to choose the boy. He needed her far more than Charles did. There would be others to lie in the long grass with

Charles, and she wept at the thought of it; but it could not be helped. She had tried to tell Charles how she felt, but she found it difficult to put into words what was in her mind. How could she say: I shall know what you are doing here; I shall know there will be others to be to you what I have been, and that will torment me. But it was always so. There were others. And I was but one of many. I shall know what is happening at home; yet how could I know what was happening to my boy in a strange land? It is with him I must be.

He had been angry with her, but sadly she had resigned herself to his anger. He had stayed with her the whole of the night before she left Chelsea. He had not cared who knew that he did so; and she, though feeling it was wrong, had always respected his wishes. It was only in this matter of leaving him that she had opposed him. He had tried to persuade her even at that late hour; he had cajoled and threatened. He had said he loved her and that he cared for no others. Then he had said that it mattered not to him if she went; she was no better, no worse than a hundred others. "Then I am glad," she had told him; and she had meant that. That was the measure of her love, had he but known it. It did not matter to her what there was for Nana; it mattered only that Nana could bring comfort to her loved ones. Let them hurt her as much as they would; she would have been less hurt than if she had been conscious of hurting them. And if he found her no better, no worse than a hundred others, then she must rejoice, for the parting would not be so sad for him.

He had grown angrier still, and then tender . . . until the dawn had come and she had said goodbye.

And now, after months in a strange land, the memories did not diminish. She feared she was a very sinful woman, for sometimes, when she thought she was remembering her happiness with Master Charles, there would seem to be another figure beside her, and it might be Pablo who was in love with Marina, or Matias who helped Pablo with the horses. She would imagine she lifted her hands and touched her lover's hair; yet it was not soft and fair as was Master Charles', but rough and thick and curly and smelling faintly of onions.

In the stables, on one occasion, Matias had come up behind her and put his hands over her breasts, caressing them; and as she wriggled free, he had turned her round and kissed her mouth.

He had spoken, and although she could not understand his words, she had, of course, understood his meaning. It was impossible for Nana not to understand that meaning in whatever language it was expressed. The warmth of Matias' black eyes made Nana feel weak and helpless.

So she had turned and run before Matias could see the very ready response which had arisen within her. She would be true to Master Charles; she had said she would be. She had given him the promise on that last night, as she might have given a sweetmeat to Felipe when he must take a dose of nasty medicine. Charles had seized it and relished it; and she was glad to have given it. She intended to keep her promise.

She had not taken into account that, during the years of her faithfulness to Charles, he had rarely left her for more than a month at a time. She remembered those occasions when he had come back and she had been like a parched creature longing for a draught of water. She had forgotten how desperate had been the longing.

But never had she been without him so long as this.

She shivered. I am a sinful woman, she thought; and life is full of temptations for such as I am.

She must stop thinking of Matias; but his image would keep presenting itself, and she found herself laughing quietly to recall the fervour of his eyes.

Oh yes, she thought, I am a very sinful woman, and life is full of temptations for those like me.

Felipe was excited. There was to be a royal wedding in Valladolid, and his parents were invited. They told him about it in their cool room behind the blinds which shut out the glare of the sun. He sat on a cushion at their feet, listening.

"The elder daughter of our great Emperor Charles is to marry Maximilian, the Archduke of Austria," his mother was saying. "And their marriage is to be celebrated in our town of Valladolid."

"It is a very good thing, then, this marriage?" Felipe wanted to know.

"Very good for Spain," said his father, and he smiled the wry, gentle smile which Felipe knew so well and loved so much. Felipe understood. What was good for Spain might not be good for England. His father's country and his mother's country were often at war with each other. Why, wondered Felipe, could they not be happy together as his mother and father were?

"Your mother and I are going to the wedding," added his father.

"You will see the great Prince Felipe," said Felipe. He was interested in the Emperor's son because he bore the same name as himself.

"I do not think we shall see Prince Philip," said his father. "He is about to set out for Barcelona. He has to travel to Flanders to see his father, the great Emperor, who is there."

"Why does he not come here for the wedding?" asked Felipe.

"He has other countries to rule as well as this one, my son. Doubtless he has much to occupy him."

"Is the Emperor a greater King than our King at home?"

"The King of England is but a little boy, Felipe, no older than yourself."

Felipe tried to think what it would be like to be a king. It was hard to believe that the great King of England, whom he had once seen riding through the City of London clad in scarlet and gold — a mighty man who made all those about him seem very small — was dead, and in his place was a boy.

"I should like to go to the wedding," he said.

"Well," said Richard, "I doubt not that Pablo will take you into Valladolid, and if you may not kiss the hands of the Infanta and her bridegroom, you will see the rejoicing of the people."

"There will be *a fiesta*, then?"

90

"Naturally there will be *a fiesta* when the Emperor's daughter marries."

"And will there be a bull-fight?"

"There is always a bull-fight. The Spaniards set bulls to fight whatever the occasion. Whether it is the victories of their armies, the canonisation of a saint or a royal wedding, there must always be bulls to help them celebrate the occasion."

"I shall ask Pablo to take me to the town then. And I shall see you in the procession doubtless."

"Doubtless," said his father.

"Shall I see the little Prince, Don Carlos?"

"I do not think you will."

Poor little Don Carlos! thought Felipe. His mother Doña Maria Manoela had died shortly after his birth through, so said Marina, eating a lemon.

He would insist on Pablo's taking him to the town that he might see the rejoicings.

Pablo was saddling the horses and he paused to touch with loving care the great curved knife in his *faja*. Pablo was angry. The hot colour burned under his skin and his black eyes flashed more wildly than usual. Felipe, watching, knew the reason. Marina was going to the *fiesta* with Tomás.

Felipe tried to comfort him. "It is a sad thing, Pablo, that you must love Marina. If you loved some woman who loved you, we should all be happier, I am sure."

"Ah! It is a wise man our little Don has become."

"Why do you not interest yourself in one of the other girls, Pablo? Sabina is very pretty; and so is Theresa."

"Love! You do not understand. It comes. There is no reason. It stays!" Pablo added significantly: "And only death can end it!"

Pablo's hand was resting on his knife. "Tomás said that if she did not go to the *fiesta* with him he would take Sabina," said Felipe.

Pablo straightened himself and snapped his fingers suddenly; then he went on saddling the horses.

When they were ready he said: "Why should we not take your Naña? Would she not like to see the sights?"

Felipe smiled. "I should like that, Pablo. But . . . she would not want to ride so far."

Pablo patted the saddle of his horse. "Why should she not ride with me, eh? Why should she not? I should be enchanted to carry the fair Naña." Pablo looked sly. "I think she might enjoy to ride with me."

"I will go and ask her, Pablo."

Nana was in his room mending his clothes.

"Naña," he said, "I am going to the *fiesta*."

She frowned. She did not like him to stray too far from her. She would never become accustomed to this strange country; it seemed to her to be full of dangers which could never lurk in an English country lane.

"Naña, I wish you to come with me."

"With you and Pablo?"

"Yes, Naña. I wish it, and Pablo wishes it." He put his arms about her neck and she thought: Oh, what pretty ways he has, my boy. He is a bit foreign, a bit like these people, but oh, what pretty ways!

"It is many miles, Felipe."

"Not so many, and you would ride with Pablo."

Her heart began to beat faster.

"Well," she said, "perhaps that would not please him. I should be a burden to him."

"No, no, Naña. He wishes it. And think — you will be with me. You will not have to be sitting here wondering whether robbers have taken me and slit my throat."

She kissed him. She was amazed at his cleverness; how could he read her thoughts so cleverly? It was almost as though he were possessed of second sight.

So, a short while after, Nana, with a red kerchief tied about her head, was riding pillion to Valladolid.

Pablo was gracious; the glances he threw over his shoulders were warm. They clearly said: It gives me great pleasure to have you with me, Naña. We are good friends; we must be better friends.

As they neared the town the crowd grew dense. Gipsies and villagers mingled together; dancing girls, water-carriers, beggars, merchants and their apprentices, market women and vagabonds were going into town for the *fiesta*. It was almost noon and the air was like that of a furnace. There was no wind and the flies were audacious.

They came to the great walls of the city and went through the Puerta. The horses' hoofs raised the heavy dust which made Felipe cough; he felt thirsty, as he was sure the acacias must be.

All were making their way to the Plaza Mayor, where, that afternoon, the bull-fight would take place. One of the matadors swaggered through the crowds — the hero of the occasion; his bold eyes selecting the prettiest of the girls, all of whom seemed almost ready to swoon with delight at the attention.

Into the great artificial lake which had been made for the *fiesta*, the less valuable bulls were being thrown so that the crowds could watch the beasts try to swim to safety while strong men who swam with them attacked them, and others rowed in boats tormenting them with spears and knives. The lake was already tinged with the colour of blood.

They were too late to see the royal procession, for already the wedding guests were in the Castle of Valladolid. In any case the crowds were too dense for Felipe to have been able to see very much. Nana clung to his hand for fear she should lose him in the press of people.

Then Pablo, realising the boy's plight, lifted him on to his shoulder that he might see the bulls in the lake; and as they stood there, Marina sidled up to them. She was alone. So, thought Felipe, she has lost Tomás. She wore a blue blouse open at the neck to show her big breasts, and her skirt was red; she wore a red flower in her black hair. She stood very close to Pablo, but Pablo, with Nana on the other side of him and Felipe on his shoulder, stared straight ahead.

Marina nestled closer, looking up at Pablo.

"So," she said, "you are here with Naña and the little Don."

Pablo did not answer.

"I knew you would come, Pablo. I looked for you. I was pleased to find you. I have left Tomás, Pablo. I have left him for you. Come . . . come and drink wine with me."

Felipe could follow what Marina was saying, quite easily. The servants did not realise that he had quickly picked up their patois. They thought he understood Spanish only as spoken by his parents, and the sober, solemn speech they used for him.

"I am in charge of the little one."

"Naña is here to look after him."

"Go back to Tomás."

"You would tell me that?"

"You came with Tomás."

"Only that I might find Pablo here."

"You lie . . ."

She looked up at him, laughing. "If you wish for the company of Naña, then you must have it."

"Nay, Marina . . ."

"You say Nay! You say Nay! Yet you do not leave her."

She lifted her hand and snapped her fingers, as Felipe had seen so many of the servants do. She tossed her head. "Very well. Then I go. And never again, Señor Pablo, shall I give you the opportunity to enjoy my company."

She turned away, but Pablo had caught her with such force that Felipe was almost jerked off his shoulder.

"One moment . . . Wait . . . Don Felipe . . . Just a little moment." He set Felipe on the ground and turned to Marina. She drew away, but he held fast to her hand. Laughing she pulled, and gradually she drew Pablo away from Nana and Felipe.

Naña was watching the bulls in the lake. The crowd closed round them, and Felipe could no longer see Marina and Pablo.

While Nana had sat on the horse with Pablo she was thinking: He is a fine man, this Pablo — a very fine man.

And when he turned his head to smile at her, she knew that her eyes shone as they should not shine. I am a sinful woman, she reminded herself.

She turned her eyes to watch the graceful figure of her boy, riding beside them. How beautiful he was! His skin had turned to a darker shade since he had lived in Spain; and with his solemn little face he might well be one of these people. Her heart was almost bursting with love for him. She wished she need not be aware of the man whose horse she shared.

There was no forgetting the desire within her. Such desire seemed more natural, more spontaneous here than at home. It was doubtless because of the heat, the lassitude which seemed to come over her. Always now she was aware of this desire. She saw it in the eyes that looked at her — the dark, smouldering eyes of the water-carrier, of the gentlemen on horse-back. The girls with the flowers in their hair, low-necked blouses, faded skirts, bare feet . . . they all reminded her, as they seemed to remind each other, of desire; passionate desire that was like thirst and hunger.

Into the town they went. They left their horses in the stables of an inn where Pablo was known. As they walked away he touched her arm lingeringly, and his black eyes glistened.

Near the Plaza Mayor the girls were dancing Andalusian dances, their eyes on the men who danced with them. Their smiles, the snap of the fingers, the rattle of castanets, their very gestures . . . all were a provocation.

When they were watching the bulls in the lake, Nana was aware of a man who stood near. He was tall for a Spaniard; his hair was thick and black, his eyes flashing and lustrous, and his smile the boldest she had ever encountered.

He reminded her of Master Charles. Why, she could not say. Master Charles was fair-haired, fair-skinned, blue-eyed, tall and slender; this man was black-haired, black-eyed with an olive skin. Though not as tall as Charles, he had a similar leanness; but it was not his looks which reminded her; it was his smile, a certain sureness in him that, were he given a few minutes alone with her, would make it impossible for her to resist him.

Nana felt as she had felt at the washtub when Master Charles had first noticed her.

The man moved closer to her; Nana kept her eyes on the lake. She moved closer to Pablo, as though for protection.

It could not have been more than a few minutes later when Felipe tugged at her hand and said: "Naña, we have lost Pablo."

She looked down at him, startled. "Lost . . . Pablo? Where did he go?"

97

"He was talking to Marina; and I cannot see them now."

"Well, he will find us."

She looked quickly to her right. She could not see the strange man now. Was she relieved, she wondered, or disappointed?

"The crowd is too dense here," said Felipe. "I can see nothing. Let us go and find Pablo. There is much to see yet, and I am tired of looking at bulls."

People looked at them curiously, since they were speaking English.

Nana said: "Yes, let us get away from here."

As they forced their way through the crowd, Felipe said he was hungry.

"Then we will go to the inn and get the food we left there. Perhaps we could find a shady spot and eat in comfort."

"Let us do that," said Felipe. "Pablo will find us."

They had pushed themselves free of the crowd and were looking about them.

"We came that way," said Felipe. "That is where the inn must be."

"Well, let us go, then."

She took his hand and they set off.

They found themselves in a maze of short alleys which opened into courts, and even as the buildings grew more and more squalid they showed evidence of Moorish architecture.

"We did not come this way, Naña," said Felipe. "I believe we have lost our way." He put his hand on a wall and withdrew it sharply. It was very hot. "Come, Naña, we must go back the way we came."

They found they were in a *cul-de-sac,* and as they turned they saw three youths of about seventeen or eighteen years of age, ragged and vicious-looking, approaching them. They and the three striplings were the only people in the small airless alley.

"Come," said Felipe, putting his hand in Nana's, for he felt frightened as the three crept towards them. Time seemed to move slowly for Felipe while his heart gave fast heavy hammer strokes. "Come, Naña," he repeated, and his voice was high-pitched with terror.

The young men were close now; they stood across the narrow alley, barring the way.

Felipe tried to pull Nana past by keeping close to the wall, but one of the men put a hand out and caught Nana's shoulder. The three of them laughed unpleasantly; they stood, their legs, in their faded cotton trousers, apart, their cotton shirts open at the neck, their knives at their waists.

"Where do you go in such haste?" said one of them.

Nana looked at Felipe, who said: "Please allow us to pass. We have to find our servant."

"Servant! Servant, eh? And who is the lady? Holy Virgin, it is the Infanta herself!"

The one who seemed slightly older than the others and was evidently the leader had said this, and the others laughed. Delighted with their laughter, the leader pushed Nana back against the hot wall.

Nana was frightened. "Let me go," she cried. "Let me go."

The men glanced at each other. "Foreigner," said one of them, and he spat on the cobbles.

The man who was holding Nana thrust his hand inside her blouse. "Yet," he said, "she's pretty." And he put his face against her neck.

Naña screamed and struggled.

Felipe cried: "Stop! stop! My father will have you punished if you do not let us go at once."

"His father!" said the leader. "And who is he? I know. The lady is the Infanta, the bride; and this is Maximilian, the bridegroom."

They all rocked with laughter at this — horrible laughter which terrified Felipe.

The ruffian who held Nana said, in the Spanish Felipe had learned from the servants: "She is fair enough. We could get a good price for her. Three pesetas. And we could speak well of her, my friends. We shall be able to test her, yes? The three of us?"

The other two came close. One grasped a strand of Nana's hair; the other pulled at her blouse; and he who had her by the shoulders lifted her suddenly and tried to fling her to the ground.

"Stop!" cried Felipe. "Stop! If you do not . . . if you do not . . ."

But they pushed him aside as though he were nothing but one of the numerous flies; he fell, scraping his hand against the wall.

He felt dizzy and very frightened. He doubted that he had ever been so much afraid in the whole of his life. It was their laughter, their mockery, that made their cruelty seem the more intense. If they had hurt him, or even Nana, in anger it would have been less frightening. He did not know what to do. He would be ready to die if he could save Nana, but he did not see how he could save her. She was lying on the ground, and her cries mingled with the coarse laughter of the men.

Felipe waited for something terrible to happen; andthen, there was another sound in the alley.

"Hey!" cried a voice. "Hey there! What is this, then? What is this?"

Felipe rose hastily to his feet and saw a man coming towards them.

"Help us!" cried Felipe. "For the love of God, help us."

The three ruffians had stood upright; they looked defiant, yet a little alarmed to be caught in their devilry.

Nana, cowering on the cobbles, looked up, and her heart gave a great bound, for there was the man whom she had seen only a short while ago in the crowds about the artificial lake. He had an air of authority; he was some years older than the eldest of the three scoundrels; there was arrogance in his walk; there was nobility in his proud features.

"What is this?" he roared; and his eyes went from Felipe to Nana, and from Nana to the three men.

Felipe ran to him.

"Oh, save us, Señor. These scoundrels have set upon us. We were looking for our horses. We have lost our servant in the crowd."

The man paused for a second to smile reassuringly at Felipe, then with a speedy gesture he drew his sword from its sheath and advanced towards the group.

101

"Begone!" he said. "Begone, you dogs."

The two younger of the men were pale and in great fear, but the leader struck a belligerent attitude; his hand flew to his knife, but before he could draw it, he let out a yell of pain, for the newcomer's sword had pierced his arm.

He turned to look with horror at the blood which stained his shirt, and as he did so, the gallant rescuer took him by his thick hair and sent him reeling down the alley.

Then, his sword in his hand, his legs wide apart, he faced the three of them.

"Come," he said. "Come . . . one and all. If you wish to feel the quality of this steel, hesitate not, for I am waiting."

But the three bullies had no wish to test their skill against a swordsman; they reserved their attacks for the unprotected. They retreated, supporting their leader, who could not take his eyes from the blood of his wound.

At the end of the alley one of them stooped and half-heartedly picked up a handful of stones, which he threw. The rescuer let out a bellow of laughter; and then yelled at them: "What . . . only stones? Out with your knives and fight. Come! I would see you lying in the dust for this. Come back, that I may make you my prisoners. I will have you hurled from the rock of Toledo. I will have you burned under a slow fire in the Plaza Mayor. I will show you what a good Spaniard will do to those who insult ladies."

But the will to fight had left them; they fled.

Then the gallant gentleman turned and bowed to Felipe and Nana.

"How can we thank you, Señor?" asked Felipe.

But the man was giving his attention to Nana, who had scrambled to her feet. He handled her with tenderness, and his gaze lingered on her torn blouse.

"Señora . . . Señor . . . I am Roderigo y Galán, at your service."

Felipe said: "I am Felipe Grendell. My father is an Englishman. We live beyond the town."

"I have heard of your father, Señor."

"And this is Naña. She came with us from England and she speaks no Spanish. She speaks only English."

Roderigo y Galán took Nana's hand and raised it to his lips, which made Nana blush. She had completely recovered from her fears; and, noticing this, Felipe wondered how she could do so.

"Tell the lady," said Roderigo, turning to Felipe, "that I deeply regret the actions of my countrymen. Tell her that she will not find many Spaniards so lacking in courtesy . . . in the knowledge of how to treat a lady."

When Felipe translated, Nana's eyes sparkled. Her eyes were soft and she could not help looking at the man; whenever she did so he seemed to be looking at her.

"We are very grateful to you, Señor," said Felipe.

"If I have been able to render the smallest service to your noble self and the lady, that is reward enough for me. I will confess I saw you by the lake, and when you came towards this part of the town — knowing the reputation of these parts — I followed. Unfortunately I lost you in this maze of narrow streets. If I had not, I should have been at your side more quickly." His eyes were still on Nana. "If you will allow me, I shall accompany you until we are far from this spot. I do not trust those ruffians."

Felipe told Nana what their rescuer had said, at which she smiled happily.

"Perhaps," said Felipe, "you will be kind enough to show us the way to the inn where we have left our horses. It is not far from the *Puerto*."

"I know it well. I will accompany you there."

He walked beside them, and Felipe noticed how he would constantly glance at Nana; and he noticed also that Nana blushed and smiled as she held up her hands to her tattered blouse.

"Tell me more," said Roderigo. "You came to Valladolid to see the celebrations with your servant?"

"Yes, and lost him."

Roderigo's brow darkened as he showed his anger against Pablo, who had allowed himself to be lost; he looked fierce and formidable; but almost immediately he had turned to Nana, and there was his flashing smile again, as though merely to look at her dispelled all anger.

Felipe said: "The crowd was so thick. He was swallowed up, it seemed."

"To leave you at such a time? That was dangerous. I swear I shall not leave you two until I know you to be in a place of safety. When you have your horses, I shall get mine . . . and then I shall escort you to your home, for, as you see, it is unsafe for you to be alone and unprotected."

"We have left a basket of food at the inn," Felipe explained. "We hoped to find a quiet spot where we might eat it. We thought we might find such a place beyond the town. Señor, if you would join us, we should be enchanted."

Roderigo inclined his head ceremoniously: "Señor, the enchantment would be mine."

"I will explain to Naña," said Felipe, and he did so. Nana was delighted with the proposal.

They found the inn, and Felipe went to the stables where the groom assured him that his horse had been given water and corn. He asked the groom to tell Pablo, when he returned for his horse, that he and Nana had found a friend who was taking them home.

Tethered to a tree beyond the town was Roderigo's horse.

"Were you not afraid it would be stolen?" asked Felipe.

Roderigo rolled his eyes heavenwards so that the very clear whites were visible. "None would dare, Señor," he said, his slim brown fingers resting on his sword. All his gestures were significant, and Felipe, like Nana, felt that he was one of the most exciting people he had ever met.

"I know where we will eat," said Roderigo. "Not far from here there is a shady spot under some trees. Come, we will make for it." He looked at Nana and smiled. Then he lifted her and set her on his horse. He mounted, and with the reins in one hand, and the other round Nana's waist, they started.

Every now and then she would turn and smile at him; he returned the smile and squeezed her tenderly.

Before long they came to the trees, dismounted and tied up the horses.

"See," said Roderigo, "it is cool here."

Nana busied herself with the food-basket. There was bread, meat, fruit and wine.

"Come, Felipe," she said, "we must look after our guest."

"What does she say?" asked Roderigo.

Felipe told him.

"Then tell her she has but to smile at me and I am well served," he said.

They were very thirsty and the wine was good. Never had bread and meat tasted as that did; never was fruit so luscious. They lay stretched out lazily in the shade.

"Señor," said Felipe, "have we interrupted your plans?"

"My plans were idle ones. Just to take a look at the *fiesta* and the crowds."

"But shall we be taking you far from your road?"

"My road is your road."

"I could look after Naña, Señor y Galán, if you feel it is too far out of your way to accompany us."

"I should never forgive myself if I did not see you safely home. I beg of you, Señor, do not ask me to deny myself that comfort and pleasure."

Nana was flicking at the flies with her kerchief. It was a long time since she had felt so happy. He was beautiful, this man; and he was kind. He had saved her from those bullies; she had not understood their words, but she had understood their intentions. They would have treated her shamefully. And then had come this hero, the most handsome man in the world, she felt sure. He was already confused in her mind with Master Charles. He was so kind, and she felt weak when he looked her way. It was irksome not to understand his words, but his eyes told her much, and his straying caresses confirmed what his eyes told her. She was happy here in the shade with her beloved boy beside her, and this new acquaintance to excite her.

He would take them back to the house and he would leave them. Nothing would happen, she assured herself, because she must be true to Master Charles. But it was pleasant to lie here beside him, with the presence of the boy her safeguard. What would happen if the boy were not there? She caught her breath imagining it. She was a very sinful woman, she knew.

"Are you on a journey, Señor?" asked Felipe.

"I am always on a journey."

"Always travelling and never reaching your destination?"

"That is so."

"That is a strange way to live."

"I am a strange man, I fear."

"Have you no home, then?"

"No, I have no home."

"But where do you sleep?"

"Wherever I find myself."

"This night you must sleep in my father's house."

"Your father would wish that?"

"He will not be there. He is at the wedding. So is my mother. But they would be angry if they learned that you, having saved Naña and me from those ruffians, were not given the hospitality of their house."

"I would not offend your honourable parents."

"Then you will stay at least one night in our house?"

"It would be churlish to refuse."

"I am so glad. Naña, Señor Roderigo y Galán will spend the night at our house."

Naña smiled at Roderigo and lowered her eyes.

"Naña is pleased?" asked Roderigo. "Ask her that?"

When Felipe asked her she said: "Yes . . . yes, I am pleased."

"She says she is pleased," said Felipe.

"Then tell her I am the happiest man in the world."

This, thought Felipe, was carrying Spanish ceremony a little too far, but he passed on Roderigo's extravagant compliment, and saw Roderigo take Nana's hand and kiss it.

After a while, refreshed and cool, they rode on to the house, with Nana on Roderigo's horse and his arm about her.

It was night. Nana opened her window that she might feel the cool air on her face. The stars had already begun to appear in the darkening sky; she could see them above the *patio*. Flowers scented the air, and she could hear the water playing in the fountains.

She was thinking of the stranger. She guessed that she was not the only one in this house who thought of him. All the serving girls were excited by his presence in the house; Nana could not understand their chatter, their sudden bursts of laughter, but she knew what they meant.

Pablo would be thinking of him, Pablo was very angry with him. They had no right, he had said, to leave the town without him. He had searched all through the heat of the afternoon. Pablo would like very much to know who the stranger was. This was the way robbers worked. Felipe had whispered to Nana the meaning of that flood of words. Pablo was very angry; all the time he scolded . . . first Felipe, then Nana . . . his fingers pulled at his knife. He was not a man to forget an insult, he would have them know.

Nana turned from the window. She undressed slowly, and lay naked on her pallet.

She thought continually of how sinful she was; but how could a woman help her thoughts? She tried to pray, but while she prayed she listened.

She was safe, she told herself. How could he come to her? Her room adjoined Felipe's, and there was no entrance but through his. Felipe's mother had said: "This is like the room you had in Chelsea, Naña. You will feel safe here." Well, Roderigo could not come through Felipe's room.

Roderigo! She knew his name. She said it to herself, smiling. So strange, so foreign; as he was himself.

She got up from her pallet and wrapped her gown about her. She opened the door and saw that Felipe was sleeping. He was tired. It had been an exhausting

109

day. She, too, was exhausted; but her excitement was stronger than exhaustion.

She shut the door and turned the key in the lock. Then she went back to her pallet. She could not sleep; she lay, staring at the window.

It was past midnight when he came. She heard his hard breathing as he climbed up the pillars to her window. Those pillars made the task an easy one. It was almost as though they had been put there for the purpose.

"Naña," he whispered. "Naña."

And there he stood outlined against the window . . . inside her room.

She gasped: "No. You should not come."

But he had leaped towards her, and, kneeling, kissed her.

"Naña," he said, "I could not come before. I feared I should be seen."

"You must not . . ." she said. "You must not."

But, as Charles had pointed out, her lips might say No but her eyes said Yes, and as he could not speak her tongue, he had only her eyes to rely on.

"It is years away," he said. "The moment by the lake . . . under the trees . . . when you were on my horse . . ."

Nana said: "You must go. You must not stay."

"I know, Naña. As I have longed for you . . . so have you longed for me. You shall teach me to speak English. Then we shall tell each other how much we love. Till then . . . we must content ourselves in other ways. That is so, my Naña?"

And Nana had her arms about him and could say no more.

Roderigo had been at the house a week.

Felipe had explained to his parents how their guest had rescued him and Nana from the three youths in the alley.

"My wife and I do not know how to thank you," said Richard.

Roderigo was charming, and all in the house were attracted by him, with the exception of Pablo, who was enraged, not only that he had brought Felipe and Nana home on the day of the *fiesta*, but by the effect Roderigo had on the women of the household. He went about muttering threats, vague prophecies, and continually sharpening his knife.

"I will have my revenge," he declared.

Richard had rebuked him. "How did you come to lose Don Felipe? You should have been doubly careful at such a time."

"Señor, I cannot say. They were there . . . and . . . they were not there."

"They might have been murdered."

"They would have been safe, Señor, had they waited by the lake, I spent the hot afternoon looking for them, and it was not until I went to the inn that I understood they had returned home."

Richard said no more, but it was clear that his faith in Pablo was shaken. After that he did not set him to look after Felipe; and wherever Felipe went, Roderigo accompanied him.

Dolores talked of their guest to her husband.

"I like him. I am certain he is a gentleman of good family. Yet there seems to be a mystery about him. He says nothing of his family. Have you noticed that?"

"I have. And I do not care to question him on a matter about which he prefers to keep silent."

"Poor Roderigo! I wonder what has happened to his family. Do you think he committed some indiscretion and was turned adrift?"

"That thought had occurred to me, I suspect it may have had something to do with a woman. There is no doubt, Dolores, that he has a way with them. Half the maids are in love with him."

"Is that why Pablo is sharpening his knife? Richard, I hope Pablo will not be foolish."

"Pablo! Nay, my love! He is a coward. He talks too much of revenge ever to attempt it. He is, of course, jealous of Roderigo. I am afraid Felipe has been completely bewitched, as has Nana . . . and others. Pablo does not like that. He is a jealous little man. Never fear; he will not go beyond sharpening his knife."

One day, when Roderigo sat drinking wine with his host and hostess, he spoke of his departure.

"We shall miss you," said Richard.

"Must you go?" asked Dolores.

"I cannot further encroach on your hospitality, my good friends; I have been here a week. This week has been the happiest I have known for a long time."

They smiled; this was the exaggerated form of Spanish courtesy, and they accepted it as such.

112

But he flashed his warm smile on them again. "I mean it. It is so. To live thus . . . graciously again . . . has been a great pleasure to me. I shall be desolate to say goodbye to dear little Felipe, to you and your household."

"Then stay a little longer."

"My friends, for a whole week I have sat at your table. I have broken bread with you, drunk your wine; and all because I did what any man would have done on finding two defenceless people being attacked. You have rewarded me well, and I would not encroach further."

"I beg of you," said Dolores, "do not talk of encroaching."

"Señora, you are good to me; your kindness to me is something I shall never forget." The flashing eyes were full of tears, which he dashed away with an eloquent gesture.

"Don Roderigo," said Richard, "you must forgive my blunt English ways, but tell me this only if you wish to. Will you return to your estates . . . to your family?"

"I have neither, Señor."

"Then, have you some destination, which you have delayed reaching in order to delight us with your company?"

"I shall ride on from here not knowing where I shall next lay my head."

"But . . ."

"I know. You wonder. You think I am not a wanderer . . . a gipsy . . . not a vagabond or a beggar. But in truth, that is what I am. I have no longer any estates or family. I live as I can. You are shocked? Forgive me. I cannot tell you more."

"So," said Dolores, "you will just take to the road again? But you must stay longer."

"Señora, I am a proud man. I cannot eat the bread of charity." He had lifted his head haughtily, but almost immediately he was smiling. He said: "I would not ask favours, but if you should need a man . . . one who could manage your household, who could see that the best wines are served at your table, who could keep your servants in order . . . You understand what I mean? If you should need such a man to serve you and yet not be a menial servant . . ."

Richard took his hand and shook it, and Roderigo's smile flashed his pleasure.

And so, from that day Roderigo became a member of the household, and there was not one person in it — with the exception of Pablo — who was displeased with the arrangement.

Roderigo became to Felipe something of what Roger had been. There was a similarity between the bold, blue-eyed English boy and the flashing-eyed adventurer turned major-domo.

"How glad I am that you have come to live with us, Roderigo," he said one day as they rode together.

"Ah, Felipe, these are the happiest days of my life."

"When we go to England, you will come with us?"

"How should I be in England? They do not love the Spaniards there."

"My mother is a Spaniard, and my father loves her dearly. So do my grandfather and my grandmother. They would love you too, Roderigo. My cousin Roger would love you very much."

"Of that you cannot be sure."

"I would make them, Roderigo. I would insist."

Roderigo laughed. He broke into song. His rich tenor voice was not the least of his attractions.

When the song was over he was thoughtful; then he said he believed he would love the English, for he loved many of them already. He loved his dear friend Felipe; he loved the master and mistress of the house; he loved Naña. He smiled sidelong at the boy, and wished he were older that he might talk of the perfections of Naña.

"You have travelled much, Roderigo?"

"The length and breadth of Spain."

"What adventures you must have had!"

"Many, many adventures."

Then he began to sing again. Life was good — to live in a great house by day, and to feel himself almost master of that house; to have for a companion this dear boy, this strange boy who was not quite Spanish and not quite English, intelligent, alert, the best of companions; and by night, to bed with Naña!

Felipe was eager to discover the secrets he sensed in his friend.

"Where were you born, Roderigo?" he asked.

"Where should I be born but in Spain?"

"Have you no father or mother?"

"I have not. They died, Felipe, and I would not speak of them, for it gives me pain."

"Forgive me, Roderigo."

"There is nothing to forgive. But you will remember not to speak of them?"

"I will never mention them again."

"Nor should you ask me of my home, Felipe, because that makes me unhappy, and I would be happy . . . happy as I am now."

"I will remember. Tell me of the places you have seen."

"I will tell you of the most beautiful place on earth, Felipe. I will tell you of Seville. The roses bloom there all the year round, and when I speak of *la tierra de Maria Santisima* I smell the orange blossom and I see the olive groves. It is said, Felipe, that he whom God loves has a house in Seville. That is true."

He loves Seville, thought Felipe, as people love their homes.

"There is the river — the great river, the Guadalquivir. I should like to sail with you up the Guadalquivir to Seville . . ."

He stopped speaking, and Felipe, seeing the tears in his eyes, said: "Tell me of other places you have seen."

But Roderigo must go on talking of Seville. "You should see the women. They are the most beautiful in the world. They sit at their windows, their high combs in their hair, their mantillas falling over their shoulders. They are like queens, Felipe, and they sit at their windows after *siesta*, fanning themselves and smiling at the men."

116

"They liked you, Roderigo, did they not?"

"Why do you say so?"

"Because I believe it to be true. All the women at home watch you. Tomás says you are lucky because all women are ready to fall in love with you."

"In Seville it is said: 'Only he is fortunate with women, of whom they take no notice.' "

"Is that true?"

"Who shall say? It is only at the end of a man's life that he can say whether or not he has been fortunate."

"Roderigo, I think you are a wise man."

Roderigo smiled and they rode on in silence.

That night when he lay beside Nana, Roderigo thought of that conversation.

Nana slept. She had a beautiful body. He was indeed fortunate to have found Nana.

There were little bits of good fortune to be met with along the road, but whither was the road leading? Should he stay here? Here he felt safe.

He kissed her lightly on the cheek, so lightly that he need not wake her. He wished to have her beside him, yet that she should sleep so that he might be alone with his thoughts.

At such times as this he liked to think of the past; at such times only could he bear to do so.

He wished that he could talk to someone, but he dared not. He could not talk to Felipe. He trusted the boy, but it was not wise to ask another to bear a secret like his. What if he said to Richard or Dolores: "I am not Roderigo y Galán. That is not my name. I dare not tell you my name. I hide myself under a false name. I am a man who must live in shadows; yet I have done no wrong. My parents, who have died most cruelly, have done no wrong." He could not say such things. He dared not. Not only for his own sake, but for theirs.

Now he looked at the sleeping Nana and compared her with Cristeta, the gipsy girl who had loved him, the girl who had saved his life. He had left Cristeta, had left the safety of the gipsy encampment to wander across Spain.

He saw the gipsy encampment again; it had been close to his father's land. Cristeta was brown-skinned, black-eyed, with great brass rings in her ears. She had lain on the grass laughing at him. She knew that he was the son of the great lord, but she was wild and free, and she cared nothing for that.

He had been with her when they had looked for him, and they had not thought to find the son of a nobleman in a gipsy encampment.

He remembered the night, every detail of it. A night in Seville. What a beautiful night it had been! In the gardens of the Alcazar there were pink berries on the pepper trees and the scent of flowers was heavy in the air. He had wandered into the grounds of his father's house. He had lain by the fountain in the *patio* and thought of Cristeta. The *patio* was covered with an awning to keep out the glare of the sun, and there it was quiet and cool. He could not rest because he was thinking of the gipsy girl. Now it seemed providential that on that night he should have left his father's house to be with her.

He had awakened to find Cristeta's father standing over them — a big gipsy with rings in his ears and a long curved knife at his belt; and he had spoken those words which were dreaded more than any other in Spain: The Inquisition.

And after that night he had no father, no mother, no land, no possessions; and in his heart was a great hatred for those black-clad, most sinister figures who came by night and took men and women from their beds; who called them heretic, and tortured them and condemned them to the fiery death. The Inquisition was growing more powerful, richer; rich families became poor that the Inquisition might become rich, for it was among the rich that it looked for its victims.

Seventeen years old he had been then, carefree, rich and beloved; and the Inquisition had come; in a single night they had robbed him of all that he loved . . . except Cristeta the gipsy. She cared for him; she hid him; she stained his skin and gave him cotton trousers and a cotton shirt; and he became one of them . . . and after that a wanderer.

He raised himself on his elbows and the tears fell from his eyes. His fists were clenched. "Naña . . . Naña . . ." he whispered. "I hate the Inquisition. Willingly would I die a thousand deaths . . . deaths such as only they can invent . . . if I might destroy the Inquisition. They took my beloved father, my dearest mother . . . my home . . . all that made my life. If they could find me they would kill me . . . though I have no riches for them to plunder. I am a fugitive, Naña . . . What have I to lose?"

He had awakened her.

"Roderigo," she said; and momentarily he was afraid. Then he remembered that she could not understand.

He kissed her and said: "It was a dream . . . It was a bad dream . . ."

Then he laughed, for he had forgotten that she could not understand.

Nana was looking at him anxiously, but he kissed her again. "Naña . . . Naña . . . I love Naña. Life is good when there are moments like this."

Pablo often saw Roderigo swing himself up to Nana's window.

"Rogue! Seducer of women!" muttered Pablo.

How he hated him! He thought of those two behind the window. Nana would hold out her arms to him and he would smile his charming smile. The women were fools about Roderigo.

It was not only Nana. There was Marina as well as Sabina . . . Maria . . . Juana . . . There was not one of the women of the house who did not hunger for him.

Pablo lifted his hands and snapped his fingers.

To think that they must take orders from him! Once he had hated Tomás; now that hatred was transferred to Roderigo. More than any he hated Roderigo, the swaggering Roderigo, with his air of nobility and his success with the women.

Pablo was the son of a horse-thief, and he hated the nobility.

Is he so handsome? Pablo asked. I think not. Is he the nobleman fallen on evil times? I think not. How I should like to expose him, to show him for the knave he is. He has taken Don Felipe from me. Don Felipe no longer comes to the stables to watch me at work. No, it is Roderigo . . . Roderigo . . . Roderigo . . . Where he goes, so must Don Felipe go. He has not time for his poor friend Pablo. And why? Because that scoundrel has turned him against me. First he persuaded the boy and silly Naña to leave the town and ride home with him that he might protect them. Protect them! That he might seduce silly Naña. What else?

He would have but to beckon Marina and she, too, would be his dear *amiga*. Yet had she a smile to give to Pablo? No! She even preferred that dolt Tomás!

Hatred grew in Pablo's heart; malice and envy nourished it.

I will kill Roderigo! he promised himself. I will kill him because he has turned the little Don Felipe from me. One day he will be sorry he came to this house.

Once when they rode out from the house, Felipe and Roderigo talked of terrible things.

Roderigo's gay face had become darkened with sorrow and anger. Felipe did not know how they began to talk of the Inquisition.

"We dare not speak of it within walls, little Felipe," he said. "It is unsafe to speak of it. It is only out of doors that one dares."

Felipe had felt his heart beat faster. He had heard talk of the Inquisition at home in England. Roger had mentioned it and how, one day, when he was a sailor, he would drive every Spanish ship off the seas; he

121

would, he had said, sail to foreign lands, and drive the Inquisition from those places in which the Spaniards set it up.

But Roderigo talked of the Inquisition differently — not with gay bravado, but with a quiet, brooding anger.

"How did it grow, Felipe? I will tell you. Once upon a time we had a great Catholic King named Ferdinand; he was a mighty conqueror and many will tell you that he made our country great. He married a Queen named Isabella and so united Castile and Aragon — which seemed a good thing to do. There were many Jews in our land, and the Jews were rich merchants; they had earned for themselves land and riches. But Ferdinand and Isabella coveted those lands and riches."

Felipe shuddered as he listened. He was reminded of a summer's day in England when he had crouched by some bushes with Roger and had watched men walk towards his grandfather's house in order to search it. If those men had found what they sought they would have taken his grandfather prisoner.

He did not want to hear more. He wanted to turn from this picture which Roderigo was about to show him, as he had wanted to run from the fire which had been lighted at the feet of Anne Askew in Smithfield Square.

"And so," went on Roderigo, "this King and Queen, with the help of a Dominican monk, Father Tomás de Torquemada, who became one of their grand inquisitors, devised tortures for rich men, that they might in their agony proclaim themselves heretics and infidels. It was to the rich they turned, Felipe, because

122

they coveted their wealth. That was why they attacked the Jews, the Moors. They were pitiless, Felipe. I wonder what the Jews and Moors have thought of the Christians, Felipe. They cursed them. That much is certain. And, Felipe, we are beginning to suffer from those curses. Our cities are not as rich as they were; our Inquisition has become bloated with riches. If you drive from your cities those who bring trade, what happens? There is no trade, and so it is that while the Inquisition grows powerful, our country suffers."

"Roderigo, I think you would rather not talk of these things. It is like Seville. It is like your parents and your home . . . You do not like to talk of these things."

Roderigo laughed. "Yes, Felipe, it is so. And I am a fool to talk. See how the sweat stands out on my brow when I talk. I have dug my nails into my palms. There is blood. I might have come from the torture chambers of the Inquisition. They come by night, Felipe . . . they come in silence . . . and they lead a man away. He is asked questions concerning his parenthood. Woe betide him if he is Moorish or there is Jewish blood in his veins. He is doomed. He is doomed in any case . . . if he is rich enough."

"Roderigo, I beg of you, talk no more. It distresses you."

"Very well, no more. Only this: they come in the dead of night. A man retires to his bed and his house is quiet, and there is a knock on the door. His servant goes to answer it. 'Open,' he is told, 'in the name of the Holy Office . . . open.' The servant is terrified. He opens. And the victim is taken away . . . taken in his

123

night-clothes, Felipe. There is no safety . . . no safety . . . no safety . . ."

"Roderigo, no more, I beg of you. Tell me about the days of famine when the harvest was a failure in the mountains of Leon and the people came south in hordes."

"That is not a happy subject either. You have a taste for horrors this day. And mayhap so have I. Shall I tell you of the lazy town of Lorca and of the terrible heat haze and the *leveche*, that death-dealing wind that covers all with a layer of dust, so that the dead birds drop like stones from the sky, and men and animals lie gasping near to death? How I hate Lorca! I will not speak of it. Shall I tell you of the dates I have picked and eaten in Elche? Or shall I tell you of wonderful Granada with its Alhambra?"

"Yes," cried Felipe, "tell me of the great cities of Spain."

But although Roderigo talked with his usual charm and gusto, Felipe was haunted by the terrible picture of men in dark robes knocking at the door by night and demanding entrance in the name of the Holy Office. For just as he had known that Seville had been the home of Roderigo, he knew now that such men had, one tragic night, knocked at the door of Roderigo's father's house.

Felipe watched Pablo, who was running his fingers lovingly along the hilt of his knife. Pablo's eyes were hot; he was thinking of Roderigo.

"You should not hate him," said Felipe. "He does not hate you."

Pablo said: "How is it you have time to spare to come to see your old friend Pablo this day? Is it that *Don* Roderigo is so busy that he has no time to talk to you?"

Felipe flushed. Pablo had spoken the truth.

"But, Pablo, I like very much to be here in the stables with you."

Pablo laughed with the utmost bitterness. "It would give me great pleasure if you and Roderigo were friends," said Felipe.

"Friends! You do not know what you say."

"But indeed I do. He wishes you no harm."

"You and Naña!" cried Pablo. "You left me in the town. You left me to spend the hot afternoon searching for you. And who is this rescuer of yours? Tell me that. What do we know of him? One day we may discover. One day we may know. There are bad men who worm their secret way into the confidence of those who are too ready to trust."

"Roderigo is not a bad man."

"And what do we know of him?"

"We know all that it is necessary to know."

"We do not know where he comes from."

"He comes from Seville."

Pablo put his head on one side. "Ah, Don Felipe, you are in his confidence."

"Pablo," said Felipe, "I wish you to be friends with Roderigo. I think he is not always so gay as he seems. I

125

do not think you should speak of him as you do. You are always saying how you would like to slit his throat."

"It is the truth."

"It is not the truth. You are not cruel, Pablo. You are just angry with him because of what happened in Valladolid. And you should not be angry because the women like him. Only they are fortunate with women of whom they take no notice. That is what they say in Seville."

"Then he is not very fortunate, is he?"

"No, Pablo, I do not think he is. Be kind to him, because a terrible thing happened to his father and mother."

"What was this?"

"I think they were taken by the Inquisition and he lost everything. There, Pablo, do not speak of it, for I do not think he wishes it to be known. But remember it and be his friend. Will you, Pablo?"

Pablo laid his hand on Felipe's head and smiled.

"I will remember it," he said.

"Naña," said Dolores, "sit beside me. I have something to tell you."

Nana sat on the stool and waited with apprehension. She wondered if her mistress had heard of her lover's coming to her each night.

"I am going to have a child, Naña."

Nana smiled.

"It will be in six months' time, Naña, and I have every hope this time."

"Oh, Mistress Dolores, I hope it will be as you wish."

"Do you think you will love Felipe's brother . . . or sister . . . as you love him?"

"No," said Nana.

"Dear Naña! You are so sure. You will help me to look after the little one, won't you?"

"Yes, Mistress Dolores."

"She will be born here, and after that we shall return to England."

Nana was not disturbed. Six months was a long time in Nana's life; she could not look ahead as far as that.

"You have become happy here in my country, Naña?"

"Oh yes, Mistress."

Dolores smiled. She knew of the love between Roderigo and Nana. Richard had said that it was inevitable. Nana must have a lover just as she must have a child to care for.

"I will show you the ornament we bought for our child when we were in Valladolid. As soon as my baby is born it shall be put about his neck . . . but perhaps it will be *her* neck. I think I should like to have a little girl."

Nana smiled. A dear little girl, she thought, a little baby. There was nothing sweeter in the whole world.

"Look, Naña. This is the ornament. This little cross on the gold chain. The baby will wear it always."

Nana went away and thought of the little baby which would be born in six months' time. There was a longing within her to hold that baby; she could almost see it, looking rather like Master Felipe when he was a baby . . . after she had saved him. She saw him, greedily reaching for her breasts, and she remembered all the love she had felt for the helpless Felipe — a different love from that which she now had for him. Now he was a healthy boy; then he had been a helpless baby. And she almost wished that he could be a baby again, to pull at her heavy breasts, to crow in her arms, and to give her that feeling of intense joy which only a baby could give Nana.

When she was with Roderigo that night she was thinking of the baby Felipe, wishing he was young again, longing to hold a baby in her arms.

Perhaps that was why, on that hot night, the child of Nana and Roderigo was conceived.

Roderigo had gone.

He went as suddenly as he had come. Everything about Roderigo, those at the house had begun to realise, had been mysterious.

He had ridden into Valladolid, his purse full of Richard's pesetas, to buy wine; and he never came back.

Felipe was to have accompanied him, but he had seemed feverish, and Nana had refused to allow him to go. Felipe had pleaded, but Nana had been firm. So Roderigo had gone forth in the early morning, and all that day Felipe and Nana had waited for his return; but night came and he was still missing.

Nana lay sleepless, waiting for a sound in the *patio*. She knew now that she was to have a child; she did not know whether Roderigo would be pleased; as for herself, she longed to have a child at her breast.

She would have to tell the mistress. But later she would do that. She would take her baby back to England. But she did not want to think of going back to England, because of Roderigo. Would he come too? Felipe had said he would come with them. He, Felipe, would insist. And then . . . what of Master Charles?

Nana's brow was wrinkled with worry at the thought.

She could not separate Roderigo and Charles in her mind. Roderigo and Charles were Man, and Felipe and the baby that was to be born were Child. Nana felt that her purpose in life was to love and serve them both.

So she lay, waiting for Roderigo's return.

Felipe said: "Father . . . Mother, Roderigo has not come back. Where can he be?"

"Doubtless something has happened to detain him in Valladolid, my son," said Richard.

"He said he would be back before the sun went down."

"He has been delayed."

Felipe went out and stood, shading his eyes against the hot glare of the sun, looking out along the stony road to Valladolid.

There was no sign of a horseman, no sound of a gay tenor's song.

The day wore on and Felipe became anxious.

"Father," he said, "there must have been an accident."

"Do not fret, my son. Roderigo will know how to take care of himself."

There was a little twist to his father's mouth. Felipe noticed it, and he knew that his father thought: Roderigo left yesterday morning, and his purse was full of money.

"Roderigo would never steal, Father," said Felipe sternly.

Richard laid his hand on the boy's head, but he said nothing.

He was thinking: The boy has made a god of the man. Well, he was attractive. Some rogues are. Perhaps he was nothing more than an adventurer. Was he, after all, a wandering beggar who deceived us with his courteous speech and fine manners?

Felipe said: "Roderigo will come back. He will come back, unless . . . unless . . ."

"Unless what, Felipe?"

"Unless he is dead."

"Don't fret, my son. Roderigo will always give a good account of himself."

"Yes, he will give a good account of himself."

And Felipe continued to stand, his eyes strained, watching . . . watching for a man on horseback, listening for the gay sound of a tenor's song.

Pablo laughed.

"Hah! So now they know. So now they understand. He has gone off — this gay *caballero*. He has gone off with our master's money in his purse." Pablo was almost choking with laughter. "Depend upon it, this is the last we shall hear of our gay Roderigo. He has robbed our master of his money and our women of

130

their honour." He glared at Marina, and snapped his fingers. "How many of our women has he thus robbed? That I would not care to guess. And if he has not robbed them all, every single one, it is not their fault. No, no! This is the end of our gallant *caballero*."

He fingered his knife.

"I am sorry he has gone. It would have given me the greatest pleasure to have slit his throat."

"Be silent!" cried Marina. "He will be back, and then we shall see who gets his throat slit."

But Pablo continued to laugh. He laughed at the anxiety of Felipe, at the red eyes of Nana; and most of all he laughed when he contemplated the distrust which sometimes showed in his master's face.

"Now," said Pablo, "they know. They know their Roderigo for what he is!"

And the weeks began to pass, and it became clear that Roderigo had slipped away from them.

Nana would lie in her room, her eyes fixed on the open window. Nana was waiting. He would come; he would surely come. She did not believe he had willingly left her.

Something had happened to keep him away, and it was because he had known this might happen that he had been sad at times. His sadness had been there often, thinly veiled by his gaiety. She, who could not understand his speech, had understood his moods.

Now her child was growing within her. She was careful to keep this secret. It was easier than it had been in Chelsea. There was no prying Betsy to worry her; the voluminous skirt she wore was helpful; and she was not afraid as she had been on that other occasion. There was about her a brooding serenity as she awaited the birth of her child.

She would tell no one. She would wait until Roderigo returned; he must be the first one she would tell.

The weeks passed; she would sit with the mistress; they would sew and talk a little; and Nana would rise often to fan away the flies.

When Dolores talked of the baby that was to be born, Nana too thought of a child, but the child she thought of was the one within her own body.

One night when Nana lay sleeping on her pallet there was a gentle knock on the door. She started from her sleep and thought: He has come. Roderigo has come.

But as she sat up she knew that could not be so, for he could not come through Felipe's room. He would have to come by way of the window.

The door opened quietly and Richard stood in the room.

He put his fingers to his lips. "I do not wish to disturb Felipe. But, Nana, will you come at once to the mistress?"

He left her, and she rose at once and put on her gown. She had been expecting this call. She had known Dolores' time was near.

She went along to the bedchamber. Dolores gave her a wan smile. The midwife was already there, and Richard was trembling and in great fear.

How he loves her! thought Nana; she felt a deep sympathy and understanding, for love was something she knew a good deal about.

She longed to comfort him, but there was no time to do anything but attend to the mistress now.

Dolores' child was born a few hours later — a little girl with a fluff of dark down on her head.

Nana held her in her arms and loved her; and it seemed to her that because Dolores' son had become as Nana's own, the child in her arms had a mystic link with the one within her.

Dolores was sleeping the sleep of the exhausted. The baby lay in the cradle which had, with loving care, been prepared for her.

Nana found Richard in a small ante-room.

"Nana," he said eagerly, "all is well? Tell me truthfully. These people . . . they think to be kind, but they keep things from me."

"There is nothing to be kept back, Master. She sleeps. She is very tired, but so are all women at such times."

"Nana!" He put his hands on her shoulders and looked into her face, and she knew then that he was aware of what had happened to her. "You also?" he said. She lowered her eyes.

"Poor Nana," he said. "Was it Roderigo?"

She nodded.

"When, Nana?"

"Less than three months, I think, Master."

"Where did he go, Nana? Did you know?"

"No, Master."

"So he gave you no warning?"

"No."

"Did he know of this child?"

"No, Master."

"I wonder."

"No . . . he could not."

"It is very strange. I would not have believed he could have left us thus. You loved him very much, did you?"

Nana felt her lips trembling; she covered her face with her hands and the tears squeezed through her fingers.

"Nana, don't cry, Nana. We will look after you and your child. You know that."

"Yes, Master."

"I am sorry it has happened to you again like this, Nana . . . because you deserve to be very happy, the joyful mother of many children, with a husband to help you care for them."

"I have Felipe," she said.

"You have indeed been a mother to him. We are grateful for your care of him, Nana — my wife and I. Will you love his sister as you love him?"

"I don't know. Perhaps there could be only one Felipe."

"You must love our daughter, Nana. You will. Now, do not be unhappy. He was irresistible, was he not? We understand, my wife and I."

She bowed her head.

134

He smiled and said: "Nana, she is really well? She will recover?"

"She is well, Master. She is better than when Felipe was born."

"Thank you, Nana; and God bless you."

"Felipe," said Nana, "you have a sister."

Felipe smiled. "That is what I wanted." He looked happier than he had since Roderigo had gone.

"Your mother is sleeping now. Later you shall see her."

"Now, Naña, we shall go back to England. My father said we should. I shall be glad. I shall start preparing now, for as soon as my mother is well we shall go." He put his arms about Nana in a sudden gesture of affectionate understanding. "Naña, we shall forget Roderigo. It will not be easy to picture him when we are in England."

"Why?"

"It might be because when we are in England he will seem a stranger. There are no people like him in England. We shall forget him, you see, Naña. And that is what we wish to do, because he will never come back. He has gone for ever."

Nana's brow was wrinkled; she was trying hard to remember England. There was the house by the river . . . the fields and the copse. There was Master Charles who had for her the same laughing eyes as Roderigo.

Yes, she too wished to go to England, for just as she had found it difficult to separate Felipe from the child

135

she had borne, so Roderigo and Charles were as one in her mind.

Dolores lay in bed, and about her were gathered every member of the household, from the master to the stable-boy. In their hands they held cups filled with wine.

"You are here," said Richard, "to drink the health of my daughter. Let us give her a good welcome to this earth."

"Long life and happiness!" cried Pablo. He was happy, now that Roderigo had gone, and people no longer talked of him.

"May the saints guard her from all ill!" murmured one of the servants.

"So be it!" echoed the others.

"May she have beauty," said Marina.

"May she have wisdom," said Tomás.

"May her life be full of light and laughter!" said Sabina.

"May she be fruitful as the vine," said Juana.

They all uttered their wishes, and all the wishes were for the peace, the prosperity and the happiness of the newborn child.

Felipe said: "May she grow up quickly, so that I may teach her to ride."

This caused much laughter; and Felipe joined in this.

But he was not completely happy, for the ghost of Roderigo lingered with him. When he put his lips to the wine, he remembered the day he had first tasted it.

When the wine had arrived, Felipe had gone with Roderigo to the cellar to see it stored there; and when they were alone with the wine stacked about them, Roderigo had talked of it.

"Wine ... wine ..." Felipe seemed to hear Roderigo's voice now. "The most delicious wine in Spain, Don Felipe. Now we will taste it. We will see if it possesses all the qualities which are claimed for it."

Felipe looked at the company assembled in his mother's bedchamber and instead he saw Roderigo, raising the cup to his lips and rolling his eyes upwards. He remembered the glistening whites of his eyes in the dark cellar. "This wine comes from Jeréz, my Felipe. Ah, Jeréz! It is small wonder that in such a paradise grow the vines which produce such nectar. Now, can you taste the flavour? What is it? Of nuts? No! It is something divine that you have never before tasted." Felipe had shaken his head.

"Ah! Your palate is not in tune, Don Felipe. It is a child's palate that needs to be cultivated ... like a child's mind. Show him a page of writing and what does he do? He shakes his head. It is nothing, he says. But ... cultivate his mind, teach him to read, and that page has wonders to offer him."

Felipe had been enchanted as he ever was by the words of Roderigo.

"So it is with the tasting of wine. It is necessary to learn ... and when we have learned, why, then all the wonders of the world are opened to us. It is the lime that blows on the gentle wind that you taste in the cup; it covers the grape; it becomes part of the grape.

Nowhere in the world, Felipe, does this happen to grapes, but in our own Jeréz. And nowhere in the world can you find such wine as this. Ah, Jeréz! I have lingered there. Beautiful . . . so beautiful, Felipe, with the blossoming orange trees and the *pimientos* . . . and the white lime on the vineyards."

Remembering this, Felipe's eyes filled with tears and he lowered his head that the tears might not be seen.

This was a day for rejoicing, not for sad memories.

Soon, he thought, we shall go back to England; and when I am there it will seem as though Roderigo was never real.

That was a happy day. It stood out for a long time in Felipe's memory. There was peace in the house. His father's fears were lifted, for he had been terrified that his wife might die giving birth to the child.

But the child was safely born and her mother was well.

Richard talked to Felipe on that day, of their return to England.

"You will be glad to see your cousin, Felipe. I wonder how much he has grown."

"I wonder too. I greatly look forward to seeing everybody at home in Chelsea. When shall we go?"

"Your mother will need some weeks in which to grow strong enough to face the journey. Perhaps in two months . . . three months, from now. By then your sister will be of a better age to travel. Yes, Felipe, I should say in three months' time."

To Felipe three months seemed a very long time.

Felipe awoke suddenly in the night. Something had awakened him, but he was not sure what it was. An unfamiliar noise in or outside the house.

He strained his ears and his heart began to beat faster because he was thinking of Roderigo. Would Roderigo come back suddenly . . . in the night?

He rose and went to the door which led to Nana's room.

"Naña?" he whispered.

She was awake.

"What awakened you?" she wanted to know.

"I am not sure. I just . . . awakened. I thought I heard noises . . . voices . . . footsteps . . ."

He had heard the joyful expectation in her voice, and he knew that she, too, was wondering whether Roderigo had returned.

"He would not have come to the house by night, Naña," he said.

She knew to whom he referred for she answered: "He would have waited in the *patio*."

She was thinking: He would have climbed to my window. He would have let me know he was back.

"Perhaps someone is ill. My mother . . ."

"Listen!" said Nana.

They thought they heard footsteps outside the house.

"It is not inside at all," said Nana.

"I would like to go and see that my mother is well."

"Nay," said Nana. "You will disturb her. Wait until morning. It was someone outside the house."

"We shall know in the morning if he has come back, Naña. I will go back to bed now. I will leave the door

open. Then if you hear anything more you can let me
know. And if I hear anything I will tell you."

They lay awake for some time listening, but they
heard no more. And when they fell asleep it was so
deeply that they did not awaken until long after their
usual time.

That was a strange morning.

A quietness filled the house. Felipe arose and went to
look at Nana. She was still sleeping, so he hastily
dressed and went downstairs.

There he saw Juana and, when he spoke to her, she
turned and hurried away.

That was strange; and immediately he recalled the
noises of the night.

He wondered whether he should go first to his
parents' room, but decided not to disturb them. Why
had Juana avoided him like that? Why had he and Nana
been allowed to sleep so late?

He went to the kitchens. No one was preparing food.
The servants sat in gloomy silence; some of them were
weeping.

Pablo stood up when he saw Felipe; he looked lost
and bewildered; his face was puckered in an odd way.

"What has happened?" asked Felipe.

Nobody answered him.

"Is . . . my mother . . . ill?"

Marina shook her head; then she came to him and
put her arms about him.

"Don Felipe . . . poor little Don Felipe!" she said.

"What has happened? Tell me quickly. I beg of you, tell me at once. I demand to know."

Marina looked at Pablo, who nodded.

"He must know," said Pablo. "It cannot be kept from him."

"Last night . . ." began Marina; then she stopped and burst into tears.

"Last night?" cried Felipe. "What happened last night? I heard voices. I heard noises in the night."

Pablo continued to nod while tears ran down his cheeks.

"Some men came last night," said Pablo. "They were robed in black. They were the *alguazils* of the Holy Inquisition. They came . . . silently and secretly."

"No," said Felipe. "*No!*" And now again it seemed that Roderigo stood before him, Roderigo who had told him of these things. "They come by night, these familiars of the Inquisition. They demand admittance in the name of the Holy Office . . . and they take a man away from his home and his family . . ."

Felipe's voice had risen to a shriek. "They cannot come here. How could they come here? My father is not a Spaniard."

He heard Roderigo's voice again: "The Holy Office does not act only against Spaniards. The Jews . . . the Moors . . . they were rich . . ."

My father and my mother are rich, reflected Felipe. He was trembling so much that he could not see with any clarity the faces about him. He was aware only of horror . . . of terror. He thought of black-clad figures who came by night . . . as robbers do . . . and stole all the gaiety, all the happiness out of people's lives.

Pablo came to him and put an arm about his shoulders.

"They came last night," he said. "They demanded admission in the name of the Holy Office."

"Whom . . . did they take?" whispered Felipe.

"Don Felipe . . . they have taken your father."

Everyone in the house was waiting; through the long days and the fearful nights they waited. And there was misery in the house.

"Pablo," cried Felipe, "what will they do to my father?"

Pablo could only shake his head and weep.

Felipe grew closer to Pablo during those days. Pablo had changed; he was gentle and never talked of killing now; he was as tender as a mother to the boy.

"How dare they take my father!" cried Felipe. "What shall we do? We must do something. They cannot take my father. He is an Englishman."

"Little master, little Don Felipe," groaned Pablo, "they care not that he is an Englishman. Here . . . in Spain . . . they do what they will . . . they take those they wish to take."

"They cannot harm him. They would not dare to harm him."

"If he is a good Catholic he will be freed," soothed Pablo.

Dolores lay in a high fever.

"Mercifully," said Juana, "she remembers nothing. She was like this soon after they took him. She fell swooning on her bed when they came. I think that she has not realised that they have taken him. That is as well, poor lady."

"The shock will kill her," said Marina. "She was weak before the birth of the child. I have seen women in this fever before. She has not once asked for the child. She lies there as though she is not of this world. I do not think she can last long thus."

Nana had taken the baby. She nursed her and gave her goats' milk. The little girl was small and wizened, remarkably like Felipe had been in those days when they had thought he could not live.

Nana fingered the cross on the chain about the baby's neck, and she could almost forget the dark tragedy which hung over the house in her love for the child.

"If only I could feed you, little sweeting," crooned Nana. "If I could feed you as once I fed Felipe."

She kept the child in her room and watched over her continually. No one attempted to interfere. All had known that it had been the will of the master and mistress that Nana should be the child's nurse.

Felipe was almost demented. He wept bitterly; then he would grow quiet, and the servants said that his silences were more alarming than his tears. There were times when he prayed that they would take him as they had taken his father. He would wait in the heat of the sun . . . watching, always watching for the return of his father.

143

He longed for Roderigo more than he had in the first days of his friend's mysterious disappearance. If Roderigo were here he could bear this more easily. Roderigo would tell him what happened to those who entered the prisons of the Inquisition, and Roderigo would have managed to bring him some comfort.

He roamed about the house — a melancholy small figure with such tragedy in his eyes that some of the women could not bear to look at him.

He went to his parents' room where Juana stood by his mother's bed, fanning her.

"Mother!" he whispered.

But she did not seem to see him. She did not know who he was. She lay on her bed like a strange woman, for indeed she no longer looked like his beautiful mother. Her face was of a yellow hue and her eyes which were sunk deep in their sockets, seemed sightless. She plucked at the bedclothes, and when he touched her hand, Felipe found it so hot that he was reminded of the wall in the alley of Valladolid at that time when the three youths had threatened himself and Nana so brutally. That in itself was a reminder of the frightening things which could suddenly confront the unwary.

He felt lost, alone and frantic with despair. He could not weep; he was conscious only of his despair.

He went to Nana for comfort. She showed him the baby, but he could not care for the baby.

During the nights he would lie awake listening for sounds that might spring up in the house. When he slept he dreamed often of men in black robes; he heard voices crying: "Open! Open in the name of the Holy Office!"

He found small comfort in pretending that Roderigo was with him and that he could talk to him, for what had happened to him had happened to Roderigo, he was sure. Those men in black had gone to Roderigo's house in the dead of night. They had taken Roderigo's father as they had taken his own.

"Oh, Roderigo," he whispered, "what do they do with those whom they take to the prisons of the Holy Office?"

Felipe lay on the grass and sobbed.

He had no mother now. She had died peacefully in her sleep, they had told him.

"Why? why?" he had demanded.

Nana took him in her lap and held his head against her breasts while she rocked him as though he were a baby.

"She did not suffer, my love," said Nana. "She did not know."

"But," he cried in wretched exasperation, "she was well. She was not going to die. Why did she die?"

"It was the fever, my sweeting. It was the fever, you see."

He clenched his hands together. "*They* killed her. They killed her when they took my father."

"Hush, hush, my boy. My darling, you must not talk thus. They are afraid of them here. They are all afraid."

"Oh, Naña, Naña, when will my father come back?"

"Soon, soon, my precious. He will be back soon."

Felipe hated the house with its ornate tiles, its carved pillars, its great staircases and its luxury. It was not his home any more.

All the servants — both men and women — whispered a good deal together. They shook their heads. They were anxious. Who was the head of the house now? they asked themselves. The master a prisoner! The mistress dead! When rich men were suspected their servants were often taken to talk of what they knew, to tell of what strange and evil practices had been going on in a house which had contained heretics. They had all heard of the *chevalet* and the pulley; they had seen those who had experienced such things, and that meant they had seen that which they dared not contemplate, which they were afraid to remember.

One of the most miserable people in a miserable household was Pablo.

He came out to Felipe when he lay on the grass.

"Don Felipe!" he cried. "Don Felipe!" And he stroked the boy's hair and wept with him. "Do not weep so, little master. It is better so. Now she is dead, she is at peace."

"She was getting well," said Felipe. "They have killed her. We were going home. Oh, how I wish we had gone, before they took my father!"

Pablo made the sign of the cross. "Your father is a good Catholic. It is only the heretics and infidels who must fear. He will be back."

"He will never be happy again . . . now that my mother is dead."

146

Then Pablo burst into violent weeping. He threw himself on to the grass, and sobs shook his body.

"Oh, Pablo, Pablo, you are my good friend. You must not weep so. It can do no good."

"Don Felipe, I did not mean this to happen. I did not mean this . . ."

"You, Pablo?"

"I wished them to take Roderigo. He was a heretic. But when the Inquisitors come to a house . . . they do not take only one . . ."

"Pablo, do you mean this is . . . because of Roderigo?"

Pablo had turned away; his eyes had grown crafty; he had said too much.

"He should never have come here, Don Felipe. I knew he would bring disaster. Oh, if only you had not left me on that day of the *fiesta* . . . how happy we should be now!"

Felipe cried: "Pablo, have they taken Roderigo too? Do you know this?"

Pablo kept his eyes hidden. "That would not surprise me, Don Felipe."

Now it was clear to Felipe. Roderigo had been hiding from the Inquisitors. That was why he had been wandering all over the country. They had found him and . . . because he had been in Felipe's father's house, they had suspected Felipe's father of heresy.

Felipe felt numbed. He rocked back and forth in his misery. He wished he could lie on the grass and die.

He had never known unhappiness like this. He had realised, on that day when men had come to search his grandfather's house, that terrible things could happen swiftly, that happiness could be dealt a death-blow in one moment.

He it was who had met and loved Roderigo, who had brought him to his father's house; and the sweet companionship of that man had led to misery. They had taken his father; he had no mother now. He had only Nana . . . Nana and his little sister.

He was the head of the house until his father returned. What ought he to do? He thought suddenly of his cousin Roger, and the longing for his friendship and advice overwhelmed him. What would Roger do at such a time? Roger would gladly shoulder responsibility. Roger would want to ride off in search of his father. That was because Roger, for all his bravery, was a child in some matters. He would try to pit his boy's strength against the might of the Inquisition. Felipe was not like Roger. He must think clearly; he must be spiritually brave. He must do something to guard Nana and his little sister.

Then he realised what he ought to have done long ago. He must send a message to his grandfather and his Uncle Charles in England. He must tell them what had happened. Looking back, they seemed to him mighty men, all-powerful, full of resource and courage. They would know what to do. They would come to Spain; they would make the Holy Office give up his father; and they would take them all back to England and safety.

"Pablo," he said, "I must find some means of telling my grandfather and my uncle what has happened. I must send a message to them."

Pablo's eyes glistened. A message to England! Here was his own salvation.

He said, after only a few seconds' hesitation: "Give me your instructions, Don Felipe. Give me your messages . . . write them down in your own tongue . . . and I will carry them across the seas. I will take them to England."

Pablo's eyes were lifted to the sky. Yes, he would go to England. I will risk my life, he told himself. I will make amends by taking the little Don's message to England.

Pablo was almost happy. He was terrified of staying in the house; he knew that those who lived within its walls were unsafe. He knew that the eyes of the Holy Office were very likely directed upon it now. Roderigo had lived under its roof and they had taken its master. And might they not consider, as their next victim, him who had informed them how to capture one who had escaped them and lived under a name not his own?

It might be decided that knowledgeable Pablo had more knowledge to impart.

He had no wish to face his questioners in the torture chambers.

Now he could deceive himself as had been his habit previously to deceive himself. "I will kill . . . kill . . ." he used to cry, when secretly he had known he was afraid of the long knives of other men. Now he said: "Don Felipe, I will serve you with my life. I will make this perilous journey to England. I will deliver your message. I will die if necessary . . ."

And in his mind a small voice said: "And you should go quickly. You should slip away from this house which is doomed, as all are doomed who lie within the grim shadow of the Holy Office of the Inquisition."

Pablo had left. So had most of those who had made up this large household. They had taken mules from the stables and ridden away.

Tomás and Marina stayed, but only because they found it difficult to make the effort necessary to leave.

The big house was being neglected. There was dust on the windows; the dead flies lay in heaps and no one removed them. The goats, which Nana milked regularly, had strayed into the *patio*; their smell mingled with that of *olla podrida*, and filled the lower rooms.

Tomás and Marina were kind, but they were concerned with their own affairs. They talked of travelling the hundred and fifty miles south to Madrid on mules they would take from the stables. But they dreaded the long and arduous journey across the arid plain; and while they feared the coming of the *alguaçils*, again and again they put off their departure.

"*Mañana*," said Marina; and Tomás was glad to postpone the journey to an indefinite "tomorrow".

Nana had taken the baby into the mistress's room, and she lay in her cradle, yellow and shrivelled, more like an old woman than a young baby. The chain with

150

the jewelled cross hung about her neck, hidden by the swaddling clothes.

She cannot live! thought Nana, and she wept bitterly.

Felipe had said: "Soon my Uncle Charles will come for us, Naña. Pablo has gone to England; he is taking a message to my grandfather and to Uncle Charles. It will not be easy for him, since he speaks no English, but I have written the name and the place where he is to go with the message; and he has taken those papers with him. They will come soon, Naña. Then they will force the Inquisitors to release my father. We shall all go back to England then. Oh, how I hate this land! How I wish we had never come here!"

Nana nodded. "Yes, Felipe. Your uncle will come and he will save your father. He will take us home."

Poor Felipe! thought Nana. It is too much for a boy of his age to suffer. What will become of him . . . and the dear little baby?

Felipe seemed scarcely to notice his little sister. Nana tried to draw his attention to her; her own care of the baby had helped her to grieve less for Roderigo, for her mistress and master. But Felipe was not so easily lured from his grief.

"Your sister is ill, Felipe," Nana told him. "I am very-anxious. She will take little milk. I do not see how she can thrive on what she takes."

"She will be better when my uncle comes."

"Yes, she will be better then."

Several weeks went by. Each day Felipe would stand on the little hillock near the house, looking in all directions, hoping that he would see his uncle.

And Nana, waiting in the house, knew that her baby was about to be born.

Marina had naturally become aware of her condition.

"Roderigo?" asked Marina.

Nana nodded.

"Ah!" said Marina. "How beautiful he was! You poor Naña! How will you manage, I wonder . . . alone in this house?"

It would be soon, thought Marina; it would be very soon.

But it was no affair of hers. As soon as possible she must ride away to Madrid with Tomás. They had delayed too long.

But Marina thought much of Nana. Could a woman leave another at such a time in such a position? Marina did not think she could. There were obligations and responsibilities one woman had towards another when she was in Nana's condition; Marina told Tomás so.

"And what if the Inquisitors should come, Marina?"

"They would not take us. They are not concerned with us. We are good Catholics, and what have we that they could need?"

There was truth in that.

Tomás was easy-going and it was pleasant living in the big house like lords. Why, it was as though he were master of the house!

"I think she does not wish the little Felipe to know," said Marina.

"It is as well that he should not," said Tomás, "until the child is born. That Roderigo is responsible for this, I doubt not!"

152

"Ah, that Roderigo!" said Marina, lowering her eyes that Tomás might not see their wistful look. "He was one to love and ride away . . . not like my good Tomás."

Then Tomás kissed her.

"As you wish it, *amiga,* we will stay until the child is born," he said.

"You are good to me . . . good to me . . ." said Nana. "You wish to go, and yet you stay to help me."

Marina knew the words expressed gratitude.

She snapped her fingers.

"Is the pain bad, then?" she whispered. "There, cling to me. Poor Naña! Poor Naña!"

How different she was, thought Marina, from the poor mistress. Naña was strong, and the mistress had had death close to her all the time. It had only needed the shock to kill her, for she had been weak, unfit to bear children.

As for the little one in the cradle, she was surely dying. Naña had anxiously signed for her to try to feed the child, but what was the use? The child would not take the goats' milk which was offered. She needed her mother, poor soul, although the good Naña had been to her all that a mother could be, except for the fact that she had been unable to feed her.

What will become of us all? thought Marina. Holy Saints preserve us!

Nana was crying out in fresh agony.

"There, Naña. There, little Naña," murmured Marina. "Holy Mother of God, how women suffer!"

"Felipe?" said Nana, looking to the window.

Marina smiled and nodded reassuringly. She understood. Nana did not wish the boy to know. The little one was at this moment fully occupied. He was on the hillock, where he would be content to remain for a long time, looking for his English friends. Poor little Felipe! What would happen to him in this house of doom?

Marina shivered. Soon she must be with Tomás on the road to Madrid. They must not delay long. As soon as Nana was up and about they must go.

Nana said: "Felipe!" again; and she put her finger to her lips to indicate secrecy.

Marina did the same, assuring Nana with nods and gestures that she understood perfectly. For the time being Felipe should be kept in ignorance of what was happening.

Nana smiled.

He must not know. It would increase his anxieties. He would remember afresh how his mother had died; he would be anxious lest the same fate overtake Nana. No, he must not have more to bear than he already had.

Nana lay waiting for the next pain, and Marina crossed to the cradle in which was the baby girl.

How quiet she was! Marina shivered. There seemed something that was supernatural in this situation; a birth and a death were about to occur in one room at almost the same hour.

Nana was refreshed. Beside her lay her child — a little girl with black hair and dark eyes. She was so like that other girl who had lain in the ribbon-decorated cradle that had they been placed side by side at the hour of their birth they might have been thought sisters.

Nana was temporarily happy to be aware of a painless body; for a brief space she could be forgetful of the tragedy about her and enjoy the triumph of motherhood. Her child was born and lay beside her; and, compared with that overwhelming fact, nothing else could seem of any importance.

She touched the baby's face gently as it lay in the crook of her arm. She looked at the cradle which she kept close to her bed and saw the wan face of Felipe's sister. The baby in the cradle lay still and silent.

Nana's brow was wrinkled and her eyes showed that she was puzzled. A strange thought had come to her; it was half a plan . . . something which she could not entirely grasp.

Later Felipe came in to see her.

"Naña, Naña," he cried. "You are ill?"

"Nay, Felipe, I am well now. Tomorrow I shall be quite well."

His eyes were on the baby in her arms, but he did not seem to see it. Nana's heart began to beat fast.

"Marina told me you were ill," he said.

"Did she tell you what was wrong with me?"

"She said you were a little sick and must stay in bed for a while. Oh, Naña . . . Naña . . . *you* are not going to die?"

"No, no. I am well. I shall be up and about tomorrow, I doubt not."

He threw his arms about her.

"There, there, my sweeting," she soothed. "Do not crush the little one, my darling."

"Oh, Naña," he said, his dark eyes filled with sorrow, "what would have become of my sister if you had not been here to look after her?"

Nana drew the child close to her. She had wrapped it in one of the rich shawls that belonged to the child in the cradle.

"Naña," went on Felipe, "if my uncle does not come, what will happen to us?"

"He will come, Felipe. Never fear."

Felipe kissed her.

"Yes, Naña, I think that he will come."

Nana was up the next day, although she felt a little weak. The peasants here walked about immediately after child-birth; she had seen them in their black clothes working in the fields, their bodies heavy; and a day later they would be at work, their babies lying on the grass beside them.

It was the same with the poor people at home. They did not lie abed.

Nor shall I! decided Nana.

Marina came to her the day after the child was born. She pointed out of the window and waved her arms to convey that she and Tomás would delay no longer.

Nana nodded and smiled her understanding.

"Very soon," said Marina, "your friends will come. Then all will be well."

Felipe bade them both goodbye very gravely and stood sadly watching them as they rode away.

Now that Tomás and Marina had left the house, there only remained Felipe, Nana, the newly born child and the child that was soon to die.

Nana now knew herself to be not only a lustful woman, but a sly and cunning one.

Her child was the most important being in the world. Roderigo was lost to her, and now in these coming months the mother would supersede the lover. This child was her own as even Felipe had never been. She had loved Felipe, so she had thought, as her own; but there had never been anyone so important to her as the child who now lay in her arms.

The baby was small, yet strong. How the master and mistress would have rejoiced, thought Nana, if they had been blessed with a child like Nana's daughter!

Nana fed her, watched her greedily reaching for Nana's milk. She laughed with pleasure at the tickling made by the small mouth.

Then she remembered the poor little baby in the cradle; and she set aside her own child and took up the other. She placed it at her breast, but the child was too weak to suck. Nana's tears fell on to the dark head which was so like that of her own baby.

It was so sad that this little one should die, while the other was so strong; and though Nana wept with pity and love for the sad little baby, how could she help rejoicing in her own?

And as Nana watched the two babies, that plan which had come into her head grew more definite; she began to see how easy it would be to carry it out. She said nothing to Felipe. He did not know that there were two babies in his mother's room. He was not now interested in his little sister. He thought continually of his father; when would his uncle come, and when could a rescue be made?

It was natural that he should not think of his little sister; and Nana continued to keep him in ignorance of the birth of her child.

Three nights after Marina and Tomás had left, Nana stood by the ornate cradle and knew that the child who lay in it was dead.

She wept afresh. It hurt her to remove the beautiful clothes and to see what was more like a skeleton than a baby beneath them.

Nana carried the baby to the window, and her tears fell on to the dead face.

How could she tell Felipe that he had now lost his little sister? He would take it as a further sign of ill fortune. She could not forget the terror in his face when he had flung his arms about her and feared that she would die.

He was too serious a boy to suffer so; he was too sensitive.

He must not know, thought Nana; and she could not but be conscious of the sly thoughts that mingled with her tender love.

It would be so easy to carry out that plan which had come into her mind. The news that the master of the house had been taken would have spread, with the result that nobody came to see them now.

She wrapped the baby in a shawl so that she could not see its poor little face, and she set it under the coverlet on her bed.

Then she laid her own child in the cradle. She looked beautiful there.

"So you *should* have a cradle, little sweeting," she said. "You should have a cross and chain about your neck."

She took the chain and cross from the dead child's neck and put it about that of her own.

Now she had admitted to herself what she intended to do. When Master Charles came — and she was sure he would come — Felipe would say to him; "This is my sister." And there would be the beautiful child with the Spanish features and the cross and the chain about her neck.

She would be a lady, this little one. She would learn from books as Felipe and Roger learned. She would grow up with them and the little girls of the household.

And the next day, when Felipe watched on the hillock for the coming of his friends. Nana took the dead baby, dug a hole near the pomegranate bushes in a lonely part of the grounds, and there she buried the baby.

When she returned to the house, she went to the mistress's room, and there in the cradle lay her own child smiling at her, the chain with the jewelled cross about her neck.

One Sunday morning when Felipe returned from the hillock there were men waiting for him.

"You are Felipe Grendell?" said one of them.

Felipe said he was. "You have brought my father back?" he cried.

"Come with me," said the man, and he led him into the big hall. The blinds had been drawn to shut out the sun and when he became accustomed to the gloom he saw that Nana was there, holding the child at her breast as though she feared these men would take her from her.

One of the men, who wore the black robes of a monk, sat at the table. His features were pale, his skin was stretched tightly across the bones of his face, his mouth was thin and straight, and all the cruelty of the fanatic was written there.

The man who had led Felipe to the room now laid a hand on his shoulder and pushed him towards the table.

Felipe stepped forward, his heart beating so that he could hear the heavy great strokes in his ears; the furniture seemed to sway and dip in an extraordinary manner; the men, Nana, and the child, seemed like figures out of a dream.

"You are Felipe Grendell?"

"Yes, Señor."

"Who is this woman?"

"She is my nurse."

"Does she speak Spanish?"

"She speaks no Spanish."

"And the child?"

"It is my sister."

"And your mother?"

"She is dead." He wanted to shout: "And you killed her!" But there was that about these men which inspired him with awe. Moreover, he wished to obtain news of his father, and he believed them to be so cruel that they would, unless he fell in with their wishes, refuse any such information.

"There are only you, the nurse and the child in this house?"

"That is all."

"You must go from here. The house and the lands are no longer your property."

"But . . . it is my parents' house. It was my grandfather's . . . For many years it has belonged to . . ."

"It no longer belongs to them."

"Do you mean we must go from here! But where will we go? Where will my uncle find us when he comes?"

"Your uncle? Who is this uncle?"

"He is my father's brother. He is coming from England."

The man at the table considered this reply.

"How do you know that he will come?"

"I sent a message to him. It is a long time ago, but the journey is long. The sea is so treacherous, and he must cross the sea. I have asked him to come and take us home."

"When did you send this message and by whom?"

"By one of the servants. It was soon after my father . . . went away. Oh, Señor, I beg of you, let me see my father."

The man lifted a hand for silence. "You are to see him. Orders have been given that you shall."

"Oh, thank you, Señor. When . . . when?"

"A week from today."

Felipe felt the tears running down his cheeks. He knelt before the man at the table and kissed his hand.

Nana, watching, thought that man's face might have been made of stone.

The man said: "A week from today a messenger will ride out to you. He will take you and the woman to the place where you will see your father. But first you must convince me that you are a good Catholic."

"I am a good Catholic," said Felipe eagerly.

"You will repeat the *Pater* and *Credo*."

"Now, Señor?"

"At this moment."

Felipe, who had never had any difficulty in learning, buoyed up by the dazzling hope of seeing his father, was able to do without hesitation what was required of him.

The man nodded, a little astonished, and for the first time his mouth softened slightly.

He rose.

He said: "You will be prepared to ride to your destination this day week. And as your English friends are coming to take you home, you may rest in this house for four weeks after that. If at the end of that time they have not come, you must leave."

Felipe could not pay much attention to what was being said. He could think of one thing only: At last he was to see his father.

The week of waiting passed more quickly than Felipe had dared hope it would. There was so much to do.

"Naña," he cried, "how dirty the house has become. Do you remember how the table used to look set out with silver dishes? There is dust on everything. What will my father think?"

"We must have it bright and shining before he comes home," said Nana.

"He will be very sad, Naña. It may be that he does not know that my mother has died. How can he know, unless those men tell him? How shall we break the news to him, Naña?"

"I do not know, Felipe. But you can remind him that he has you . . . you and the little one."

"Shall we be enough, when he has been thinking he had us all?"

"He will be glad to be home."

"Naña, they said we must not stay here. Why not? Why is it no longer our home?"

"I do not understand them and their ways. I did not like them, Felipe. They had cold, stone faces. They were not good men."

"I did not like them, Naña. But they are taking me to my father . . . and I could like them for that."

"Come, Felipe, we must make the house beautiful. He will be shocked to find the servants are gone."

"I will help you, Naña."

"No, my darling. Sit here and hold your sister. Talk to me while I polish the silver dishes."

It pleased her to see him there, holding the baby.

"How little she is, Naña!"

"She is young yet."

"Is she like me, Naña? I believe she is a little."

"She is very like you," said Nana. She took the baby from him and held her tightly in her arms, smothering her face with kisses.

"Oh, Naña!" cried Felipe. "If only my mother were here, I do not believe he would mind about anything then."

He began to weep quietly, and Nana put her free arm about him. "There, there, my love," she soothed. "He has his son . . . his little Felipe, and he has . . . this little darling."

"We will comfort him, Naña. You . . . I . . . and the baby . . . we will comfort him."

Nana smiled, and it seemed indeed true that out of evil good could come.

At last the day arrived. Felipe was up when the first sign of the dawn was in the sky. "This is the day I shall see my father," he said.

He dressed with care; then went down to the stables to prepare the mules. He was almost happy; he felt ready to sing, although on the day his mother had died he had thought he would never do so again.

"Naña," he called. "Naña, wake up."

He went to the room which had been his parents'. Nana was lying in the bed which she had used since his mother had died and she had taken sole charge of the baby.

Nana was wide awake.

"Is it time to get up, then?" she asked.

164

"It is early yet. But we must be ready. Oh, Naña, I can scarcely believe it. I said yesterday: 'Tomorrow I shall see my father!' And now the day has come when I may say: 'today I shall see him.'"

Nana rose, and they ate a hasty meal of the bread Nana had baked a few days ago; but neither could drink the wine which Roderigo had bought and of which there was still plenty in the cellar.

It was early when the men arrived. There were two of them and they wore monks' robes. They were courteous and behaved with great solemnity.

"Are you ready to leave?" asked one of them of Felipe.

"Quite ready."

Nana had strapped the baby to her back, and the child cried fretfully to find herself in such an unfamiliar position.

"There is no time to be lost," went on the man. "We have a long ride before us and there will be many on the road today."

Felipe was surprised that they did not take the road to Valladolid. Instead they turned south. The dust and the flies made Nana cough; the baby cried; but Felipe exulted, thinking: Soon . . . soon . . . I shall see my father. The monks said nothing as they rode on — one leading the way, the other taking up his place at the rear of the little party.

When they had been riding some time they fell in with crowds of people, all of whom were heading in one direction, and Felipe guessed that they must be nearing a town. He was reminded of that day when he had

165

ridden into Valladolid to see the celebrations for the Infanta's wedding.

But that had been long ago. Then his mother had been alive and she and his father had been so happy.

But he must not think of his mother. He must think only of his father. He would say to him: "Father, you have my sister and you have me. We will make up to you for the loss of our mother."

They came to a walled town and rode through the gate.

Now the crowd was dense. This was some sort of *fiesta,* and yet it was unlike the day of rejoicing at Valladolid. Was it not a Sunday? Did that mean it was a religious feast?

They rode into the town square, where a platform had been erected, about which had been placed an elaborate tapestry awning; on this platform seats had been set, and a few of these were already occupied, some by monks, others by men in elaborate robes.

As they neared the platform, one of the monks who had ridden with them said: "Let the woman remain here. You will come with me."

Nana was glad to dismount and fuss over the baby, while Felipe, under the instructions of the monk, tied the mules to staples which had been fixed in the ground for that purpose. And while Nana unstrapped the baby and sat down to feed her, Felipe went with the man on to the platform.

There he was made to stand before a man who wore the robes of a monk and who was seated on one of the chairs.

"This is the boy," said the man who had brought him. "The Englishman's son."

The monk nodded.

"Please," pleaded Felipe, "may I see my father now?"

The monk lifted his hand for silence. "Soon you shall see him. I hope you will profit by the sight."

"Oh, Señor, Señor, when . . . when?" Felipe's voice broke on a sob.

"All in good time. You are a good Catholic, my son?"

"Yes, yes, Señor. So is my father."

"You will see for yourself."

Felipe was bewildered.

"Keep the boy here on the platform," said the man who was seated. "I wish to observe him."

The tolling of the bells seemed to come from every part of the town. Felipe looked about him with great curiosity. He had imagined this day's adventure would be so different; he had thought they would take him to the prison, and that there he would see his father, and, when they had embraced, his father would come away with him. He had not imagined anything like this.

Now he noticed the poles which had been set up in the centre of the square. He looked about him. Nana was squatting on the cobbles, and there were so many people round about that she was almost lost to sight. She seemed absorbed in the baby.

"You will not have long to wait," said the man. "Ah . . ."

Soldiers were forcing back the crowds to make a passage, and through this, some limping, some carried on chairs, came a procession of strange figures. Felipe

167

did not know whether they were men or women, for they were dressed alike in yellow robes of coarse wool. On these garments were painted lurid symbols and designs.

In a moment Felipe was reminded of Smithfield Square. He looked in horror from that column in hideous yellow to the wooden poles which had been erected in the centre of the square.

Beside the procession of yellow-robed people walked two men in the swinging black garments of monks.

"Repent!" they cried. "Repent while there is yet time."

In ghastly understanding Felipe realised what he was about to see and, in feverish eagerness, he craned forward as the people in yellow drew nearer. He felt certain that among them he would find his father's face.

But it was not easy to see their faces, for now another procession of men on horseback came riding beside them. These were the dignitaries of the Church; their lips were smiling, their eyes upraised; their rich ecclesiastical garments made a startling contrast with the hideous yellow of the degraded victims.

The chanting voices went on: "Repent and be reconciled. Repent and be reconciled."

Felipe scanned the faces of those yellow-clad figures, while nausea mixed with his fear. They were not like the faces of men. They were drained of all colour, except where the blood had dried on their scars. The broken arms of some hung limply at their sides. Some had been blinded. Felipe knew that they had suffered torture which was beyond his imagining.

And he was sure now that his father was among them.

He felt a hand on his shoulder, and heard a voice in his ear.

"Those who are to suffer the flames are wearing the caps. You see them?"

Felipe saw them. They wore pointed caps which were disfigured with pictures of grotesque devils. For a moment he was tempted to cover his eyes.

"All," said the voice, "wear the *sanbenito*, the yellow robe of shame, for all have been guilty of heresy. Some have repented."

"My . . . my father . . ." said Felipe.

"Look for him. Not all those in the *sanbenito* will die. Look at those with the red crosses on their garments. They are to do penance and suffer imprisonment, for their sins have not been so great as other's. Can you see the pictures on their robes? Can you see the heads and busts painted there? They are being consumed by flames, those heads and busts. The flames are pointing upwards. They are too far away for you to see that clearly, perhaps. If the flames are pointing upwards, that means the one who wears that robe has recanted; therefore he will die mercifully. He will be strangled before he feels the flames. Now see . . . there are others. On their robes the busts are depicted with the flames *downwards*. Hideous devils fan those flames . . ."

"And . . . my father?"

"You will see. You have been brought here, my son, by those who wish you well. Your youth demands compassion. That which you see today will assure you of the virtues of the Catholic Faith. You will, in this *Quemadero,* be purged of any evil which you may have inherited."

"Let me see my father. I beg of you, let me see my father."

He could not endure it. He could not sit here. He leaped forward, but a hand gripped his shoulder and a voice, soft and gentle, said in his ear: "No, no, my son. You must be patient. You will see. If you are a good Catholic, you will rejoice in this day's work, as do all good Catholics."

Now the Inquisitors themselves were coming into the square. They carried the scarlet sarcenet — the colour of the blood which they sacrificed to their God — the banner that was emblazoned with the arms of their most Catholic Majesties, Ferdinand and Isabella, who had done so much to make the Inquisition the mighty monster it was, and also with the heraldic bearings of the Inquisition.

Behind them the people closed in, alert, eager to witness the sufferings of others. This was better than a bull-fight. Here torture and suffering — *human* suffering — could be witnessed, and all with the approval of Almighty God. Prayers would be chanted; they would mingle with the screams of agony; and those in the crowd could look on with fascinated eyes and say: "Thank God I am not as other men. Here is a circus, here is excitement such as surpasses that

170

provided by the games of the Romans, and all done under the eyes of God which are so terrible when fixed on these victims, so benign when watching the pleasure of His servants."

Now the great Inquisitors had taken their places on the platform. None of them took any notice of Felipe, cowering at the feet of the man in black, who not for a moment released his grip on the boy's shoulder.

There was silence over the square. A Bishop who had been seated at the front of the platform rose and began to deliver a sermon.

Felipe vaguely heard the words. He knew they concerned the greatness of the Holy Office and the determination within it to stamp out heresy. The boy's eyes were frantically searching among the victims for one face.

When the Bishop had finished his long discourse, he sat down, and the Grand Inquisitor rose. His robes, richly embroidered, proclaimed him an Archbishop. He lifted his hand and, in the silent square, the people fell instantly to their knees.

The Inquisitor then administered the oath of the Inquisition, which the people must repeat after him. They swore to defend the Inquisition in Spain against all who attacked it. They swore to be faithful to it, to give their eyes if necessary, their hands, their lives in its defence.

Strangely enough the sound of those chanting voices seemed to Felipe more terrible than anything he had yet witnessed.

There was silence. The hot sun burned down on them. There was no sound but the buzzing of flies in the air. Felipe felt he had entered Hell itself, and that whatever there was beyond this life, nothing could be more evil, more terrifying than what was in it.

The Great Inquisitor then took a long scroll from a monk who stood beside him, and began to read out the names inscribed thereon. He read with each name an account of its owner's wrongdoing and what punishment should be inflicted. As the names were called, those to whom they belonged must kneel and proclaim their guilt aloud.

The voices were ringing through the square. All those now being called were those who were guilty of the lesser heresies and who had repented. The Inquisitor read their sentences; they were all condemned to long terms of imprisonment with penances, and their lands and goods were to be confiscated.

The dreary list went on and on, and when the voice of the Inquisitor paused, he had still not mentioned Felipe's father.

Those whose names had been called stood up, and guards came forward to lead them away. About twenty men in yellow were left. Felipe concluded that among these who remained was his father. They were maimed; they could not stand; they already seemed more dead than alive.

Now the Inquisitor continued with his reading. Felipe listened. "Condemned to the flames . . ." "Condemned to the flames . . ."

And then: "Richard Grendell, Englishman and heretic, condemned to die by fire without mercy of strangulation. Confiscation of estates . . ."

Felipe staggered forward; he shrieked in his high treble: "Father!"

"Be silent," said the voice in his ear. "It will be the worse for you . . . and him . . . if you are not."

The grip on his shoulder was painful; the heat was overpowering. The smell of people, the hideousness of the *Quemadero* . . . he could not bear it. It was a nightmare. It must be. Soon he would awaken in his room in Chelsea and his cousin Roger would be standing beside him. Roger would say: "What a nightmare!" And when he heard what it was about: "That was due to my talk of Spaniards."

He was lying at the feet of the man who held him. But he must not faint. He must look again. He must assure himself. They would not do this thing to his father . . . his noble father, who had never harmed anyone, whom he loved more than anyone in the world.

He opened his eyes. The glare from the sky hurt him. He was going to faint again.

The words of the Inquisitor droned on, but he did not heed them. The prisoners were now being handed over to the secular magistrate, for the holy men of the Inquisition did not sully their souls with the deaths of their victims. They merely recommended the sentence, which the officials of the state dared not hesitate to carry out. The heretics, said the holy ones, were not fit to live, and God could only be appeased if His loyal followers sent them out of this world in the cruellest

173

manner they could invent. The Holy Inquisition set men on the *chevalet,* in the great collar, dislocated their limbs on the pulley, all in the name of God and righteousness that they might confess their faults and lead the Inquisitors to those of like thinking; but the actual carrying-out of the sentence must be by order of the secular law. And if any magistrate should refuse to enforce that sentence as proclaimed by the Inquisition, it could but mean that that man was himself a heretic and needed the attention of those men of the lower chambers who knew best how to extort men's secrets from them.

Felipe had seen his father, but he would not have recognised him had he not heard his name called and seen him forced to his knees by the friar who stood near him. His arms were useless; his mouth was shapeless. No, thought Felipe in anguish, that man could not be his father.

"What . . . what have they done to my beloved father?" he cried. "I hate them. I will kill them. I will never rest until I have had my revenge on you all for what you have done to my father."

He spoke in English, which was fortunate for him. The cold, glittering eyes of his captor surveyed him with anger. "Be silent, little fool!" he said. "Do you wish to join them there?"

To join them there? Yes, he thought. Yes, I do. For I cannot endure this. I cannot remain here while they do terrible things to my father. I cannot live after this.

The tears were running down his cheeks. His heart was broken and he longed for death.

And as he looked again at the group of doomed men, he saw among them one whom he thought he recognised. It was the set of the head, the innate jauntiness which could not desert the man even at such a time.

"Roderigo!" gasped Felipe.

And in that moment his surprise was greater than his misery.

Roderigo . . . here . . . with his father! Could it be possible?

The name which had been called was not that of Roderigo; but perhaps Roderigo y Galán was not his real name.

So here was additional torture. Not only his beloved father, but his dear friend Roderigo was doomed. Yet the sight of Roderigo filled him with anger, and it was as though Roderigo and Roger spoke to him simultaneously. "Be careful," they seemed to say. "What good would it do to die? Live . . . live and fight those who murdered your father and your friend. Fight them in every way you can."

He was silent while the torches were set to the pile of faggots. But when the smoke rose and the anguished cries of the sufferers mingled with the exulting shrieks of the multitude, Felipe fell fainting at the feet of the man who held him.

Slowly, mournfully they had ridden back to the house — Felipe, Nana and the baby.

To Felipe the days and nights were an interminable stretch of gloomy time. Nana, the practical one, devoting herself to the boy and the baby, feeding them, crooning over them, had something to live for.

She understood though that they would soon be turned out of the house, which was now the property of the Inquisition, as was all the property of men condemned to the flames.

Nana had seen what had happened to the master and Roderigo, and she wished that she had been struck blind before she had seen it, for always it would be with her, never completely banished. It would appear at odd moments, staining all future happiness with horror. The blind were fortunate, for they could not have seen what she had seen; the deaf were lucky, for they could not have heard the anguished cries of martyrs nor the hypocritical preaching of men who called themselves the servants of God.

Felipe was ill and she feared for his life. He lay listlessly on his bed. Sometimes he wept; at others he lay wide-eyed, saying nothing. She knew that instead of the room he saw the hideous square with a sky above like molten brass; he saw the flies, the mob crazy for blood; he heard the terrible cries of men in agony; he saw the smoke which put a merciful screen between the cruel eyes and loved ones in agony.

At other times Nana would have said: "What will become of us all?"

But, oddly enough, now it did not seem to matter. Providing the two children did not suffer, it was immaterial whether they lived or died. Those men in the square had made her feel that life was not important.

176

Roderigo was in her thoughts continually, yet, because of the children's need of her, she could keep her sanity.

Then one day men again came riding to the house. Felipe heard them, but he did not rise from his bed. He thought fleetingly: Now they have come to take me, to do to me what they have done to my father. Or perhaps they have come to take our house and turn us out to wander under the hot sun or in the bleak winds. Let them come. I care not.

But it was not the members of the Inquisition who came.

Nana saw a tall man dismounting from his horse, and it seemed to her that Roderigo had returned. But it was not, of course, Roderigo. She had seen what had happened to him at the *auto-da-fé*.

With this man were two others; one was Pablo, the other a man whom she had known in the long ago days in England.

"Nana!" cried Charles. "At last we are here."

He lifted her in his arms and kissed her while she clung to him and wept. He was gentle and soothing. He said to her: "Felipe? What of Felipe?"

Felipe was coming down the staircase. He stood still when he saw his uncle.

He looked blank for a moment and then, as he recognised Charles, a light came into his face. He ran to his uncle and embraced him. He was like a child who has awakened from a nightmare and now knows that the bad dream is over, even though it will haunt him for the rest of his life.

177

When Charles heard the terrible story, his face grew pale. He would demand retribution, he vowed. They should suffer for this. They should die for this.

Felipe listened sadly and hopelessly. He had seen the might of the Inquisition. He had heard the dread oath. He had stood under a burning sun and seen the people of Spain fall on their knees and repeat their oath of allegiance to the Spanish monster of iniquity.

"Let us go quickly, Uncle," he said. "Let us leave this cruel land for ever."

And all that night he sat with his uncle and talked to him of the things he had seen; and he begged his uncle to take him back to England without delay, for he feared what might happen to any of them if they delayed longer in this land.

"Uncle . . . save us. You do not know how cruel they can be. You did not see. Save Naña and my little sister . . . save me . . . yourself . . . Save us all from these inhuman Inquisitors."

Then Charles began to understand.

He said: "We will go at once. Tomorrow we will set out, and we will not delay until we have left this accursed land behind us."

CHAPTER
FOUR

Sir Ralph Grendell was sitting on the wicker seat gazing across the river. The spring sun warmed him, and he could have taken pleasure in the scene if it had not reminded him of a similar day. It had been more than seventeen years ago, he reflected, for Felipe was now seventeen, and Ralph remembered distinctly that, at that time, the boy had not been born — although he had been expected hourly. He, Ralph, had sat here; the baby Roger had lain at his feet; Dolores and Cecily had joined him and together they had watched the arrival of Herr Pretzel.

Jane had cursed that day, for she believed that when Pretzel had tied up his boat at the privy steps and come to their house, he had brought trouble with him. Trouble had certainly come. Felipe had saved them that day when the men had come to search the house. Poor Felipe! He had had an early acquaintance with tragedy. He had returned from Spain a different boy from the one who had left England a year or so before.

The veins would stand out on Ralph's temples when he thought of what Felipe had suffered. He, a mild man, wanted to kill those who had tortured and murdered his son and made his young grandson suffer

179

such agony. As for Jane — he could not bear to recall her grief. This house had been a sad place when that little party had returned from Spain. The pleasant sense of security had vanished; he and Jane had been constantly on the alert. Hatred prevailed in the house, which had now become fiercely Protestant. It could never forget what the Catholics had done to its sons. On Richard they had imposed the most foul and degrading torture before they condemned him to a fiery death; they had subjected young Felipe to the most cruel mental torture; they had let him live, but they had done that to him which would haunt him for the rest of his life.

Felipe was now not as other boys. There had been times, it was true, when Roger had been able to make him laugh, but his grandparents were conscious of his ever-present melancholy. The boy seemed unable to free himself from the memory of his father's sufferings.

"Why did we ever let them go to Spain?" That was a question he and Jane asked each other many a time.

Dolores was dead; Richard cruelly tortured and murdered; Felipe severely shocked; and even Nana was bound to carry the scars of her dreadful experience.

It was small wonder that Jane wept bitter tears by night.

But there was one joy which had come out of Spain; that was his small granddaughter, the best loved of all his children — Donna, the dainty little Anglo-Spaniard.

He could see her now; she was standing on the bank looking at the river. Her black hair, which hung loose about her shoulders, was as unruly as she was. She was dressed in scarlet and she had tied a sash of cloth of gold about her waist. No doubt she had begged Kate for this, for she could do what she would with Kate.

Donna was small for her age — she was not quite seven — a child, yet a young lady. Coquettish, aware of her charm, she already made good use of those dark eyes of hers. She was warm-hearted and wilful, generous and hot-tempered. Ralph often thought her a typical Spaniard; she was ready to give all she had to those she loved, and to kick and bite those whom she hated. She could not veil her feelings. She loved fiercely; and she was a stormy and enchanting creature.

She was not in the least like the granddaughter Ralph had dreamed of. He had thought Dolores' daughter should be as gentle as Dolores had been. This flashing-eyed little girl was unlike Dolores, unlike Richard; yet it seemed to Ralph that she was perfect.

He loved her best of all his grandchildren, and that he felt to be wrong. Dear Kate, who was kind, gentle and always to be relied upon, should have been his favourite; the choice of some grandparents might have fallen on the dashing young man whom Roger had become; on the other hand, out of his pity for Felipe, there might have grown the greatest love. But it must be the youngest of them all — this little creature of fierce loves and fierce hates — whom he must love the best.

She it was who had been his comfort during the years of mourning. She had lain at his feet, as Roger had once done, studying him with her great dark eyes; and to baby Donna he talked often, talked of his sorrow and the pitilessness of life. And she would kick and laugh and flash her big eyes at him. When she was a little older it became a habit of hers to climb all over him, to pull his beard, his ears, his nose, to bite him in anger and almost suffocate him with her loving arms when she gave vent to her passionate affection.

As he watched her there by the river, he could deem the Spanish marriage of his younger son worth while in spite of all the sorrow it had brought.

Nana adored the child; and it was to Nana she went in moments of real trouble. Nana had mothered her from babyhood, as she had Felipe. But this naughty creature had, Ralph believed, overshadowed even Felipe in Nana's affections. Kate loved the child too. He was glad of that, for Kate was a good girl, the best in the world, quiet, gentle always ready to forgive. He wondered if Kate would have been able to forgive the Spanish Catholics for what they had done, had she been in Felipe's place. Her nature was such that he believed she would. She had a habit of wrinkling her brow — so that there were already lines on it, although she was but fourteen — and trying to see every side of a question. That was admirable; that was logical; it brought about a placidity which should have enchanted all — and it did in a way. But it was the wayward ones, with their unexpected behaviour, who won his affections. He loved Roger, the gay young rip, another such as his father. For Felipe he felt a different kind of affection, at the core of which was a great tenderness. He watched the boy closely; he continually wondered to what that underlying streak of melancholy would turn.

Felipe was quiet and gentle, yet beneath his gentleness was hatred, a smouldering fire. What could a grandfather know of a boy's mind when that boy had witnessed horror such as it was difficult to imagine?

He had two other grandchildren — Ceci and Lucie. Lucie, the younger girl, was a frivolous creature — gay, light-hearted and vain of her prettiness; her thoughts were continually of her own personal charms and the husband she would have; her grandfather could not share her excitement about these matters.

And Ceci? Ceci seemed to him a reincarnation of her mother. Cecily had died of a fever shortly after Richard and Dolores had gone to Spain, but she had lived long enough to imbue her eldest daughter with her own ideas. To see Ceci in the kitchen with her maids, to watch her about the house and garden, was to imagine that Cecily was still alive. There was the same assurance that all she did was right, and that what others did, if different, was wrong; there was that calm contempt for the weakness of others, that deft hand with pastry, that sharp tongue for the maids, the heavy hand for delinquents. Cecily had died, but she had left her personality behind in her eldest daughter.

These were his grandchildren — Roger and his three sisters, Felipe and little Donna. He would have no more, he felt sure, for Charles would not marry again. Why should he? One taste of marriage had been enough for him, and he had Nana. Ralph could imagine the comfort of Nana. But even she had changed as the result of her stay in Spain. She had been there; her eyes had seen what Felipe's had seen. And no one, Ralph opined, not even such as Nana, could look on such scenes and be the same person afterwards.

He must not think of it. When he did so, mists of hatred swam before his eyes, and he, a comfort-loving gentleman, wanted to take his sword and go to that cruel land; he wanted to find the men who had murdered his son, who had been responsible for the death of his daughter-in-law and planted a brooding melancholy in the eyes of his grandson.

He shaded his eyes from the sun. There were tears in them.

He felt a movement beneath the seat. He looked down and there, peeping up at him, was the face of Donna. She put her fingers to her lips. He looked at her with that delight which never failed to possess him when she was near him.

"Shush!" she whispered. "Do not look down here, Grandfather. You have not seen me. Remember that."

Then he understood, for he heard Ceci's voice calling: "Donna! Donna!"

Donna! he thought. The sweetest of names, and an odd one. Nana had insisted it was the child's name. It could not have been the name they had intended for her. Nana, who had learned but a few words of Spanish, must have picked up *Doña* and thought it was the child's name. Well, Nana had called her Donna — so had Charles and Felipe — and by the time they had reached England, that was what she had become. It suited her. It was strange and inconsequential, just as she herself was.

Ceci came into view. Her hair, the colour Cecily's had been, was well hidden under her headdress; she looked prim, and perhaps because he had been thinking of the past, he was more struck than ever by her resemblance to her mother.

"I'm looking for that child," she said.

"What is that, Ceci?" he answered.

"Donna. She should be at her lessons. And she shall be whipped for this. Mr Heath has but to leave her for a moment and she runs off."

"Ah, Ceci, she is young. She has plenty of time to learn her lessons."

"You excuse her," said Ceci angrily. "That is why she is so bad. She will flatter Kate until Kate helps her with her lessons; she will burst into tears and have Mr Heath feeling he is harsh and cruel and that she is to be pitied. I know her. I thought you might have seen the way she went."

Ralph felt Donna's fingers pinching his leg.

"I doubt not that you will find her," he said.

"It may be that she is hiding in the house. She has a fancy for the cellars. I expect she is playing there. I shall lock her in one day and let her stay there. Then perhaps she will not have such a fancy for them."

"Do not be too hard on her, Ceci. She is young."

Ceci clicked her tongue. "That is what you all say. She is not too young to play her tricks, and whipped she shall be."

Ceci walked off impatiently to the house, and after a short pause Donna said: "Grandfather, has she gone?"

"Come out," he said. "She has gone."

She stood before him, laughing. There was a smudge of dirt on her gown. She did not know of it; she would be concerned if she did, for she was very vain about her appearance.

"I was afraid you would betray me," she said. "If you had I should have *hated* you!"

He caught her and held her against him. "You are a bad child," he said.

She laughed and put her arms about his neck. She brought her face close to his so that, to him, hers was a blur. He felt that he wanted to hold her tightly, never let her go, never let her know there was anything more terrible in life than to have to hide from Ceci.

He said: "Why do you do these things, you bad Donna? Why do you run away at lesson times?"

She drew back in astonishment. "*Everybody* runs away at lesson times."

"Everybody?"

"Roger did."

"Roger is not everybody."

"No, but he is Roger."

"He should not tell you these things."

"Everybody should tell me things."

"Why should they tell *you* things?"

"Because I'm Donna."

She laughed, sure in her charm and her youth that all she desired would be hers.

"Now," he said, "you should go back to your lessons. For when Ceci finds you are not in the cellars she will come out here again, and you cannot expect every time to use a kind grandfather for your shield."

"Knights have shields," she said. "They are shining things . . . not grandfathers." She laughed in the clear, joyous way which was hers alone.

He fought the temptation to keep her with him. "Go back to your books," he said sternly. "At once. You should never have left them. It was very wrong."

"Wouldn't you like me to stay and talk with you?"

"No."

She looked hurt, and he added quickly: "Another time. Not in lesson time. If you do not go I shall have to tell Ceci when she comes out again."

"Why?"

"Because that is the right thing to do."

"Do you always do the right thing, Grandfather?"

"I'm afraid not."

"Then you are bad, too." She put her arms round him and hugged him. "Does Roger? Does Felipe?"

"You talk too much. I did not betray you, did I? Now you must reward me for that. You must go back to your lessons to please me."

She considered him. "Do people always have to pay for the good things with something bad?"

"Perhaps."

She looked at him solemnly for a few moments; then she nodded and ran off.

She paused after a while to look back at him. She threw him a kiss, and he loved her dearly for it. She had dispersed his gloom, as she had so many times before; she had made him forget his sadness. Spain, which had taken his son and his daughter-in-law, had given him Donna.

His wife Jane came and sat beside him. She was uneasy. Ralph took her hand and pressed it. "What ails you, Jane?"

She was silent for a few moments, then she said: "I am fanciful today. Something in the air . . . It reminds me of the day those men came to search the house. It was nine years ago. The boys were about nine and ten then. I suppose we should consider ourselves fortunate that nothing else followed . . . at least not here."

"Do not let us speak of Richard, Jane," said Ralph. "I have been thinking of him as I sat here. No good can come of thinking. We cannot control our thoughts, but do not let us utter them."

"No, Ralph, we will not."

"We were indeed fortunate not to be troubled further. Mayhap that was because the King died and there was a new King — a Protestant King. I know how your thoughts run, Jane. You are uneasy because that young King is dying."

She bowed her head in assent.

"You ask who will follow him," he went on. "If it is Mary . . ."

"And surely," she put in, "it must be Mary."

"There is talk of the Lady Jane Grey."

"Ralph, it is not possible. The people would not have her."

"Would they prefer a Catholic on the throne?"

"Why should they not?" cried Jane passionately. "They have not been to Spain. Their sons . . . Ah, now I have spoken of it."

"Dear Jane, it is near the surface of our thoughts. We do not mean to speak of it, but it slips out."

"Hatred . . . hatred, Ralph. How can we not hate, remembering Richard . . . Dolores . . . Felipe?"

"Jane, do not let us talk thus. Let us pray that Mary never mounts the throne. It is the King's wish that Jane Grey should follow him."

She said fearfully: "These people who come here . . . These meetings . . . these talks you have with them . . . These are against Mary."

"Have no fear, my dearest. All will be well. King Henry declared his marriage to his first Catharine null and void; so how could his daughter ascend the throne? She is a bastard. So is Elizabeth. The crown must pass to Lady Jane. Her grandmother, don't forget, was Henry's sister. She is in the direct line."

"But Mary is Henry's elder daughter! She is Edward's sister."

"His illegitimate sister."

"There are many who believe Henry's marriage with Catharine of Aragon was a true marriage and that their daughter is the rightful heir to the throne."

"She must not come to the throne, Jane. She must not."

"I pray she will not. Everyone in this house does the same. What will happen, think you, should she become our Queen?"

"We shall have Spanish ways here. She is half Spaniard. That is enough to make us hate her."

"You forget, Ralph. You are not yourself, your serene self, when you talk of these matters. Little Donna is half Spanish too."

"*Dolores* was her mother." His voice broke, and he covered his face with his hands.

Must it always be thus? wondered Jane. After seven years, must it be as fresh as yesterday?

There was no escape for either of them. Had not Richard been their son, their beloved son? Perhaps they had loved him more than their elder son; he had been quiet, sensitive and had seemed to need their love more than the self-sufficient Charles. Once Ralph had been lazy — the laziest man in England, she had lovingly called him. But now the cancer of hate was in his mind; it was polluting the pure contentment which had once been his; it was replacing love of serenity with a desire for revenge.

He was a Protestant now, whereas once he had been inclined to stand aloof from religious differences. She herself wished to remain aloof. She had lost her son, and she would never forgive those who had murdered him; but she had the rest of her family to love and cherish, and she trembled for them. As a warning she had reminded Ralph of poor Joan Bocher, who had been called Joan of Kent and who had been burned for her religious opinions. She also recalled to his mind the case of George Van Parre, who had denied the divinity of Christ and had been burned for that. Jane wanted to take no sides.

Her code was a simple one. She wanted to help those about her; she wished to do kindness whenever she could. She could not give her allegiance to any sect which condemned a difference of opinions in others; she was repelled by those who practised brutality in any way whatever. "Love your fellow men" seemed to her all-important; it was not necessary to be Catholic or Protestant to do that; either could do it equally well. And, she asked herself, how could any man who persecuted another call himself a Christian?

Once Ralph had held similar views to her own, but hatred had coloured his life and had altered his opinions. He was a Protestant now because Protestants were the enemies of the Catholics who had murdered his son and had submitted his grandson to torture such as few of tender age were called upon to suffer.

Now she said: "We must not think of it. It happened a long time ago. I watch Donna growing up, and I feel that Time makes the pain less acute."

"You are right," said Ralph. "It is wrong to think of it."

"Our grandchildren will be marrying soon, I dare swear," she went on, hoping to turn his thoughts in a happier direction. "They will be having children. Oh, Ralph, it will make me very happy to see them running about these gardens."

She was talking rapidly, partly to draw his attention away from the old tragedy, partly to reassure herself. She could not help remembering with fear that day when men had come to search the house. How she wished that Emil Pretzel had never come to them. Perhaps if he had not come, Richard would have remained a staunch Catholic. How could she ever forget her younger son? How could she shut from her mind the pictures of him in a dreary prison? Those men who had tortured him would have been the cause of his repudiating utterly the Catholic Faith; for, like his father, he would ask himself whether any religion, which could do such things to a man's body, was capable or worthy of ministering to his soul.

There was constant discussion regarding doctrines and schisms. What did it all mean and how could it be of such great importance as some men believed it to be? What greater commandment could there be but "Love one another"? To occupy oneself with the care of others, with kindness towards a neighbour was surely a better way of life than compelling them to accept doctrines by force instead of reason. But she would not be indiscreet. She had made up her mind to that on the day of The Search.

"I should like to see the grandchildren married," said Ralph. "That would please me mightily."

"Kate loves Felipe," said Jane almost happily, for now he was smiling, seeing these gardens made merry by the sounds of children's voices, instead of the *Quemadero*, the brutish faces of the participators in that scene of horror, the terrible physical sufferings of one beloved man and the mental anguish of an equally beloved child.

Jane settled herself cosily beside him. "They are alike, are they not, Felipe and Kate?" she went on. "Kate is as kind and gentle as Felipe is."

"I think Kate could help him to forget."

Jane said quickly: "She loves him already. She is only thirteen, but she loves him."

"Perhaps when she is sixteen . . ."

"Three more years."

"And Felipe? Do you think he loves Kate?"

Jane looked thoughtful. "He is fond of her. Who could help being fond of Kate? But at the present time she may seem to him like a sister."

"She is his cousin."

"Yes, but it will come. He cannot fail to love her as she so clearly loves him. Perhaps in three years' time . . . or even two. Fifteen is an age for a girl to marry."

"Dear Jane, a good deal can happen in three years . . . or even two."

"And Roger? He should marry soon?"

"Indeed yes. He is lusty, and I doubt not that a good wife is necessary to him. His father has talked of this. Roger's behaviour with the village girls gives him some cause for anxiety."

"Ah," said Jane, with a rueful smile, "these manners which Charles deplores have doubtless been inherited from him."

"That, my dear, is no doubt why they give him cause for alarm. He knows to what trouble Roger's adventures may lead him."

"I had thought that Donna would make a good wife for Roger."

"Donna!" There was the faintest note of indignation in Ralph's voice.

"She is a child yet . . . but would you not like to see your two beloved grandchildren united?"

"Nay!" He laughed. "The difference in their ages is too great. Roger would never wait for a wife until Donna grows up. She is seven. He is eighteen. It will be eight years before she is marriageable."

"I think both Donna and Roger will be marriageable at an earlier age than most."

"You would want to make the marriage of our children a family affair?"

"That would ensure keeping them all together . . . under one roof."

"Frightened, Jane?"

"Cautious. I want the family together . . . snug and safe."

"Dear Jane!"

"But do you not think that if Felipe married Kate, and Donna married Roger, that would be an ideal arrangement?"

"Roger will not, I fear, be a faithful husband. He is a buccaneer by nature. He is a rover, a wanderer. I doubt whether Donna would accept the conditions Roger would impose on a wife."

"But Donna is one to impose her own conditions."

"I should tremble to contemplate a union between Roger and Donna."

"I should tremble to contemplate a union between Roger and anyone but Donna, and between Donna and anyone but Roger."

"What strange ideas you have today, Jane. You look too far into the future."

"I think perhaps you are right." She took his hand. "Here is a beautiful spring day. The lilac has a lovely scent. How gently the river laps the bank. Today we are happy. Let that suffice."

And as she drew closer to him he put an arm about her; and they sat still looking out over the peaceful scene.

Lucie and Kate sat on the window-seat. Each was busy with her embroidery. Kate worked deftly, Lucie fitfully, glancing out of the window every few minutes to see if a boat should draw up at the privy stairs.

Donna sat on a stool at their feet. She was frowning over a piece of needlework which Ceci had said she must complete. Donna hated Ceci, for Ceci was the one person in the household whom she could not charm. It would be no use smiling at Ceci when she handed her the cobbled canvas; it would be no use saying: "Oh, Ceci, if I could but use my needle as you do!" Ceci would take one look at the work and, unmoved by entreaty, would calmly sit on the stool on which Donna now sat, roughly pull Donna towards her, put her across her knees and beat her with a stick.

In vain would Donna kick and scream. And although everyone would be sorry for her, they would all shake their heads and be grateful to Ceci for giving Donna what they knew she deserved.

That was a gloomy prospect for Donna.

She looked at Kate. Kate's fair hair was almost hidden under her linen cap, which came to a point in the centre of her forehead. Her dress was open in the front and showed her under-dress. Her stiff bodice fitted closely to her figure. She was plump and already womanly, looking more than her thirteen years.

Kate seemed to Donna the kindest person in the world, and she would ask her to put her needlework to rights, for although Donna was accustomed to Ceci's whippings, she hated them, more for the indignity they imposed than the pain. She was a dignified person, and what she could never forgive was being laughed at or humiliated in any way.

She sat now listening and watching the girls. She knew that Lucie was hoping to see young Henry Braxton, who sometimes came to the house with his father.

Yesterday Donna had seen Lucie and Henry in the orchard together. Lucie had run away from Henry, and Henry had run after her; but when Henry had caught her and kissed her, Lucie had merely protested crossly, although she had not looked in the least cross. Donna had thought it advisable to remain hidden and observe more of this strange conduct which was similar to that which she had seen take place between the serving men and maids — and particularly when Pablo was involved.

Lucie now held up the collar she was stitching, to admire it.

"There! Is it not pretty? It will go with my blue bodice."

"It is beautiful," said Kate.

"Kate, what do you think Henry's father and our father and Grandfather talk about when they are together?"

"The affairs of the country, I doubt not," said Kate.

"I don't believe it."

Donna kept very still. She was interested in the affairs of grown-up people. So often they would be talking and then grow silent when they noticed her. Donna was sure that there was a wonderful world of grown-up people of which she knew little, and which

196

would, if she could but explore it, unfold great secrets. Donna loved secrets.

Felipe would talk to her of the past. He would show her where their ancestors had hidden during the great Wars of the Roses. He showed her where a man named Wat Tyler had stood to challenge the King, and he had told her how Jack Cade had rebelled. Sometimes she could get him to talk of Spain — that land which was partly theirs and did not belong to Roger, Kate and the rest of them. They were different — she and Felipe. They were half Spanish. He could tell her fascinating things about Spain. He told of Alhambra and Alcazar, of the ladies of Seville with their combs and mantillas. It was one of her greatest pleasures to lure him to talk of Spain, because when he did so he was a different Felipe — not the quiet young man whom the others knew, but almost a stranger.

"Felipe," she had once said, "tell me of when you were in Seville." And he had answered: "I was never there. I never saw Seville." Yet he had spoken of it as though he knew it; and that was strange, for it seemed to Donna's alert and eagerly curious mind that another person had spoken through Felipe's mouth, someone who had seen all those places of which he had told her.

Felipe, she had decided, was the best brother in the world; she loved him better than anyone, even better than Grandfather or Nana, and certainly more than Roger. She hated Roger; but she had always found a fierce joy in hating him, which gave her almost as much pleasure as her love for Felipe gave her.

Now she was listening eagerly, that she might discover more regarding the relationship between Lucie and Henry Braxton; she knew that Lucie intended to talk of Henry because she never lost an opportunity of doing so.

Kate had something on her mind. "Lucie," she was saying, "it may be that Sir James talks to Father of you and Henry, but . . ."

"But what?" interrupted Lucie shrilly and almost angrily.

"They talk of the King's illness and who will follow him. I know it. That is why Sir James is here so often . . . and others also."

"Oh that!" said Lucie scornfully. "There is always such talk."

"Indeed there is not," said Kate gently. "It is not every day that a King is dying, and there are differences of opinion as to the succession."

This was talk such as Donna loved. She sat as still as a lizard on a rock who fears he may be detected.

"It may be that they talk of other things," said Lucie petulantly. "Other more interesting things."

"Lucie, you are too young for marriage."

"I do not feel too young. I am fourteen."

"You will have to wait at least a year, I fear."

"What nonsense! I believe Henry's father and our father talk of us. I do indeed. Why not? It would be a good match."

"Do you wish to marry so soon?"

"Of course. Don't you?"

Donna took a sly glance at Kate and saw her blush as she bent over her needlework. "Not for years!" said Kate.

She lies! thought Donna wonderingly. What could make good Kate lie about such a silly matter? Kate was, after all, one of those grown-up people who did unaccountable things.

Kate went on almost tartly: "You talk about your . . . flirtation as important! But these matters of which they speak are of the greatest import. They come here that they may discuss what they will do should the King die and Mary Tudor come to the throne. Lucie, I think our grandfather and grandmother are anxious."

"Why should they be?"

"Oh, Lucie, you think of nothing but flirting with Henry Braxton. They are afraid because if Mary came to the throne the *Catholics* would be in power."

"Henry is a Protestant," said Lucie. "He is a staunch Protestant."

Catholics . . . Protestants! thought Donna. Long words which held some sinister meaning. Protestants were noble people like Felipe, Roger, her grandfather, her Uncle Charles, Sir James Braxton, Henry Braxton and all the ladies and gentlemen who came to the house to be friends with her family. What were Catholics? Horrible people . . . ugly people like the old witch who lived in a hut in the woods, like the humpbacked man who gathered watercress by the river. Catholics were all ugly and would all go to hell. There was a wicked, ugly woman — a *Catholic* — named

Mary who must not be allowed to be Queen when the King died.

It was exciting, and she wanted to hear more. But no one would talk to her about Catholics and Protestants. When she tried to talk of them, people turned away. Once she had said to Felipe: "Felipe, what do Catholics *do*? Do they hurt people?" And his face had grown white and a terrible sadness had come into his eyes. He had put her gently aside and walked away from her. She had guessed it was because he was going to cry and did not wish her to see.

"They would have no objection if you were older," Kate was saying. "But I feel sure they would not discuss your marriage when they are so concerned about . . ."

"They are not concerned!"

"Lucie, they are. Think what it would mean. Sometimes I lie in bed and shiver to think about it. What if some people try to put Mary on the throne? What if there were civil war? Think of it! Our house might be burned. And if Mary won, what would happen to Grandfather, to Father . . . to all of us? They would take everything we have. They would turn us out. It has happened before."

Donna forgot the need for control. She leaped to her feet. "We must not let them, Kate. We must not let them. Roger will stop them." She flung herself at Kate; she had started to weep bitterly, for she had seen it all so clearly. The house taken from them by hideous Catholics — ugly cruel people, like the witch in the wood and the watercress-gatherer.

"Donna! Donna!" cried Kate aghast. "Do not cry. It won't happen. We won't let it happen. Why did you sit so quietly there? It's not like you to be so quiet. It won't happen, will it, Lucie?"

"It won't happen," Lucie assured her. "Donna dear, don't cry, and I'll tell you all about the dress I shall wear at my wedding."

Donna lifted her face and looked from one to the other. Kate was alarmed, whatever she said. Kate believed that their house would be taken from them if the wicked Mary took the crown. Kate believed in that story just as Lucie believed she would have a beautiful wedding dress.

"Why," said Kate, "look at your work! Oh, Donna! You had better let me see this."

"We won't let Mary take the crown, will we?" said Donna.

"No, of course not."

"Is Felipe frightened that Mary will take it?"

"Nobody is frightened."

But they could not deceive her. They would not talk to her because she was too young. She was sorry; but she would have to listen as much as she could. She would have to discover what was going on about her.

She nodded and held out her needlework to Kate, for if they could have secrets so could she.

She sat listening to Lucie's description of the dress she would wear when she married Henry Braxton, while Kate clicked and clucked indulgently over Donna's needlework; and all the time Donna was thinking of the queer look which came into Felipe's face when she talked of Catholics.

Nana took out jugs of ale to the men and maidens who were haymaking. She stood, shading her eyes, watching them. They lay about, snatching a few moments from their work.

Nana smiled. "Here, Jennet. Here, Betty. You look hot, Tansy."

"This is good ale," said Betty, who came from a cottage in the village to help with the hay. Betty was a saucy wench. Pablo was lying beside her now, near the hedge. He talked in his queer English, which made Betty giggle uncontrollably.

Nana sighed. There was that about Betty which reminded her of her own youth. Betty was only fifteen, but her bold eyes had a tale to tell. Nana had heard gossip about Betty. Her mother would sit at her cottage door at dusk smiling at passersby. It was said that she invited many in for a drink on a hot and dusty day; and that when they were inside they did not leave without paying for something more than their ale or cider.

And Betty was another such as her mother. Her bold eyes were on every man.

Well, who was Nana to blame Betty? It was not all who were fortunate enough to be taken in by as good a master and mistress as Nana's.

Nana was worried about Pablo. His eyes followed her still. Sometimes she thought of a hot day when she had ridden pillion into Valladolid. He too remembered, she was sure. It was not that Pablo tempted her. She had her man, and that was all she asked; for she and Master Charles had resumed their relationship from the time he came to Spain, just as though there had not been a break of a year or more.

He had sat up all that night of his arrival, it was true, talking to Felipe, mourning the death of his brother. He had been a sad and melancholy man until they left that house; but during the journey to the coast they had become lovers again; and lying there in the darkness of the Spanish night, she had been greatly comforted to know that everything was well between them. She had known that she loved him — even as she had loved Roderigo. While they were in Spain, Master Charles had been so much the foreigner there, that she could not confuse the two men in her mind, and Nana had not been sure whether her sorrow for the loss of Roderigo was greater than her rejoicing in the reunion with her English lover. And when they had been on the sea and the storms had come and the boat had rolled, her feelings had been such that at one moment she had rejoiced in the safety of her lover's arms, and the next she longed for death that she might not live to remember the last time she had seen Roderigo.

But then they had come home, and home was so different from that strange land. Everything at home seemed right, as everything should be. That was the only way in which she could explain it to herself. The sun should not be too hot; the countryside should be green, and the flowers neither too spare nor too profuse. There should be people who spoke her own tongue, people whom she understood. And no sooner was she in England than her sorrow had begun to recede.

So had her fears. For she had been afraid. She had always known herself to be a sinful woman. That had been apparent from the time Master Charles had first noticed her at the wash-tub. But there were sins other than that overwhelming sensuality, that feeling of sinking into a quicksand in which her willpower fought a losing battle against her desire. She had known she was full of that sort of sin. Master Charles had discovered it; Pablo had guessed at it; so had Matias. She knew that, had Roderigo not appeared, with his strong fascination, she would have allowed herself to sink into that caressing and delightful quicksand with Matias or Pablo. Pablo knew this, and that was why he watched her now; he was waiting for an opportunity. But she had no fear of him while Master Charles was at hand. She was a woman who could be faithful to her lover, providing they were not separated too long.

Yes, she was fully aware of her carnal sins. But there was this other sin. There was the delight and terror of her existence; there was Donna.

For Donna she would be ready to die; they could do to her what they had done to Master Richard and to Roderigo, and for Donna's sake she would endure it and not complain. Love was to her what Faith was to others. So she allowed her sin, the sin she had committed for Donna, to haunt her.

How had she slipped into such sin? She could not rightly say. She had not meant to. She had meant to try the cross and chain on her baby's throat. She had just wished to see how Donna looked in the fine clothes of a child of gentle birth. That was all. And there was sin, waiting for her, as Master Charles might have waited, as Pablo, Matias and Roderigo waited . . . beckoning her, making it so that she could not resist.

There is nothing too good for my baby, she had thought.

And she had seen Jennet's boy working in the kitchens — Jennet's bastard. Such a life was not for the daughter of her noble Roderigo.

So, into her mind had crept the thought like the snake in the garden of Eden: My baby shall be brought up as though she is Felipe's sister.

She had heard them call Dolores, "Doña Dolores". "Donna," she had said to Felipe. "That is pretty. Why do they call your mother that?" He had said: "It is just a name. It is like saying, 'Lady Dolores'." She could not say it as they said it, so she called her baby Donna; and she let them all think that Donna was Felipe's sister.

At first she had thought how easy it was, but now, every day, there seemed something to remind her of Roderigo. Nana had to think . . . to brood. Sometimes she would look at Donna and see Roderigo in the flash of her eyes. She would try then not to remember him as she had last seen him; but the memory was there like a mist on the river, shutting out the brightness. Sometimes it was hazy; sometimes it was scarcely there at all. And each day it seemed to her that Donna grew more and more like the man who had begotten her.

He had been proud, she would remind herself. He would have been angry if his daughter had been made to sleep on the floor with the maids, to fetch water for the kitchens, to be at the beck and call of everyone in the kitchen and think herself lucky if she found a ploughman or a gardener to marry her.

It had to be, it had to be! thought Nana fiercely; and she wished there was someone to whom she could confide her secret, for it was a heavy one for Nana to carry alone.

Then she would think of Donna, growing haughty and proud; and she would think of how they all loved her — all of them except Ceci, and Ceci loved no one but herself. Nana believed that her Donna was more loved than any of those who were believed to be her cousins — perhaps more than Roger who would be the head of the house one day, more than Felipe to whom they were all so gentle.

Nana told herself that one day, when she was an old woman, she would see Donna mistress of this house. That was what she wanted: her Donna to marry Roger and be Lady Grendell. For that was what Roderigo would have wished.

When Nana thought thus she was happy, because she could always be happy knowing that her sinful actions would bring pleasure to others.

Returning to the house with the empty jugs, she put them in the buttery and went upstairs to the big bedroom which Donna shared with Kate, Lucie and Ceci. Her Donna slept in Kate's bed; Lucie and Ceci shared another. Nana smiled. It was right that her Donna should share a bed with kind Mistress Kate, her cousin; yes, her cousin. Nana smoothed the counterpane and thought of that lovely face lying on the bolster, the cheeks faintly flushed so that the big dark eyes looked more lustrous than ever. Poor Kate! she would look very insignificant there, but everyone must be insignificant when compared with Donna.

She went to the chest and looked at the child's clothes. Did anything need to be mended? Was all tidy? Mistress Ceci made sudden inspections of Donna's chest, and if she found any garment in need of a stitch, or anything not carefully folded, she would throw Donna across the bed and whip her. Nana could not bear to contemplate it. Once when she had heard the little one's screams through an open window she had sat on the wicker seat and covered her face with her hands, with the result that she had not noticed Sir Ralph, who came and sat down beside her. "Poor Nana!" he had said. "But she is a wilful child, our Donna. A whipping will do her no harm. It is good that Mistress Ceci can do that which you and I would flinch from doing." Nana had trembled then, terrified that he might look into her eyes and read her secret. But he had not done so. He had thought she loved the child as she loved Felipe; and because Donna was so beautiful, he might believe that her love for the little girl was greater even than that which she had for the boy.

She smiled on seeing the sash of cloth of gold. How her little one loved fine clothes! There was the scarlet gown which so became her and which Ceci said was far too bright. There was the little rent in the hem-line where the impatient feet had caught it.

Nana mended the gown and, as she put it back into the chest, she saw there, in a little silver box, the cross on the chain.

She stared at it in dismay. The cross and chain should be nowhere but on the neck of Donna. Nana saw it as a symbol. She had felt there was something miraculous about the cross and chain and that when Donna wore it she was really the daughter of Richard and Dolores.

Nana was superstitious, and she was now frightened. She must find the child and insist on her putting the cross and chain about her neck at once. She must tell her that it was the last wish of her mother that she would wear it always. That would move Donna. She was easily moved; she wept and laughed as frequently as Roderigo had wept and laughed.

Nana put the cross and chain into the box, placed it at the bottom of the chest and went to look for Donna.

She could not find her in the house, so she went out of doors. Donna was not in the hayfield; she might be in the copse, for it was a favourite haunt of hers; she climbed trees and pretended that she lived up there.

As Nana approached the copse she heard the sound of laughter. She did not call, for if Donna did not wish to be found she would hide. So it was that she came upon Roger and Betty, and those two, being so wrapped up in their affairs, did not see Nana although she saw them quite clearly.

Betty was behind a tree, peeping round it at Roger, who was half amused, half angry. Betty was teasing;

Roger was impatient. He looked remarkably like his father, although she, Nana, had never teased. Now Roger made a lunge at her and almost caught her; but she had skipped to the next tree and was peering round it, laughing at him.

"Enough of this," he said sulkily.

Betty put out her tongue, as no girl of her station would dare do unless . . .

"Tonight," she said. "Perhaps . . ."

Nana waited to hear no more.

So tonight he would go to Betty's house. He was his father all over again; but his father loved Nana. Donna was no Nana. She would not endure infidelities. She was fiery of temper; she was a Spaniard. Nana remembered Roderigo's sudden flashing anger and the way in which he had run his sword through the arm of the man who had attacked her in the alley at Valladolid.

Her Donna would love fiercely and she would know how to hate. And Roger was born to philander. Was he the man to make Donna happy?

Donna and Roger were too wild. She saw that clearly now. Donna needed someone kind and gentle, someone understanding . . . like Felipe. But they all thought that Felipe was her brother, so it could not be Felipe.

Now she was beset by unhappy thoughts.

Her brow was wrinkled; her eyes were bewildered. There was no one to whom she could explain her thoughts, and that was a frightening thing for Nana.

She was sure now that a miracle had happened when she had put the cross and chain about Donna's neck, because as soon as it was removed everything started to go wrong.

She must put the cross and chain about Donna's neck as soon as possible.

Yes, thought Nana, but Roger may not be the one for her. Felipe would be better. But how can she marry Felipe whom she believes . . . and all believe . . . to be her brother?

Donna had picked a red rose and, taking off the cap which Ceci made her wear, she shook out her thick black hair and tucked the rose behind her ear. Now, she thought, I look like one of the ladies of Seville. Felipe had told her about them. "They are the most beautiful in the world," he had said. "They sit at their windows, fanning themselves and smiling at the men."

In her imagination Donna was sitting at a window, fanning herself and smiling at the men.

She had her castanets which Pablo had made for her. She always carried them in the pocket of her dress because she liked to use them at odd moments. This was one of those moments; the red rose had reminded her.

She went into the shade of the copse and began to dance the *jota* which Pablo had, in secret, taught her. "Now," Pablo had said, "when you dance the *jota*, you will remind me of my country, for, little Doña (and he pronounced her name differently from the others), you are of Spain. As sure as the sun shines, you are of Spain."

210

She lifted her skirts and sang as she danced and rattled her castanets; and as she danced she thought of the ladies of Seville, sitting at their windows — the most beautiful women in the world.

She did not see Roger.

He was lying full length in the long grass. He was annoyed, frustrated. Betty had bothered him and behaved in a most unsatisfactory manner. "Tonight," she had said. The urgent moment was all-important. He might not find her so desirable in her mother's frowsty cottage as he did in the hayfield or the quiet of the wood.

And then he saw Donna. He caught his breath at the sight of her, because she was so beautiful. She was like a sapling, not yet grown, innocent and lovely; and yet she seemed provocative, seductive — a woman in miniature.

She was unconscious of being watched. She came nearer; he could see her lips parted showing her white teeth; and her dark eyes sparkled. She was far away in the sunny town of Seville, which Felipe had shown her, dancing beside a fountain in a shady *patio* while she was admired and applauded.

Roger thought momentarily of the coarse-haired, coarse-skinned Betty, and he was not displeased with her refusal. Then Donna occupied his thoughts completely.

That coquettish twirl of the skirt, those languishing glances; could a little girl of seven intentionally behave so? She excited and angered him. She was a wild thing, in need of control. If she behaved thus, what might

211

happen to her? There was surely an invitation in the sidelong glance. Where had she learned such ways? But had she learned them or did they come naturally to her?

She was exotic and would ripen earlier than English girls. Could it possibly be that she had ripened already?

The blood was hot in his head, and he could feel the burning heat of his cheeks which rested on his hands. He would not admit to himself the nature of his feelings. He could not possibly feel thus for little Donna. He was fond of her. Who could help being attracted by her? He had always found a certain enchantment in her beauty and amusing ways. But this was different. He felt as disturbed by her youth as, a little while ago, he had been by Betty's teasing coquetry.

He tried to shake off the strange emotions which she provoked. He would remind himself that this was only his young cousin Donna, whom he delighted to tease.

He leaped up suddenly and confronted her. She stopped dancing immediately, and because she knew that he had watched her while she had been unaware of him, anger flared into her eyes.

"What is the meaning of this cavorting?" he asked with a grin.

"Where were you?" she demanded.

"I asked you a question. Children must not answer questions with questions. Have you not learned that?"

"You spied on me," she said scornfully.

212

"Oh, were you not hoping for spectators? Don't tell me that you went to all that trouble just for the birds and the bees."

She turned haughtily away, but he would not let her go. He wanted to have her near him, to look into her angry but lovely face. He caught her by the arm.

"Let me go," she cried.

He laughed, and she kicked him. That made him laugh all the more, and seizing her in a grip from which it was not possible to extricate herself, he held her from him, laughing mockingly. But he was studying the perfect contours of her little face; he noted the glistening black of her hair and the fine texture of her skin.

She was trying to wriggle away; her eyes blazed at him.

"How dare you!" she demanded.

"It does not take a great deal of courage to hold you thus," he told her.

"I hate you, Roger."

"Then you should be punished for your sins, for it is a sin to hate your relations."

"Let me go. If you do not . . ." But she was too full of rage to find words. He had seen her dance, had seen her smile at those watchers in the *patio*; he had penetrated her private world while he lay sneering in the grass, slyly hidden. For that she hated him.

"Well," he encouraged, "what will you do?"

Her eyes flashed and he pulled her towards him. He wanted to hold her close to him for a moment. She beat on his chest with her head.

213

"You'll hurt yourself, Donna," he said almost tenderly.

"I'll hurt you."

He longed to caress her. He thought impatiently: This is due to Betty. Curse that wench! Had she behaved reasonably I should not be here with my little cousin.

He held her at arms' length and looked sternly at her. "You are not to go about behaving like a gipsy. Do you hear?"

"I . . . a gipsy!"

"Decking yourself thus . . . with a flower behind your ear!" He could hold her with one hand, and with the other he deftly caught the rose and ground his heel upon it.

"I hate you," she declared. "I'll kill you."

"They are too soft with you, Donna. They do not whip you enough. You think it is only necessary to set a rose behind your ear and smile, and all will be well. That is far from the truth." Her cheeks were scarlet and her eyes enormous; he wanted to make her angrier; he wanted to keep her close to him, but to keep her angry, because he felt it would be unwise to make her smile.

"So!" she cried. "So you will go to Ceci, I doubt not. You will tell her I have danced when I ought to be stitching."

"Oh, so you should be at your needlework! Then that makes your conduct doubly sinful. You play truant from your stitching to steal roses from the garden and to dance like a gipsy in the wood."

"I hate you, Roger. If Felipe were here . . ."

"What if Felipe were here?"

"He . . . he would make you behave like a gentleman."

"It is a sad thing for you then, Donna, that Felipe is not here."

"Let me go."

"What! Unpunished!"

"I shall tell Felipe. I shall tell Grandfather."

"Will you tell them that you played truant to dance in the wood?"

"I shall tell them how you treat me."

"Then, Mistress Donna, here is something else to tell them."

With a quick movement he had picked her up and, tucking her head under an arm so that her legs shot into the air, he began to beat her with hard, angry strokes.

She screamed, more in fury than in pain; she pummelled him; and she was all the more angry when she found that her fists made no impression on him. He went on angrily, telling himself that he was doing his duty, that she must be made to understand she could not wander into lonely places dancing in that way. It was for her own good. She was a wild, uncontrollable creature — and the loveliest he had ever seen.

He was breathless when he put her on her feet.

There were traces of tears on her cheeks now and her eyes flashed such hatred at him as he had never seen before.

"I'll never forgive you!" she said.

Then she ran off and left him.

He laughed and flung himself down on to the grass. He was uneasy, and the mood of frustration was stronger than ever.

A plague on Betty! But really he had forgotten her. He could not escape from the memory of Donna.

There was excitement in the house. Donna knew far more about it than the others believed. Tomorrow was a great day because Queen Jane would make the journey which was traditional with all English Sovereigns, and enter the Tower of London in state.

Grandfather, Grandmother and Uncle Charles all had their parts to play, and as soon as the first streaks of dawn were in the sky they would set out in the barge, that they might be among those to do homage to the new Queen.

Ceci had said that, as a punishment for leaving her needlework, Donna should not be allowed to ride out with the others; she should stay in and finish what Ceci had set her to do. Donna was rebellious, for she knew that by the time she had finished the appointed task, Queen Jane would have entered the Tower, have received the keys and the crown, and there would be no grand ceremony to be seen.

Donna had determined to find some way of seeing Queen Jane.

She lay still, for Ceci had doused the candle. Lucie squealed, for Lucie was always the last in bed, dawdling to admire herself in the mirror.

216

"You have had ample time to get to bed," admonished Ceci. "I have told you before that if you wish to preen yourself, you must do so in the dark."

It was not quite dark, Donna saw. There was a slip of moonlight coming through the leaded panes. Donna was glad. She was afraid of the dark even when the others were present.

She lay still, thinking of the day, hating Roger. She had hated him all day, and she would hate him for ever. She believed that he had complained to Ceci of her behaviour, because Ceci had told her she was the wickedest girl she had ever seen, far wickeder than Lucie. Lucie was vain, and Ceci was sure she would receive great punishment one day; but Donna was almost as vain as Lucie, and she was guilty of other sins besides.

Lucie was excited. She could not keep quiet. She had to talk about tomorrow.

"The Duke has promised Henry a place in his household," she chattered. "Henry told me so. He said that might lead to great things . . ."

"Who is the Duke?" asked Donna.

"Be silent and go to sleep," said Ceci. "This is not the time for chattering."

"Kate," whispered Donna, "who is the Duke?"

Kate murmured that he was the Duke of Northumberland, and that his son Lord Guildford Dudley had married the Lady Jane, who was to be crowned Queen.

"So you see, Donna," said Lucie, "the Duke will be one of the foremost men of the realm, and those who are in his household will be most happily placed."

"And so will their wives be," said Kate indulgently.

Dear Kate! thought Donna. She always tried to please as now she was trying to please Lucie.

Lucie laughed. "It would not surprise me if Henry were to get a dukedom himself one day."

"Perhaps," said Ceci caustically, "they will offer him the crown."

"But that is Queen Jane's," said Donna quickly. "So how could it be anyone else's?"

"It might well be someone else's ere long," said Ceci; and Donna noticed that, even though she knew it was important for her family that the crown should remain Jane's, she sounded pleased at the thought of Queen Jane's possible misfortune.

Ceci was happiest when she was thinking of the unworthiness of other people and the trouble they were setting up for themselves.

Lucie said: "After the coronation we shall be married."

"You are too young," snapped Ceci.

"Poor Ceci!" retorted Lucie. "I know you are older than I am, but that does not mean I am too young."

Ceci was angry suddenly. There was the sharp sound of a slap.

Lucie said: "You are so quick-tempered, Ceci. Perhaps that is why you have no lover."

"If I wished for a lover I should have one."

"Wishing does not bring them," answered Lucie. "Nor does making bread and looking after the maids . . ."

"I have no doubt," said Ceci, "that when the time comes for us to marry, our father will find husbands for us." Ceci's voice was sharp with a fear which was not lost on Kate. Poor Ceci! thought Kate. She was so sharp, so eager to show them all their faults, and it was all because she herself lacked that which she most longed to possess — the power to make people love her. Lucie had it in some measure, frivolous as she was; Donna undoubtedly had it; and perhaps she, Kate, had it in some small way; perhaps it was in her very meekness. But poor Ceci possessed it not at all.

Kate covered her ears. She did not like to hear sharp words between her sisters. She herself was uneasy. She was thinking of Felipe. She was always thinking of Felipe. She could blush in the darkness of her bedroom. Dear Felipe! He was a little melancholy when great events were about to take place. She had noticed that at such times memories of the past were revived.

She loved Felipe; her happiest days were those when she could make him smile. She was not naturally clever, except in domestic matters, although not so clever in those as Ceci was; and yet she had made herself learn Spanish so that she might surprise Felipe with her knowledge of that language which was almost his native tongue. She could make him laugh by talking Spanish with him. Her pronunciation amused him. "No, no, Kate," he would say. "Like this. But no . . . It is charming as you say it." That made Kate very happy.

Tomorrow he would ride along the river bank; he would mingle with the crowds; she wished she could be with him, to speak the carefully chosen word, to comfort him. How much happier they could be if, instead of going to see the Queen, they turned aside into the fields and meadows and lay in the grass, he talking his fluent Spanish, she stumbling perhaps more than she need, in order to amuse him.

She was very happy now as she thought of Felipe, and when Lucie talked of Henry Braxton, and Ceci talked of their father's finding husbands for them, she could hug her secret to herself. She was confident that they intended to give her Felipe.

Her grandmother had dropped hints. She had said: "You love Felipe, do you not, Kate?" And Kate had said she did. "I am glad," her grandmother had gone on. "We are all glad you love Felipe, Kate, for he will need you. I think Felipe loves you too."

Oh, to be grown up! Not to be fourteen. To be fifteen, sixteen. When she was sixteen they would marry. Felipe would be twenty then. They would live here for ever. They would make hay in the summer for years and years, just as it had been made this year; they would walk together in the gardens; they would admire the roses; they would sail down the river in the barge. And she would keep him safe, safe from all state matters. She would weave about him a little cocoon of safety; and eventually she would make him forget what he had seen in a cruel and barbarous land.

Donna must have said something, for Ceci was admonishing her.

"You shall stay in all day tomorrow. You shall be locked in until you have finished your needlework. You shall learn that you cannot run away from your tasks . . ."

Donna said nothing, and Kate put out a hand to take that of the little girl. She pressed it reassuringly, and that pressure meant: I shall help you with your needlework. Don't think you must stay in all day.

Donna returned the pressure; then she moved close to Kate and put her arms about her.

All along the river the barges were sailing on their way to the Tower of London. Some were decorated with banners; there were brilliant ones of cloth of gold and arras; and some were decorated with silver bells which tinkled as the wind caught them.

It was a hot July day and there was a sultriness in the air.

At dawn Sir Ralph and Jane, with their son Charles, had set out in their barge for Durham House, where they would join the party of the Duke of Northumberland.

Jane was reluctant. How much better, she believed, it would have been to have stayed at home on that July day. She wished she could remind Ralph of the words of Sir Thomas More: "You do well there . . . lying in the shade, friend Grendell." Now they were no longer lying in the shade; they had moved out to that arena where great prizes could be won and where great danger could be met with. Yet Ralph was at heart a lazy man; it was not ambition that drove him; it was hatred.

He and Charles were both touched with hatred. They were ready to fight for Queen Jane, not because they believed she had a greater right to the throne than Princess Mary, but because they hated the Catholics. This was not because of religious beliefs; it was because of the desire to stamp out those Catholics, who had tortured and murdered one beloved member of this household and set another to watch the final scene.

Now Sir Ralph had thrown off his lethargy. He would no longer lie in the shade. When he did so, he slept; and when he slept he dreamed; and in those dreams were the echoes of his son's agonised cries, in them was the brooding horror apparent now and then in the eyes of his grandson.

So . . . they were for Queen Jane. They would join the retinue of the Duke of Northumberland, that most ambitious of men who, wishing to set a crown on his son's head, had married him to the Lady Jane Grey, had induced King Edward to name Jane as his successor, and, some said, had hastened Edward's end with a timely dose.

Jane shivered.

How much happier she would have been sitting on a wicker seat watching the pageant go by!

But the quiet days were over. Hatred had never brought peace, and there was hatred in this house.

Donna was at her window watching the departure of her grandparents and her uncle. Henry Braxton had begged to be allowed to take Lucie in his barge; and Ceci had gone with her as chaperon.

Kate could have gone, but someone must be at home to look after household matters; and Kate did not care for the pageantry, she said.

Most of the serving-men and maids, the grooms and the gardeners had gone out to mingle with the crowds, and as Donna sat at the window, looking over the deserted gardens, intensely aware of the quiet house, she could hear the shouts of the people.

Ceci had locked her in, set her a long task, and threatened her with severe punishment if the work was not completed at the end of the day.

Donna had stamped her feet, had wept a little. How she longed to be out of doors with the revellers. She longed to see Queen Jane, of whom she had heard so much. It was cruel to shut her in, and she hated Ceci. She hated her almost as much as she hated Roger.

She was wondering whether she should escape by means of the window, when she heard the key turn in her lock, and swinging round she gave a cry of pleasure, for there stood Felipe smiling at her.

"Felipe!" She ran to him and put her arms about him. He lifted her and kissed her. Dear Felipe! He was the best and dearest of brothers.

"I'm going to take you to the Tower of London!" he said in a voice of thunder. She squealed with delight. He knew how she enjoyed a game of pretence. For the moment she let herself believe that she was a prisoner and was going to be kept captive in that most gloomy of all buildings which never failed to make her shiver when she looked towards it. But this was no day for gloom; there must be only pleasure today.

"You cannot go dressed thus," he said. "Go and get into your riding clothes."

"Kate . . ." she began.

"Kate said I was to take you, that you were breaking your heart up here. We cannot have that, little sister."

She jumped up to kiss him, twice. "One for Kate," she said. "And one for you. I love you both as much as I hate Roger."

He smiled. He was amused by her habit of declaring the state of her affections. The fact that it changed frequently did not make the declaration less amusing.

"Quickly," he said. "We do not want to arrive when it is all over."

She ran to the bedroom to put on her riding-habit. She was so excited that she trembled. When she was ready she ran downstairs. In the buttery, Kate was talking to Felipe. They spoke in Spanish and Felipe was laughing. Donna flew at Kate and kissed her; she kissed Felipe also. "Now!" she cried. "Come, Felipe. We must not be late."

Felipe and Kate smiled at her impatience. They both thought how delightful she looked in her little cap with its feather. Already she was conscious of her beauty, conscious enough to wear it as though unconsciously. She was a strangely grown-up girl for seven.

"Well, since she commands us," said Felipe, smiling at Kate, "we dare not delay. Kate, can you not come with us?"

"Nay, Felipe. Someone must be here. There is much to do."

224

Felipe nodded. How like Kate! She knew how the maids had longed to mingle with the revellers that day, and she it was who had sent them out and taken on necessary tasks.

But perhaps, thought Felipe, she really preferred to stay behind. Kate was the most sensitive of girls. She was afraid of this pageantry, this revelry. She would know that while the people threw their caps in the air and shouted for Queen Jane they were really shouting for a holiday. They would as readily shout for Queen Mary tomorrow. Kate, who loved her family perhaps more than any of them, who wished above all things to keep them close beside her, was happier in the house on this day.

He understood. He too would have preferred to stay at home; but Kate had said that Donna longed to see the sights; and he, who understood the feelings of others as well as Kate did, knew full well what torture young Donna would be suffering shut up in her room on such a day. So of course he must take Donna to see Queen Jane.

"Then let us go. Farewell, Kate."

Donna was already running to the stables. She saddled her own pony, for the grooms had deserted the stables today to take their stand along the river bank.

In a short time they were riding out together.

"What is the Queen like, Felipe?" asked Donna.

"Young and very beautiful."

"How young, Felipe?"

"She is the same age as I am."

"That is not young!" She laughed, and he laughed with her.

She felt very happy at having escaped from the schoolroom and to be riding out accompanied by her beloved brother to see the Queen. Everything seemed beautiful to her this summer morning. She felt a desire to loiter, to pick the blue harebells and armfuls of meadowsweet. That was simply because she wished to make every moment of this day doubly long; really she was all impatience to see the Queen.

They had ridden for less than ten minutes when her happiness was shattered.

"Hello!" cried a voice. "Wait for me."

Donna's eyes had become narrowed with anger. Felipe pulled up.

"Why . . . Roger!" he said.

Roger rode beside them. His face was tanned a light brown which made his blue eyes look the colour of the scabious in the hedge. He smiled with malicious pleasure when he saw the effect on Donna of his arrival.

"So, Felipe, you have the child with you!"

"Naturally Donna must do what most people are doing today."

"I thought she was to be at home," said Roger, deliberately turning his head from the little girl and smiling at Felipe. "I gathered she had tasks to perform."

"What . . . on such a day!" said Felipe.

He started to move forward, and the others followed. Roger brought his horse round to the other side of

Donna; now he had turned his malicious eyes upon her.

"Do you not think we should take her back?"

"Felipe!" cried Donna, unable to keep silent any longer. "Take no notice of him. Let us ride without him." She spurred her horse to a gallop. Roger was beside her. He had laid a powerful hand on her pony's bridle.

"Are you mad?" he demanded. "You foolish one! Do you want to break your neck? To gallop in a lane like this . . ."

"I would rid myself of you at any cost."

"Even at the risk of a broken neck? How vehement you are!"

Felipe rode up to them.

"What happened?"

"Pony out of control."

"It was not out of control. I was controlling him. I . . ."

Roger was smiling in a superior way at Felipe, as though to say: Let us humour the child. Very well, we will take her with us. But we must watch her. Remember what a foolish little thing she is.

They rode on in silence for some time. It was only her anger that kept Donna from weeping with disappointment. But as they came along the Strand and saw the crowds making their way eastwards, as they heard the cannons' roaring from the turrets of Durham House — the home, Felipe explained to Donna, of that Duke of Northumberland whose son had married the new Queen — she was caught up in the excitement all about her and refused to be put out by Roger's presence.

They rode on through the crowds; people on foot, beggars, thieves, apprentices and their masters, young serving-men and women made way for those on horseback. Donna was glad, as she felt the eyes of those people upon her, that she was not alone.

Roger rode a little ahead. Many eyes were turned to watch him. He was very tall and he looked noble on his horse. Donna had to admit that grudgingly, and she could not help feeling a certain pride in him. She noticed how the girls and women smiled and tried to catch his eye. One plump and pretty girl at a window called: "God save Your Grace!" at which Roger turned and doffed his cap as though he were Lord Guildford Dudley himself.

Now they could see the bridge and beyond it the Tower. It was difficult to see the river, so crowded was it with wherries and barges of all types. In some sat minstrels, and the sweet notes from their shalms and sackbuts floated over the air.

Roger had led them through the crowd which grew more dense now that they were in the vicinity of the Tower. The people pressed about them. Some turned anxious eyes up to the sky, which had become overcast. The heat was oppressive, but a downpour of rain would be most unwelcome, especially if it were accompanied by thunder and lightning.

"An evil omen!" shouted someone above the murmuring of the crowd; and all looked up at the sky.

228

Donna looked at the man who had spoken; he was a hunchbacked beggar, and it hurt her to see his deformed limbs and his ragged clothing. She wished she had money to give him.

The bridge was crowded with people, and from the windows of the houses there pennants hung limply in the still air. They would have looked more beautiful, thought Donna, if there had been a breeze to stir them and sunshine to show up their bright colours. The beggar was right. There surely must be an evil omen, for in spite of the crowds out to enjoy themselves no one seemed to shout "God Save the Queen."

And now the great moment had arrived, for Queen Jane was setting out from her father-in-law's house — where she had sat down to a magnificent banquet — and the Duke and his retinue would escort her to the Tower. Among them, Felipe had told Donna, she might see members of her own family.

"Why do they take her to a prison?" Donna wanted to know.

"There is a palace as well as a prison."

"It looks like a prison. I hate it."

"All Kings and Queens of England must spend the first few days of their reign in the Tower of London," explained Felipe. "It is a tradition."

He called her attention to the river, for now the advance guard of halberdiers were disembarking and lining the path which the Queen would follow when she stepped from her barge and walked to the Tower. They looked very grand, their halberd staves covered in scarlet velvet which was secured with nails of gilt. Their black and tawny hose, their blue doublets, their velvet caps ornamented with silver, made them look tall and imposing. They were laying a carpet on the ground for the Queen to walk on.

The trumpets sounded a fanfare and the musicians in the boats on the river began to play. Down the river from Durham House came the state barge.

Donna looked about her at the crowded river and its banks; the spires and towers of the churches rose high in the smokeless air; she saw the gabled houses in the narrow streets, the taverns, the inns, the towers of Baynard's Castle, the bridge, and dominating all, inspiring and beautiful, the forbidding grey walls of the Tower of London.

Now came the royal barge itself, and as it passed beneath the bridge the ordnance roared. It was a magnificent sight; on its banners were displayed the royal arms, and metal escutcheons adorned its sides; its decks were covered with brilliantly coloured silks and velvets. Accompanying it were smaller barges, only slightly less colourful.

Fascinated, Donna watched the barge draw up close to the first line of halberdiers. Then she saw the Queen — a beautiful young girl who did not look much older than Kate. Donna thought she had never seen anyone so beautiful as Queen Jane in her rich gown of cloth of gold on which pearls had been set; her stomacher was ablaze with diamonds, and her surcoat was of purple velvet and ermine. Her coif was trimmed with pearls and held in place by a circlet of gold. Her mother, the Duchess of Suffolk, carried her purple velvet and ermine train as they swept over the carpet which had been laid for them.

Donna wanted to cheer, to cry "God Save the Queen!" but she was aware of a silence among the people. She noticed that many kept their caps on their heads; and it seemed to her that these people were as sullen as the skies above them.

Several men in black velvet with gold chains about their necks were greeting the Queen. Two lovely girls — surely no older than Kate — walked before the Queen. One was her sister, Felipe whispered, the other her husband's sister. They were beautiful, but none, in Donna's opinion, could be compared with the Queen.

Felipe pointed out the notable people in the procession.

"Look! There are my lords Cranmer and Ridley. And there is the Constable of the Tower and his lieutenant. There is my lord of Suffolk, the bride's father. And, look Donna, there is Lord Guildford Dudley, the Queen's husband, and with him my lord of Northumberland."

"Where is Grandfather?"

"I cannot see him. But keep watch and doubtless you will."

Someone in the crowd said: "Cranmer and Ridley . . . but for the grace of God they might lie where Gardiner and Bonner lie this day."

"But for the grace of Northumberland!" growled another.

"She is a lovely girl," said a woman. "So young. I heard she was reluctant to take the crown."

Another answered her: "That is because she is wise. She knows she should not take that which by right belongs to another."

Donna felt her heart beat fast. Here was the conflict which she had sensed in her own home. Here was Catholic against Protestant.

She shouted impulsively: "God bless Queen Jane! Down with Mary and her Catholics!"

There was a sudden hush about her. A man shouted. Two men moved towards her. Then another . . . and another. One of them seized Donna and before she realised what was happening she was pulled from her pony.

Lying on the ground, she became aware of angry faces looking down at her. She thought these people intended to trample her to death.

"Felipe!" she cried in panic. "Felipe!"

A man bent over her and caught her by the neck of her habit. He tore it, and the chain and cross which Nana insisted she should always wear swung into sight. The man caught the chain and pulled it.

"God save Queen Mary!" he cried.

It was all over in a very short time, for Roger was standing above her. He had pushed his way through those who surrounded her, sending the thief sprawling. But he was more angry with her than with anyone else. He took her arm very roughly and jerked her to her feet. He dragged her through the crowd. Then she saw Felipe's white face.

"What happened?" he asked anxiously.

232

Roger said curtly: "The little fool! Come, we'll get away from the crowds."

Her pony was not to be found, and Roger lifted Donna and set her on his horse before springing up behind her.

The crowd tittered and roared suddenly with laughter. Its angry mood had passed as quickly as it had come.

"I want to find Jasper!" cried Donna. "I want my pony."

But Roger was angrily pushing his horse through the crowd.

"What happened?" asked Felipe.

"Someone has taken the opportunity to steal her pony," said Roger. "Never mind that now. We'll get away. God knows what she may have started. Did you notice the mood of the crowd?"

"They were certainly ready for trouble," said Felipe.

"And this foolish child might have started a riot there and then. She did her best. I told you we should not have brought her."

"I . . . only said . . ."

"Be quiet."

"I will speak."

"You will speak only when spoken to. And be still. Do you want to have us both thrown?"

"I don't mind . . . if it kills you."

"What did she do?" asked Felipe.

"Did you not hear? 'Long live Queen Jane!' Hers was the only voice to shout that in the great crowd. And she must follow it with 'Down with Mary!' when she was in the midst of Mary's supporters. I shall whip her till her blood flows. I shall teach her some sense, though it will be difficult, I doubt not."

"You are too hard on her," said Felipe. "It was those vagabonds about us. They had their eyes open for what they could steal. They were waiting for an opportunity."

"Well, they have her pony. It was gone in a trice. I did not see it go. I wondered what they would do to her. Not that she did not deserve to be punished."

"Should we not look for the pony?"

"My dear Felipe, you can rest assured there was more than one horse-thief in the crowd. He seized his opportunity. We can do nothing now. I did not like the mood of the crowd. Had we been alone it would have been different. But with this foolish child . . ."

Donna could not move; his grip hurt her and she knew that he intended to hurt her. He had meant to spoil her happiness. She hated him more than she hated those terrible people who had pulled her to the ground.

Felipe said: "Let me take Donna."

"Nay!" said Roger. "I'll not give her up."

"I wish to ride with Felipe," said Donna.

"Then that matter is settled," Roger told her. "You shall ride with me. A pony lost! A nice state of affairs. What will your grandfather say? Your saddle . . . your pony . . . oh, and where is your fine feathered cap? So you left that with the mob, did you? You are the most foolish child I ever saw, yet you have the arrogance to imagine yourself a little woman. That is it. And it is your arrogance that I shall beat out of you."

"She has had enough, Roger," said Felipe. "Leave her in peace."

Then Donna, putting her hand to her neck and feeling that the cross and chain, which her mother had wished her to wear always, was not there, began to cry. They were tears of sorrow as well as anger, of fury as well as of humiliation. This was to have been one of the happiest days of her life, and this hated Roger had spoiled it.

Her sobs shook her, and Roger drew up his horse. Felipe dismounted and took her in his arms.

"It is all over, Donna," he said soothingly. "How were you to know? What you did, any of us might have done. Never mind about the pony. Grandfather will be glad to have *you* safe, I doubt not."

She had her arms about Felipe's neck and her hot wet face was pressed against his.

"Felipe," she murmured, "I love you. Best in all the world, Felipe, I love you."

Then Felipe put her on his horse and they rode slowly home; and Roger did not protest, but rode silently beside them.

Four days after Jane Grey had made her formal entry into the Tower there was a banquet at the Grendells' house in Chelsea to celebrate the betrothal of Lucie and Henry Braxton.

Jane and Ralph sat in their room before the arrival of the guests.

Ralph knew that Jane was uneasy. Her disquiet had grown since they had attended the ceremony of the new Queen's entry into the Tower.

"I cannot drive the picture of her face out of my mind," she said. "She seemed resigned. Did you not think so? She seemed as though she looked on the crown as a fearful thing, that she longed to decline it, and since those about her would not allow her to do so, she accepted it with reluctance."

"She is young," Ralph answered. "And it is a great responsibility to wear a crown."

"She is wise enough to understand the terrible danger she is in, I am sure."

"Hush, Jane. That's no way to talk."

"Did you not appreciate the temper of the crowd? Think of Donna. What would have happened to her if Roger or Felipe had not been with her?"

"I dare not think. By God, I do not wish to have another of my family murdered by those scoundrels."

"She was none the worse, Ralph. Perhaps she is the better for her fright. It will teach her caution. Ralph, how long will the people allow Queen Jane to wear the crown, think you?"

"Until she dies."

"And when will she . . . die?"

"She is young. There are many years left to her."

"And Mary?"

"The people cannot want that bigot on the throne."

"That bigot! Ralph, they do not know what we know. They do not know what suffering she would bring."

"She must not mount the throne. If not Jane, then it must be Elizabeth."

"How could it be, while Mary lives?"

They looked at each other.

"Mary has already laid claim to the throne," said Jane. "She did so on the day Edward died."

"Jane," said Ralph slowly, "I heard that she is gathering an army in the eastern counties. If she should try to enter London . . ."

Jane nodded. "War! Civil war!" But she did not really believe that possible. There would be war only if the people did not want Catholic Mary. She remembered the sullen silence which had greeted Queen Jane. Jane was beautiful, wise and good, but she was not the rightful heir to the throne. The people were convinced of it. There would not be war because there would be so few to fight for Jane, for what did the people of England know of the horrors of Catholic rule? They had not lost their sons to the Inquisition.

Why cannot we be happy? Jane asked herself passionately. She wished she had never heard of the Reformed Faith; she wished that Emil Pretzel had never come to the house that summer's day. She wished she could turn the thoughts of her son and husband away from such matters.

She tried to change the subject. "How happy the young people are!" she said.

"But it is a pity we shall lose Lucie," answered Ralph. "Henry will not live here, alas."

"I fear he will not."

"No. He is an ambitious young man."

"I am fearful for the ambitious."

"He'll take good care of himself. The Duke has promised him a high place in his service. Why, there is none who could do him more good."

"Or more harm . . . if aught should go wrong," said Jane, going to the window. "I thought I heard arrivals. There is a barge at the privy steps. Doubtless Sir James and Henry have come."

The door had opened and Donna stood before them. She was wearing a scarlet gown and a sash of cloth of gold. She stood smiling at them, and Jane was aware of the change in her husband's face as he looked at the little girl.

"Grandfather, I want to dance at the betrothal."

"Well, and why should you not?"

"Ceci says that I am too young. Grandfather, I am not too young, am I?"

"You are not very old, Donna."

She pouted and stood on tiptoe, smiling at him. She knew how to charm, thought Jane.

"Grandfather, I *do* want to dance at the betrothal."

"Well," said Ralph, "perhaps you shall . . . this once."

And he was smiling as he took the child's hand in his and went down to greet his friends.

Nana sat in her room listening to the music from the hall below. Usually she liked music. She liked to picture the minstrels' gallery and everyone dancing in the hall — her little Donna among them.

But she was worried.

Charles had said to her last night: "Nana, what ails you? Something is wrong. Tell me."

"No, no," she had said. "Nothing."

But she wished she could have told him.

Donna had come home from her jaunt to London to see the Queen, unkempt and subdued. Nana had embraced her, scolded, petted and fondled her.

"It was in the crowd, Nana," the little girl explained. "I was pulled from my horse. Felipe . . . and Roger . . . saved me."

Donna had looked defiant, as she did when she told a lie. Nana knew her well enough to realise that it had probably been Roger who had saved her, but because she hated Roger she wished Felipe at least to share in that honour.

She should not hate Roger. She must love Roger. Roger was to be her husband.

It was worrying. It set wrinkles on Nana's brow. She tried to look into the future, and she was afraid of what it might bring to her child.

And then Donna had told her the frightening news.

"Nana . . . they stole my pony. And they stole my cross and chain."

Nana had pulled open her darling's habit, had explored the little neck.

"You . . . you've lost it!"

"Yes, Nana. They stole it. A horrible man took the chain in his hands and pulled. He snapped the chain . . . and stole it."

Nana knew that here was a bad omen.

The cross and chain had meant that Donna was the child of Richard and Dolores. Without it, the spell was broken.

It was hot in the hall. They had all feasted well. Donna had been allowed a place at the table. "For this," said her grandfather, "is a great day, and the youngest as well as the eldest should share in its pleasure."

Donna's one annoyance was that she had been set beside Roger. And as she sat there and looked along the table at the smiling faces of Lucie and Henry Braxton, who, like herself and Roger, sat side by side, a feeling of apprehension came to her.

She and Roger were cousins, and Roger would be the head of the house one day. Her grandfather loved him dearly and looked upon him as his heir; and Donna knew that her grandfather, who also loved her dearly, had selected her as Roger's wife, and that one day she would be expected to sit at a table like this as Lucie and Henry did; and beside her would be the hated Roger.

Her grandfather would surely never force her into a marriage which she hated. But what if Ceci insisted! What if Ceci shut her in the cellar until she obeyed?

"What is the matter?" whispered Roger. "You look suddenly afraid."

"It is nothing," she answered.

He laid a hand on her shoulder and she smelt the wine on his breath, for he had put his face close to hers.

"I know," he said. "The baron of beef was poisoned . . . and you have eaten more of it than any."

"You lie. I have not."

"Hush! Remember your manners before our guests."

She turned away from him, but he had his arm about her, and she felt those strong fingers forcing her to turn her face to his.

"Donna," he said, "I do not believe you love your cousin Roger."

She did not answer. She looked with interest at the dainties on the table: the dish of roast quails which were so delicious, the calvered salmon, the venison pie, the capons and peacocks.

"You have eaten enough for two of your size," went on Roger. "Now you must look at me."

She did not wish him to know how frightened she was, so she lifted her face to his.

He said: "You think yourself very wise, Mistress Donna."

She did not answer. Then he put his hand on her thigh and squeezed it so hard that she winced.

"Now," he said, "will you answer me? Do you think yourself wise?"

"No. Yes . . . yes, I do then."

"And . . . beautiful? Do you know, Donna, I believe you think you are more beautiful than any lady present." The pressure on her thigh was increased. "Do you?"

"No. I think Lucie is . . . and Kate."

"You must not lie to me, Donna. I am determined to teach you better ways. You are a foolish little maid. Did you know that? I cannot have you growing up in the way you have begun. Do you know why?"

Her heart began to hammer against her ribs. "No," she said.

"I'll tell you. It is because we are going to be married one day."

"I am not going to marry you," she said in a whisper.

"But you are. Did you not know that it was arranged?"

"I will not arrange it."

"It is not for you to do so, foolish one. You merely have to be an obedient wife."

"I will not."

"Then I shall whip you every night."

"I hate you."

"You have said that too many times for it to be effective. And lower your voice, or our grandfather's guests will think he has a savage for a granddaughter."

"I am going to marry Felipe. It is Felipe whom I love."

He lifted his cup and his eyes mocked her above it. They were like pieces of blue glass, she thought, with the fierce sun's rays upon it. They held, besides cruelty, something she did not understand.

"Silly Donna! You cannot marry your brother. Do you not know that? Felipe is for Kate, and you are for me. Do not forget it. You had better start obeying me at once. Then you will make a habit of it."

Donna said nothing, but she thought: I will die rather. I will die . . . but I will not marry Roger.

Roger ceased to tease her then, for something unexpected was happening. A messenger was brought into the hall and her grandfather rose to greet him. He must, said this messenger, speak with Sir Ralph alone and at once.

Ralph went out and a hush fell over the table. Charles got up and followed his father. After a little while they came back, and it was obvious from their faces, that they were anxious.

They stood by the table and all were silent, waiting for Sir Ralph to speak.

"I have news," he said. "The Lady Mary's forces are advancing from the eastern counties. The Duke's men have deserted him."

There was a murmur along the table.

"This means war . . ."

"We shall never have Mary as our Queen."

But Ralph had held up his hand. He said slowly: "Northumberland has met Mary at Cambridge. He has proclaimed her the Queen of this realm."

There was a stunned silence then. Donna watched the faces of those at the table. Felipe's was white. Her grandparents' were stricken.

Sir James Braxton had risen to his feet. "Methinks," he said, "that there are some of us who should retire to our country estates for a while. London will be an unhealthy spot now that Northumberland has turned traitor."

Donna was puzzled. She looked at Roger, but he did not seem aware of her. His eyes blazed and his hand was on the hilt of his sword; and in spite of the fact that she knew a terrible thing had happened, she was glad because Roger had ceased to think of her.

The guests had dispersed. Lucie was white-faced and frightened. Her Henry must leave with his father and go to the country. If this news of Northumberland's betrayal was true, what of all the fine promises he had made to Henry? What use would Northumberland's promises be if Mary were Queen? The very fact of Northumberland's favour would put her lover's life in danger. Here was a fine ending to her ceremonial betrothal. Lucie wanted to lie on her bed and cry. Kate went with her to comfort her, to say the kind things which Kate always said to those in distress.

Ceci was in the kitchen, seeing that the remains of the feast were not all eaten by the servants. Ceci looked pleased. Donna knew that she had been angry because Lucie was to have a husband and she had none. If only Ceci could have Roger, thought Donna, how happy she, Donna, would be! What a pity that brothers and sisters could not marry, then Roger could have Ceci and she, Donna, could have Felipe.

Everyone seemed to be standing about in groups, talking of what had happened and what was likely to happen next.

Donna went to Nana, who was in the little room next to the big bedroom which the girls shared. Nana was mending one of Donna's dresses. She looked up as Donna entered, and when she saw the little girl's face, she laid aside her work and held out her arms.

Donna ran to her, and the feel of Nana's arms about her, and the soft pillow of Nana's bosom, made her feel that she was a baby again. To Nana she had gone for comfort in the old days. Nana had been a goddess, big, strong, and ever-loving, all-powerful against the forces of evil. Donna began to sob tempestuously.

"What is it, my love? What is it, my Donna?" asked Nana. "Tell Nana, my sweeting. Who has hurt my Donna?"

"Nana, it is Roger."

The fear which had lately been haunting Nana showed in her eyes.

"Tell Nana," she said quietly.

"I hate him, Nana. He is cruel to me. He hurts me. And he says that I must marry him and that he will beat me every night if I do not obey him."

"Tish . . . tish!" said Nana, in the old way which used to amuse Donna when she was very small. But Nana's "tish tish" had lost its magic.

"Your grandfather would never let it happen if you did not wish it, darling."

"But Roger wishes it, and he says it must be."

"They would not let it be if it made you sad, sweetheart."

"But *he* wishes it, Nana. I believe he does everything he wants to. I believe no one could stop him."

Nana tried to soothe herself as well as Donna. "Your grandfather would never let you be sad, little one."

And Nana thought: What if he died? And what if Roger were master of this house? And what if Roger determined on this marriage? What would happen to her little one?

How like her father she was! There was the constant reminder in the eyes that flashed so dangerously, the sudden tears, the sudden laughter, the anger that could be so violent. What did the future hold for Donna as Roger's wife? Nana could see no happiness for her little one.

"Nana, I love Felipe. I wish he could be my husband. I wish brothers and sisters could marry. That is what I wish, Nana. Then I would run away with Felipe and we would not come back until we were married, and then I would have nothing to fear, for Roger would not be able to be cruel to me then."

With sudden illumination, Nana saw the enormity of her sin.

Felipe and Donna! Felipe with his melancholy gentleness, with his kindness, his understanding, to curb her wildness; and Donna all brightness, gaiety and charm to lure him from his melancholy.

And so it could be, for Felipe was no more her brother than Roger was.

Nana rocked Donna in her arms.

"There, my sweeting. Don't you fret. Nana will look after you. Nana won't let Roger hurt you."

Nana's fear was greater than that of the child whom she soothed, for, she thought, the chain which bore the cross is broken, and the spell with it.

Twelve uneasy days had passed since Queen Jane had been proclaimed Queen of England.

Nana did not know what was happening in the outside world; her own world was shadowed by a

246

terrible problem. It haunted her; she thought of nothing else.

She had many times been on the point of telling Charles of her sin. Tomorrow I will tell, she would assure herself; but she did not tell.

It was a gloomy household; everyone, it seemed, was apprehensively awaiting events.

Lucie continued to weep for her lover who had gone into the country and had sent no message for her. He and his father were so deeply involved in the Duke of Northumberland's affairs that it was probable that they were in hourly danger. Northumberland, in spite of his turning traitor, had been arrested at Cambridge. Queen Jane and Lord Guildford Dudley had made yet another journey to the Tower, this time as prisoners. Jane Grey's twelve days' reign was over.

All along the river the barges were gay, decked out with arras, cloth of gold and tinkling bells. The citizens of London were rejoicing; their shouts could be heard. They were congregating to greet their new Sovereign, who was to make her triumphal entry into the capital. There would be many to throw their caps into the air and shout: "God save the Queen!" "Here is the rightful heir to the throne," they would say. "Here is good King Harry's own daughter!"

Ralph brooded on these matters as he sat on his favourite wicker seat. He would let none of his family ride into the city this day. It would be unsafe to do so.

It was Jane's wish — and he was with her in this — that they should remain in the house; they dared no longer tempt fate. They must keep aloof from state matters.

"Let us go to the Mass," Jane had said. "What matters it if we seem Catholic? Who can know our secret thoughts? For the love of God, let us have no more tragedy in this family. Was not Richard's death enough?"

And Ralph agreed with Jane.

They would be quiet and still while the storms passed over them. He prayed that the Braxtons' loyalty to the dethroned Protestant Queen had not been too noticeable. He hoped that none of his enemies would remember that he, with his wife and son, had been in that retinue which had accompanied Northumberland on the traditional journey to the Tower.

He had comforted Jane by assuring her that they were too insignificant. It was the important ones, those who played for high stakes and enjoyed great power, who ran great risks.

"We are fortunate, Jane," he had said, paraphrasing his old friend Sir Thomas More, "we are fortunate, lying in the shade . . ." Jane had said nothing, but he who read her thoughts so well knew that she thought: It was long ago when we were in the shade. Now we have left the shade; we have come out into the bright light.

And as he sat there it seemed to him that the sounds which floated along the river had an ominous ring. The shouts of the people disturbed him; the pealing of bells seemed to sound a warning; the thunder of gunfire made his heart beat faster.

You people of London who welcome Mary, he thought, do not know what you do. *Your* sons did not die the martyr's death in a Spanish square.

Nana had come to him. She was standing before him, her eyes wide and frightened, her red hands plucking at her gown.

"Nana?" he said.

"Sir Ralph . . . Master . . . I would say much to you."

"Something has happened, Nana." She heard the sharp note of fear in his voice.

"Yes, Master."

He could not speak. He visualised terrible things. They had come for Charles perhaps. For one of the boys — Roger? Felipe? He would not let them be taken. He would run his sword through the heart of any who tried to take his boys from him.

Nana said: "'Tis Donna, Master."

"Donna!" All the love, all the tenderness he bore towards the child was revealed to Nana. It comforted her. It gave her the courage she needed to continue.

Nana knelt at his feet and buried her face in her hands.

She felt his gentle fingers touching her hair.

"You love her, Master," she said. "You love her more than you love the others."

"Nana," he said, "for God's sake tell me."

"She is well. She is safe. No harm shall come to her. She must not suffer. You love her, Master. You would let nothing stand in the way of your love for her?"

"You must tell me what this is, Nana," he said. "I do not understand what you are trying to tell me."

Nana could not speak. I dare not! she thought. There is yet time. I dare not tell him.

Then she remembered seeing Felipe and Donna together this day. Donna had leaned from the window of the schoolroom to call him as he stood below in the gardens. Her face had been alight with love for Felipe. Nana had known at that moment that she dared not delay.

"Master," she said, "Donna is my child."

He did not understand at first. Had she not always said that Felipe was hers? He turned his kindly, puzzled eyes upon her, and she saw with a shock how he had aged during the last week. She thought: He will not live for ever. He will not always be there to protect my Donna, to save her from a marriage she would hate and which might end in something so terrible that I dare not think of it.

"I am her mother," said Nana. "Her father was a Spanish nobleman. Master Richard's little girl died. I tried to save her. I did indeed. I fed her Donna's milk . . . but it was too late. She was not strong like Donna, and when Mistress Dolores died there was nothing we could do to save her. And I had my Donna and I took the chain and cross and put it about her neck. Oh, Master . . . Master . . . what will you do?"

Ralph said nothing. He had looked into Nana's face, and he could not doubt that she spoke the truth.

"Her father died," said Nana. "He died with Master Richard. They took him first. They did to him what they did to Master Richard."

Ralph was still staring at Nana in silence. In her few words she had conjured up a picture for him; he saw it more clearly than he had ever seen it before: the hideous *Quemadero*, the Inquisitors, the victims in their yellow robes . . . and Donna's father had been one of them. At Donna's father's feet they had arranged the faggots as they had at Richard's; the smoke had risen about him; the cruel flames had licked his flesh and his screams of agony had risen from the Spanish fires.

Donna's father. An unknown man. Not Richard.

No, never had he seen it so clearly — that most cruel, that most wicked of spectacles.

And as he sat there staring at the weeping woman before him, as he listened to the roar of cannons and the pealing of the bells, he knew that Queen Mary, the bigot, was making her ceremonial entry into the capital city.

CHAPTER
FIVE

For weeks the sounds of rejoicing were heard along the river. There was much celebration in London in honour of the country's new Queen. Her coronation had been arranged to take place in October, and her people seemed satisfied with her. She was a good woman, they said; she was a pious woman; she was not vindictive. It was true that Northumberland had lost his head on Tower Hill, but that was reasonable. Lady Jane and her husband were merely kept as prisoners in the Tower, and it was said that the Queen was prepared to show leniency towards them.

In the Grendell household the coming of a Catholic Queen seemed a minor matter since Nana had uncovered her secret.

Ralph had broken the news first to Jane, to whom he had gone immediately after he had left Nana. He was greatly shocked, bewildered and uncertain how to act.

Jane was not so surprised as he had been. "Now we know this," she said, "I realise that she has nothing of Richard or Dolores in her. I wonder what her father was like."

"He was a martyr with Richard. We know that much."

"Ralph, what shall we do?"

"What *can* we do?"

"This is a great shock for you, my dearest. You love her. Of all your grandchildren she is the one you loved best."

"You talk as though she were dead . . . as though she were no more."

"As your grandchild she is no more. She is the child of Nana."

"And of a man who died as Richard died . . . who suffered as Richard did. We shall have to care for Donna as though she is our own, for that reason if for no other."

Jane smiled. "I knew you would feel that. Of course this must make as little difference as possible. She has grown accustomed to living as a daughter of this house. That could not be altered now. Will you keep this secret?"

"No. I do not think so. Secrets cause trouble. I think all should know who thc child is."

"And the child herself?"

"She should know it too."

"Poor Nana!"

"Nana, like most of us, must pay for her sins."

"Poor Donna! How will she feel, think you?"

"It is better for her to know the truth now than to discover it later. I would not have her shielded too much. She is a bold spirit. She will survive the shock."

So it was revealed to the whole household that Donna was the daughter of a Spanish nobleman who had died with Felipe's father; and the news was so

253

startling that they forgot to marvel because a Protestant Queen lay in the Tower while the City rejoiced in the accession of a Catholic one.

Donna was subdued. She had wept a little. Her dear grandfather was not after all her grandfather; Felipe was not her brother.

Nana could only look at her with big, sorrowful eyes. Poor Nana! she had been very sinful. She told Donna so; and Donna wanted to know more.

"Nana, you are my mother?"

"Yes, my love."

"Why did you lie, Nana? Tell me the story."

It was an exciting story. Donna wanted to hear it again and again. There was the death of Felipe's little sister, and Donna herself born secretly in a quiet house; there was the cradle with the ribbons in which Donna had been laid, and there was the cross and chain which Nana fixed about her neck.

"Nana, who was my father?"

"A handsome gentleman, a nobleman."

"More noble than grandfather, more handsome than Felipe?"

"Yes, Donna, I believe so," answered Nana. "He was very noble and very handsome."

"Where is he now?"

"He died, my sweeting."

Nana cried and would not tell the manner of his dying. But she sparkled as she talked of him; she told Donna how he had rescued her and Felipe from the ruffians in Spain.

254

Nana could not stop talking of him now. It was as though a great burden, which she had been forced to carry on her shoulders, had been removed. She sang as she mended Donna's clothes.

It was Felipe who told Donna more about her father.

"You loved him, Felipe," she said; and Felipe admitted that he had loved him.

"Will you love me just the same, now that I am not your real sister?"

"Yes, Donna. Just the same."

"Tell me more of him."

"He lived with us for a while. He and I often rode together. He used to talk to me about Spain. I never knew anyone talk as he talked."

"He was the one who told you about Seville and the ladies in mantillas, was he not?"

"How did you know that?"

Her only answer was a laugh.

She never tired of hearing about her father; she did not regret that he was not Felipe's father. If Felipe loved her the same as before, what did it matter? She had never known her father, and her mother was Nana. It was better to have a mother whom she could love, and who could comfort her, than one who had died when she was born.

But she was apprehensive when, for the first time since the disclosure, she was alone with Roger.

She was on her favourite perch in one of the trees in the nuttery when Roger passed by. He did not see her and she could have remained hidden; but, on impulse, she pulled aside the branches, and for a few seconds they stared at each other without speaking.

She could not resist saying pertly then what was in her mind. "I can marry Felipe now."

He laughed with cruel sarcasm.

"What!" he answered. "A low-born bastard marry my noble cousin! Indeed you cannot!"

Now he had frightened her. A low-born bastard! What was that?

"You set too high a value on yourself, Mistress Donna," he went on. "Such as Felipe could not mate with a low-born bastard."

"What is that?"

"It is what you are."

"I? I am myself."

"Indeed you are. The daughter of a serving woman! My grandfather allows you to live in the house, but do not think that he will allow you to marry one of his grandsons."

"You lie."

"Mind your manners. Remember to whom you speak."

She was silent. He had, as usual, planted an anxiety within her. What did he mean? Could it be that there was a difference? Her grandfather was not her grandfather. Felipe was not her brother. At least she knew what low-born meant.

"My father," she said with dignity, "was a nobleman. He was more noble than your father and more handsome than Felipe."

"But he did not marry your mother, my child. And if he was more handsome than Felipe, was he as handsome as Roger?" He looked up at her, grinning mischievously.

"You are not handsome. You are as ugly as a . . . a Catholic. I hate you, and I'll never marry you."

"Have no fear . . . or hope, Donna. There could be no question of marriage between us now."

He walked off and left her staring after him uneasily.

But when she went to Felipe for reassurance, he cheered her.

"Felipe, what is a bastard?"

He answered: "A child whose parents did not marry."

"I am that."

"Yes. They say the Queen is, and the Lady Elizabeth also. But do not, for the love of God, talk of that."

"So I am like the Queen and the Lady Elizabeth?"

Felipe nodded, smiling at her.

"Then," she said, "it is not a bad thing to be, is it?"

"How can it be when it was a matter which was decided before you were born?"

"Do you love me as much as you did when I was your sister? Are you sure of that?"

"I do and I am sure."

"So it makes no difference to you that I am a . . . bastard?"

"It makes no difference, Donna."

"It is a good thing, Felipe, in some ways, that I am not your sister."

"Is it?"

She looked wise, and he stooped and kissed her. She was happy. He had made her forget Roger's insults.

Donna and Lucie were at work on the tapestry which was to form part of the hangings in the hall. All the women of the household had worked a piece of tapestry, and when it was completed it was hung up. There were many pieces, for the Grendell women had been working on tapestry for many years.

Donna must take a hand in it. The little piece which she had worked would stand out from among the neat embroidery of Kate and Ceci; and that of Lucie too, for although Lucie was not as clever with the needle as her sisters were, she was not as bad as Donna.

But, thought Donna, I am still to work on the tapestry as though I were really one of them.

Lucie talked as they worked. Lucie's talk was, as ever, of love and marriage. Donna enjoyed hearing of such things.

"Donna," said Lucie, "can you keep a secret?"

Donna eagerly said she could.

"Do you know where Felipe has gone?"

"He is riding out to stay with some friends of Grandfather."

"Yes. But what friends?"

Donna admitted she did not know.

"He is riding into Kent. Keep this very secret, Donna. He is riding to Sir James' house to tell him how matters are in London."

"Lucie," said Donna, "why did Henry and his family go so quickly?"

"Because they thought they were in danger."

"And were they?"

"No. They think of nothing but danger . . . Grandfather and Sir James, I mean."

"Was it because of Queen Mary?"

Lucie nodded.

"Poor Queen Jane is in the Tower," said Donna. "I hope they are not hurting her there. She is a prisoner."

"You must not speak of Queen Jane. You know what happened to you when you did."

Donna was silent. She thought of lying on the ground, the man's hand grasping the chain about her neck, the blazing blue eyes of Roger; and that led her to what Roger had said to her in the nuttery. Was it true that since she was not one of the family and because she was what they called a bastard, she could not marry Felipe? It might be true. Roger, who she was sure had wanted to marry her when he thought she was Felipe's sister, now no longer wished to do so.

Perhaps she could worm something out of Lucie.

"Felipe has ridden into Kent to tell the Braxtons it is safe to return," went on Lucie.

"That is why you are so happy. You will see Henry again."

"Felipe told me. He is a dear boy, Felipe. He said: 'Lucie, here's a secret. Tell no one. But I am riding to Braxton Hall, and if you would like me to take a message to anyone there, I shall be most happy to do so.'" Lucie laughed. "You see, he *knew*."

"And did you send a message?"

"Why yes. I said 'Tell Henry I am well . . . and lonely.' "

"He will come back and you will be happy, Lucie. Perhaps there will be a wedding."

"That may well be."

"I am glad, Lucie."

Lucie kissed her warmly. "Bless you, Donna. And here is another secret. Will you keep this as well?"

"Yes."

"Henry's father has a ward. She is very beautiful and her name is Meliora. Is that not a pretty name?"

"It is very pretty."

"I think a match is being arranged between Meliora and Roger."

"You are pleased?"

"Of course. It will unite our families still more closely."

"Does Grandfather want them united?"

"Of course he does. I shall live in Henry's house, and Meliora will come here."

"Does she love Roger?"

"She has not seen him yet, but she will love him."

"Why?"

"Any woman would love Roger."

"I hate him."

"That is because he teases you. If he put himself out to be charming to you, you would love him like the rest."

"I never would. I shall hate him till I die."

"Well, that would be safest, perhaps."

"Does he love Meliora?"

"He will. She is pretty and has a fair fortune. She is a good *partie*."

"What is that?"

"A good match."

"Does a girl have to be pretty and have a fair fortune to be one?"

"Not necessarily both. The fortune is good enough; but if she be pretty, that is very pleasant for the husband. Oh, we shall see some marriages soon, I doubt not. I trust mine will be the first. Grandfather longs to see children in this house. If some of us leave it, he will want babies to grow up and take our places. But I shall be first . . . before Roger . . . before Felipe."

"Felipe will have to wait a long time."

"Oh, not so long. He grows old, you know."

"Yes, but . . ."

"Kate will be ready in two years' time."

"*Kate!*"

Lucie put her fingers to her lips. "Not a word. I talk too much. Kate is shy about these matters. I wonder why. I enjoy thinking about my marriage."

"Kate," said Donna. "Kate . . . and Felipe!"

Lucie went on talking quickly. Donna was a wise little thing. Did she know that they had meant her for Roger? It might well be that she did. Then she would learn that those arrangements would have to be cancelled. Nana's daughter — even though she were allowed to live as one of the family — could not mate with the heir of the Grendells.

Lucie kissed her impulsively.

"Don't fret, Donna. I know that, when the time is ripe, a fine husband will be found for you."

But Donna was not listening.

Weddings were in the air. Queen Mary, it was rumoured, was thinking very seriously of marriage. Rumours were circulating throughout the land concerning herself and Edward Courtenay, whom she had made the Duke of Devonshire.

Sir James Braxton, who had come to stay at the house in Chelsea with his son, his ward and some of their servants, for the celebrations of the nuptials of Henry and Lucie, talked continually, as he sat at table, of the Queen's marriage.

"Weddings," he said, smiling at his son and Lucie, "rarely come singly."

Lucie blushed and looked at her platter while Henry smiled a little sheepishly. They were very happy, and the entire household was indulgent towards them. Ceci had busied herself with preparations for the feast, and rarely had there been such activity in the kitchen quarters.

There was more to be celebrated than Lucie's wedding, and Jane in particular felt this to be an occasion for thanksgiving. Danger had receded, for it seemed that the Queen wished to bring happiness to her subjects, as, apart from the imprisonment of a few who had proclaimed themselves her enemies, there had been no great number of arrests.

Now, thought Jane, will we keep snug and safe in our backwater.

But she was a little alarmed when she listened to Sir James' garrulity. He was not the man to live quietly, and when he talked freely of the Queen and her affairs, Jane wanted to cry out: "Later! When we are in the gardens ... when we are out of earshot of the servants!"

"They say she looks on young Courtenay with great favour," Sir James was saying. "He is a handsome young man and grateful enough to marry her ageing Majesty, I doubt not."

"Let us hope this will come about," said Charles, "for if it does not ..." He shrugged his shoulders.

"If it does not," pursued Sir James, "then I doubt not that she will accept that other suitor, and, my friends, it would be hard for us to stand aside and let such a marriage take place."

Jane looked nervously about her. Pablo was helping Jennet and Betsy to serve. Jane knew what was coming, and she did not wish it said before the Spaniard.

Charles, seeing the anxiety in his mother's face, said quickly: "Why should it not be Courtenay? He is royal enough."

"Royal and grateful," said Henry.

"And who would not be grateful in his place?" put in Ralph. "Why, he has spent almost all his life in the Tower ... a prisoner. And then Her Majesty ascends the throne, and one of her first acts is to give him his freedom and a dukedom to boot."

"He is very handsome, they say," said Roger.

"Handsome, my boy!" cried Sir James. "He is indeed. He is like his great-grandfather, they tell me.

That was King Edward the Fourth. If he is like his royal ancestor in matters other than looks, her gracious Majesty will have to hold him with a strong rein."

"Why was he in prison all that time, Sir James?" Donna asked.

"You should not speak unless spoken to," chided Ceci; but she was less severe than she had been at one time to the little girl. Now she could think: Poor Donna! For all her beauty, she is but a bastard! Because of this Ceci felt less inclination to punish her; but she still kept a firm hand upon her and wished her to know that it was not for her to interrupt the table-talk of her betters.

"But I want to know," persisted Donna, smiling at Sir James, who, like most people, was attracted by her.

"Well, Donna, my dear, he was sent to prison . . . when was it? Why, it must be sixteen or seventeen years ago."

"When Felipe was born," she said. "Or soon after. That is a long time to be in prison."

"Yes. They chopped off his father's head and they sent Edward Courtenay to prison."

"Why did they chop off his head?"

"Why, bless you, I cannot remember. But I'll dare swear it was because he had a good claim to the throne. Now let me see, his grandmother was the young daughter of King Edward the Fourth, and that meant of course that as a descendant of the House of York he was not greatly liked by Tudor King Henry."

Donna was enjoying this. It was pleasant to have the important Sir James talking to her and her alone.

264

Moreover there was nothing she liked so much as to listen to tales of the past.

All eyes were on Donna now. Ralph thought: How I wish she had been Richard's daughter! But it makes no difference. One cannot divert love.

Jane wondered what her father had been like. The child had something of Nana; the rest might be of him. She made the other girls seem almost insignificant . . . even Lucie who had grown so pretty in love.

Charles thought of Nana in Spain with Donna's father. What had he been like? How much had Nana loved him? How could he, he asked himself, have expected faithfulness from Nana? He could no more expect it than he could give it. He was wishing that Donna was his daughter . . . his and Nana's. She must be a continual reminder to Nana of her father.

Felipe smiled to see her so delighted. Egoistic in the extreme, she was enjoying this talk with Sir James. He hoped Sir James would go on talking to her. There was little that gave him as much enjoyment as watching the delight of Donna. He felt so old sometimes, so weary; he felt that there was nothing in the world that could make him really happy again. He would forget for a while, but memories would return, and so vividly would he see that hot square with its smell of people, with the sound of the buzzing flies, the awful silence, the sepulchral voice of the Inquisitor. Now all those things were fixed in his mind, and there they would remain for ever, he feared. He could never completely forget. Yet to see Donna's enjoyment at this moment or to watch her sometimes running across a strip of grass, to hear her high laughter, to see her utter abandonment to delight — all those things brought him back to the days before the tragedy. And now that he knew she was Roderigo's daughter, she awakened happy memories of Roderigo — not as he had last seen him, but gay and dashing — the Roderigo who had enchanted him and had, he supposed, been one of the most loved companions of his life.

Roger also watched her. He thought: The knowledge of who she is has not changed her at all. She is as proud as ever, as watchful of her dignity.

It was a delight to look at her. She was in his thoughts a good deal. His latest *inamorata* was a gay village girl with dark hair and dark eyes, the daughter of respectable parents, and young. It was wrong to have seduced her, but when he had seen her run across the meadow, her movements had reminded him of Donna. He was repentant, for he did not love the girl, and he saw himself as a heartless seducer. Yet he could never restrain himself, and she had been a ready, though a somewhat frightened partner. He would ask his father to find a husband for her; he would look after her. And meanwhile . . . Donna. He, who knew so well how to charm, had made no attempt to charm her. He wondered what would have happened if he had. Would she have been as blatantly affectionate towards him as she was to Felipe? Poor Felipe! It must be embarrassing to be loved so ostentatiously by such as Donna. He, Roger, knew that he must content himself with the joy of teasing her.

266

What would become of her? he wondered. He guessed that his grandfather — or his father — would try to marry her well. To a doctor or perhaps an attorney. It was difficult to imagine Donna's settling down.

And why should he concern himself with Donna? Here was Meliora Langridge — Sir James' ward — a young heiress of noble birth, just past sixteen and marriageable. He knew why Meliora had been brought on this visit.

He appraised her. As a man of experience in such matters, he knew her type. She would be a faithful wife, but although she was pretty enough, she seemed to him insipid. He was being ungrateful. She would bring him a fortune, which, together with his own inheritance, would make him a richer man than his father.

He saw that his father was watching Donna almost wistfully. Was he a connoisseur even as his son was, assessing the incomparable child? It was her Spanish blood perhaps that made her seem already a woman. They grew to maturity quickly in those hot countries. She was nearly eight. That was the equivalent of twelve or fourteen in an English girl; and English girls of fourteen — as he had discovered on more than one occasion — could be ripe and ready.

He thought of his mother, whom he remembered well. His father had married her because she was a good *partie*, just as, he supposed, he would marry Meliora. But he had been led to believe that he would have Donna, for he knew that his grandparents had intended a match between them, in spite of the necessary delay before the child would be old enough to marry. He had been contented, for he had proved that he could amuse himself adequately during the period of waiting. Alas, now plans had to be changed. It was one thing to marry a Grendell cousin, but quite another to marry the bastard daughter of his cousin's nurse.

Sly Nana! Who would have believed it possible that she could have passed her bastard off as a Grendell. Roger laughed inwardly at her audacity. His father was disturbed too. That was not surprising. He must wonder continually what sort of a lover Nana had found for herself in Spain to enable her to produce a daughter like Donna.

And here were his thoughts dwelling on Donna. He must not think of her. She was in a sort of no-man's-land. Because she was the bastard daughter of his cousin's nurse, he could not marry her; and because his grandfather had decided that she should still be treated as one of the family, he could never seduce her. Therefore it was better not to think of Donna. He tried to turn his thoughts to the shy and blushing Meliora — the heiress — and he imagined marriage with her and the marriage bed, which would be important to him; and as he saw it, ornate and magnificent with the rich curtains drawn back, it was Donna he could but see there, not the young lady of fortune whom they had found for him.

They should not have put the idea of marriage with Donna into his head, for once having had it implanted there, how could he uproot it?

268

He would marry Meliora, of course, and he would be persistently unfaithful to her, no matter what good resolutions he made. There would doubtless be a Nana in his life, as there was in his father's. Yet, had they married him to Donna . . .

Ralph was talking now. He could not let Donna monopolise Sir James. Moreover, Ralph considered that when James Braxton talked of royalty he talked dangerously.

Sir James continued to talk dangerously.

"Well, Simon Renard calls himself the ambassador of his Imperial Majesty the Emperor Charles, but he is in reality a spy at the Court, and they say . . ."

Jane looked fearfully over her shoulder, but Sir James went on: "They say he will fight the Courtenay marriage with all his might. And we know why . . ."

"Why?" demanded Donna.

Ceci said: "Donna, I think you should leave the table now."

"Oh, but . . ."

"Go at once," said Ceci.

Donna looked appealingly to Ralph; she was aware of Roger's sardonic eyes upon her.

Ralph smiled at her gently. "You must obey Ceci, Donna my dear."

Donna lowered her eyes, pouting; and Kate rose from the table to lead her away.

"Ha," said Sir James when she had gone, "what a lovely child! A charmer, eh . . . when her time comes. But that is a long way off. She is but a baby yet."

It is indeed a long way off, pondered Roger. And perhaps that is as well. I declare, if she were older, I might be tempted to marry her, bastard or not.

When the meal was over, Lucie took Meliora to her bedroom to show her her wedding clothes. Kate and Donna were there, and the four of them chattered together about weddings.

The men walked in the gardens, talking about weddings too; but the wedding which was most important to them was the Queen's wedding. If she married Edward Courtenay, although she remained a Catholic, she might continue in her tolerant way; but if, as they feared she might under the influence of that spy and emissary from Spain, Simon Renard, she married a foreigner, then the days of peace for England would be in jeopardy.

Felipe listened to their talk and shuddered, for the man whom they feared the Queen would marry was the Emperor's son, Don Philip of Spain.

Lucie was married in late September.

During the previous day the serving girls had decorated the hall with oak leaves and scarlet hips and haws. From the kitchens came the smell of baking meats and pastries. Ceci meant to surpass herself, to show the guests that if only one of them had the good sense to offer for *her*, he would have a worthy bargain.

Lucie was, as Ceci said, almost silly with excitement. She had tried on her wedding dress ten times, and that, all knew, was courting bad fortune. Lucie could not help it; she could neither eat properly nor rest, so did she long for her wedding day.

Kate tried to soothe her by talking indulgently, agreeing that Henry Braxton was the most handsome, the most amusing, the most distinguished of men. Donna was almost as excited as Lucie. She had deserted the schoolroom, for even Ceci did not wish her to study on such a day.

She could only think of weddings — of Roger's with the pretty Meliora, of her own wedding, of Kate's, of the Queen's, as well as that of Lucie and Henry.

She was worried about Kate. Lucie thought that Felipe would marry Kate; but Lucie was not to be taken very seriously at this time. Lucie was so excited about her own wedding that she wanted everyone to have one. She had looked around her for a bridegroom for Kate and, because there was no one else, she had decided on Felipe.

Donna did not intend to remain in suspense. At the first opportunity she would talk to Felipe and ask him whether he loved her or Kate, and which of them he would want to share his wedding.

The house was full of guests, and many of them had attended the ceremonial entrance of Queen Jane to the Tower on her accession. Many of them wondered, as Ralph did, how long the calm would last. They could not forget that Northumberland had lost his head, that Jane Grey and Guildford Dudley were prisoners in the Tower. The quiet was unnatural. Next month the Queen's coronation would take place. Was she waiting until after that event before wreaking her vengeance?

But theirs was an age of uneasiness. The only way in which they could live was by facing each day as it came along. The present was all-important, and this was a day for rejoicing.

The ceremony over, the guests gathered about the banqueting table, which was laden with silver dishes and platters heavily loaded with every delicacy that could be thought of. Venison; beef; pasties; quails; salmon; peacocks; and wine that was worthy of them. In the gallery the minstrels played as the party feasted, and the great hall rang with the sounds of merriment.

It was during these festivities that Charles and his son strolled into the gardens. Both were mellow with much good food and wine, and knew that the other was thus; and each had chosen this moment to broach a subject which they feared might need a delicate handling.

Roger began: "Father, I wish to find a husband for one of the village girls . . . Moll Gentry."

Charles understood. How often in the past had he made a similar request to his father!

"It is time you were married," he said.

"Do you think that would be a . . . deterrent?"

"It should be."

"Was it so for you, Father?"

They looked at each other and smiled. There was a great affection between them, a bond of understanding. They were of a kind; light-hearted, they found themselves irresistible to women because women were irresistible to them; they were good-natured; they meant no harm to anyone; yet they were careless and

272

lazy, quick to anger, quick to forgive. How could Charles blame his son for making the same trouble which he in his feckless youth had made? Charles understood the temptations of Roger. He could therefore have nothing but sympathy to offer his wayward son. It was not for him, he felt, to admonish; he could only offer helpful suggestions; and the best he could offer was marriage with Meliora, the young heiress. But Meliora would not provide a solution. Cecily had not done so in his own case. Yet, thought Charles, if Roger loved Meliora as he, Charles, loved Nana . . . But he had no great belief that this would be so. The heiresses, such as Cecily and Meliora, could not turn a man from his sensual habits. Yet Nana had turned Charles from his. But was that due to his increasing years? How could he say? He could only say this: He had come to such peace with Nana that he could give her the faithfulness for which she had not asked and which she did not expect. Life was ironical.

"You may be a better man than I am, Roger," he said.

"I doubt that, Father. In fact I am sure I'm not."

They walked arm-in-arm to the river's edge. "This Moll, are you in love with her?" asked Charles.

"She is a pretty wench."

"It is over, then . . . your little love affair?"

"That's the pity of it. It was over almost before it began. It is always thus. They seem so desirable before . . . enchanting, desirable. And afterwards they become merely serving girls or cottage wenches. It is as though I am blinded temporarily, and then I see. I would I might see clearly beforehand; then there would be no desire which must be satisfied, and I should be as virtuous as my cousin Felipe."

His father laughed. "I will tell you something, but forget I said it and don't repeat it. I'd rather have you as you are, than as your cousin. But when you are married it will be different."

"I would I could think it might be."

"Meliora Langridge is a charming girl. You could not at any time think her a cottage wench or a serving maid."

"No. But *now* she is just a mildly pretty girl who moves me hardly at all. Afterwards she would still be just that. You see, there is not even that temporary blindness."

"There is a good dowry to compensate you."

"Why should I concern myself with that? I have enough here for my needs. There was a time when I thought you had decided I was to have Donna."

"That was your grandfather's wish. He doted on the child."

"Doted! He dotes still, Father."

"Yes. The fact that she is not his granddaughter has altered little, as far as he is concerned."

"I had become accustomed to the idea of marrying her."

"You could not marry Nana's illegitimate daughter."

"Yet Grandfather can keep her here, living among us, as one of us?"

"She is too young for you, my son."

"I had reconciled myself to waiting."

"You are more than ten years her senior. You would have to wait until you were twenty-five before marrying."

"Twenty-four. Or even twenty-three. Donna is half Spanish, and the Spaniards, I believe, mature earlier than our English girls."

"You would wish that? You would wish to wait?"

"I am in no hurry."

"But let me be frank. A bastard?"

"If Grandfather can forget that, why should I remember it? She will be educated. If the secret of her birth had not been discovered, I should have had her."

"Roger, you mean that you are determined to have this child?"

He was silent for a while. Then he said: "No. It is folly, I suppose. She is a bastard. Moreover, when they have finished educating her they will have turned her into another Meliora."

"Without Meliora's fortune! I daresay your grandfather will give her a dowry, but anything that she brings you will be what was intended for you and Felipe. My son, there is another matter. Your grandfather and I would wish to see you married before the year is out. We live in troublous times."

"You have heard something?"

"I firmly believe that life cannot go on as smoothly as it does now. Trouble is brewing, and if there is trouble, who knows? Your grandfather and I would like to feel that you are getting children . . . children who will carry on the family line."

"I see," said Roger.

"If you married Meliora, I think you would find as much satisfaction in marriage as most men find. She is gentle — your mother was not that. Think about it. But don't take too long to think."

"I will think about it."

"They will be leaving here in a few days' time for Kent. Sir James will ask us to return with them for a short visit. If during that visit you should find you wish to marry Meliora, you would give great pleasure to us all."

They turned and went thoughtfully back to the house.

Donna had lured Felipe to another part of the gardens. "Felipe," she said, "I must talk to you. And I want to give this pastry to my favourite peacock. He loves it, and he is so greedy that it is fun to watch him forget how beautiful he is and gobble it up."

"We should not leave the guests, Donna."

"We can slip away. They will not notice. You first, and I will follow. To the old seat by the stone wall. You know."

He could not resist her eager excitement, that abandonment to enjoyment.

"It's very important," she said, her eyes round and shining. "It's a secret. It's our secret, Felipe."

"I'll go now."

"In a few minutes I shall be beside you."

He went out into the dusk. It was a beautiful evening, quiet and still, and there was no breeze to stir the trees. He thought: In a day or so they will all be

276

busy in the orchards. It was at such times that he felt almost at peace and nearer forgetfulness. Haymaking, harvesting the fruit . . . that was what he looked forward to, the peace of this pleasant house. But that was not all peace. He looked along the river to London Bridge and the bastions of the Tower, and shivered. Who could know what was waiting for him? He longed for the gaiety of his boyhood. But had he ever been gay? He had always been quiet and studious and had never possessed Roger's gusto. He envied his cousin. Sometimes he would hear Roger's booming baritone, usually out of tune, remarkable in nothing but its power and its capacity for conveying a deep joy of living; and he would long to be like Roger, amusing and easily amused, gay and making others gay. But perhaps little Moll Gentry was not very gay just now. Everyone understood Roger; that was why they loved him. There was nothing deep or subtle in his nature; he had not looked on the cruel death of a beloved father.

But he must not think of that day of horror; and here was Donna, and to be with Donna was to forget more easily than with anyone else. That was strange. He wished to forget Spain; yet Donna, who was half Spanish, could help him more than anyone to forget.

"Felipe . . . so you are here."

"I am here, Donna. What is this secret?"

"Sit down there. Now I am going to sit beside you, and you must tell me the truth."

"I am all eagerness to share your secret."

"It is really a question which you have to answer truthfully. Which of us do you love best in the world?"

"Donna! What a question! It is hard to say."

"It is not hard for me to say, so you, who are much older and cleverer, should find it just as easy. Felipe, I love you best in the world."

"Oh, Donna," he said, and his voice sounded to her a little odd. "Why do you, and how can you?"

She considered these questions. "Perhaps it is because at first I thought you were my brother, and it seemed right that I should love you most. But it's not that really, I should have hated Roger even if he had been my brother."

"Why do you hate Roger?"

"Because he hates me."

"I don't think he does."

"He does. Once when he was in the wood and I was there, he beat me . . . and just because I left my stitching and danced."

"That's not like Roger."

"It is. It is just like him. Then he was unkind when we went to see Queen Jane."

"He may have saved your life then, Donna."

"No, Felipe, that was you."

"Donna, who is being truthful now?"

She wriggled. "I believe it was really you, Felipe."

"You are not looking at this clearly, Donna, if you believe that."

She took his hand and kissed it.

"It was Roger," he insisted, "who forced his way through the crowd, picked you up, set you on his horse and rode away with you. He is quicker, more alert than I am. I was there, but I did not see the danger."

278

"I hate him," she said stubbornly.

"You must try to like him."

"When he thought he was to marry me he said he would whip me every night."

"That was teasing."

"I do not wish to be teased; and I think he meant it, because it is just the spiteful thing he would do. So I hate him and I love you, and I am glad you are not my brother."

"Why?"

"You have not answered *my* question. Do you love me best in the world, Felipe? You should, because I love you best."

"Oh Donna," he said, "I believe I do."

"You like Kate, very much, do you not?"

She waited breathlessly for his answer.

"Very much."

"But you love me best. Felipe, you will marry me? Will you wait for me? I am not very old and you are, but now that we are not brother and sister we can marry."

"But, Donna," he said, "you are only eight. It is too young to think of marrying."

"It is not too young. You said you loved me best. So you must wait. Here." She took a ring from her finger. "Grandmother gave me this, but it will do. I want you to put it on my finger. It will be plighting our troth, and everyone knows that's as good as a marriage. Come, Felipe, do as I say."

He took the ring and smiled at her eager, childish face.

"Come along," she said impatiently.

He put the ring on her ringer. "Dear little Donna," he said.

"It's very serious, you know," she told him. "In six years we shall be married."

He took her face in his hands and kissed it.

"Six years!" he said tenderly. "You will find, dearest Donna, that much can happen in a day . . . in an hour . . . and that six years is a very long time."

It seemed to Meliora Langridge that the day of Lucie's marriage was the happiest of her life. She was sixteen years old, and until a year ago she had lived the simple life of the daughter of a country squire. Her father had been a rich man; he had died before Boulogne, whither he had gone in the service of King Henry VIII; and Meliora, his only surviving child, was his sole heiress.

She could remember the day, nearly ten years before, when she had heard of her father's death. She remembered the grief which had swept through the house, and how her mother had relied on Sir James Braxton, a friend and distant relative of her husband's, to settle her affairs.

Life had gone on simply in Dorsetshire; they were far from the Court, and the events which were of such importance there hardly affected them at all. Meliora spent much time working on her embroidery with her mother, playing the virginals, studying under a tutor, or visiting the poor on the estate; she knew little of life beyond her village.

She had read stories of the Knights of the Round Table, and, being a romantic girl, she imagined that one of these knights would come courting her. He was handsome and young, possessed of all the virtues; he was Sir Lancelot, Sir Galahad and King Arthur all in one.

Her parents had been ideally happy in their marriage, and marriage had consequently been idealised by Meliora until the daughter of a neighbouring squire, whom she had known all her life, and who was no more than two years older than herself, was married.

The husband who had been found for this girl was thirty years older than she was, a roué who, to his young bride, seemed hideously repulsive. Meliora, who had attended the wedding, had received her confidences; and the night before the wedding Meliora had shared the bed of the bride-to-be, who had lain shivering in Meliora's arms; and in the morning Meliora had watched her, white-faced and frightened, pondering whether it might not be wiser to drown herself in the moat than to enter into such a marriage. Meliora knew without a doubt that had she been in her friend's place she would have chosen the moat.

But the marriage had taken place, and when Meliora had next seen her friend she had worn a look of resignation which had seemed more tragic than death to the romantic Meliora, who had visualised marriage as an idyll shared with a partner in shining armour.

That was a startling experience, and Meliora's dreams were tinged with apprehension after it.

Her mother had died a year later, and when Meliora had to leave her simple country life and visit her guardian in Kent, life became different. Braxton Hall was nearer to London and there was much coming and going of important personages. There was always excitement at the Hall; Sir James was a busy, meddling, talkative man.

She had believed he might arrange a match for her with his son Henry. She did not wish for that; she liked Henry well enough, but he did not fit in with her picture of the knight who would one day come for her. Nor was it to be Henry, for he was already destined for Lucie Grendell. Meliora knew that as an heiress she would be expected to marry; she knew that she would be considered desirable for that reason; she had known that when she reached the age of sixteen her marriage could not long be delayed.

Felipe had ridden to Braxton Hall after the accession of Mary; he had come with an important message for Sir James. She did not know what the message was, for she knew little of events; she had never been taught to take an interest in them, and she did not know what difference it could make to her whether Jane or Mary ruled.

Felipe was charming; he was quiet and she liked him; but he, no more than Henry Braxton, fitted into her picture of the incomparable knight.

And then she had come to Chelsea for the wedding celebrations, and it was here that she had found him. She had never seen anyone so tall and handsome; so skilled in games. She had watched him fencing with his cousin Felipe, laughingly flicking the sword out of Felipe's hand while he pointed his own at his cousin, shouting with mock ferocity: "Beg for your life, sirrah, or die." In the game of tennis he would beat everyone and not seem to care for the victory. She had watched him ride, looking distinguished, noble, the most handsome of knights with the bluest eyes she had ever seen.

Moreover, he was kind to her. He smiled at her as though her presence in his home gave him great pleasure; he looked at her in a manner which made her heart beat fast.

Meliora had found her knight, and his name was Roger Grendell.

"You are happy?" asked Jane of her husband on their granddaughter's wedding night. "You are pleased with this marriage?"

"Pleased, yes. But sorry to lose Lucie."

"Well, soon you will doubtless have Meliora in her place."

"She is a sweet and simple girl, Meliora."

"Has Roger promised to ask her?"

"Charles said he was a little evasive, but I think he will. He has been most attentive to her all day; did you notice?"

"I did. It is to be hoped that the plight of poor little Moll does not come to her ears."

"Ah! She must understand that a young man will sow his wild oats before he settles down in marriage."

"The sowing of such as Roger is apt to be prolonged. However, as you say, little Meliora must accept this, as others have had to do."

Ralph was silent for a while. Then he said: "Charles said that Roger mentioned Donna when he talked to him. Roger said he had grown accustomed to the thought of marrying Donna. He sees the impossibility of that, of course; but I am rather sorry I put the idea into his head."

"It will be long ere you need concern yourself with Donna's marriage."

"It is odd that I should feel as I do towards her, when she is not one of our family."

"Ah, but Donna is supremely attractive. When will Felipe marry?"

"I suppose it is my duty to speak to Felipe, but I hesitate to do so. He is so sensitive. I would rather the thought of marriage came to him of its own accord. I think it would be unwise to try to plant an idea in his head. He loves his cousin Kate, and I suppose he has guessed that we expect them to marry one day."

"So you will say nothing to him of marriage?"

"Not yet. But now that Lucie is married and Roger will soon be betrothed, Felipe will want to be married too; and there will be Kate . . . waiting for him."

"I am glad we are returning to Kent with the Braxtons. Perhaps Roger will ask Meliora while we are there; and if Felipe too becomes enamoured of the idea of marriage, our journey will have other results besides the sweetening of the house."

284

"Jane, think how wonderful it will be to see our great-grandsons about the house! Roger's sons! Will they be like him, I wonder? And Felipe's? Marriage could do for Felipe what nothing else has been able to do. If he has sons of his own, he would cease to brood as I feel sure he does."

"The time passes, and yet he seems unable to forget."

"Children would help him to forget. Sons to distract him and sweet Kate to soothe him. The sooner the better, Jane. The sooner the better!"

"Ah, Ralph," said Jane wistfully, "if only we could direct those we love in the way we wish them to take."

"What troubles you now, sweetheart? On what road would you direct me?"

"On the road to peace and quiet. James talks continually of the Queen's suggested Spanish marriage. If they should try to put that into effect . . ."

"Jane, we should not trouble ourselves with this matter. As yet nothing is settled."

But Jane went on: "He said he and others would do all in their power to stop this marriage. Ralph, *you* would not be one of those who tried to stop it?"

"You fret too much, Jane. You have been fretting for years. And look you! Here we are. In the same bed . . . in the same house . . . happy together. The marriages of our children make happier talk than the marriage of the Queen."

She agreed with him, for she was too happy to entertain uneasiness for long on that night.

Lucie was enchanted by the old timber-framed mansion with its gables and diamond-paned windows. The great hall dominated the house and extended to the roof, which was magnificently carved and decorated with the figures of angels among white and rose-tinted clouds on a dark blue background. The huge table, which, in its turn, dominated this hall, had evidently been put there in the days when the servants had sat at table with the family. Sir James was modern in outlook; he was a man who liked to follow the fashion; he had enlarged his house, extending the servants' quarters; and the family now ate in a private room except when there was a banquet. Two elaborate staircases ascended from either end of the hall to the gallery; and in this gallery, which was hung with tapestry, were the many doors which led to the upper rooms of the vast house. At one end of the hall was a great carved door which led to the servants' wing, including the kitchens, pantry, buttery, bolting house and those apartments in which the servants slept.

The home farm was extensive, and the farmhouse a building of timber and plaster with a thatched roof.

It was pleasant to ride round the estate in Henry's company while the villagers curtsied or touched their forelocks and gaped at Lucie, who would one day be the lady of the Manor.

Lucie was in love with Braxton Hall, the Braxton estate, and still more so with Henry and her new life.

Meliora had grown more beautiful since the visit to Chelsea. During the journey to Kent it was Roger who had ridden beside her, attentive and charming. The miracle had happened, and the blue-eyed knight loved her; she contemplated a marriage as idyllic as she believed her parents' had been.

Roger was resigned. Meliora was a gentle girl who would suit him well. He remembered the quarrels between his father and mother; and although he had been only eleven years old when his mother had died, he had been old enough to know something of her character; and he now realised that Meliora was a different kind of person. She would be sweet and forgiving; and it was comforting to believe that if he strayed she would forgive. There was a gentleness about her which pleased him.

Even Ceci had lost some of her asperity. With all this talk of marriage, they would find a husband for her, she did not doubt; and ere long she would have her own house, which she could keep in perfect order. She would have children who would be models of virtue; and she would no longer fret because she feared she lacked the attractive frivolity of Lucie, the gentleness of Kate and the charm of Donna, which everyone seemed to prefer to her own good sense.

Kate was happy. She felt cosy and safe within the circle of her family. Kent was not so far from Chelsea, and she, foresaw many happy visits between the two families. Lucie would have babies. There would be young people in the family. It would multiply and they would all be happy together. Roger would marry that sweet girl Meliora, who was like a nervous fawn. Kate longed to protect her, to take her under her care and to make her happy at Chelsea; she was going to love her sister-in-law. And Meliora and Roger would have children to run about the lawns at Chelsea, to roll in the hay and feed the peacocks. And Kate herself was growing up. Felipe was fond of her, she knew. This was what Kate wanted: Felipe — and happiness and security for them all.

Donna's happiness was greater than that of the others because her emotions were always more intense than those of other people. She loved riding near Felipe, smiling at him now and then to remind him of his promise. Ours, thought Donna, will be the best wedding of all.

But there was Kate to give her a twinge of anxiety.

If Kate loved Felipe, how would she feel when she knew that he was betrothed to Donna?

But Donna would not allow her happiness to be even faintly impaired; she would find a lover for Kate. She had heard that Sir James kept open house at Braxton Hall. There would be many to choose from, Donna felt sure. And Donna would choose the best, the most handsome, the most kind and the richest — and he should be Kate's.

It was the happiest day Meliora had ever known, and she doubted whether she could ever know a happier. It was December, but the air was mild and the scene bright with winter sunshine.

It happened in the pond garden, whither she had gone, knowing that he would follow. During the past week she had lived in a daze of alternate uncertainty and delight. At one moment she had believed that it had been settled and that at the first opportunity he would speak to her; but the opportunity came, and still he did not speak; then she was overwhelmed with uncertainty.

If he did not wish to marry her — and she could feel sure that it must be he who was holding back, for his parents and her guardian wished it — then she would be the unhappiest girl in the world. She would go through life unfulfilled; she would go into a convent, give her fortune to good causes. That would be the only life for her. But if he asked her to marry him — then would she know perfect bliss.

She felt so unworthy of him. He was gay and witty; people sought his company; he was beloved of his family, and Sir James showed his approval in many ways. Roger was perfect, and to think of his many attractions humbled her, made her uneasily conscious of her own shortcomings.

And then came that December afternoon in the pond garden. She was sitting on a little seat by the statue when she saw him coming through the gap in the fir trees which gave entrance to the garden.

She feigned unconsciousness of his approach, but her flaming cheeks betrayed her.

"Why," he said, "it's Meliora. You look disturbed to see me."

"No . . . indeed I . . . I am not disturbed."

He smiled and sat down beside her.

She could not look at him. This was the moment for which she had longed and yet feared. She felt she would die of happiness at this moment, for he was taking her hand.

"Meliora," he said, "you do not know very much of me, do you?"

"I . . . I . . ." She was tongue-tied in his presence. She lifted her eyes to meet his brilliant blue gaze.

"No," he went on, "you do not really know much of me; but I know enough of you to know that I want to marry you."

He put an arm about her, and when he felt her tremble, he released her.

"Meliora," he said, "you are so young and so sweet; and I'll warrant you know little of the ways of the world. If you would rather I did not speak further, say so, and I shall respect your wishes."

She thought: How kind he is! How gentle! He who is gay and charming and never at a loss for a word, would sacrifice all he hoped to achieve rather than make me uneasy.

Here it seemed to her was Chaucer's "perfect, gentle knight".

He had moved closer to her. "But if you do not wish it, Meliora, pray tell me, for I would not cause your heart to flutter so. You are young and good and pure, and I am quite unworthy; so, if you would that I should desist, I could not find it in my heart to go on."

Now she looked at him, and there seemed to be an entreaty in his face. She thought he was entreating her to allow him to continue.

She put out her hand and he took it.

"Please . . . it would make me happy if you were to go on with what you have to say to me."

He was silent for a moment. He sat back on the seat, still holding her hand, and as he gazed at the plants on the pond, he seemed lost in a melancholy contemplation.

Then he laughed, and all his natural gaiety returned.

"Then, Meliora," he said, "you and I will marry, and with God's help I will do my best to please you."

He raised her hand to his lips, and then, looking into her face, he said: "Meliora, the thought of marriage frightens you, does it not?"

"It is not the thought of marriage," she said, "but the fear that I shall disappoint you."

Then he put his arm about her and kissed her cheek tenderly.

"Have no fear, Meliora; we shall make a success of this marriage of ours. We shall, I tell you. We shall."

Then he sat back, and they were silent. He reached for her hand again, and for a long time they were still, gazing — without seeing them — at the plants on the lily-pond.

There was much coming and going at Braxton Hall. It would soon be Christmas, and Donna found life exciting. She must still work at her lessons, for her tutor had accompanied them. Ceci did not persecute her as she had once done, and Roger was betrothed to Meliora, which was a blessing, for he now scarcely looked her way, and for that Donna was grateful. She pitied poor Meliora, who was to marry him, yet Meliora seemed happy about it. She was continually gossiping with Lucie, and there was talk of celebrating the marriage during the Christmas festivities, before the Grendells and their servants returned to Chelsea. Then Meliora, as the wife of Roger, would travel with them to her new home.

That was very satisfactory, but there was the problem of Kate's future to bother Donna, for so far Donna had not succeeded in finding Kate a husband, and until she had done that she could not be completely happy.

On the day after the betrothal of Roger and Meliora had been announced, Donna had mounted her horse and was riding about the Braxton estate, brooding on this matter, and so earnestly did she brood that she strayed farther from the Hall than she was permitted to when she was alone.

She was not lost. She knew perfectly well which way she could return, but the countryside, being unfamiliar to her, seemed exciting, and because it was out of bounds, she longed to explore it. Providing she made sure of the way she had come, she would be able to make her way back. She was not the baby they sometimes thought her.

She was in a narrow lane admiring the red berries on a holly bush when a man came riding towards her. As he approached she was struck by his handsome face; indeed, he seemed to her one of the most handsome gentlemen she had ever seen; the richness of his garments proclaimed him a man of rank.

It was necessary to make slow progress along the narrow, winding lane, and their horses almost touched as they were about to pass.

The man smiled at her and doffed his cap.

"Good morrow to you," he said.

"Good morrow," she answered.

He paused. Doubtless he was wondering what a well-dressed girl of her tender years was doing unaccompanied.

Donna made a quick decision. Her heart was beating very fast because, the more she saw of this young man, the more impressed she was with his fine clothes and handsome countenance. She decided he would be the best possible substitute for Felipe.

"Sir," she began, "can you help me? I have lost my way."

He drew up at once, and she felt gleeful. If he would conduct her back to Braxton Hall, if he would fall in love with Kate and Kate with him, Donna's purpose would be achieved.

"I am at your service, my little maid," he said.

His eyes twinkled, and she was aware of that admiration, that amusement, to which she was accustomed. He was ready to give her that attention which she had come to regard as her right.

"I fear I have strayed too far," she said.

"Then we must remedy that. Where do you live?"

"In Chelsea."

"In Chelsea!" He looked disturbed. "Then you have indeed come far."

"Nay! My family is staying at Braxton Hall."

"Braxton Hall! I know it well. It is not very far away, and you have strayed but a mile or so."

"Then would you please . . . if it is not out of your way . . ."

"With the greatest pleasure."

"It would not take you from your way?"

"Indeed it would not. I had intended calling on Sir James Braxton some time in the near future."

"Why should it not be this day?" she said artfully.

"Why not indeed! I will ride to Braxton Hall with you, and pay my call on Sir James this day."

"I am very fortunate to have met you, sir."

"It is I who am fortunate, methinks, for it is a great pleasure to be of service to you."

They rode on together under lime trees that glinted red in the pale sunlight.

The young man thought what a beautiful child she was; and as for Donna, she was more and more impressed with his courtly grace as their acquaintance ripened. He was the very man for Kate, she decided.

"So you are staying in Kent?" he said. "How do you like our county?"

"It is very beautiful."

"You should see it in the spring, when the fruit trees are in blossom. I trust you will prolong your stay till then."

"I doubt we shall stay so long. This is not the way I came, sir."

"I want to show you one of the loveliest views in Kent. It is very little out of our way."

They had come to open country, and he pointed out a church tower and the walls and turrets of a castle glittering in the sunshine.

"There!" he said. "One of the loveliest of Kentish villages. That is Hever Castle and St Peter's church. You see the stream running through the valley there? That is the River Eden. The name suits it, think you not?"

"Yes, sir. It is very beautiful." She thought that this was an enchanted morning. The sun was so brilliant in spite of the time of year; and the church with the cottages about it, the castle and the gleaming river, made a picture she felt she would never forget. But more interesting still was the young man beside her.

"Is it your castle?" she asked.

"Nay. I live at Allingham Castle. It is not very far from here. My father was a frequent visitor to Hever Castle. A Queen lived there."

"Not Queen Jane?" said Donna quickly.

"Nay, little one. Queen Anne. Queen Anne Boleyn. She, poor lady, lost her head."

"I know of it," said Donna.

"My father loved her dearly. He often went to Hever Castle in his youth . . . to play games with her and her brother and sister."

"Does it make you sad to think of your father?"

"It does indeed, for he is dead. And as I sit here on my horse beside you, I needs must think of him. Many times must he have been at this very spot with a lady beside him, gazing on Hever."

Donna surveyed him happily. "Come," she said, "I fear they will miss me."

She was all eagerness to lead him to Kate.

As they rode on he told her his name was Thomas Wyatt, and he hoped that she and her family would visit him at Allingham Castle during their stay in Kent.

Christmas was near, and during this season the marriage of Roger and Meliora was to be celebrated.

Sir Thomas Wyatt paid many visits to Braxton Hall after the day when Donna brought him there. She continued to admire him, but he disappointed her; it was not that he proved less handsome or charming on closer acquaintance; it was simply that he showed no interest in Kate. When he came to the Hall it was his custom to seek out the men and confer with them. He seemed particularly to enjoy the company of Roger. Donna was afraid she would have to look elsewhere for Kate's husband.

If Sir Thomas Wyatt brought disappointment to Donna, his presence at Braxton Hall filled Jane with apprehension.

It seemed to her that James and his son Henry were quite unable to learn from experience. It was but a short while ago — on Mary's accession — that it had been necessary for them to lie low; now they were ready to associate themselves with the mad schemes of this firebrand Wyatt.

Jane knew what was brewing, because Ralph could not keep anything from her. Wyatt was a Catholic — he insisted on that — but as a boy he had lived in Spain during the period when his father, the poet, had been on an embassy there and in acute danger from the Inquisition.

"I shall never forget the risk my father ran," said young Thomas, his eyes flashing. "Nor will I forget what I have seen in that barbarous land. I will resist the union of England and Spain while I am capable of holding a sword."

He was rousing the men of Kent to march on London. If they were successful it might be possible to depose Mary and put the Princess Elizabeth on the throne. There was more than a touch of the fanatic about young Wyatt. He had idealised his father, and it might be because his father had loved Elizabeth's mother that he wished to have a hand in making the Princess Queen of England. His zeal was contagious, and Jane saw that the men of the house were ready to follow Wyatt in his ambitious adventure.

Felipe alone was aloof. That was strange. Felipe had suffered as had Wyatt, but whereas Wyatt's suffering arose through fear of what might come to pass, Felipe had witnessed the reality. The effect on Wyatt had been a wild urge to rebellion, even though there was a great danger of failure; but the effect on Felipe had been to make him loathe and shun violence of any sort. Even Sir James, who wished to stir everyone to action, agreed that Felipe should not be pressed to join the revolt, for he realised that none of them could know the depth of Felipe's agony; nor could they fathom the effect this might have had on a young and impressionable mind.

As for Roger, he threw himself into Wyatt's schemes with enthusiasm — a fact which terrified Jane no less because she felt that Roger's desire was not so much to thwart the Queen in her marriage or to see Elizabeth on the throne, as to throw himself into some activity, that he might not think of his own marriage.

So during those December days the men at Braxton Hall saw much of Wyatt, and often one or more of them would ride to Allingham Castle for a conference. Messages constantly went back and forth between Braxton and Allingham; and Pablo, who was often the messenger, started a love affair with a girl in the Allingham kitchens.

Meanwhile preparations for the wedding went on. Lucie was a little superior, taking Meliora under her wing, offering advice. Lucie, as a young matron, was more charming than she had been as a maiden. Ceci watched the domestic arrangements of the Hall and gleefully congratulated herself that they suffered in comparison with those of the Grendell household. Kate shared Lucie's pleasure in her new home; and they were oblivious of the dangerous activity of the men, as they discussed the coming wedding at every hour of the day.

Donna lured Felipe out to ride with her. They went hunting and hawking with the others, but Felipe preferred to ride alone with her. He did not like hunting anything; he was never happy to see his falcon with its prey; he hated to use his own crossbow, to hear his dogs barking at stag, hart or otter. He was strange, unlike other people; but Donna felt that was how he should be.

He preferred to ride aimlessly in the woods in which King Henry had hunted on his way to Hever Castle to visit his love. To Felipe the countryside seemed more beautiful in the pale wintry light, and the stark black branches outlined against a mottled sky suggested a peace which he felt was far away, since conspirators congregated close at hand to plot against the Queen.

As was her custom, Jane waited to talk to Ralph until they lay in their bed together, when the silence of the night had fallen over the house.

"Ralph, what now? What part have you in these plans?"

"One that need cause you no anxiety."

"Need you join with these men?"

"Jane, what can I say to you? Think of Richard. Think of what happened to him. What if the men of this country were in danger . . . continual danger of sharing his fate?"

"How can we prevent it?"

"By refusing to allow this marriage."

"You have no power to do that."

"We could fight for the power. We know now that the Queen has decided against Courtenay, in favour of Philip of Spain. There are many in this country, Jane, who are ready to give their life-blood to prevent that marriage."

"But not you, Ralph. Not Charles nor Roger."

He was silent for a while.

Then he said: "Elizabeth is the hope of the Protestants. She has shown a fondness for Courtenay.

Do not imagine there will not be other rebellions besides this one in Kent. Suffolk will lead the men from the Midlands, and Sir Peter Carew in the West Country. They will meet, and march on London."

"Suffolk will wish to set Jane Grey on the throne. Yet Wyatt and Carew wish to place Elizabeth there. Don't you see, Ralph? There will be no end to these troubles. Jane has no right to the throne. Elizabeth is a bastard. The Queen had to declare her so, if her own mother's marriage to the King was to be made valid."

"There are many who have said that Mary is a bastard."

"This is folly, Ralph. Let well alone."

"Do you realise what may happen to this country if Mary marries Philip of Spain? Tyranny, murder, will be as common-place here as they are in Spain. We shall be ruled by that gloomy Spanish tyrant. They will set up the Inquisition here."

"There is nothing we can do to prevent it."

"We can fight against it. There are many in this land who would die rather than submit to the Spanish yoke."

"Ralph, I beg of you, keep out of danger. You promised me you would."

"Oh, Jane, what can I say?"

"They do not need you. We have lost Richard in this futile religious war. Let us guard well what we have left to us."

"We will guard well what we have left," said Ralph vehemently.

"Then as soon as the wedding of Roger and Meliora has been celebrated, we shall return to Chelsea?"

"Yes, Jane. It shall be as you wish."

"I do wish it," said Jane fervently.

Ralph lay awake after she slept. He had not told her that it was arranged that he and his family should return to Chelsea immediately after the wedding, that Sir Thomas would almost immediately march on London and, when he had taken that city, he would need loyal supporters at hand in order that he might consolidate his gains.

Ralph was involved in this; his son Charles was involved; so was Roger — particularly Roger, whose task it would be to raise the men of his neighbourhood and stand ready to support the rebels when they were in control of the City of London.

Jane did not understand. There was a mighty conflict raging throughout the world from which it was impossible to stand aside. They had lost Richard; they must indeed guard well what was left to them; but they dared not stand aside.

In the great hall the wedding guests made merry.

Sir James had invited many of his friends to feast and dance at the wedding of his ward. Among them was Sir Thomas Wyatt. Only a few days would elapse before he would be ready to march on London.

The bride was shy and very happy. She dreamed of the life which lay before her; she would one day be mistress of the house in Chelsea. Meliora did not wish to interfere with anyone's wishes; she wanted all to be as happy as herself; and she had made up her mind that

Ceci should continue to manage the household affairs in Chelsea for as long as she liked.

She stole a glance at her bridegroom. He was more handsome than ever in his wedding garments, but he was unusually quiet.

He was as happy as she was, thought Meliora; and that was a miracle, for although anyone could understand why she loved him, it was difficult to realise that he could care for a girl as insignificant as herself.

Dreams would persist. She could not shut from her mind those glimpses of a rosy future. She saw her family growing up about her in the house at Chelsea, and the love between herself and Roger strengthened by the years, as it had been between her beloved parents.

Roger looked about the table. The food was displayed in a manner to tempt the appetite, but he had lost his. The buttered fish, the great meat pies whose crust was done to a golden brown, the wild boar which had been soaked in vinegar with juniper berries and garlic for several weeks before it was roasted, the great baron of beef, the peacocks and carp, the various cheeses . . . nothing could tempt him. But he was drinking a good deal. The bragget brewed in Braxton Hall was good. It was strong, this Kentish ale, and flavoured with honey and herbs it was not only delicious but potent; it eased his melancholy.

He caught Meliora's eyes upon him and smiled tenderly. He wished that the poor girl would not look on him so dotingly. She did not know, poor soul, with what kind of a husband they had provided her. What would she say if she knew that since his betrothal he had been unfaithful to her? But he would be faithful after the marriage, after this day. He could smile ironically at himself. He had intended to be faithful after the betrothal. As he had sat on the seat in the pond garden he had made all sorts of resolutions. And then one of the serving girls had raised her eyes to his . . . and his vows were forgotten.

His father's eyes gleamed with affection when he raised his goblet of wine to drink the young couple's health. He understood. So must he have made his resolutions twenty years ago. Roger almost wished that he had reached his father's age, that he had found comfort with a peaceful serving girl like Nana, who was ever ready and who made no demands. But there were many years to be lived through before he reached that state of acceptance and understanding of life.

He would not meet Meliora's eyes, for there had come to him a great desire to tell her of himself, to beg her not to set him upon a pedestal, but to see him as he was — a sensual man who had taken his pleasure at will, and would doubtless, no matter how he tried, fall into further temptation.

How could he explain that? What did she know of such as he was? They should never have allowed her to marry him. She should be warned. But she knew nothing . . . nothing . . . and the awakening would be rude.

I will be a faithful husband from now on, he resolved. I will overcome all temptation. I will. I swear it.

But he knew that he was vowing the impossible. He would fall, and when he had fallen, because she was as she was, he would suffer great remorse; and he did not want to feel remorse. He wanted a wife who understood him as his father understood him. He wished Meliora could be made to understand that this was a marriage of convenience; she never would, this simple girl from the country who had endowed him with qualities which he could never possess, who expected too much of him and from their marriage.

But soon there would be other matters than a marriage to occupy him. He looked at Wyatt, who was drinking and talking earnestly. Wyatt's eyes were ablaze with the fanaticism of one who believes he has a mission to fulfil. Roger smiled with something like disdain. He was not greatly interested in the quarrels between Catholics and Protestants, for he was not at heart a religious man. What was he? He did not himself know. Tonight he could only think of himself as a sensual man, a man whose appetites came on him suddenly and must be appeased. Women were necessary to him as was food to a starving man; and when the desire was with him he had few scruples.

He was almost glad that Wyatt would march on London, and that he would be there — with his grandfather and father and others like them — secretly waiting until the right moment came to succour Wyatt and dethrone the Queen, so that England might never, through a Spanish marriage, bear the yoke of Spain.

His grandfather was saying that Donna would dance for them. She sat beside him, and his hands fondled her long black hair, for he doted on her still. It made no difference that she was not his own flesh and blood, that she was Nana's bastard. He loved her now as he always had.

Her black hair hung loose about her shoulders, and in her gown of scarlet velvet she was very beautiful. Her beauty grew, thought Roger; it would never diminish.

She would dance the *jota*, she said. Pablo should play his lute for her.

So Pablo came forward and played his sensuous music, and Donna took a rose made of scarlet silk, and set it behind her ear. She took the castanets from her pocket, and danced as Roger had seen her dance in the woods.

With what abandon she lifted her arms! With what grace she lifted her skirts! Her movements displayed her grace and beauty. The clatter of the castanets played on Roger's nerves, and he longed to go to her and seize her as he had that day in the wood.

She danced down the hall, smiling at them all as she passed.

Thomas Wyatt seemed temporarily to have forgotten the great project before him as he watched her. Felipe was indulgent, seeing her as a child. Roger met his father's eyes, and there was a quick understanding between them. Charles realised why his son wanted to marry Donna and had been prepared to wait for her.

Donna was close to Roger now; her eyes mocked him and told him how she hated him; but her hatred was less fierce than it had been. She would remember, as he remembered, that incident in the wood; and it was as though her eyes said to him: "You would not dare to touch me now!"

She was daring to challenge him. Sometimes he wondered how much she knew of his feelings. Was she the child her age declared her to be?

Now Pablo's music stopped and Donna was momentarily still in an attitude of the utmost grace. She bowed to the applause and the cries of Bravo.

Then — a little girl once more — she went demurely to sit by Sir Ralph.

Roger determined to look her way no more. Yet, as he smiled at Meliora, he was seeing Donna's small dazzling figure, the satin slippers, the red velvet gown; and he could not rid himself of the sound of castanets.

His father was beside him.

"Tactless, Father," said Roger. "A Spanish dance . . . at such a time!"

"Hush, my son!" said Charles.

Roger went on angrily: "They all seem bemused!"

His father pressed his arm, and in that pressure there was sympathy.

In the nuptial chamber, Roger had blown out the last candle. He stood by the bed; he could sense her trembling.

"Meliora," he said, "Meliora, you must not be afraid."

"No . . . no . . . it is just that . . ."

He bent over her and put his lips to her forehead. She did not move him except by exciting his pity.

"You are afraid, my poor Meliora."

"I am so foolish."

"No, no," he said. "It is natural to be afraid."

"You are so kind. You are the kindest man in the world. The kindest and the best, as well as the most handsome, the most noble, the most brave . . ."

He laughed harshly. "Do not say such things, I beg of you."

"But they are true. I know them to be true."

"Nay, they are false."

She shook her head and he went on: "Meliora, you must not be frightened."

"No," she said. "I will try."

"I would not frighten you for the world."

"I know. I know." She was crying quietly.

He said: "Please do not cry. I will lie here at the foot of the bed. Then you will be happy."

She did not answer, and he stretched himself out at her feet. After a while she ceased to tremble.

"You are not frightened now, Meliora?" he asked.

"No. I am not frightened, only happy . . . so happy."

"Stay happy, Meliora. That is what I wish. And . . . after a while you will grow accustomed to being married to me . . . and then you will know . . . you will understand."

"Yes," she said.

"Can you sleep now?"

"I think so."

"Good night, Meliora. Good night, sweet wife."

"Good night, dearest Roger."

His eyes were hot, but there was no feeling in him but relief. She moved him only with pity. Tomorrow he would feel different. It was Donna with her accursed dance who had upset him; he could not get her red skirts and her castanets out of his mind.

And Meliora lay thinking of this wonderful man who was her husband, this very perfect, gentle knight.

Before they arrived back in Chelsea, the news was spreading through the countryside that Wyatt had issued a proclamation in the square at Maidstone against the proposed Spanish marriage. As they rode through the villages they saw knots of people discussing the news. In the inns at which they rested people were whispering of the need to keep the dread Inquisition at bay.

Ralph smiled to himself. So the people of England were not insensible of threatened disaster. They might not have lost a son to the Inquisition, but they had heard of the tortures, the fiery revenge it demanded on those called heretics.

"There will be no Spanish marriage!" Ralph prophesied as they came within sight of London.

But when they crossed the Bridge and were in the heart of the City they saw that London was preparing itself to stand firm behind the Queen. It did not like the Spanish marriage, but it liked rebellion less; and London was determined to see the rightful heir upon the throne. Queen Jane was not the rightful heir; nor was Elizabeth, while Mary lived.

There was activity everywhere. The City gates were to be defended with ordnance; cannons were set up about the Tower of London; and in its turrets and battlements stood men at arms, ready for the attack. Everywhere, it seemed, were the Queen's soldiers.

The family passed safely through the defences, and on reaching Chelsea in great secrecy the men set about gathering together all those loyal to their cause, making sure that each man understood that he must wait in his home for the call to arms.

News was not long in coming. Suffolk had proclaimed Jane Queen in Leicestershire, but his revolt in that quarter was quickly suppressed; Carew was beaten in the West of England and immediately fled to France; only Wyatt prospered. He came marching triumphantly through Kent with everything in his favour. Captain Brett, who was in charge of the London trained bands on whom Mary believed she could rely, was in reality a supporter of Wyatt. He set out — as the Queen thought — to attack Wyatt, but when their forces met it was not as enemies. They marched together to Deptford.

There was tension in Chelsea. Wyatt would take London; then would come the signal, by means of a messenger, to rise and go forth to support Wyatt.

There were many rumours abroad. It was said that that sly witch, the Princess Elizabeth, was the cause of the trouble. Had she not flirted with Courtenay, and lured him from her ageing sister? Had she not convinced him that marriage with herself and the promise of a crown were far more desirable than marriage with Mary and the certainty of it? The Queen had shown herself all too willing to mate with the handsome Duke who was — some would say — more royal than herself. But the Spanish Ambassador had betrayed to the Queen the relationship between her lover and her sister, the Princess Elizabeth, and had so inflamed Mary's anger that she would have had the heads of the Duke and the Princess had she not been restrained by her more cautious ministers.

It was because of this that Elizabeth had been banished from the Court to Ashridge and Courtenay was in disgrace; and, rashly, the outraged Queen had given Renard, the Spanish Ambassador, permission to write to his royal master that the marriage with Don Philip would be acceptable to her.

Though the Queen was willing, her people were not. And all through the fair county of Kent they were showing their disapproval. But the people of London waited, grim and relentless about the person of the Queen, ready to defend her because her claim to the throne was the only one they recognised.

The Duke of Norfolk, the zealots Gardiner and Bonner, the ever-faithful Sir Henry Bedingfeld, who had saved her life on more than one occasion, and whom she trusted as she trusted no other, were about her, advising her, ever watchful, realising the danger of her position, swearing to defend her with their lives.

When Wyatt reached the city he found the defences unassailable and was forced to retreat to Southwark; a fierce battle took place outside Whitehall, which the Queen, showing great bravery, witnessed from the Holbein gallery of that palace.

The suspense in Chelsea was only just bearable.

Roger sharpened his sword, wishing he had never agreed to wait, for he greatly desired to be in the thick of the fight. He longed to escape from the house, from the period of waiting, but he was soldier enough to know that any action on his part at such a stage must cause confusion. A soldier must obey commands; Wyatt was in charge and the instructions were to wait for orders from him.

During the last days Roger had overcome his awkwardness with his bride and had made gentle love with her. She was fair enough, and it had never been difficult for Roger to make love to a woman. No searing passion this, just a gentle affection. It was all she desired; and he must try to be content with it.

But the hunt ever attracted him. If he could not hunt women, he must hunt the Queen's men. But he chafed against the inactive part to which he was committed.

He rode out along the river bank, but not too far, lest the messenger should come during his absence. He brought his horse to a standstill and looked at the great fortress, that by its very appearance seemed to scorn attack. Now it was twelve acres of fortifications. He came near enough to see the moat sparkling in the frosty air. The bridge was drawn, and he could see the embattled towers of the Lion's Gate, and beyond it a tower with mighty bastions on either side and a double portcullis. He looked at the high weather-washed walls and shivered at the thought of being imprisoned in that place, as so many noble and notable people had been. He could not see it, but he pictured the church of St Peter ad Vincula with the green before it on the grass of which had been spilt the blood of two of King Henry's Queens. If Wyatt failed, he doubted not that the blood of yet another Queen would stain the grass — for Jane was a Queen, even if she had only reigned twelve days.

These were gloomy thoughts. But he was alternately gloomy and buoyant.

He wondered at himself. He was not the man he had been a short while ago. Once he would have laughed to scorn the idea of failure.

He turned away and galloped swiftly back to Chelsea.

He saw Tom Bassett's cottage in the distance. Tom Bassett was the blacksmith who had accepted a sum of money and his blessing to make an honest woman of Moll Gentry. The marriage had taken place in time to allow Moll's child to be born in wedlock.

He thought of Moll now with heightened interest, and he knew what was wrong with him. He had not been himself; instead he had been trying to live up to a false ideal based on Meliora's fine pictures of him. He was no saint. He was merely a lusty man.

As he passed the blacksmith's shop he gave a low whistle. So had he called her out of her own cottage in the days when he had desired her company. It is just to have a word with her, to ask a civil question about the child, he thought, deceiving himself as he would not have done a month ago.

She came to the door of the adjoining cottage. She was not as pretty as she had been. Life with the blacksmith had robbed her of something; but as he looked at her more closely, he was not sure that it had not added something too.

She had coarsened, and the lacing across her bodice was broken.

He felt excitement rising as memories came back.

She bobbed a curtsy, and a strand of her hair fell across her face.

"And how's the child, Moll?"

"Bonny, Master."

"That is well, then. Good day to you, Moll."

He walked his horse away. He remembered too much about her; and he remembered that on their first encounter she had reminded him of Donna. Oddly enough, she still did. What was it? There was no likeness of feature between them. It was some quality in them both, some inner knowledge of their power which an immense sensuality had given them. The dainty Donna, the child who as yet could not be aware of that power which was hers . . . and Moll, become a slattern, none too clean, the wife of the hairy blacksmith — both were possessed of the same power.

Perhaps he knew that when he reached the wood she would be there before him by means of the short cut which led from the back of the cottages. She had collected a few sticks, which she carried in her apron for appearances' sake.

She stood before him, smiling that knowledgeable smile.

He was angry, and yet he was glad. He was going to say goodbye to gloom and be himself.

"Moll!" he murmured.

"Yes, Master," she answered, bending her head submissively. It was that submissiveness which made it impossible for him to resist her. Clearly he remembered the day he had seduced her, when she had been an innocent girl, and he desired her now as fiercely as he had desired her then.

He dismounted deliberately and tied his horse to a tree. The quiet way in which she waited inflamed him. It was no use thinking of his noble resolutions: he must be himself.

He laughed and seized her, and as he did so he felt her body respond. It must be here . . . on the grass . . . in open daylight, doubtless with Wyatt's messenger on the way — and to the devil with the consequences.

This was himself as he had always been, as he knew he always would be.

Gloom hung over the house at Chelsea. Everyone was waiting. Now and then one of the servants would run out of the house and would stand on the hillock shading his or her eyes to look along the road, straining the ears for the sounds of horses' hoofs.

The spring in all its glory had spread itself over the land, but it seemed to many that there had never been a more tragic spring for England than that spring of 1554.

This must be a lesson to them, thought Jane. If we come through this with no greater tragedy than that about which we already know, then must we learn our lesson. If we do not, then surely we deserve whatever further pain we are called upon to suffer.

314

There had been no call from Wyatt to the men of the house. In that fact lay their greatest hope. It might be that their enemies had never discovered what part they had intended to play in the great rebellion.

For, right at what had appeared to be the very height of success, Wyatt had failed. London had decided in favour of the Queen, and it was useless for any to pit their strength against that of London. Wyatt had failed to break through Ludgate, where he had expected to find good friends; his men were tired, footsore and muddy from the march; and when they were forced back along Fleet Street, they lost heart at the sight of the numbers arrayed against them. Wyatt, seeing his men falling about him, knew himself lost; in despair he sat down on a fish-stall in the yard of the Bel Savage Inn, and there he was arrested.

Now — with Wyatt a prisoner in the Tower — the Queen and London celebrated their victory; but there was no rejoicing in the house at Chelsea.

As soon as darkness fell, bonfires could be seen from far beyond the city's walls and there was the sound of music and roistering along the river. Oxen were being roasted whole in the fields, and the odour was carried along on the breeze; firework displays illumined the darkness and barrels of pitch burned on the battlements of the tower and some of the great houses.

In the dungeons of the Tower Wyatt's men were crowded together. There were many executions and numbers died in the dark chambers at the hands of the sworn tormentors. The rack creaked perpetually; the Scavenger's Daughter fervently embraced victim after victim. Men who had fought against the Queen were hung in the doorways of their houses, and their corpses were left dangling there for all to see what happened to those who worked against the Queen.

Lady Jane Grey with her father, the Duke of Suffolk, and her husband Lord Guildford Dudley, had been three of the first to lay their heads upon the block. Wyatt, under torture, had implicated Courtenay, who with the Princess Elizabeth was placed under arrest.

The Queen's marriage treaty with Philip of Spain had been signed.

"What good will come of this rebellion?" asked Kate of Felipe. "It has brought nothing but suffering to all those who took part in it."

"Fighting and killing one another is not the way," said Felipe. "I do not know how we can turn men and women from this cruelty, but to fight is not the way. Perhaps to talk to them with persuasive words . . . But they would not listen. They have such arrogant faith that they believe themselves to be always right."

"Felipe, what if they should come for you . . . or Roger, or Father and Grandfather? They might. Hourly men are taken to the Tower for their share in this fruitless enterprise."

"Then, Kate, we shall join those who have already suffered."

"Felipe, I could not bear it."

He took her hand and kissed it, and he thought of death by the swift stroke of the axe. That seemed easy; it was what might precede such easy death which troubled him.

316

He had heard the story of Wyatt — that brave man and reckless soldier. Now he was a tortured wreck. They had broken him on the rack; they had destroyed his fine body, and they had crushed his fine spirits when they had crushed his limbs. In the extremity of torture they had wrung from him a confession that Courtenay was involved in the plot. At the instigation of the Spanish Ambassador, they had tried to force him to implicate the Princess Elizabeth; but that he had bravely refused to do.

Jane was afraid to leave her husband's side. She sat with him on the wicker seat in their peaceful garden. Peace! There was no peace. It was a false peace the garden showed her, with its green lawns and the river gently lapping at its privy stairs. All through the days and nights she was aware of those sounds of revelry. Every sound of a horseman on the road, every boat on the river that passed near the garden, filled her with fear.

"Of what use was it all?" was her constant cry.

And Ralph answered her gently: "The plan failed, Jane. Had it succeeded there would have been no Spanish marriage."

"Yet what difference does it make? What difference has it made? Our friends are tortured . . . dead or dying. And we know that at any moment there may be a knock on *our* door; a barge may draw up at *our* privy steps . . . and take you or one of the boys."

"What difference?" said Ralph. "How can we know? But we know this: our country will now be united with one which is known to be ruled by the cruellest institution that ever was invented by man." He did his best to comfort her. "But . . . we are safe, Jane. We are safe in our backwater."

Then they would listen to the sounds on the road.

"Poor Wyatt!" said Jane. "So fine and handsome he was. I cannot forget him. And now he lies in a dungeon . . . maimed. Will he be able to walk to the scaffold tomorrow, think you? I am glad he did not betray Elizabeth. I cannot get him out of my mind. We saw so much of him; and he was certain of success, was he not? I wonder, when those cruel men had him on the rack and tried to make him betray the Princess Elizabeth, whether he was sustained by the memory of his father, who loved Elizabeth's mother. I am glad he did not betray her. And I am glad he has withdrawn what he said against Courtenay. He will go to the scaffold happier for that. Poor Wyatt! Only twenty-three years of age . . . and tomorrow he will die."

"Jane, I beg of you be calm."

"How can I? It might have been you . . . or Charles . . . or Roger, or Felipe. How can I be calm! Why cannot we rest here as we did of old! Why do we fight? Why cannot we be calm and happy in the enjoyment of the sunshine and the green fields?"

He tried to soothe her, but there was no soothing Jane. She was listening for the ominous sounds — the footsteps of men who had come to rob her of her family.

And on that April day when Thomas Wyatt laid his head upon the block, horsemen rode into the stable

318

yard, and everyone in the house waited in trepidation to see who came.

There were six or seven riders, and with them a pale-faced girl.

It was difficult to recognise her as the frivolous bride of a few weeks ago.

Her father was the first to embrace her.

"Lucie," he murmured. "Lucie, my little girl."

And Lucie clung to Charles, and she who had in the past wept so easily because a collar did not fit, because she had broken her fan, had no tears to shed.

They crowded about her, and she looked at them with blank eyes, not seeing them individually, but simply as her family, those who had helped her bear her sorrows in the past and would do so now, who would care for her and comfort her. There was dear Kate, whose eyes were brimming with tears; Ceci grown unusually gentle; little Donna to take her hand and kiss it. Roger, Felipe, her grandparents.

"Lucie, dearest, you are home now. You are home, my love."

She did not know which one said it, but she wanted to cry out: "No, home was in Kent. Home should be on Tower Hill now . . . with Henry!" But she could not speak of Henry; she dared not think of him, so recently warm and loving, now a headless corpse; she could not think of Braxton Hall, of which once she had been so proud, because when she did so she must see the body of Sir James hanging lifeless in the porch.

They took her to her room, where Ceci had made a wood fire; and Kate sat by the bed holding her hand.

And that night sorrow reigned over the house in Chelsea.

Jane said to Ralph when at length they were alone: "They killed your son Richard. They killed your son-in-law Henry. Is that not enough?"

And Ralph, covering his face with his hands, wept bitterly.

"You are right, Jane. It is enough. God helping us, we will risk no more. If He will let us ride this storm without further loss, I swear to you we will return to our backwater. We will find peace again."

CHAPTER
SIX

It was July.

Three months had passed since Lucie, the widow, had returned to Chelsea. Everyone was now breathing more freely. The Wyatt rebellion seemed to have taken place a long time ago, and the sudden arrests, which had unnerved those families who had something to fear, had ceased.

The heat was great that year; but to most of the people in the house at Chelsea the hot weeks seemed comforting, because with the passing of each one, the danger was fading.

Now there was excitement throughout the land because a royal wedding was about to be celebrated on English soil. The people were not pleased with the bridegroom, but the marriage by proxy had already taken place, and the people of England were not accustomed to rail against what was done and could not be mended. They deplored the marriage, but it was better, they supposed, to have any marriage than no marriage; they had heard that the might of Spain would be beside them against their perennial enemies, the French; and it was certainly time that the ageing Queen was married, if she was to provide an heir. More than

321

anything the people longed for an heir. Doubts as to the succession meant trouble. It had always been the case, and it always would be. Had the matrimonial affairs of the six-times-married Henry been more lucid there might not have been this recent and distressing rebellion.

As Ralph looked along the big dining-table at which his family was assembled, he congratulated himself that his loss had not been so great as he had at one time feared it might be. It was nearly nine years since he had lost Richard and Dolores. He had his poor Lucie back, and although she had been heartbroken at the time of Henry's execution, already there were signs of recovery; she was becoming interested in the set of a headdress and the placing of an ornament on a gown. Lucie was light-hearted by nature. Doubtless ere long she would find another husband. Sometimes, though, he noticed the shadow in her eyes; but that would pass. Ceci no longer cosseted her as she had when she had first come home. Poor Cecil Was she growing envious again? Did she think that Lucie the widow was more charming than Lucie the young girl had been?

He had, too, a new granddaughter to take the place of Dolores in his affections, and he was fond of quiet little Meliora. He had prayed fervently during that anxious period that Roger might not be taken. It had seemed more important that Roger should be safe than Felipe, for if Roger were taken, if they did to him what they had done to Henry, Meliora would never recover, as Lucie was doing. No, if Meliora lost Roger she would have no wish to live. Ralph sighed as he contemplated that blind adoration. No one should be worshipped in quite that way — certainly not one so full of human weakness as his beloved grandson Roger.

If she had loved Roger for his faults, I should feel happier, he thought. But she loves him for the shining virtues with which she has endowed the image she carries in her imagination.

Talk round the table was of the Queen's marriage. That was not dangerous talk provided no one raised a voice against it. He had kept his word to Jane and had seen that the others helped him in this. Indeed, not to have talked of the Queen's marriage would have seemed treasonable; so now they discussed it as they would have discussed the hay crop, the apple harvest or the weather.

Donna was saying: "Felipe, when the Queen and her new husband ride into London, will you take me to see the procession?"

Ralph's eyes were on Felipe's face. He must not go, Ralph was thinking. He must not see the Spanish grandees and their ceremonial manners. That would inevitably bring back painful memories.

"I wished Felipe to help me on that day," he said; and Felipe gave him a smile of understanding.

"What if I took you?" asked Roger of Donna.

"Thank you," said Donna sedately, "but mayhap I will not go, after all."

Roger grimaced. He was his old self now; he did not ignore her, but was beginning to tease her as he had once so shamefully done.

Donna chattered about the marriage by proxy and asked many questions. Why were they not being married in London? Why had the ceremony been performed in Winchester? Why did the people not like the new Prince? He would be a great King, would he not, when his father died?

"Now, Donna," said Ralph, "you talk too much, and that means you neglect your food."

Donna was silent then. She longed to see the entry of the Queen into London. She had never seen the Queen. She no longer believed that all Catholics were hump-backed and cross-eyed; but the Queen seemed to her a sinister figure. She was not so unobservant of affairs as they believed her to be. She knew what had happened to Lucie's Henry and to Sir James; she knew that Sir Thomas Wyatt had lost his head. That had shocked her deeply. Life could, she was sure, be both terrifying and exciting; and she was impatient with her youth and inexperience, for she wished to know more of that terror and excitement.

She was determined to see the Queen, and if Felipe could not take her, she would ask Pablo to accompany her.

Pablo and she were great friends; he had always told her that she was a little bit of home to him. She reminded him of much that he missed; and when she laughed — so said Pablo — she laughed as a Spaniard laughed; and when she set a rose in her hair and danced — why, then he could believe he was back in his sunny land.

Pablo spoke quaint English. He was amusing. Nana liked him, Donna was sure, although she pretended not to. And Pablo liked Nana; she, too, seemed to remind him of something that pleased him. All the maids liked Pablo, and one of them had a child — a little black-haired, black-eyed boy who was very beautiful and on whom Pablo doted.

Ceci hated him, for he was the sort of person Ceci would hate. There were some sins which did not arouse Ceci's indignation half as much as others; and Pablo's were those which Ceci deplored more than any.

To the stables went Donna.

"Ah!" said Pablo, bowing at the sight of her, and his bow was gay and solemn all at once. "It is the little Señorita come to pay me a visit."

"Pablo, you will go to London to see the Queen's husband?"

Pablo's eyes flashed and he snapped his fingers. "I will go. Yes! It will be as a breath from my native land."

"Pablo, I must go too. I will go with you."

Pablo assented. He wondered whether she had been forbidden to ride out to see the procession. He knew that there were many intrigues in this house. He knew of its sorrows, of its feelings towards the Queen's Spanish marriage.

Pablo was fond of this family which had given him a home. He was fond of Felipe, who had never reproached him for the betrayal of Roderigo. He was fond of Nana — very fond. She was growing older now; she was over-plump; but the ladies of his country grew plump, and plumpness did not, in his opinion, detract from a woman's charms. He had thought he understood Nana; he had discovered he did not.

Nana was the faithful mistress of one of the masters of this house. Yet he could not forget how she had been when riding to Valladolid one hot day. Then he had believed she would soon be his mistress; he had thought he sensed in her the same urgent desire which he himself felt; and faithfulness was not part of the natures of such as he knew himself to be and had believed Nana to be. Therefore she puzzled him; but she did not interest him the less for that.

Always he hoped that one day he would prove himself to be right. Anticipation of this was one of the pleasures of his life. Meanwhile he did not allow his longing for Nana to interfere with his enjoyment of that consolation which other women were ready to offer him. Here he was more popular than he had been in Spain; here he was different, exotic, and his strange rendering of the English tongue amused; his manners seemed courtly and gentle. He had no Matias, no Tomás as rivals here.

Now, looking at Donna, he told himself that if the family did not wish her to ride into the town to see the Queen and her husband, he should not take her; but the prospect of having beside him such a beautiful child, to be in charge of her, was more than he could resist. Moreover, if she pleaded as she undoubtedly would, how could he say no?

So on that day in August when the Queen, after her marriage in Winchester and her sojourn at Windsor and Richmond, having spent the previous night at Suffolk Place, was due to enter London, Donna slipped out to the stables, where Pablo had her horse waiting for her, and silently they made their escape and rode towards London.

But before they had gone far along the road, they were hailed and, as on another occasion, Donna, turning, saw Roger riding up to them.

He looked sternly from Pablo to Donna, and Donna was filled with anger against him because, behind that affected sternness, she detected the desire to tease and humiliate.

"So," said Roger, "you are riding to London to see the Queen and her husband?"

"Your grace, your honour," said Pablo in his quaint accent, "I had no command not so to do."

"And you?" asked Roger, turning to Donna.

"What I do," she said, "I do. I do not ask you. Come, Pablo."

Roger rode on beside them.

"It is understandable, Pablo, that you should wish to see your countrymen."

"Si, Señor. Si, honoured sir."

"Pablo, you may go ahead. You may relinquish your charge to me. I will look after her."

Pablo doffed his cap and rode on.

Roger turned to Donna. "It is well that I guessed your plans."

"It is not well for me."

"I trust you will not disgrace yourself, as you did on that other occasion. Do you remember? You came home minus a pony."

"I see that you have decided I shall not forget it."

"Donna," he said gently.

She turned her head.

"I can enjoy this . . . riding into the City with you," he went on. "Why did you not accept my invitation in the first place? Should I not have been as fitting a companion as a groom?"

"I prefer Pablo."

He sighed. "Perhaps it is natural. You . . . the daughter of a serving girl, would, I dare swear, prefer a groom to a gentleman."

"It would seem to me that Pablo's manners are more like those of a gentleman than are your own."

She whipped her horse, but he was beside her, keeping pace with her.

"As headstrong as ever!" he said. "It is as well that you have me beside you."

They rode on in silence.

As they rode through the London streets she was reminded very much of that other occasion; she remembered how frightened she had been when pulled from her pony, and she was glad that Roger rode beside her. Roger would defend her with his sword if need be. Pablo, she knew, was, not brave.

They pressed their way through Cheapside and Canwick Street and reached the river once more. They had found a good spot near the Bridge when the cavalcade came in sight.

The bridegroom was not handsome. His clothes were of sombre black velvet, but his *berret* was decorated with gold and a feather. His weak blue eyes looked out coldly on the English scene. The Queen was so richly dressed that she seemed beautiful; her gown of cloth of gold was decorated with so many jewels that she was dazzling to look upon. Her kirtle, which was visible beneath her gown, was of the richest satin and embroidered in silver; her coif was so large and elaborate, so lavishly ornamented, that it distracted attention from a face made plain by ill health.

Guarding the royal pair came the cavalcade of horsemen and archers in the Queen's colours, with whom mingled the black-clad men of Spain.

The watching crowd was silent, as they had been when they had watched Jane Grey's entry into the Tower of London to receive the crown. Yet there was a difference. They did not like the Queen's Spanish husband, but they accepted him — as they had never accepted Jane Grey — because their lawful Queen had made him her lawful husband.

As Spanish Philip passed so close to her that she could see his face, Donna felt a shiver run through her, and turning, she looked at Roger, straight, tall, with his thick fair hair, his fresh complexion and his eyes of a blue that seemed almost the colour of lapis lazuli when compared with the pale orbs of the Spaniard.

She thought: What a King Roger would make! Although I hate him, I think he must be the handsomest man in the world. Pablo saw the procession from another point of vantage, and the sight of his own countrymen filled him with a longing for his own country.

Could I but go back to Spain, he told himself, I should be a happy man.

But, as usual, he deceived himself.

He knew that he would not dare set foot in his native land. Had he not called the attention of the Inquisition to himself? And was it not a fact that none could call himself safe when that had happened? Not for a hundred pesetas would he set foot in his native land. True, he had returned to it with Master Charles in order to conduct him to Felipe and Nana. But that was because it would be even more dangerous to let the English family know what part he had played in their tragedy than to return to Spain. He was a humble man, and it was a fact that the Inquisition did not concern itself with the poor and humble unless they could be the means of providing rich and important victims. He had lived in terror until they had set foot in England. But now he had been long in England, and it was pleasant to see himself as a homesick foreigner. The women were so sorry for him, and he enjoyed the pity of women almost as much as their love; and in any case he had often proved that one was a stepping stone to the other.

So now he watched the grandees and the great Prince who was the son of the greatest Emperor in the world, and who would one day rule Spain; and he allowed the tears to fill his eyes.

When the procession had passed and the crowd had begun to disperse, he went his way through the narrow streets to a tavern in a courtyard near the river; he looked up at the sign creaking on its hinges which proclaimed the inn to be *The Spanish Princess*. This was doubtless a compliment to the first wife of King Henry VIII. He went inside and called for a jug of ale.

The tavern was full of an excited crowd. Now the procession was over the roistering would begin. The shopkeepers were setting up shutters in preparation for the revelry. These people of London might not wish to celebrate the arrival of the Queen's Spanish husband, but they were ready for a holiday at any time.

At length he was served, and by the busy lady of the house — a plump creature with merry black eyes and strands of dark hair straying from under her mob cap.

Pablo's eyes were warmly appreciative as she brought his ale and set it before him.

"Ah," he said. "A grand day, this. A great day."

"And good for custom," she answered, while her smiling eyes told him she liked him as well as he liked her.

"Señora, it is your black eyes, rather than the Queen's husband, that bring the custom here."

She liked that. "You are a foreigner," she said.

He stood up and bowed. "I come from the same country as Don Philip."

She had been about to hurry on with her serving, but she stood still, her eyes round with wonder as she surveyed him.

"A Spaniard!" she said.

"It does not please you? You like us not? Then I am sad. For the sake of those black eyes I would relinquish country . . . faith . . . my place at Court."

How could she, a humble woman, only recently become a widow, resist such a handsome courtly gentleman?

She knew that when foreign princes came to England they brought their followers with them. On other occasions she had had the foreign quality in her inn before they learned that *The Spanish Princess* was not a suitable place for men of breeding. But this one . . . he was humbly clad, yet he was undoubtedly a foreigner; and what black eyes, and what a way he had with the English tongue!

"I have travelled far," he said, "and never have I seen such sparkling eyes as yours."

"Marry, and I'll not believe you," she said with a laugh.

But she was very ready to believe, and soon she summoned one of her maids to take her place that she might sit beside the fascinating foreigner while he told her of his estates in Spain, and how he had made his way across the water in the retinue of the Queen's Spanish husband.

The crafty widow did not intend to surrender at once, and so provide a fitting ending to Pablo's adventure at *The Spanish Princess*; but she gave him hopes of speedily achieving his desires, and he would certainly, in the guise of a Spanish gentleman, pay another visit to *The Spanish Princess*.

A year had passed since the coming of Philip of Spain to England; it had been an uneasy year.

The unpopularity of the Queen's husband was undisguised throughout the land. Children playing in the streets fought battles with one another — the English against the Spaniards. On one occasion a boy who had been designated to play the part of Philip of Spain was set upon so roughly that he would have been killed if not rescued in time.

The Queen, longing for an heir, imagined herself to be pregnant. Her hopes were disappointed. Philip disliked her, so said the rumours, and many were the scandals concerning him. He would have preferred the younger Elizabeth, with whose name rumour had often concerned itself. Thomas Seymour's name was recalled as well as Courtenay's; and now it was said that the wily Spaniard's intentions were to get Elizabeth with child, poison his wife, marry Elizabeth and keep possession of the English throne, at the same time securing a younger and more comely wife.

But there were matters of greater importance than these scandals. Queen Mary believed that a wife should obey her husband in all things, and it was well known that the Queen's husband was a devoted adherent to the Catholic Faith, and the setting up of the Inquisition all over Europe was what he desired even more than an heir to Spain and England.

He already had a son — Don Carlos, a mad boy, so rumour had it — and the people of England wanted none of his heirs to rule them. Deeply was the Spanish marriage regretted, and great was the fear that the people of England would have a chance of proving the terrible stories they had heard concerning the Inquisition.

Uneasiness grew. Many of the laws which Henry VIII had made against the Pope were repealed, and the persecution of heretics was set in motion.

The fires of Smithfield were about to be kindled.

Hot August came, and during one sweltering day a man lay down in the Poultry and died. The same day two more died — one in Canwick Street and the other in Old Jewry.

The plague had come to London Town.

In the surrounding villages people heard the news with apprehension. They watched each other closely for the first signs.

Roger was restless.

He longed for adventure. He had heard tales of the men who sailed the seas, and he wished to travel with them.

There were many Spaniards now in England. These men, lacking the stature of the English, seeming less hardy in English eyes, had made great discoveries. Cortes had discovered Mexico, and Pizarro Peru. Spain was rich in her conquests. Why should not England follow in her wake?

He had talked or these matters with his father and his grandfather. They did not wish him to leave their house. But what was there for a young man in England if his family were suspected of following the Protestant Faith, and a Catholic Queen reigned?

One day Roger would go away from Chelsea; he would fulfil the dreams he had had in his childhood. It was unnatural for a young man to stay at home, to occupy himself with the life of a simple country gentleman, when he was filled with the love of adventure.

His cousin Felipe seemed content. Roger felt irritated with his cousin, for Felipe was one of the reasons for this parental restraint. It was the Spanish marriage of Felipe's father which had been the cause of trouble, as he supposed all marriages of English and Spanish must be. But for that they would not have gone to Spain, and that which had happened to his Uncle Richard would not have happened. But all that had taken place long ago and, as Roger saw it, the world was a place in which, while great torment could be suffered, great pleasure could be enjoyed. It was a mistake to hide from life. He was twenty; he despised the quiet life; he did not seek peace but adventure.

He often thought of foreign lands, of plunder, of gold and silver treasure . . . and women; and all the women he dreamed of were foreign . . . like Donna.

But when he broached the subject of adventure, of leaving Chelsea, he would be aware of the pain in his grandfather's eyes and the fear in those of his grandmother, of his father's desire that he should not leave them.

He did not understand himself. He had thought himself strong, ruthless, yet the pleading in their eyes moved him deeply and had so far caused him to abandon his plans.

But what should he do? His marriage was not satisfactory, although he was undoubtedly fond of Meliora. Was it possible for one of his conceit to be insensible to such adoration? It naturally pleased him that she should think so highly of him. He wished she could have a child. It was a strange, perverse nature which gave him children by other women who should not have them, and denied him legitimate heirs!

Moll was to have another baby.

He supposed his liaison with Moll was known to everybody but Meliora. Strange that she should not see what others saw so clearly. She had endowed him with such virtue, and she could only see him as the possessor of that virtue; and one who possessed it would certainly not be guilty of immoral intrigue with a woman whom he had had to marry to a blacksmith because she was to have his child.

To think of Moll was to want her. She was as eager for him as he was for her. There were times when he, wishing to bear some resemblance to Meliora's perfect knight, stayed away from her for a long time. But after that the meetings were more frequent than ever; they were like two thirsty people who had been denied drink and must take copious draughts because of such abstention.

The blacksmith husband was complaisant.

He had discovered that having a wife who was the mistress of a rich man was a profitable arrangement. The cottage adjoining the forge showed signs of opulence which other cottages did not possess. There was always a welcome for Roger in that cottage, and the blacksmith would busy himself in the forge until his own and his wife's benefactor took his leave.

A bad state of affairs, and I will end it! thought Roger, twenty times a day.

And then he would dream of adventures on the Spanish Main and of the laughing foreign women; or he would watch Donna running across the lawns. Then he would go back and back again to the comfort Moll could give him.

There was plague in the village. Ceci had discovered this. She caught Roger as he came through the porch, and so frightened was she that she did not hesitate to upbraid him.

"You have been with Moll!" she cried.

Meliora was gathering honeysuckle which grew high in the hedge; she had had to climb the low stone wall to reach it, and it was impossible to get down quickly.

Meliora heard the angry words of Ceci, and almost immediately Roger's retort.

"What of it?" he demanded.

"There's plague in the cottages."

"Plague!" said Roger uneasily.

Meliora put her hand over her loudly beating heart. He had been to the cottages doubtless to help some poor villager in distress, and there was plague there. He might be ill and die of it.

Ceci said: "Old Harry Green is sick, so I heard. The Greens' cottage is near enough to the blacksmith's." Ceci's voice was shrill with anger. She hated Moll; and she considered that her brother was guilty of the greatest of all sins . . . adultery! She was certain that God had severe punishment in store for him.

Ceci was frightened. It was no use isolating Roger now. If he had caught the plague he would probably have already passed it on to other members of the household. Being afraid, Ceci let loose all the righteous indignation which she had been bottling up for years.

"You could not stay away from her, I suppose. You are the most licentious . . . the most wicked of men. We all know why you go to the cottage . . . It is disgusting. It is vile. Have you not a wife? Cannot Meliora satisfy you? Must you have the blacksmith's slut . . . and others? Already she has borne your child, and will bear another . . ."

"Be silent, Ceci. Be silent, I say."

"I will be silent no more. Father knows what you are. So does Grandfather. I do not understand why they do not punish you. You have always been the same. I remember you when you were but fourteen. I saw you . . ."

"So you spied on me, my pure Ceci!"

"Yes, I spied. I know you for what you are . . . what you have always been. Lust, lust. You think of nothing else. You cannot resist a doxy who is, like as not, infected with the plague."

He was angry with her because, although he could have forgiven her any lapse of virtue, he could not endure her self-righteousness. He would rather any sinner than those who folded their hands, piously raised their eyes to Heaven and said: "Thank God I am not as other men."

338

"Oh Ceci!" he cried. "My sweet, pure sister Ceci; you should not be angry because no man fancies you. If one had, you might not be so ready to condemn the lapses of others."

"How dare you!" she cried. "Oh, how dare you! I suppose you will deny that Moll is to have your child . . . and that you married the slut to the blacksmith that you might continue to make use of her?"

"Why should I deny it?" he said. "And be quiet. Do you realise you are shouting, and the servants will hear?"

"I should be telling them nothing that they did not know already. How many of them are Moll's rivals, and poor Meliora's, I should like to know."

"What? Do you not know? I thought you kept a closer watch on my movements."

"And so," she went on, "you cannot leave her alone . . . even though there is plague in the cottages."

"She said nothing to me of plague. She would have told me."

"I'll swear there was little time to talk of such matters. That which you and she must do together occupies all time . . . all thought."

"Ceci, your purity overwhelms me."

"You do not believe me, do you? You do not believe that there is plague in the cottages?"

"I believe that you hope there is and that I may be taught a lesson."

"I wish that you may have caught the plague from her, but not that you should die of it, because that would hurt others in this house. But I should like to see you disfigured . . . so that you were repulsive to these women."

"Be careful, Ceci. You will betray your thoughts, and they are so pure, my sweet sister. They should be guarded as you imagine you guard that precious virginity of yours. It is easy, is it not, to guard that which no one considers worth taking?"

"You will be punished for this!" she cried.

He went to his bedroom and shut the door.

He was laughing when Meliora came in. Moll . . . the plague? That was absurd. She was as lusty and healthful as ever. He laughed wryly. Had there been a plague spot on her she would not have been able to hide it from him. He thought of the dark living-room, the none-too-clean rushes on the floor, and Moll lying naked on the pallet. Forced to see himself through Ceci's eyes, he was faintly disgusted with Moll and with himself. He was, as she said, vile. He believed that the very drabness of the cottage appealed to him. Was it repulsion from his own elaborate bed with the silken curtains? Such a contrast they presented, as did Moll naked and eager, compared with gentle Meliora, who must be made love to in the dark.

He hated himself at times. He wished he could leave this house, leave London, sail away on a voyage of discovery, join in the sack of a town, have his women, sail away and forget them.

But Meliora had come in, and she looked as though she were walking in her sleep.

He said: "Meliora, my love?"

340

She stood still, leaning against the hangings, her trembling fingers plucking at them, her great eyes staring at him incredulously.

"Your love?" she said.

He was perplexed.

She went on in a quiet voice: "I heard what was said . . . what Ceci said. I could not help it. I was on the wall close to the porch, gathering honeysuckle; and I could not get down in time . . . before she had begun."

He felt numb with misery, and out of his numbness there came an anger against Meliora. She was a fool to have made a hero of him. She should have had the sense to know that he was not in the least like the picture she had made of him.

It had always been a fault of his that, when ashamed, sick at heart and sorry, he would vent his anger on others, eager to make excuses for himself, to blame others because his shame was intolerable.

"So . . ." he said. "You were eavesdropping!"

He saw with a shock that she had scarcely heard him. She must be thinking of him and Moll together. Her picture of him had changed drastically.

She was silent, and he was determined to make her speak. Meekness was something he could not endure; if she were going to smile and forgive him, he would feel more ashamed than ever.

He said harshly: "What a little fool you are! You, who should know me better than anyone else — to think that I could reform my ways! Or perhaps you thought there was no need of reformation?"

She said the most unwise thing she could have said. "I'm sorry, Roger. I'm afraid I've failed."

If she had cursed him, he could have understood and been gentle with her, but to take the blame on herself for the failure of their marriage was more than he would endure. Moreover, if she were not such a fool she would see that the marriage was by no means a failure. Even his mother, whom he had known to be a shrew, realised his father's need of women other than herself.

"Failed?" he said. "There is no failure. Our marriage has been all I expected it to be. I have been unfaithful to you from the beginning. I never expected to be anything else. You have been a simpleton, Meliora . . . a simple village girl. You know nothing of life. Did you expect me to be satisfied with what there has been between us?"

She did not look at him; she stared blankly before her, still with the air of a sleepwalker.

In a low voice she said: "It is not true. It is not true, is it?"

"What Ceci said? Indeed it is true. I have been with Moll a hundred times. I have been . . . seeing her for a long time. She is going to have a child. Her eldest is mine too. Meliora, be reasonable. These things are. They must be accepted."

"I see that the fault is mine," she said.

The veins stood out on his temples.

"I beg of you, do not take on that hypocritical tone. You know full well what I am. What did you overhear Ceci call me? Lecher, was it? Well, if it was not, that will

342

do. I lust after women. I have always done so. I shall always do so. Moll is not the only one who has borne my children, nor will she be the last."

She did not answer; she walked to the door.

"Meliora," he said more gently.

But she had gone.

He stared after her. What a fool I am! he thought. Why could I not have been something like the man she thought me?

He covered his face with his hands, but he could not shut out of his mind the memory of sad Meliora. He remembered her in her wedding dress, and the night when he had lain at the foot of the bed.

What had he done to her?

He cursed Ceci and her virtue. But he knew that it was himself and his lechery which were to blame.

Why did Meliora marry me? he wondered. Why am I what I am?

As dinner, over which they sat at the big table in the dining-hall, was begun at eleven, and it was often one o'clock before they rose from the table, the family were ready for a hearty supper at six.

There was a certain apprehension among them on that hot August day when they came down to supper. They had heard from Ceci the rumours that there was plague in the village.

Ralph suggested that there might be no truth in the story.

"Should we not go there to find out?" Donna wanted to know.

"No," said Ralph. "If it were true, that would not be a wise thing to do. Let us wait until we hear definitely — meanwhile taking all care in the house; and until we are sure, let us believe that these rumours are untrue."

"I was in the village this day," said Roger.

"And you heard nothing?" asked Charles.

"Nothing."

"Then, depend upon it, rumour lies. Where is Meliora?"

Ralph was looking along the table at which they had all seated themselves. He saw the fear in Roger's eyes. Roger had not seen Meliora since her outburst in their bedroom, and that had been about four o'clock.

Ralph said: "Donna, my dear, do you go to Meliora's bedroom and see if she is there. It is unlike her to be late."

Donna went, but she returned very shortly to say that the bedroom which Meliora shared with Roger was empty.

"Well," said Jane, "I'll warrant she is somewhere in the garden and has forgotten the time."

"It is not like *her* to forget her manners," Ceci said, shooting a malicious glance at Roger. Ceci had seen Meliora come in with her arms full of honeysuckle; and one look at her face had been enough to tell Ceci that she had heard at least some of Ceci's righteous reproaches; she would at last have learned something of the true nature of the man whom she had married. Ceci was glad because, she told herself, it was ridiculous to be as foolishly blind as Meliora pretended to be.

344

"Well, let us begin," said Ralph. "She will forgive us, I doubt not."

Conversation ensued and as Meliora, when she was present, contributed little to it, her absence was more quickly forgotten than that of any other person would have been. But Roger could not forget. He found it difficult to eat any of the pork or beef, the goose, capon, venison, with which the table was laden. Ceci noticed his discomfiture, and was glad the rake was uneasy.

When supper was over, Meliora had still not put in an appearance, and as they were about to leave the table, Pablo came in. His face was pale.

"Señors," he said. "Señoras . . ." He still addressed them thus when perturbed. "There is bad news. Jennet was warned when she went to the cottages. Harry Green is dying of the plague."

There was silence in the hall.

Pablo continued: "Jennet is staying in the barn, Señors. We will not let her enter the house for fear she brings this plague to us."

"You did right, Pablo," said Ralph. "Let us know if anyone shows signs of illness."

He saw the panic in Jane's eyes. The plague could destroy whole families. It was to be feared as much as the Inquisition.

Roger went to the door, where he paused and said: "I think I should go to my room. Let no one come to me. I feel well. I feel nothing can be wrong with me, but I was in one of the cottages this afternoon. Do not let Meliora come near me."

He went to the bedroom and his remorse was great.

If the plague has come to this house, he accused himself, I shall have brought it.

It was as though the house was in a state of siege. Ceci organised the kitchens, drew up the rules and saw that they were enforced. She looked to the provisions stored in the buttery and pantry, the bolting house and the kitchens. The house could endure a state of siege for several weeks.

They were filled with apprehension because that night and all next day Meliora had not returned.

Donna remembered that she had seen her running through the woods.

"It was yesterday," said Donna. "I was in a tree, and I called her, but she did not hear me. She did not even look round when I shouted after her."

"Which way was she going?" asked Jane fearfully.

"Through the woods."

"In the direction of the village!"

That could have been so, Donna thought.

No one spoke. They did not care to say what was in their minds.

"We must search for her," said Jane. "Everywhere possible we must search."

So they searched through the house, through the grounds and beyond; but they did not, of course, go to the village.

They did not find Meliora, and all that day and the next she did not return.

346

Jane went to Roger's room on the third day, for she had to tell him about Meliora.

"Not come home!" he cried. "But where is she? Where can she be?"

"Donna thought she saw her going to the village."

"To the village! But . . ."

"We searched everywhere except the village. We are afraid."

Roger said: "She may be ill. She may be dying . . ."

"We can only think that she went to the village," said Jane, "and knowing that it would be dangerous to come back to us . . . has not done so. Oh, Roger, she may be safe . . . she may be well. It may be that she just fears to come back among us for a while . . ."

"If she is ill," said Roger, "I must find her . . . I must look after her."

She could not stop him. He went past her; he ran out of the house into the gardens; he ran through the nuttery calling her name. There were tears on his cheeks. He longed for Meliora. It seemed to him the most important thing in the world that he find her and tell her he loved her.

Donna saw him running wildly through the grounds. There was that in his distress which moved her deeply.

"Roger," she cried, "I will help you find Meliora. We must go to the village and look for her there."

All Donna's hatred for him had gone now; she could only be sorry for him because he was clearly so unhappy.

"I will come with you, Roger. I will nurse her. I will help to make her well."

347

"No, Donna. You must go back to the house. You must tell them that I have gone to the village to look for her. Tell them that I shall not come back until I am sure I can do so quite safely."

"Let me come with you, Roger."

"You must not. Dear Donna, you must not."

"But I will. I . . ."

He was his old self suddenly. "You foolish child," he said. "Go back at once. Have you no sense? If one of us has to die of the plague, then so be it. But it is folly to die without cause."

"I would not die. I love Meliora. I want to help find her."

"I am the one who must go, Donna. Please go back. For the sake of them all, go back, and let me do this alone."

She was about to protest again, but something in his face deterred her; and then, obediently, she ran back to the house.

He went as fast as he could across the bridge, across the fields, the way he had come many times before, eager for Moll, on an interlude of infidelity to Meliora.

The cottages looked the same as usual in the hot August haze. The pigs, which were being fattened for the November kill, grunted as they always grunted; he could smell the evil odour from their sties. He saw, though, that there was no one working and the plots of land were deserted, and that in one spot the earth showed signs of having been newly dug. As he drew nearer he saw the fresh mound in the shape of a grave.

Moll must have seen his approach. She came running out of her cottage. She stood still and called to him to come no further.

"Moll," he cried. "Moll!"

"Meg Green has followed Harry. Come no further, Master."

But Moll had more to tell than that. Her voice was shrill. She was terrified on his account. Did she really love him? Was she afraid that his manly body, which could so delight her, might be lost to a rival, the plague?

He would not obey her. He must find Meliora, and he was convinced now that Moll could tell him something.

"Moll," he said, "my wife . . . where is she?"

"Please stop there. If you do, Master, I will tell you."

He obeyed, and stood still, waiting with apprehension for Moll to continue.

When Meliora had left the house she had run to the nuttery, there to hide herself among the trees. She lay on the grass and put her hot face against the earth.

She was but seventeen, and half an hour ago she had known little of the world. She was frightened by what that half-hour had taught her.

The revelation had come too suddenly. She had known, of course, that brutality was rife in the world. She knew how Sir James, Henry, and Sir Thomas Wyatt had died. That had been terrible, but she had felt that life which contained love such as she had for Roger — and she had believed he had for her — made worthwhile everything else.

And then quite suddenly she had felt that there was nothing good in life. There was cruelty and torture; there was pain and death; but there was no real love.

She had been slow to learn. To everyone else it had been apparent; but she had been blind. She remembered fragments of conversation she had overheard between the serving girls: she recalled their ribald laughter. There was much slapping and pinching among the men and women, much creeping out into the darkness of the stables; there was laughter, giggles and sighs. And this she had thought of as innocent flirtation.

Roger had taken part in these shameful games. With whom had he played them? With Moll, the big-bosomed, fat-buttocked wife of the blacksmith, who had already borne him one child and was to bear him another. "Cannot Meliora satisfy you?" Ceci had asked. "Must you have the blacksmith's wife?" "Why should I deny it?" he had answered. He knew it was foolish to deny what all but his simple wife knew to be true.

It was the pictures which came into her mind which hurt her most. The dark cottage next to the forge . . . the giggles . . . the sly pinching and slapping. He had been almost diffident with her. It had seemed that what they did was solely for the purpose of procreation. It had been like a solemn ceremony, a religious rite.

And he had despised her because he could not love her. He must have his Moll . . . his serving girls. Which of them? Any of them. All of them!

How could she live in that house? How could she look at him again? She felt that all must see the pictures that she saw. Even little Donna knew more of him than she did.

He was a monster, this gallant knight of hers; he was a lecher in the guise of a Galahad. His mind was as evil as his body was beautiful; and he practised evil things in the darkness. No, not the darkness — in the light of day. The darkness was for his relationship with her, and she no longer wished to live.

People had told Lucie: "If you wait awhile, the greatest tragedy must grow less burdensome."

But she, Meliora, could not wait. She would have to wait too long before she attained a life which would be tolerable to her. Her dreams had been too beautiful, and they had become too sullied.

It would please her to lie in the cool, shallow stream that flowed into the river; to lie with her face down among the pebbles and the water-plants, hidden by the willows. But one must not choose that way. It was the coward's way, they said.

Then she went over the scene again. She was climbing the low wall, and the sweet scent of honeysuckle was in her nostrils. She was the happiest wife in the world. Then Ceci spoke. The sun still shone hotly and the scent of honeysuckle was as sweet, but Ceci spoke and killed her happiness as the stroke of the executioner's axe will kill a man who has been alive and well a few seconds before.

"You have been with Moll." "What of it?" "There is plague in the cottages . . ."

Plague in the cottages. If there had not been, she would not have been disillusioned. She would have gone on dreaming her beautiful dreams in an evil, sordid world.

She knew what she would do. There was plague in the cottages. Well, she would go to the cottages instead of to the sweet, cool river.

She felt almost happy, having decided what to do. She ran through the nuttery. Someone called her name, but she did not stop. She ran fast across the bridge and through the meadows.

This was the way he came, she supposed, when he sought Moll.

She stopped at the cottage by the blacksmith's forge and looked in at the open door. A woman was there. This must be Moll. Her body was already thick with his child. Her black hair was loose and a curl hung from beneath her cap.

This is the woman, thought Meliora; and she stared fascinated at the big breasts that seemed to resent the lacing across them. This was the woman who could give what Meliora could not.

"Mistress . . . Mistress . . ." began Moll.

"There is plague in the cottages?" said Meliora.

"You should not be here, Mistress, for 'tis so. Go . . . go quickly."

"Which cottage?" asked Meliora.

"Harry Green's . . . the last one. Do not go near it. Go quickly, Mistress. It is not safe for you to be here."

Meliora did not move. "When did you know?" she asked.

"When . . . did I know?"

"Did you know . . . while my husband was here?"
She must know whether their desire was so intense that
even the fear of plague could not suppress it.

Moll did not answer that. She said: "Harry Green is
struck down. Mistress, go . . . go and tell them. And
. . . keep away."

Meliora turned and, as she walked past the cottages,
past the sties and the fowls and the tilled land, she kept
picturing him in that cottage with that woman.

Now she could make clearer pictures. She had seen
the woman; she had seen the cottage. She must brood
on those pictures because by doing so, she was
determined to go on with what she had planned to do.

All her life she had been warned against the plague,
protected from it. Once, during her childhood, it had
come to the village in which she had lived, and she and
her mother had had to leave in a hurry for one of their
other houses. She would never forget the haste of that
journey, the fear she had discovered in her mother.

But she would not fear the plague. She wished to go
to it gladly.

She found the cottage and pushed open the door. A
man was lying in the rushes. His face was purple and he
was sweating. Beside him lay a woman, and, although
she was not so far gone as the man, it was easy to see
that she was suffering from the plague. Crouching in a
corner was a girl of about sixteen.

The girl rose as Meliora entered.

"Go away!" she cried. "The plague! The plague!"

But Meliora came to her. "I have come to help you,"
she said. "We must nurse these people. Who are they?"

"You are mad," said the girl. "They are dying. And I dare not go out. All will shun me, as *you* should."

Meliora stood close to the girl. "They should be nursed," she said.

"There is death in this place."

"I know. And I care not for death."

"You look like one of the ladies of the House. Are you? Or are you an angel? Am I already in Heaven?"

"There is nothing wrong with you but fear," said Meliora. "We must nurse these people."

"They are my father and mother, yet I dare not go near them."

"They should be given nourishment."

"How could we nourish those who are dying of the plague? They cannot eat."

"Is there nothing that they can drink? The woman murmurs that she is parched with thirst."

The girl drew back shivering. "I dare not go near them. There is some ale on the table there."

Meliora went to the table and took the jug of ale. She poured some into a cup and put it to the lips of the woman, who drank it eagerly.

Then she went to the man.

"You are mad . . . mad," said the girl. "You are doomed . . . we are all doomed."

"I will stay with you," said Meliora.

And she saw that the girl was comforted.

She had lost count of time. She was not sure how many days and nights she spent in the cottage. She had tried to bathe the faces of the man and woman; she had tried to make them a little comfortable. In doing these things she could subdue her grief.

She and the girl sat side by side on the rushes. The man and the woman had ceased their groaning, but the horrible plague spots were visible on their faces.

"Why did you come?" asked the girl. "I am glad you came . . . but why did you come? It was folly . . . madness."

Meliora did not answer; and the girl rose to light a rush, for the night had come again.

Meliora sat looking at the room in the faint flickering light and tried not to see Roger and Moll in a similar room.

After a long time the girl went to the man and peered into his face. "He is dead," she said. "We must bury him quickly. We will make a big grave . . . big enough for me as well."

"And for me," said Meliora.

She and the girl dug a deep grave. Once they looked up and saw a light in a window of one of the cottages. They would have been seen with their spades digging a grave by the light of a lanthorn and all would know the meaning of that.

By the time they had buried the man, the woman was dead; so they brought her out and buried her in the grave.

Meliora prayed as she had been praying all the time since she entered the cottage: "Let me die. Let this affliction come to me. Let me receive this terrible contagion, for it is my only salvation." She longed to die, for in her death alone could she escape from her melancholy.

And when they had covered up the bodies she gave a great cry of joy, for she knew that her prayers had been answered. She fell across the grave and lay there in ecstasy.

The girl said: "You have caught it. I knew you would. I shall follow you. For me it is different. They are my own. But you . . . why did you do this thing?"

Meliora did not answer.

She lay dazed, unsure where she was. The stars came out and the cool air fanned her burning body. She thought the earth was her marriage bed with the rich silk curtains about it; and the embrace of death in the darkness was like that of a perfect gentle knight.

CHAPTER
SEVEN

Pablo had continued to visit *The Spanish Princess*. The widow could not believe in his protestations of devotion when she saw how his eyes strayed to the pretty pot-girl. She was attracted by him, but she did not entirely trust foreigners. If he thought he was going to marry her and share her bed and the profits of *The Spanish Princess*, he was mistaken.

Still, she liked to listen to his gay and innocently bawdy compliments; and his queer manner of speech amused her as much as it had when she had first heard it.

So, while the little Spanish gentleman was still a welcome visitor, her favours were reserved for John Kimber, who had been courting her assiduously since she had become a widow and who, when she decided to bestow her hand in marriage, would know how to manage a tavern, and not be afraid of hard work.

John Kimber, big of body and strong as a horse, able to deal adequately with rowdy customers, was at times tempted to lay his hands on this little Spanish monkey, as he called Pablo.

Pablo knew this; he also knew that he had the protection of the mistress. She would be displeased if

John Kimber harmed her courtly Spaniard; so John's attacks were confined to words; and the patrons of *The Spanish Princess* would listen with enjoyment to the arguments and abuse these two exchanged on those occasions when Pablo could slip away and ride into London.

"You do not come often," complained the widow.

"My affairs at Court, Señora!" he explained, trying to express with gestures the burdens of a gentleman as highly placed at Court as he was.

He had told a fine tale about himself — how he had chatted with the Queen, advised her on State matters; how Philip had sworn he could not do without his dear friend Pablo.

"I'll warrant the Spanish Philip takes you with him on his whoring," said the widow.

"And I'll warrant your friend Pablo gives a good account of himself," said John Kimber, glancing significantly at the widow.

All those in the tavern would take up the ribald song of the moment; and in it was all their hatred for the Queen's husband. They sang of Philip's taste for the low-born, his amorous adventurings into the low life of London.

"The baker's daughter in her russet gown,
He'd rather have than Mary, without her crown."

Pablo was angry. "I'll have you show greater respect to my master!" he cried.

358

Then he would tell them of the splendours of the Court, the excitement of his life, his adventures in Spain.

But now he was faced with a problem, for Philip had left for Spain. Pablo must either give up his pleasant adventures at *The Spanish Princess*, or he must confess that his royal master had left him behind.

He was loth to give up so much pleasure; and he had the utmost faith in his ability to pull wool over the eyes of these simple revellers.

So back to *The Spanish Princess* he went.

They were all discussing the departure of Philip. The Emperor Charles had suddenly decided to abdicate in favour of his son, and it was necessary for Philip to return to his native land to take over the duties of ruler. Many of the revellers had been to Greenwich to see him take farewell of his wife before embarking for Spain, to mutter curses after him, and to express the hope that he would never return. Already men were imprisoned because they did not accept the faith of Philip of Spain; the acrid smell of English martyrs' burning flesh was often in the nostrils of Londoners, and they were growing restive.

Pablo was greeted with mingling cheers and jeers.

"What, then, have you not set out for Spain?"

"My friends, I begged to be allowed to stay. I love England too well. I could not leave this fair land and . . . I have Philip's business to attend to while he is absent."

"It surprises us," said the widow, looking for a compliment, "that you should not take the opportunity of returning to your own country."

Pablo's answer so pleased her that she filled his cup with the very best she could give him.

She sat beside him, and others gathered about them. He believed he had succeeded in duping them. They fired questions at him. They would know more of Philip's business. And he talked as he never had before. They were his dear friends, he said; and he loved them all.

They gave him ale, and the ale of *The Spanish Princess* was notoriously potent. He wept a good deal; he embraced the widow; he even embraced John Kimber.

"Nay, I will never leave you," he declared. "I will never return to Spain. Señors . . . Señora . . . I will stay here with my good friends as I have stayed with them since I have spurned my native land . . ."

It was not long before he was telling them tales of the Inquisition and how he had brought young Felipe to England.

He was growing more and more incoherent. He had talked of the house near Valladolid, of Richard Grendell and his Spanish wife, of how the Inquisition had taken Richard Grendell, and that it was all due to a certain Roderigo.

They taunted him; they did not believe him now any more than they had believed him before.

But only the widow noticed the two men who sat silently listening and drank scarcely any of her good ale. She signed to John Kimber. All knew the methods that were being practised in England now. Gardiner and Bonner had their spies everywhere, and it was said that they were always looking for "faggots" to feed the Smithfield fires. They did not hesitate to take the lowly with the high-born; indeed, poor men provided material for the fires more often than did the rich; for the powerful families could appeal to the Queen on behalf of their members and frequently obtain a pardon. The Queen, suffering great agony of body, knowing that her husband did not love her, trying to believe that the swelling of her body was due to pregnancy and not some dreaded disease, was a fanatic, but she was not eager to see her subjects burned at the stake. She only wished to please her husband and her ministers.

And now strange men in *The Spanish Princess* were watching the drunken Pablo.

The hour grew late, and the widow said: "We must put him on his horse. Perhaps one of you gentlemen would ride back with him."

The two strangers rose. "We are going his way," they said. "We will look after him and see that he arrives safely where he belongs."

"It is over in Chelsea," said the widow; and she began to tremble because she believed that she would never see her little Spaniard again.

"At the house of the Grendells," said one of the men. "We know it."

And they took him out and set him upon his horse.

As they rode away a quietness fell over *The Spanish Princess*.

Nana was alarmed. Pablo had disappeared, and it seemed to her that what had happened long ago in

Spain was about to happen again. That other tragedy had begun in a similar way. Vividly she recalled that night when she had lain in her room, her window open, waiting for Roderigo to call her name. In vain had she waited. "He will come tomorrow," she had told herself then. But he had not come; and the next time she had seen him had been when he was in the *Quemadero*, that square of pain and misery — quite a different Roderigo from the man who had been her lover.

And when would she next see Pablo?

Charles said to her: "You are sad because that fellow Pablo has deserted us. Nana . . . why? I demand to know why."

Nana was silent.

"You were fond of him, were you not, Nana?"

He was angry; she still had the power to make him jealous.

"No . . . no . . ." she said. "It is because it is like another time."

Then Nana talked, as she had never talked before, of those days in Spain when Roderigo had disappeared, and of all the misery which had followed on his disappearance.

"That is why I am sad," she said. "He is gone, as Roderigo went, and I am afraid for you . . . for Felipe . . . for Roger . . . for Donna. It is because it reminds me, that I am afraid of what will happen next."

He soothed her with tenderness and passion; and for a while she was comforted; but as the days followed each other she would sit over her mending, her brow wrinkled; and every time she heard voices below her window she would rise and look down, hoping that Pablo had returned and that the terrible disaster which she felt hanging over the house would not fall upon it after all.

After the first fright Pablo had become accustomed to his surroundings.

He had awakened to find himself lying on the cold stone floor of a cell, and knowing that he had been drunk and talked freely, he guessed that he had been indiscreet; he was terrified. That which he had feared more than anything was upon him.

He waited fearfully for torture and death; but the days passed and nothing happened.

He missed his good food, for his jailer brought him nothing but bread and water; but during those first few days he would have been too frightened to eat whatever good things were brought to him.

The Tower in which he knew himself to be incarcerated was crowded with prisoners. Some, he supposed, were left in their cells and forgotten. To lie here for ever! It was a dismal prospect, but not so dismal when compared with that of torture and death by fire.

No one came to question him; he asked his jailer why he was here, but the fellow said he knew nothing. He thought it was doubtless because Pablo was a heretic, as the Tower was full of heretics at this time. The man only shrugged when Pablo insisted that he was a good Catholic.

There was a small opening at the top of the wall just below the roof of his cell, and across this were thick iron bars. When Pablo climbed up to it and looked through it he saw that the window was on a level with a path.

Often he heard footsteps along that path, and he whiled away his time looking through it. Adventure with women had always played a big part in Pablo's life. Coward though he was, even on the point of death he could not be unconscious of a pretty woman. It therefore seemed inevitable that he must become enamoured — poor prisoner that he was — of a dainty pair of feet which he saw one day passing along the path outside his window.

He watched them and found that they passed regularly, and one day he called out: "Fair lady, I beg of you. A glimpse of your face."

The feet stopped. "Prisoner?" said a woman's voice.

Pablo answered: "I am a poor prisoner. Lighten my life with a glimpse of your sweet face."

There was a pause, and then at the bars of the window he saw the plump, good-natured face of a woman in her mid-thirties; he saw, too, that he had pleased her, and that being a poor prisoner had in no way impaired his way with women.

"I have seen you," he said. "Now I can die happy."

Their acquaintance grew in the days that passed. She had been hailed by prisoners in that cell before; most of them had begged for food; he was the first who had asked for a glimpse of her face.

She was the wife of the head cook, she told him. They had their quarters close to the great kitchen in which meals were prepared for the royal household when the Queen was in residence at the Palace of the Tower; her husband and his men cooked also for the warders and officials of the Tower. He was an excellent cook. Pablo himself soon tested the truth of this, for it became a habit of the lady to thrust the most excellent fare through the bars of his prison.

He professed undying devotion to her, declaring he would be happy to be a prisoner all his life, since prison had brought him into touch with her.

So, there were compensations to enliven his captivity, and he gradually grew reconciled to his fate.

The weeks passed. With the coming of winter the cook's wife gave him a warm shawl. He was not doing so badly, and he had now ceased to tremble and sweat with fear every time the door was opened.

The winter passed, and life was more comfortable in the spring.

He and the cook's wife were devoted to one another by this time. The bars of his prison alone, he was sure, prevented them from consummating their love. But what could not be shown by caresses was conveyed in tender words; and a good wedge of beef, he was bound to admit, was a suitable substitute for more passionate satisfaction.

He was therefore unprepared for what came to him. Those who had put him where he was seemed suddenly, after months of neglect, to remember him;

perhaps they were short of victims. One day his cell door was opened, and through it came two men.

"You will follow me," said one of them.

They both, he noticed, carried halberds.

He was very frightened. He feared they would take him to another cell where he would be deprived of the attention of the cook's wife. What would she do when she came and called him and found him gone? More tragic still, what would he do if they placed him in another cell which was not accessible to her?

But soon those fears were replaced by others, for he was led down a staircase, through narrow passages and down more stairs until he knew that he must be in the underground chambers of the Tower. Nervously he touched the sweating walls; the damp smell of the river made him want to retch. He knew that he was being conducted to that chamber to which men were taken when they were required to answer questions.

The man who was leading the way paused before a door which he opened with one of his keys. He stood aside for Pablo to enter.

Now Pablo began to tremble more than ever, for he knew himself to be in the torture chamber. Beneath a sheet which was dark red in colour, doubtless so that the bloodstains would not show, he saw a shape, huddled and horrible, which he guessed to be a man. As he watched, the board on which the figure lay was picked up by two men and carried out of the chamber.

Pablo watched it, shuddering.

He was startled by the hideous instruments arranged about this chamber. The Scavenger's Daughter, which bent a man's body double and sent the blood spouting from his nose, mouth and ears, was standing as though waiting to embrace her next victim. There was the Spanish Collar, the Thumbscrews, the Gauntlets and . . . most hideous of all . . . the Rack.

"A Spaniard, eh?" said a man who was seated at a table. "Well, put the Spanish Collar on him. He will feel at home in that."

They stripped him of his shirt, and he was naked to the waist. He was glad he was wearing his rosary. This he was allowed to remove. They put the collar about his neck; and at his least movement the sharp spikes pricked his skin.

He was almost fainting with fear.

These English, he had always known, did not understand the refinements of torture as did the Spaniards. He knew that the tortures inflicted by the Inquisition were more barbarous than those practised in this country. But here was torture enough to unnerve him. There was not a man living in Spain who had not in some nightmare dreamed he was in such a position. The Inquisition was a nightmare to them all . . . even the most devout Catholics.

He had believed he had escaped from it when he came to England. Now he believed he was destined to suffer. He had betrayed Roderigo to this; he had betrayed a kind master and little Don Felipe to a different kind of suffering. For that he must pay.

He thought of the sweetness of life, of boasting of great deeds, of digging his teeth into pastry brought to him by the cook's wife; he thought of lying in a *patio* with the fountains playing, of lifting his face to the warm rays of the sun, and loving women. To him life was very sweet.

"If you answer the questions put to you, you will have nothing to fear," he was told.

He said: "I will answer all."

"Do you follow the doctrines of the Holy Catholic Church?"

"I am a good Catholic. I have never been anything else. I would die the fiery death rather than renounce my religion."

"Yet you serve heretics."

"I know nothing of their faith. I am but a servant. I was born in the Holy Catholic Faith, and I shall stay in it till I die."

They believed him. He had been watched, and he had always behaved like a good Catholic. When they looked at their records they knew that he had not been called to protest his faith. He had been called to bear witness against others.

"You are in the service of Sir Ralph Grendell?"

"Yes, Señor."

"And he is a heretic?"

"As far as my knowledge carries me, sir, he is a Catholic."

"What part did his son and grandsons play in the Wyatt rebellion against Her Majesty?"

"None that I know, Señor . . . sir . . . your honour. His daughter married Sir James Braxton's son . . . and for that we journeyed to Kent."

368

"You paid many visits to Sir Thomas Wyatt's castle at Allingham."

"I was in love with a serving girl there."

They smiled.

"That was your sole reason for going there?"

"It was. I swear it was."

"It was not to take messages?"

"I swear it was not, Señor."

"How long have you been in England?"

"It must be nine . . . yes, nine years, sir."

"How did you arrive in England?"

"We . . . we escaped with Master Felipe. Señor."

The man at the table began to write. "Escape? From what did you escape?"

"The Inquisition. They . . . it was thought that they would take the boy. It has been known, Señor."

"Why should they take the boy?"

Pablo was sweating. He had not meant to talk. This was the most dangerous thing he could say. He knew that Spain and England were one now. The King of Spain was the ruler of England. He would have power, would he not, to take an Englishman if the Inquisition demanded it? There was no one in Spain who gave more whole-hearted support to the Inquisition than Philip who was now the King of Spain. What was he saying? Had he not brought misery enough on Master Felipe? He sought refuge in Spanish. "You must forgive, Señor. My English it is not good."

"Release the collar," said the man at the table.

Pablo breathed with relief. That was good. They understood he could not help them. He had come through.

But they were leading him towards that instrument which was shaped like a trough. He stared down at the windlasses with the ropes attached.

One of the men said: "Perhaps a spell on the rack will improve his English."

"Señor . . . no . . . I beg of you. I will speak English. I will tell you all I know."

The men looked at each other.

"You are a wise man," said the one at the table. "It is better to talk before torture than afterwards. For talk you will. You are too wise a man to refuse to speak. I saw that at once. You are a wise man who will talk and avoid the pain."

Pablo fell on his knees; he lifted his hands in supplication. "I will tell you all, Señor. I will tell you all you wish to know."

"Come back to the table, then. If what you have to tell me is what we wish to know, I promise you your freedom, for I have reason to believe you are a good Catholic."

"I am a good Catholic, sir, I am . . . I am . . ."

"Then it is your duty to expose heretics, is it not?"

"Yes, Señor. It is. It is. I swear I will."

Then he told the story; he told how he, the good Catholic, had betrayed the heretic Roderigo, how Roderigo had perished with his heretic master, Richard Grendell.

"And Felipe?" they wanted to know.

"He witnessed the death of his father. The good Catholics thought that thereby they would save his soul."

"And did they save his soul?"

Pablo was silent, and they did not press him then.

"He escaped to England, did he, because he was afraid that he, not being a good Catholic, might meet his father's fate?"

What could Pablo say? They were menacing him. He had not yet escaped. They offered him his freedom. All he need do was tell them Felipe was not a Catholic. They were going to torture him if he did not say those words. He knew it. What could he say? How could he meet their challenge, he who was a brave man only in his thoughts?

"Will you tell us the truth?" they asked, and although their voices were gentle, their eyes were menacing.

"Yes, yes, I will tell you all you want to know."

"Felipe Grendell is a heretic?"

Pablo hesitated, but only for a moment.

"Well, señor, yes ... yes ... I suppose he is a heretic."

They smiled. He had said what they wished him to say; he had bought the key to freedom.

They took him back to his cell; and he lay there, weeping bitterly. He thought of the little boy whom, in his way, he had loved; he thought of the boy's father for whom he had had great respect.

For the second time he was the betrayer. He was the Judas.

But he would not have sold his master for silver —
only for freedom . . . freedom from pain . . . freedom
from torture and death.

And when the cook's wife came to visit him, he had
no smile for her. He could only lie and weep until he
had no more tears to shed.

The garden was full of sunshine. It brightened the
purple nettles and the flowering pyramids of loosestrife
down by the river's edge; it shone on the barge which
had stopped at the privy steps.

Four men got out of the barge and walked in single
file up the bank, across the lawns to the house.

Ceci saw them coming and cried out in alarm.

Similar scenes were taking place all over England.
The fires of Smithfield must be kept burning.

"Open . . . open in the name of the Queen."

Ceci had gone to them. She did not lack courage.
She opened the door which she had locked when she
had watched their approach across the lawns.

"What do you wish?" she asked coldly.

"Felipe Grendell is here?"

"No," said Ceci, the colour flaming in her cheeks.
"No, no. He is not here."

The men stepped past her into the hall. They were
preparing to mount the stairs, when Ralph appeared in
the gallery.

"What is this?" he asked.

"We come in the Queen's name," said one of the
men. "It will be well for you if you lead us at once to
Felipe Grendell."

372

Jane had come to stand beside her husband in the gallery. Ralph was conscious of her white hands gripping the rail.

"Oh no . . . no," she murmured. "Oh, God, save him. God save us all."

"He is not here," said Ralph; but he knew he was being foolish.

Felipe had heard the men. He came into the gallery. His face was pale but he held his head high.

"I am Felipe Grendell," he said. "What do you wish with me?"

When Donna heard that they had taken Felipe, she went into the woods and lay down on the soft grass.

The house was a house of mourning. Continually Ralph looked towards that grim fortress; he watched the smoke rising above Smithfield Square.

Roger came out to the woods and found Donna there. He lay beside her. He was angry . . . too angry for tears.

"Why Felipe?" he demanded. "What harm has he done? If they had taken any, I should be the one. I was the chief mover in the rebellion. Why do they take the innocent one? Why do they take Felipe?"

Angrily he pulled up handfuls of grass and threw them from him.

His anger suited Donna's mood, as the blank misery of Kate and the tearful sorrow of the others could not.

"Oh, Roger, what can we do? You could do something, Roger."

"I swear I will do something. I swear they shall not have him. I will do something, Donna."

Then she began to cry, bitterly and angrily; and he smoothed her hair with gentle fingers.

"Donna, dearest Donna, don't cry. I will save him for you."

She lifted her eyes to his.

"You will do it, Roger. I know you will do it, because you are brave and strong. You are the bravest, strongest man in the world, and you do not hate me any more."

"I never hated you, Donna. I loved you."

She looked at him wonderingly.

"Donna," he went on, "you are not the child you seem. You are more beautiful than anyone I know. That is why I love you."

She shook her head. "You hated me. I hated you."

"It had to be hate, Donna, because you were too young for love. I will show you how much I love you. I will bring Felipe to you. Somehow I will bring him to you. I will die doing it if necessary, but I will do it."

"You must not die," she said.

"I deserve to die. I killed Meliora."

"You did not. It was the plague that killed her."

"I sent her to her death. You do not understand, Donna. It was because of you. Yes, it was. But for you, I might have been faithful to her. You drove me to Moll and others. It was always Donna . . . Donna . . . And I hated you because I dared not love you."

She thought: He is mad. Meliora's death has made him so.

He stood up.

"Donna," he said, "we will not despair as the others do. I will bring back Felipe to you."

The weeks passed and the year faded. There was no news of Felipe. They knew that he was a prisoner, but they could discover nothing more.

The Bishops, Ridley and Latimer, had been burned to death.

People said that it would not be long before Cranmer joined them. The fires of Smithfield were burning steadily, and the people of London were growing sullen. How long, they asked themselves, for they dared not ask each other, will the fires continue? When will our ears be free from the cries of the suffering?

The Queen was sick unto death, it was said; and many cursed her and prayed that she would die.

All over the country the stakes were set up and the torches were applied to the faggots. Never had there been such persecution in the land of England. Never had her people felt so ashamed.

Cranmer's turn came; and he died with dignity, stretching out to the flames that right hand with which he had signed the document of recantation, that all who beheld him might know that he repented of his weakness and died in the faith in which he had lived.

Each day in the house at Chelsea they waited for the news that Felipe's time had come. There were many victims awaiting death by the flames. And then Pablo came back to them.

He was strangely altered. He was thin and his brown face had turned yellow as leaves in autumn through his long incarceration. But he had been fortunate; he had been sustained by his good friend, the cook's wife.

Everyone at the house welcomed him; they were very kind, and he knew still greater shame, because he could not forget his second betrayal.

Now, as before, he longed to help them; he longed to do some heroic deed that would make him a proud man again. But he could do no such thing, and he never would because he was a heroic man only in his thoughts and in the brave words he said to women.

But there was something he could do.

He could visit the kitchens at the Tower as a guest of the cook's wife.

He told Roger of this advantage which was his. "I know the warders. I received gentle treatment on account of my beloved friend. I may discover where they are keeping Master Felipe. I may be able to do something for him . . . as much was done for me."

"You are right, Pablo. You are right. You must go to the kitchens and discover all you can. And when you know where he is, we must find some means of making his escape possible."

Pablo was happy. He spent much time with his friends at the Tower. He was known to the warders. They winked at each other as they let him through. The cook's wife was a merry dame, and it was she who really ruled the kitchens. It was as well, if you were to receive titbits from the pantry, to be on the best of terms with the cook's wife.

Pablo longed to be the means of rescuing Felipe, that he might soothe his conscience.

He was not entirely unsuccessful.

He confided his mission to the cook's wife and she, indefatigable in her efforts to please him, discovered that Felipe was in the Bowyer Tower, that so far he had been unmolested and, it would seem, had been forgotten, as so many were brought to this gloomy prison at this time.

Pablo passed on this good news to Roger, who made a plan which, though wild and difficult to carry out, he felt might not be impossible.

Felipe had lost count of time. He lay in his dungeon and waited for death.

There were times when he was scarcely aware of his body; it had grown light and thin on a diet of water and dry bread.

The stone walls which shut him in, he knew, had witnessed great misery. Some prisoners had scratched their names on the stones; they had written heartrending words which betrayed their sufferings. The rats came to his cell, fierce hungry rats; they waited for him to grow weaker that they might successfully attack him. Vicious as they would be if they dared, they were not so cruel as those men he had seen in a square in Spain. Those men he would never forget; and he was not sorry in his heart that he had come to this. When he was dead he would not have to think of what had happened in Spain; he would not have it brought back to him by a hundred reminders — the buzz of a fly, the heat on a stone wall, the horrible pall that hung over Smithfield. Death would be an escape from that which had haunted him since he had witnessed it; death would free him from the knowledge of the inhumanity of men.

He felt light-hearted and light-headed. There would be the swift pain at the stake — for he was too weak to live long and endure his agony — and after that, forgetfulness.

He wondered now whether he had always known that he must come to this; he prayed that when his time came he would be given the same courage which his father had shown.

At last they came for him. He did not know how long he had been in prison, but he guessed it must have been some months. His jailer was a silent man who laid his food down and went away; but he had fancied he had seen a gleam of pity in the man's eyes, and that gleam had cheered him like the sun on a wintry day.

They led him down to the torture chamber. He scarcely noticed the grim scenes he passed on the way. He could walk only with difficulty after his long confinement, and one of the jailers was obliged to support him through passages damp with the river's slime.

The sworn tormentors, the chirurgeon, and the examiner were waiting for him; the first, to inflict torture; the second, to make sure that he did not remain unconscious too long; and the last, to write down the confession it was hoped to extort from him.

About him were the dreaded instruments of torture about which he had often heard.

He was taken to the table at which the examiner sat. They gave him a stool because it was obvious that he was too weak to stand.

"Your name is Felipe Grendell?"

"That is my name."

"What is your faith?"

"I do not know."

"You do not know! Come, come, that will not do. You have denounced the Mass, have you not?"

"I do not think of the Mass."

"You deny the divinity of the Sacrament?"

"I have not denied it."

"Do you accept the Holy Catholic Faith?"

"I do not accept it."

"Then you are a heretic?"

"If by heretic you mean that I accept the teachings of Martin Luther, I would say that I do not accept them either."

They were bewildered. This was unexpected, and they were not sure how to act. People were either good Catholics or heretics. This man seemed to have no faith. He had said so.

As Felipe waited he thought: This is what happened to my father. What matters it whether it was in a prison at Valladolid or Madrid . . . or beneath the Tower of London? He faced it as I must face it now.

What would they do to him? He could see the hideous rack with its ropes and pulleys, and he knew that once a man had been racked, those ropes attached to his wrists and ankles, those windlasses turned, he was never the same again; he might die on the rack; he might never walk again even if he survived; his arms and legs might be useless ever after.

The examiner said: "We have a way of dealing with heretics here."

"I know. You burn them at the stake."

"If you repent you will save yourself. Will you accept the true faith?"

"The Catholic faith?"

"The true faith. The only true faith. The Catholic faith, of course."

Felipe considered this. What mattered it? I would not die for their doctrines, he thought. Should I allow them to break my limbs for Luther . . . for Calvin? Both these men are intolerant in their turn. I would not suffer for a faith. I accept no faith.

He had never seen it as clearly as he saw it now. He did not believe that any who tortured their fellow men had a faith worth suffering for.

"I accept the Catholic faith," he said.

The examiner smiled. Here was a coward, as many were when they came to this chamber. It was gloomy here; the only light came from the lamp hanging from the ceiling. The place seemed haunted by all those who had suffered in it. Men came into it bold, determined to fight for their beliefs; and it had often happened that merely to confront them with these instruments of torture was enough to deter them.

"You show wisdom, Felipe Grendell. I see that you are a good Catholic. There is one other matter which we have to discuss with you. You live in Chelsea with your family?"

"I do."

"They are heretics."

"No."

"They are Catholics?"

"Yes."

"They have been under suspicion."

"The house was searched once when many houses were searched. Nothing was found. There has never been any suspicion since then."

"Were you concerned in the Wyatt rebellion?"

"No."

"Some members of your family were."

"No."

"We believe that to be false. You have a cousin, Roger Grendell?"

"Yes."

"He was directly concerned in the rebellion?"

"That is not so."

"We have information to the contrary."

"You have been misinformed."

"You lie, and you know you lie."

"I do not lie."

"We do not believe you, and if you do not tell us the truth, we shall have to press you to do so. You are a sensible man. You are a good Catholic — you told us so. Carry your wisdom a little further and tell us what part your cousin played in the Wyatt rebellion. And what part was played by your uncle and your grandfather? We would know that also."

Felipe was afraid. He heard the menace in their voices. He had thought he could be brave; he had thought he would welcome death; but being faced with it made brave men tremble.

He was trembling now.

"Strip him," said the examiner; and the tormentors stood, one on either side of him.

They hustled him to the rack. He prayed for strength, for courage.

They placed his body on the rack; they tied the ropes about his wrists and ankles; and the ropes were attached to the rollers. Each of his tormentors took an oar and fitted it into the notches on the windlasses, ready to turn at the examiner's signal.

The examiner was now standing over Felipe.

"Don't be a fool," he said. "Tell us the truth."

"I have nothing to say."

"You have denied your faith. You were not brave enough to defend your heresies. Yet you will not tell the truth about this slight matter."

Felipe closed his eyes.

No, he thought, I will not speak. *This* is *my* faith: My love for them. It is stronger than a belief in an afterlife. Love is a worthy cause for which to suffer ... for which to die. Now I know my faith. Oh God — the God of love who must look with abhorrence on these cruel tormentors who work in His name — give me courage to be worthy of the faith of love.

"Begin," said the examiner.

Here was agony. It seemed as though his arms and thighs were being gradually torn from his trunk. He had never known there was agony like this.

Mercifully unconsciousness enveloped him.

But they would not leave him thus. The chirurgeon was bending over him; they were dashing some unguent into his face; its harsh pungency dragged him back to torture.

"Your cousin, Roger Grendell, was involved in the Wyatt rebellion? Answer . . . Answer."

"No, no. He was not. He knew nothing of it."

"So! He has not had enough. Turn once more . . . sharper. You have been too gentle with him."

Every nerve in his body seemed raw; pain beat in his brain. He wanted to beg them to stop, to tell them anything if they would cease to torture him.

But he said nothing.

He had fainted again, and once more they were restoring him to consciousness. He must be dying. He could not endure much more.

"Give it to him. Harder . . . We have been too soft."

Pain was all over his body; it was a thousand gnawing insects that tore at his nerves, a million knives that stabbed him. Pain . . . pain . . . and then the revival to face more pain.

This is for faith, he thought. This is my faith. Faith . . . Hope and Charity. And Charity was Love, and the greatest of these was Love, it had been said. What did these people — the Queen Mary whom people had begun to call "Bloody", Philip her husband — what did they know of Love? They had faith, it was said; they had hope. What hope? That their souls would be received into paradise because they had faith and had tortured the bodies of men and women with burning pincers, with their racks and their pulleys; they had roasted men's bodies over slow fires; they had burned them at the stake; they had inflicted many tortures upon them, and for that they should be received into Heaven, and the angels would sing for them.

But the greatest was Love. And what love had they but love of their own souls, their own welfare within the Promised Land?

He heard a voice from a long way off say: "He can stand little more, sir. He is nigh to death."

Death. Forgetfulness. Sleep and darkness.

He had won. He knew it. He had won a battle for love. He had come to understanding. He would not suffer the torture for the sake of his own soul; but he had suffered it for the sake of those he loved.

Love was the answer then. He had found the true reason for living.

They untied the ropes and threw his broken body on the floor. He did not feel the jar. He lay there, oblivious of the evil-faced men about him, of the hideous chamber.

He was unaware of the journey back to his cell.

In the little room close to the kitchen of the Tower, Roger dressed himself in the uniform of a warder, while Pablo watched him. Pablo was smiling with glee. He had expiated his sin; but for him, this would not be possible.

384

They trusted him, these good friends of his in the cook's kitchen. He was one of them. He had asked a favour, and they were merry people who liked to help a friend. The cook's wife, moreover, insisted that they should do this small thing. What was it? Simply that her Pablo's friend should be given a uniform belonging to one of the warders and without suspicion thus enter the cell of his cousin and speak with him for ten minutes. It was not much to ask. Who would know? Thomas Lee, whose duty it was to guard that section of the Bowyer Tower in which the prisoner was kept, would conduct the supposed warder to the cell, would unlock the door, let him in, allow him to enjoy a short conversation with his cousin and let him out again.

It would be by no means the first time such a thing had been done.

And now they were ready.

Roger had donned the uniform of a man of almost exactly the same size as himself, and they stepped out by the light of a lanthorn.

It was almost dark, but a faint crescent moon gave a little light to the September sky, and a few stars were visible. Roger looked up at the weather-washed walls and thought of Felipe within. He knew that he had given himself a task which many would say was impossible of achievement; but he felt powerful; never had he been so sure of his ability to succeed.

"This way," said Thomas Lee. "And do not speak, sir, except to mutter a greeting if any hail us. Beyond that . . . nothing."

"It shall be so," whispered Roger.

Thomas took a bunch of keys from his pocket and opened a studded door. They stepped inside the Bowyer Tower.

Thomas held the lanthorn high above his head and Roger followed him cautiously through narrow passages and down a spiral staircase. The close atmosphere seemed stifling to Roger, and the smell from the river, foul.

Thomas paused at the door of a cell and, taking his keys, opened it. Roger went in and Thomas locked the door behind him.

It was some seconds before Roger's eyes grew accustomed to the darkness. Then he saw a bundle on the floor; it was covered with a cloth.

"Felipe!" he whispered. "It is I . . . Roger."

There was no answer.

"Felipe . . . It is Roger . . ."

He fancied the bundle moved. Roger went to it and knelt beside it.

"Felipe . . . Felipe . . . Quick! There is not a moment to lose . . ."

"Roger," muttered Felipe. "Roger . . ."

"You are bewildered. Of course you would be. There is so little time. Listen. Get up. I am wearing the uniform of a warder. You are to put this on . . . pretend that you are Roger Grendell. Imitate my voice and as soon as you are outside this Tower, run . . . run as fast as you can. You will get through as you are wearing warder's clothes. Felipe . . . Felipe . . . why do you not move?"

Roger shook his cousin and, as Felipe groaned in agony, Roger understood.

"Roger," said Felipe. "Dearest cousin, you come too late."

"Torture . . ." stammered Roger.

"They have racked me. I could not stand upon my feet."

Roger was dumbfounded. His plan was of no avail. It had seemed so clever, infallible. He was to come into the cell in the warder's clothes; Felipe was to go out in them.

"Do not tell them," said Felipe. "Do not tell Grandfather . . . Donna . . . Naña . . . Kate . . ."

"Felipe, what will they do to you now?"

"I do not know. Mayhap they will leave me here. I have told them I am a Catholic. They do not burn Catholics, do they?"

"The monsters! I would I could kill them. I would I could do to them what they have done to you."

"They are doing it to hundreds, Roger. Here . . . in England. They are doing it to thousands . . . in Spain. Roger, your plan was noble. What of yourself? What did you plan for yourself?"

"To take your place awhile. I would have found a way of escape."

"You have found the way, Roger. You too. You have found it. It is love . . . greater than faith, greater than hope."

Roger thought he wandered in his pain; and he wished for vengeance on those who had tortured his cousin.

"Felipe," he cried in anguish, "is there nothing I can do? Cannot I carry you out?"

"You could never get out with me, Roger."

"I have my sword. I would fight my way through."

"You are brave, but you could not take me out. You must get out of here quickly, and you must go away. They are planning to bring you here . . . and to do to you what they have done to me."

"I will not leave you here."

"You must. There is nothing else to be done."

"But I came to save you."

"If I die, I shall die happy . . . knowing that you came."

The warder was unlocking the door.

"Time to go," he said.

Baffled, frustrated, Roger left the cell; bemused and bewildered he followed the warder through the passages and out through the heavy door.

Donna read the letter he had left for her. He had said: "Read it an hour after I have gone and tell no one of its contents. It is our secret, Donna, yours and mine."

"My dearest Donna,

"Very soon I think you will see Felipe. I want you to see that there is a horse ready for him in the stables. He will come straight to the stables, and he will not have time to tell you much. You must not delay him with questions. Say nothing to anyone, but have food ready for him. He will ride away at once. None of the family must see him, and you must make sure that the servants do not. He will have to hide himself at once. But that I shall tell him when I see him. I have found a way of getting into his prison. I shall have to take his place, but never fear I shall soon find a way out.

"I love you, Donna; and if I never see you again, remember what I told you. It was not real hate; it had to seem so because you were too young to love. Roger."

And when Donna read that letter she was filled with a terrible fear, because she believed she would never see Roger again. In the two years since Felipe had been taken, she had grown up; and she knew that she would never be really happy if she did not see Roger again.

She went to the stable, saddled the horse and waited.

It seemed a long time before she heard the sound of a horse's hoofs, and a man came riding into the stable yard.

"Felipe!" she whispered.

But it was not Felipe. It was Roger.

She could not help it, but the happiness which the sight of him gave her was, for a brief moment, her only feeling.

During that wet October and the early mists of November, great was the rejoicing in the City of London, for the Queen was dying.

This was the end of Bloody Mary and her Spanish husband. This was the end of Papist rule. Never again, said the people, would they accept a Catholic monarch. If such a misfortune was ever threatened, the people would remember the fires of Smithfield. They would tell their children's children, and they in turn should tell their children.

The courtiers were deserting the Court and riding out to Hatfield, where the new Queen resided — a young woman who had always had a gracious smile for the people. They were ready to love her for her youth, her beauty and her gaiety, and ... because her reign would mean an end to the Smithfield fires. She was to be the means of releasing them from the Spanish yoke, so that there should no longer be a link with Spain and its Inquisition.

The great news was proclaimed. Mary was dead.

"Long live the Queen!" cried the joyful people.

The new Queen came riding from Hatfield to London with a great retinue of lords and ladies, and as she approached the metropolis the people ran out to meet her, to follow her and bless her.

From the Charter House along the Barbican to Cripplegate she rode in a magnificent chariot; and in Cripplegate she left the chariot that she might ride on horseback to the Tower of London.

Beautiful she looked in her rich riding-dress of purple velvet; beside her rode the handsome Robert Dudley, and before her, the Lord Mayor and Garter King-of-Arms.

All the fortifications were decorated with silks and velvets; tapestry hung from windows; the bells rang and the guns boomed. The people cheered her; they were mad with joy; they were sure that they had come out of the dark horror of the Marian persecutions and that the golden-haired Queen would lead them to a golden age.

She was gracious to her subjects, fully aware that she owed her state to them, determined to take possession of their love and respect, that she might retain possession of the throne. Her sister's reign of blood and terror was a warning and a lesson to her.

And so she entered the Tower of London; and as she stood within its great walls, she addressed those who were assembled about her, saying: "Some have fallen from being Princes in this land, to be prisoners in this place; I am raised from being prisoner in this place to be Prince of this land. That dejection was a work of God's justice; this advancement is a work of His mercy. So must I bear myself — thankful to God, and to men merciful."

And there was great hope among the people, and particularly in the hearts of those who feared for loved ones lying under the threat of death.

Many prisoners were released on that day, and among them was Felipe.

It was Roger who brought him home to Chelsea. Felipe rode on Roger's horse, and their progress was slow.

And when they came home, it was Roger who, supporting his cousin, helped him into the great hall.

Felipe lay, exhausted by the journey, on a couch which had been prepared to receive him.

He would be lamed for life; it was doubtful whether he would ever regain the health he had enjoyed before his imprisonment; his body was broken, but Ralph and Jane saw that his mind was healed of his sad memories.

It was not easy to understand how his physical suffering could bring peace to his mind; perhaps he would explain to them one day. In the meantime he was home.

Kate, standing there with the others, suddenly flung herself down by the couch and very tenderly placed her arms about him.

Painfully he stretched out his hand to touch her hair; and she, lifting her face, smiled at him through her tears.

And there was Donna at Roger's side. They both looked at Kate and Felipe. Donna sought Roger's hand; he took hers and gripped it tightly.

Through the windows they could hear the songs and shouts of revelry, the sound of joyful music coming from the barges on the river.

The Death of King Arthur

Peter Ackroyd

An immortal story of love, adventure, chivalry, treachery and death brought to new life for our times. The legend of King Arthur has retained its appeal and popularity through the ages: Mordred's treason, the knightly exploits of Tristan, Lancelot's fatally divided loyalties and his love for Guinevere, the quest for the Holy Grail. Now retold by Peter Ackroyd with his signature clarity, charm and truth to the spirit of the text, the result is not only one of the most readable accounts of the knights of the Round Table but also one of the most moving.

ISBN 978-0-7531-8900-9 (hb)
ISBN 978-0-7531-8901-6 (pb)

Crown of Aloes

Norah Lofts

Isabella of Spain was a great woman, a great Queen. Crown of Aloes is presented as a personal chronicle. Within the framework of known fact and detail drawn from hitherto unexploited contemporary Spanish sources, a novelist's imagination and understanding have provided motives, thoughts, and private conversations, helping to build up the fascinating character Isabella must have been. Her fortunes were varied indeed: she knew acute poverty, faced anxiety and danger with high courage, gave much, suffered much, lived to the full. At the end she was mainly aware of her failures. It was left to others to realise how spectacular her successes had been.

ISBN 978-0-7531-8834-7 (hb)
ISBN 978-0-7531-8835-4 (pb)

Madonna of the Seven Hills

Jean Plaidy

In a castle in the mountains outside Rome, Lucrezia Borgia is born into history's most notorious family. Her father, who is to become Pope Alexander VI, receives his first daughter warmly, and her brothers, Cesare and Giovanni, are devoted to her. But on the corrupt and violent streets of the capital it is a very different story: the Borgia family is feared, and Lucrezia's father lives up to the reputation as "the most carnal man of his age".

As Lucrezia matures into a beautiful young woman, her brothers grow ever more protective and become fierce rivals for her attention. Amid glorious celebrations their father is made Pope, and shortly afterwards Lucrezia is married — but as Borgias, the lives of the Pope's children are destined to be marred by scandal and tragedy, and that is a fate that Lucrezia cannot hope to escape . . .

ISBN 978-0-7531-8842-2 (hb)
ISBN 978-0-7531-8843-9 (pb)

The Heart of the Lion

Jean Plaidy

At the age of 32, Richard the Lionheart has finally succeeded Henry II to the English throne. And, against his father's wishes, he intends to make Berengaria, daughter of the King of Navarre, his Queen.

But first he must fulfil his vow to his country to win back Jerusalem for the Christian world. Leaving England to begin his crusade, Richard entrusts his kingdom to his brother, John, who casts covetous eyes on the crown, and his sister, Joanna, who is willing to defy even a king.

ISBN 978-0-7531-8580-3 (hb)
ISBN 978-0-7531-8581-0 (pb)